Second Best

A Novel

Jessica Dettmann

HarperAvenue

Second Best

Published by Harper Avenue, an imprint of HarperCollins Publishers Ltd

First Canadian edition

Originally published in Australia in 2018 by HarperCollins*Publishers* Australia Pty Limited in slightly different form as *How to Be Second Best*. First published in Canada in 2019 by Harper Avenue, an imprint of HarperCollins Publishers Ltd, in this original trade paperback edition.

HarperCollins books may be purchased for educational, business, or sales promotional use through our Special Markets Department.

HarperCollins Publishers Ltd
Bay Adelaide Centre, East Tower
22 Adelaide Street West, 41st Floor
Toronto, Ontario, Canada
M5H 4E3

www.harpercollins.ca

Library and Archives Canada Cataloguing in Publication information is available upon request.

ISBN 978-1-4434-6011-8

Printed and bound in the United States
LSC/H 9 8 7 6 5 4 3 2 1

For my mother, Carol, and my grandmother Mims.
Two of a kind, and two of the kindest.

Chapter One

I am in the kitchen making tea for my husband's current wife. He's my ex-husband, not my husband. I wonder if I'll ever get used to calling him that.

His wife's name is Helen and she is very particular about her tea. No bags. No caffeine. The water slightly off the boil. Not really resembling tea in any way.

Helen's very comfortable in my kitchen. She's draped her leggy frame all over one of the mismatched wooden chairs and she's absent-mindedly running her hands through her smooth, gently waved blonde hair.

'Have you got something with dandelion?' she asks. 'It's amazing for bloating.' She pats her flat belly.

Instinctively I glance down and tighten what remains of my own stomach muscles. It's disheartening how little effect that has these days.

I start taking everything out of the pantry, stacking boxes and packets on the counter, pretty sure that somewhere in there is a box of what appear to be dried lawn clippings. I find it—'Lactation Tea', the label says, but that's surely rubbish.

I brew a pot of sticks and leaves. It smells like what happens when you get too enthusiastic at the fruit and vegetable store and it all turns to brown soup in the crisper.

Helen waits calmly—calm is her default mode—her hands now folded and resting on an alarmingly thick document she has prepared for me. It's all about how I am to care for her daughter while she and my husband, who's now her husband, are in Ubud next week, having massages and aha moments and sex.

It's kind of her to be so thorough. I mean, if we didn't have daughters the same age, I might not know what it takes to keep a three-year-old alive. Yes, that's correct, our daughters are the same age. They are half-sisters, born three weeks apart.

Helen's daughter, Lola, came first. I didn't know about her until after my daughter, Freya, was born.

In movies, a woman often finds out her husband has been unfaithful when he calls her by the wrong name in bed. I discovered it when my husband called our baby the wrong name.

I was lying on the sofa, the first evening home from the hospital. Tim, our three-year-old son, was asleep in his bed. Before me on the coffee table was a plate of runny brie with crackers, and a glass of wine I didn't really feel like drinking.

Troy had several hundred pieces of the new double stroller laid out carefully on the carpet, and he was poring over the instruction manual.

Freya wasn't feeding as easily as her big brother had. As I wrestled my nipple into her tiny shrieking mouth, her father reached over and stroked her little soft head. His eyes were still on the page explaining how to adjust the height of the stroller's handle. He wasn't even remotely up to the point of adjusting the stroller's handle.

'There you go, little one,' he said. 'Have a big drink. That's right, Lola, darling.'

'Lola?' I said. 'Who's Lola?'

Lola, as anyone knows, is a showgirl's name. Lola is a sociopath in a children's book and TV series, sister of Charlie, one of the great long-suffering brothers of literature. People called Lola hang out in bars where the champagne tastes like cherry cola.

Lola hadn't ever been on our list of potential baby names.

Troy might have got away with it too, explained it as a slip of the very tired tongue, except he was so exhausted, what with being the proud and terrified father of two newborns living one suburb apart, that the strain of the lie was too much.

If he hadn't also been trying to assemble a double stroller at the time, a task that could undo just about anyone, he might have had the wherewithal to keep his mouth shut.

But as it was, he just sat there on our living room floor, surrounded by small plastic bags containing seemingly identical but actually distinct and crucial bits of dark grey plastic, and told me everything.

When he'd gone out that afternoon to buy milk and bread with five-day-old Freya in the BabyBjörn, he'd actually taken her to meet her three-week-old big sister. That was why he'd forgotten the milk and bread.

For a long time afterwards the part of this that I couldn't stop thinking about, the part that made my heart feel as if bits of it were peeling off like flakes of rust, was the idea of him walking up our street. Past the café where we bought our coffee every day and our breakfast every Saturday, past the bakery, the pharmacy, the liquor store and the corner store, through our life and out the other side of the suburb to his other life.

Afterwards I did wonder if he'd taken Lola for the same walk when she'd come home from hospital. Did Ron the storeowner come out to congratulate him? Did Natalia the pharmacist wave to him? Did they think that baby was my baby? How could he lie to those people? How did he think he was going to get away with any of this?

There hadn't been much thought involved, as it turned out. Just a lot of emotion.

He had fallen in love, he told me, with his twenty-six-year-old Pilates instructor. Troy was forty years old. The cliché hurt almost as much as the betrayal.

I'd thought we were immune to that sort of thing. We used to laugh at the men we'd see driving to the beach in European convertibles—menoporsches, we'd called them—with their over-long grey hair blowing in the wind as they dangled one arm over the bare brown shoulder of an unfeasibly attractive woman half their age.

How could he be considering joining their ranks? It made no sense.

'But love doesn't make sense, Em,' he'd explained tearfully that night. 'I never planned to fall in love again. I'm already in love. I love you. God, I didn't even know you could be in love with two people at once. Did you know that, Emma? It's actually possible.'

I didn't know that.

It's hard to explain how elated he was, and how somehow at the same time that this news was lifting me up and repeatedly smashing me onto rocks, filling my lungs with sand and horror and grief, I was also riding the wave of his excitement.

I didn't take the news lying down, you'll be pleased to hear. Hell had nothing on my fury that night. He kept trying to explain it all to me, as if it was ever going to make sense.

'I wanted to tell you about her, about this connection I'd made, because, Em, you know you're everything to me. We're a team. It was the weirdest thing in the world to keep this amazing thing that was happening in my life from you. But I didn't know what "it" was, you know? I couldn't tell if it was okay or not okay. It was intense.'

'Well here's a tip for the future,' I spat back at him. 'If you have to describe your relationship with a woman who's not your wife as "this amazing thing" and you wonder if it's okay or not, then it's probably not fucking okay.'

For the next few hours, Troy told me everything that had happened. In far too much detail. It was like he was high.

And it was when I realized he sounded like he was on drugs that I made a decision. This was an addiction. He was addicted to this woman, or the feelings or sex or the serotonin and dopamine, or some hideous combination of all of that.

You don't abandon someone because they are an addict. I mean, not right away. You help them. You support them through whatever they're going through, and hope they'll come out the other side and you'll get back the person they once were.

It sounded crazy, what he was telling me. You can't love two people at once, not in the same way. That's the sort of bullshit that cheating husbands feed their idiot wives. No one in her right mind would believe that.

Or can you? I didn't know how much I could love until I met Troy, so who's to say the capacity isn't there to feel that love twice? (Although it did seem far more likely that this was all the love hormones talking.)

'It's like your children,' he said, as he sat beside me on the sofa, his eyes wide and so bright, gripping both my hands with his. 'Remember when Tim was born? Do you remember we used to say he'd have to be an only child because there was no way we could love another baby even close to how much we loved him? But we do! *You* do! *I* do! As soon as we saw Freya we loved her just as much and didn't that completely blow your mind, Emma?'

That did make sense. In a way. I can remember thinking that he must have been falling in love with both baby Freya and Lola at the same time, shortly after falling for Helen, and so obviously he suddenly had an unshakeable belief in his boundless capacity for love.

So he was in love with both Helen and me, it seemed. He hadn't gone looking for someone because he'd stopped loving me. That was a positive. But he was planning to go live with Helen and Lola. That wasn't as good.

I asked him about that decision. About why, if he loved both of us so much, he was choosing her over me.

'Em, I can only do this because you are extraordinary. You can do this,' he said, stroking my snotty, tear-stained face. 'I'm going to live with Helen because I know you'll be fine. You are the strongest person I know, and the best mother, and I wouldn't go if I didn't think that. Helen's not like you. She is totally freaked out about having a baby. I don't think she'd manage on her own.'

As compliments go, that one took quite a few go overs with the orbital sander and the truth turpentine to reveal that it was, in fact, not a compliment at all.

Perhaps I can blame the oxytocin for the way I accepted what Troy said that night. I was devastated, completely in pieces, but what he said left me feeling, somehow, quite noble and strong.

And to the outside world, that's how I have remained for the three years from that day to this. While behind closed doors there was more screaming into pillows, crying and rending of breast than I had foreseen would occur in my daughter's first months of life, outside I held it together.

In a staggering display of magnanimity, I helped Troy, who was floating on a cloud, to pack his bags and move in with his new family, into Helen's house in Grace Park, the next suburb east.

Together we explained to our families, including poor little baffled Tim, that Troy was going to have an extra family, and that while Daddy still loved us, he also loved Helen and baby Lola now.

As far as break-ups go, ours went beautifully, for Troy. He didn't have to move into the nasty red-brick block of apartments overlooking the train station, known locally as the Home for Disgraced Husbands. The place that does short-term rentals and smells like microwaved lasagna and regret.

Instead he got to go a couple of kilometres down the road to a charming cottage with windows full of shiny dangling crystals and a back garden that fairly jangled with wind chimes, complete with a repurposed swimming pool full of lotus and waterlilies that Helen called her Serenity Lagoon.

Three years down the track, they are married and I am not. I am a single mother.

It has taken me three years to fully accept that what Troy told me that night was, largely, complete bullshit. Three years. Was I in shock? Can shock last that long? I truly can't believe I fell for it. I think Troy believed it, though, because it made things a fair bit easier for him, and I suppose for a while it made things easier for me to believe it too.

It meant that after he left, I helped him with his new baby. He was right about Helen not being a natural mother. She was pretty alarmed by all that went along with having a tiny baby.

She didn't cope very well with sleep deprivation, Troy told me, and instead of screaming back 'Welcome to the fucking club,' I decided it was no big deal for me to stop by a few times a week, when Tim was at preschool and I was going for a walk anyway, and pop Lola in the other side of the double stroller with Freya. (I had ended up assembling the double stroller.)

Long walks with two babies are much the same as long walks with one baby, with maybe a few extra stops to change nappies and feed one with a bottle and one with a boob. While I walked the babies, Helen could catch up on sleep.

Looking back, I can only assume it was my own chronic sleep deprivation that made this arrangement seem like a reasonable idea.

Before any of us knew it, Lola and Freya had bonded and they were happier together than apart. Tim liked them both, as much as any three-year-olds like any babies, and once Helen resumed teaching Pilates, it just seemed to make sense to everyone for Lola to come to me when her mother was at work.

Outsiders assume it takes a staggering amount of goodwill and personal largesse for me to care for my husband and his new wife's child like this, and that assumption, though wrong, is fine by me. If people want to think I'm a wonderful person for minding Lola, they're very welcome. Frankly, I'd rather they thought that than the truth, which is that I am a pushover.

Once the girls turned two, and Tim started school, the arrangement did actually start to make practical sense for me. It's easier to entertain two toddlers than one.

One toddler wants to do whatever you are doing. Two of them just need you to provide a Milk Arrowroot biscuit for each hand and apple slices at regular intervals. You have to keep enough of an eye on them that they don't accidentally off themselves, and adjudicate the odd skirmish. Other than that they don't want you involved much at all. That works for me.

So I never went back to work full-time. Troy gave me more than than he legally had to in our divorce settlement. I got our house, our nearly-new car, and a pretty generous chunk of child support each month.

At the time we split, I was grateful. The money meant I didn't have to face the fact that my own earning power had withered since Tim was born. Troy had, back then, been adamant that one of us should stay home full-time with our baby. 'Babies need one of their parents,' he always said. 'Why bother having kids if you're just going to let some daycare worker raise them?'

When Tim turned one, it became apparent that what he meant by 'one of their parents' was me. 'Think about it,' he argued. 'Practically your whole salary would go on childcare costs. Why put yourself through all the stress of daycare when you can just do a bit of work from home while he naps?'

When I look back, I don't understand why I didn't point out that no, in fact my whole salary wouldn't go on childcare costs, because only fifty per cent of the price of the care would be mine. Neither did I see it as strange that he believed the stress of daycare would be my burden alone. I just looked at our life, and saw that Troy's business was starting to take off. Of course I couldn't expect him to be the one to take days off when a sick child couldn't go to daycare. He seemed right: I should stay at home another year.

By the time Tim was two, we were trying for another baby, so again, it made no sense for me to go back to work. Besides, by then I no longer had a job to return to, and I would have had to negotiate some sort of part-time role. It all seemed a bit hard.

Troy's business was booming, too, so I just kept on as I had, doing the odd editing job here and there, when I could fit it in.

Weirdly, after all the shit with Helen went down, and I washed up on the shore of my new life, somehow clutching three kids instead of two, I found it easier to work, because the girls entertained each other.

These days I feel like if I could do the minding-Lola part without having to deal with her parents, that would be ideal.

It's been a gradual process, realizing I am no longer loved by Troy. A bit like a piece of clothing fading until one day you refer to your smart black sweater and the person you are talking to looks confused until they figure out that you are gesturing to the tattered, threadbare grey thing tied around your waist.

I mean, how do you even know if you are loved or not? He certainly hasn't told me, since the night he told me about Lola and Helen. But there have been looks, kind words. Initially, when we weren't used to not touching any more, he'd rest a hand on my waist as we tucked one or other of the babies into the stroller. And there were a few hello or goodbye kisses where we accidentally defaulted to lip contact, and I still felt the spark I always had.

It seems absurd that such tiny physical gestures sustained hope in my heart. But the heart can be fairly idiotic. It believes what it wants to believe. Maybe it does it to protect you. Maybe I wouldn't have survived if my heart had shattered that night. Maybe the only way for me to get from there to here was a very gradual acceptance of Troy's betrayal and his rejection of me.

But whether you're lowered down gently or dropped from a great height, the end result is the same, ultimately. You find yourself on the cold hard ground of reality. I'm just splattered into fewer pieces.

Tonight, in my cluttered kitchen, as Helen sips her tea, there's really no point any longer in my pretending that I'm anything other than just a very gullible woman scorned.

Helen clears her throat and starts reading out her manifesto.

'So, no screen time, obviously. That includes all devices. No parabens in her bath products—I mean, I've packed the things she can use but I know you sometimes like to throw all the kids in together so—'

'Helen, it's okay, I can go through that. You don't have to read it alou—'

'Lola has ballet on Tuesday, gymnastics on Wednesday, swimming Thursday afternoon and karate on Saturday morning. French is now just Thursday morning. We were worried we were over-scheduling her so we cut one class back. That won't clash with any of Tim's and Freya's activities, will it?' Helen cocks her head to the side, her eyes wide and innocent.

I gently grip the edges of my chair. 'No.'

'Still holding firm about under-scheduling them? Good on *you*. It's such a natural way to raise kids. I wish I was brave enough to do it but I just worry she won't have the advantages the other children at school have. I love that you can get past that.'

There's no point answering this in an appropriate way, because that would involve upending the teapot on her lap.

I take a quiet, deep breath and remind myself that I am a strong, resilient, independent woman and she is a ninny named Helen who married a man named Troy and didn't realize there was anything funny about that. She still doesn't.

Besides, she is sort of right. I don't take Freya to nineteen activities, because she's only just three and she'd rather be at home pulling seedlings out of their pots and wedging important bits of her brother's Lego into the gaps between the floorboards.

Tim is six and I don't take him to anything except swimming lessons, because he goes to school now.

He's in first class, which seems to be academically roughly the equivalent of what the first year of high school was like when I was a kid.

As far as I recall, for seven years of elementary school all we did was learn to read, and recite our times tables as far as six—maybe up to ten if you'd been tapped as gifted and talented—and do quite a lot of projects about colonial history, presented on wall-sized sheets of cardboard. Being advanced meant figuring out the spacing of your bubble writing before you crashed into the right-hand margin and had to redo your whole heading.

It's not like that any more. Tim has homework every day. He has to do projects that involve more engineering knowledge than is required to build an Olympic velodrome.

Unfortunately, since he is only six, I have to do most of this, while simultaneously trying to make it look like he did the work himself and imparting enough information about what I'm doing that he can convincingly pass himself off as the architect of whatever hovercraft, cantilevered sports stadium, or space vessel we're constructing from toilet paper rolls and plastic milk bottle lids. That means I have to 'show the working' as I go, like some sort of Cyrano de Bergerac of craft.

So no, I don't spend a lot of time and money taking Tim to soccer and mixed martial arts or African drumming workshops or Lego classes.

Handily for Helen and Troy, this leaves plenty of time for me to ferry Lola to all her lessons while her parents are out kicking career goals and ticking off achievements on their five-year plans.

I realize Helen is still talking, and I tune back in to find her explaining something about refined sugar and the inflammation it causes in young cells, which is absolutely nothing compared to the inflammation caused by her talking about this to me in my own kitchen, where I will be feeding her child for the next ten days out of the goodness of my own heart.

The girls go to the same local preschool, because a year after Troy had vacated our marriage, Helen sold her place and they bought the house three doors down from me. It made things more convenient for them.

Lots of their friends admire this set-up. We are generally regarded as the model of a high-functioning divorced couple. I know people have used us as an example to their freshly separated friends. 'Our friends Emma and Troy split up,' they say. 'And they co-parent *brilliantly*.'

It's actually an awful set-up, only made bearable by Troy earning lots of money.

His bottled juice company—Lord of the Juice, you'll have seen their chartreuse trucks driving around—has done so well in the past few years that he could afford to give our house to me in the divorce settlement and buy another, nearly identical house for him and Helen and Lola to live in.

I say nearly identical, but his new place is a superior version of mine. They're matching Edwardian houses, like our whole street, but his has been renovated.

I'm glad for Lola that she doesn't have to live somewhere awful, and I'm pleased our situation works for the kids, because their happiness is The Most Important Thing, as people are fond of telling you when you've been dumped.

My phone buzzes somewhere on the table and I rifle through several colouring books and school newsletters before I find it.

There's a text message from my sister, Laura. It has no words, just a martini emoji and a question mark.

'Excuse me, Helen,' I interrupt. 'This is work. I've got to quickly sort something out.'

'I totally understand,' she says. 'The small business never sleeps!'

I give her the double 'you know it' finger guns as I back out to the hall. I text the phone emoji to Laura and within ten seconds my phone rings.

'Hello, Emma speaking. Yes, right, of course,' I tell my imaginary work caller. 'Tonight? Well, it'll be a stretch but I can manage, if it's urgent. I'll start right now and have it to you by midnight. Tell me the brief.'

Helen mouths 'I'll go' at me and starts an exaggerated tiptoe out of the room. I give her the thumbs-up and a whispered 'Sorry!'

She motions that she'll call me later and I wave to her as we walk to the front door, picking our way through an abandoned Matchbox car rally and over what seems to be an attempt to bring all the puzzle pieces in the house into one mashed-together jigsaw EU.

It's very helpful that Helen doesn't understand how my job works. I am a freelance book editor, and freelance book editors rarely get calls at eight o'clock at night asking them to do something in the next hour. Editing a book takes many, many days.

Often the many days it should take are squashed into fewer

days than are ideally required, but the industry doesn't typically operate with the urgency of, say, a hospital trauma unit. It suits me that Helen doesn't understand this.

When Laura hears the door close, she says, 'Has that woman gone? Have you made sure you've ordered the right kind of air for Lola to breathe next week?'

'Yes, it's fair trade air. Cruelty-free.'

'Perfect. Not like that factory-farmed air you give your kids. Am I coming round for a drink?'

'Tomorrow,' I tell her. 'I'm too tired tonight and I have to get up early to finish writing Tim's speech on ecosystems for his news in class tomorrow.'

* * *

Before I go to bed, I clear a safe access path from the front door to the bedrooms. I'm not going to put everything away, because it will all be out again within ten minutes of the kids waking tomorrow, but this is my concession to good housekeeping: to make sure we can get out without breaking our necks if there's a fire.

I make another promise to myself to sort this mess out next time I get a weekend without the kids. If I had a dollar for every time I had made such a promise I would use all the dollars as kindling and burn this place to the ground.

With my feet in ballet's first position I snowplow the toys along the hall and look into my children's bedrooms.

Tim is lying on his back, the sheets tucked neatly around his long straight form. Beside him lies one toy, a long-limbed stuffed mouse called Desmond Tutu. Tim sleeps like a vampire in a coffin, with his hands neatly clasped over his chest. He has done this since he was a baby. I've always found it funny. He'll wake up in eight hours' time in the same position.

In Freya's room are matching single beds. Lola used to nap here, and now she sleeps over a fair bit, but tonight her bed stands empty, and Freya sprawls on hers like she has been dropped from a plane, arms and legs splayed. Her rounded little tummy rises and falls and she appears to be chewing something in a dream. She is wearing tiger-print pyjamas, and she's surrounded by a dozen stuffed tigers of varying sizes and styles. All have names, and I am frequently reproached for confusing the tiger called Jonathan with the tiger called Orange.

Clutched in Freya's hand, as always, is her prized possession: a copy of *The Tiger Who Came to Tea*. I had this book as a child too, but it never captured my heart the way it has Freya's. Perhaps that was because my mother read the whole thing to me, whereas I have glued the final two pages together. I just think it has the wrong ending.

The story is of a tiger who comes to a little girl's house and eats and drinks everything they have. When her dad comes home they get to go out for dinner because the cupboards are bare. The next day the mother takes the little girl shopping to replenish their supplies, and they buy a big tin of tiger food, in case he returns. That, in my opinion, is a lovely ending. It's hopeful. Everyone is happy and prepared and optimistic about the future.

Then for reasons I don't understand, there is another page, which tells you that the tiger never again came to tea. Why? Why shut down the possibility of a repeat of what was a terrific adventure for the little girl? It's such a downer. My kids have had enough downers in their short lives. So I've never read it aloud, I've made that page disappear, and we are all just fine with that.

I read it at least twice a day to Freya, and have done for a year now. She's somewhat obsessed. The book calms her when she's upset and she falls asleep holding it most nights.

This deep sleep, the kind where a loving parent can stand in the same room and breathe without waking the children, is a relatively new development in our home.

As babies, my kids were nocturnal. With Tim, Troy and I spent hours, days, weeks gently rocking him in our arms, bouncing softly on a fitball or, on the advice of one baby health nurse, rocking the stroller back and forth across a rolled up bath towel, a movement designed to mimic the joins in the pavement.

Tim seemed to have arrived with a finely tuned internal altimeter, and if I ever lowered him to the cot before he was deeply, deeply asleep, a wailing siren would sound.

I spend my days longing for bedtime, for the constant self-narration of their lives to pause, but then when I see my children like this—asleep, peaceful, quiet—I miss their awake selves. It can be lonely here at night.

Back in the kitchen I sweep the detritus from the table and into a plastic tub that I shove into a cupboard. I scrub dried-on bran cereal from the table, leaving a fresh canvas for the bran cereal to dry on in the morning, lock the back door and turn out the light.

It's not even nine o'clock. My children now sleep through the night so I no longer feel the pressure to go to sleep immediately—a fact that still thrills me. Less thrilling are my options at this point in the evening.

I am now the prisoner of my good sleepers. At least when they used to be dreadful at going to bed I had an excuse to bundle them into the double stroller and walk around the suburb in the dark.

That was useful. Putting one foot in front of the other was soothing to my shell-shocked brain. Some people do a lot of thinking when they walk. I do a lot of walking when I walk. I find it allows me to not think at all. And for the past few years, I haven't wanted to think.

But now, at night, it's quiet and still in my house. I've had to find new ways to not think. Books are okay for this, but television is better.

I climb into bed and fire up my laptop. According to Helen, who would have got it from someone on Instagram, it's terrible for your sleep quality to have electronic devices in your bedroom at night, and it's more or less a slow suicide to let yourself fall asleep with a TV show playing.

If that's the case, then start digging my grave, I say. The day I stop falling asleep to an episode of a Scandinavian murder mystery will be my last.

The one I'm watching now is a Swedish show called *The Devil's Heirs*. A young detective inspector, Tilde, is struggling to make sense of a series of brutal murders of middle-aged women in their homes. The victims are all single, well-educated professionals. It's pleasingly chilling and suspenseful, though I find myself distracted by Tilde's very neat hair. Her curls are casually tousled, yet never frizzy. There must be very low humidity in Luleå. Within fifteen minutes I fall asleep, wondering both how to get my hair to do that, and whether there's enough Lego still on the floor to injure an intruder if someone broke in to murder me in my sleep.

Chapter Two

The next evening I'm scraping the remains of the spaghetti bolognese into the bin. It's mostly tiny pieces of carrot, which all three children have meticulously removed from the sauce and left on the side of the plate. They'll all happily eat carrots raw, but they have taken a mystifying united stand against its inclusion in bolognese sauce.

Why I persist in putting carrot in the bolognese every time I cook it is unclear to me, and I'm wondering whether these thoughts count as leading an examined life when I hear my sister's key in the lock.

'In here,' I call.

'I've found you a boyfriend,' she calls back. Laura has never been one for preamble. She started talking to me as soon as Mum and Dad brought me home from the hospital and has rarely paused for breath since.

I hear her stop in the living room. 'Hey, guys. Hi, Lola.' They mutter something in reply, inaudible over the TV. Laura continues to the kitchen.

'Why's Lola still here?' she asks.

'I'm going out—which means you can't stay for ages, by the way—and when she heard my guys were having a babysitter Lola asked if she could have a sleepover. I couldn't think of a reason to say no,' I tell her.

'I'll bet you a hundred bucks Helen and Troy put her up to it,' Laura says with contempt. 'Those two can smell a sleep-in a mile off.'

I haven't got a comeback for that so I go back to her earlier announcement. 'What was that about a boyfriend for me? I'm not looking for a boyfriend, by the way.'

She drops her bag on the floor by the table, in a spot that almost certainly has at least a sprinkling of parmesan cheese and some sauce, pulls out a chair and sits.

'Oh, for fuck's sake, Emma,' she says. She gives the same look of disappointment she has been giving me since I turned her B-52's cassette into a pile of mangled brown ribbon in a terrible rewinding accident when I was nine. 'How remarried-to-someone-else does Troy have to be before you'll accept that he really, truly doesn't want to be with you ever again?'

'Thank you for your sensitivity at this difficult time,' I tell her. 'I know he's not coming back. But that doesn't mean I'm ready for anyone else to get the chance to reject me.'

'Oh, you big idiot,' she says, more kindly now. 'It's time to get back on the horse. It's been three years. I know it's only been a few months in your huge dumb head, because you believed him about loving both of you and all that shit. But really, it's been three years and you can't stay off the market any longer. It's like property. You've got to buy and sell in the same market, or otherwise all the stock will seem like overpriced crap once you finally do start looking again.'

Laura's married to a real estate agent. A local one who sells overpriced crap hand over fist.

'This fellow I've found you, he's your type.' She takes a long drink. Like most things she does, Laura drinks like there's a timer on her life and if she doesn't finish before the buzzer she'll be sent home and won't get to compete for the holiday in Fiji.

'A manipulative adulterer?' I ask. 'My type is a terrible type. I need to move away from my type.'

'No, he's a very tall vet. I met him yesterday. Had to take Bled in because he ate another part of a brick.'

Along with her real estate agent husband, Mark, and their three sons, Laura shares her home with a remarkably stupid dog, a fat black Labrador called Bledisloe.

That Bledisloe is still alive is against the odds. The whole family could travel to Europe every year for what they spend having random indigestible objects removed from that animal.

'Emma, are you listening? He's a vet! Remember the list?'

She means the list we tried to make about fifteen years ago of professions that we thought only attracted good people. We only ended up with one entry. Vet.

'I remember. Tell me about this very tall vet. How tall are we talking? Jeff Goldblum tall? Andre the Giant?'

'Normal tall. Like, six two or something. He's divorced, one kid—'

'And I'm going to stop you right there. Too complicated.'

Laura gives me the busted cassette look again.

'Em, you're going to need to broaden your horizons, or drop your standards or something. You're thirty-six. Everyone available is divorced with a kid. You're divorced with *two* kids. It's the second go round. Everyone's second-hand at this point.'

This conversation always ends up in the same place. Stuck in the cul-de-sac of my stubborn refusal to consider a relationship with someone else who is divorced with kids.

Laura thinks I'm being snotty. She thinks this is related to my intense dislike of thrift stores. There is some truth to that.

In second-hand clothing stores, the previous owners are still, always, present in some way. You can smell them. Or you can feel them, in the worn areas of the jeans or the way the fabric has stretched.

I realize this is both irrational and tantamount to being an environmental terrorist, because apparently we all need to save the planet by wearing each other's horrible tatty old clothes, but I can't help it.

The same applies to men. I don't really want a musty, faded man who still smells like someone else.

I don't know when I started feeling like this. Back at university, a boyfriend who had already had a few girlfriends was sought after. You wanted someone with few clicks on the odometer.

At some point though, experience turned into baggage, probably when I was busy being cheated on by my husband. A relationship with baggage, I can do without.

'What about school?' Laura isn't going to let this drop. 'There must be loads of hot single dads at the school. That's what you're going to need. Someone in the same boat as you.'

'Which boat's that? The life raft of people who have been chucked out of other, better boats? You think that's the best I can do?'

'It's not a question of the best you can do. It's a question of practicality. You need someone with kids.'

'I don't need any more kids. I have enough of my own and other people's to look after already. *The Brady Bunch* always seemed like a complete nightmare to me. I don't really like other people's kids. Sometimes I barely even like my own kids. Why can't I have someone footloose and fancy-free?'

'Because men without kids don't want to look after other people's kids. Men don't even really want to look after their own kids. Except penguins. That's biology.'

'Laura, if there's one thing I'm even more certain about than not dating a weirdly tall, divorced vet, it's that I don't want to go out with a parent from Tim's school,' I tell her firmly. 'This suburb's too small as it is. I've been the scandal of Shorewood once already. I'm not doing it again. If I'm going to go out with anyone, it's going to have to be someone from, I don't know, truly far away. Like Denmark.'

'Western Australia?'

'No, proper Denmark. Someone who has no place in this life. A dad from around here is going to an ex-wife around here. He's going to have his version of me. I don't want to know any more versions of me.'

'Well that's a point,' says Laura. 'You've already got one Helen. I'm just not sure how you're going to find a never-married Danish man around here. You only ever go to the school and the mall. I suppose there's always the gym.'

'There isn't even the gym,' I say glumly. 'Troy got the gym. I haven't set foot in there since before Freya was born. Do you know he and Helen go there to celebrate their anniversary?'

'That is disgusting,' Laura says. 'It strengthens my point though: you only go two places. And they're not exactly magnets for hot, single Scandinavians.'

'Tonight I'm going somewhere else,' I tell her. 'I'm going to a book launch.'

Laura wrinkles her nose. 'Book launches are full of women. Always. You won't meet anyone there.'

'I'm not going there to pick up,' I tell her. 'I don't care if I meet anyone there. This is my point.'

'Fine,' she says. 'It's your funeral. Which will happen sooner than it needs to, because I read that married people live longer than single people.'

'That's not true,' I reply. 'It just feels longer.'

* * *

What I don't tell Laura, but I suspect she knows anyway because she's my sister and likes to rummage about in my head without my permission, is that I am still, three years down the track, far too frightened to go out on a date with anyone.

What happened to my marriage came so out of the blue. Only from my perspective, obviously. Troy had some inkling it was coming.

I could never understand those stories you'd hear about people who led double lives and got away with it. How does someone not notice that their partner is running another family somewhere? It's a logistical nightmare. You'd have to be a highly organized sociopath to pull it off.

Or, as it turns out, you just have to be a sociopath and your new girlfriend can be the highly organized one. That's an unstoppable combination.

Helen and Troy had met at the gym, where she was teaching the Pilates mat class. Troy was in that class because he'd put his back out from bouncing Tim to sleep. So really it's Tim's fault, what happened. I'll save that up to tell him when he's old enough to understand.

Helen wasn't single either. She had a long-term boyfriend to whom she gave the elbow some time in that first year she and Troy were sleeping together. That poor fellow. I think they'd been together for a while, too. Maybe he and I should have gone for a drink and commiserated about our respective dumpings.

I wonder if her boyfriend had any idea of what was going on. Looking back now, I can see things that should have made me worry. Troy's sudden interest in how he looked. Suddenly dealing with the weird foot fungus thing he had been ignoring for years, despite my telling him it was disgusting and quite probably contagious. The working late.

It really did seem, after the fact, as if Troy had been following some sort of guide to cheating that included all the classic hits.

When Tim was two, just as sleep was starting to look like it hadn't left us forever, and the idea of a shag no longer seemed, as it had in the earliest days of parenthood, like something only slightly preferable to bleaching the bathroom, Troy started working late. A lot.

Instead of coming home from the office around six, walking in right after the toddler was fed and bathed, just in time to rev him up before bed, Troy started arriving later and later each evening. It was gradual, but once I found out I was pregnant again it really struck me. At least four nights a week he wasn't home before nine or ten.

But he was running a small business, a start-up that was growing fast. I could put his absence down to that. And with me being pregnant, if he wasn't home by seven it didn't really make much difference to me whether he came home at eight o'clock or three the next morning. I was out for the count as soon as I had Tim asleep.

That was probably something he learned in his *Affairs for Dummies* manual: cheat on your wife while she's pregnant. She'll be too tired to notice, and if she does get suspicious you can reassure her that it's her hormones talking.

Sometimes I wonder if Troy will do to Helen what he did to me. Once a cheater, always a cheater, isn't that what they say? Perhaps I should make Helen a handy list of warning signs to look out for. But then again, why should I?

* * *

When Charlotte the babysitter arrives—half an hour late—Laura takes off. Charlotte is a fifteen-year-old who lives around the corner. She is my last choice of babysitter, owing to her constant lateness, which is a symptom of her pathological inability to give a shit about anything. She drawls every word she deigns to utter, plays with her hair too much, and is never off her phone. But she's cheap, and local enough that I don't have to give her a lift home. And she was the only one available tonight.

She wanders into the living room and flops down on the sofa with the kids while I order an Uber and dash about giving instructions she will almost certainly disregard. The kids should be in bed by now, but since I was busy being harassed by Laura I've dropped the ball a bit. Charlotte is the sort of babysitter who will see I've dropped the ball this evening and languidly watch it roll under the couch.

But it's already six-thirty and the speeches start at seven, so I haven't got time to give her a lecture about her work ethic. I kiss the kids, who are lobbying against tooth-brushing and bed, and leap into the waiting car.

The launch is for a new thriller by Wanda Forthwright, the woman who invented being famous for being famous. American by birth, she moved from a small town in Vermont to New York City in the early 1960s to become a model, and spent the rest of that decade sleeping with pretty much every musician, artist, writer and actor of note. She ended up doing a bit of everything they did—a sexually transmitted career, really. She released albums, exhibited paintings, starred in films and then, ten years ago, she married an Australian man, moved to the Noosa hinterland and began turning out thrillers of impressive quality with equally astonishing frequency. She was a publisher's dream come true.

My old boss, Carmen, is that publisher, and so I worked on the final edits of a couple of Wanda's books back before I had kids, when I worked full-time, in an office, wearing makeup, and pants that were hardly ever what I'd slept in the night before.

Since returning to work as a freelancer, I've worked on two more of her novels, and we have a pretty nice little author–editor relationship going. Which is to say, I've met her on more than two occasions, I'm invited to her book launches, and she sends me a bottle of French champagne at Christmas every year.

Although of course I'm keen to witness Wanda's new book being released into the world, I really want to see her tonight so I can figure out why her next book, a memoir, which was meant to come to me for editing three months ago, is still nowhere to be seen. Titled *Affairs in Order,* it's supposed to be a chronological account of Wanda's love life: a warts-and-all catalogue of the mischief and mayhem she's been involved in over the past half-century.

The publishers want it out for Christmas this year, a plan that is growing ever less likely with each missed deadline, since—quite apart from the time it will take to edit the book—the thing will have to be scrutinized by a team of the finest lawyers in the land as it is almost certain to be largely made up of potentially defamatory statements about other famous people.

Every few weeks Carmen calls Wanda and politely inquires after its progress, and each time there's not much to report. Not surprisingly, every time I'm informed that the dates have been pushed back again, the tone of Carmen's emails becomes ever more panicky.

The delay is wreaking havoc with my schedule too. The weeks around the time I've put aside for this project I've filled up with other work, and whenever I get another email saying 'Sorry, I know we said the manuscript was going be with you next week, but it's going to be another month,' I fly into a panic about what I'll do with the projects that are already booked in for that date. It's a bundle of laughs, working for yourself.

Tonight's launch is at the Justice and Police Museum, which is where Wanda has set this novel, *After the Fact*. It's about an archivist who realizes, as she is researching old crimes for an exhibition, that someone is recreating those crimes around the city.

Even though it's late there's still traffic, and I have forgotten, or maybe I never knew, since I so rarely go anywhere, that Ubers can't use bus lanes. A trip that would take fifteen minutes in a cab takes forty-five, and by the time I jump out of the car and run up the steps of the museum, the speeches are in full swing.

Sophie, the managing director of the publishing house, is at the podium, heaping praise on Wanda, so I quietly wedge myself into the back row. A tall man with a shock of salt-and-pepper hair shuffles to the side, making room for me.

I look up to thank him and he smiles. He has startling blue eyes. I smile at him, then we both look to the front again.

When the MD finishes, Carmen steps up. She starts to speak, and the man beside me reaches over to a waiter who is standing by the wall and takes a glass of champagne from his tray. He passes it to me without a word.

I smile at him and take a sip. She's a valuable author, so this is proper champagne. It's so delicious I want to knock back the whole glass, but then I remember I haven't had dinner. Standing beside the drinks waiter is another waiter, this one holding a tray of what are almost certainly duck spring rolls. I try not to think about them, but my eyes must flick over there a few too many times, because the blue-eyed man reaches over again, takes a napkin from the fanned out pile and puts two spring rolls on it. He passes them over, again without a word, and motions for me to give him my glass so I have enough hands free to eat.

I wolf the spring rolls down gratefully, then, seemingly without taking his eyes off the stage at the front, he leans over and passes me two more.

I don't listen to Carmen. I've been to enough of these to know what she'll be saying. Wanda's outdone herself, every time they think she's done her best work, she surpasses it, blah blah blah. It's not entirely bullshit, Wanda does get better with each book, but the number of times Carmen's said this you'd think Wanda would have won a Nobel Prize for Literature by now.

Wanda's loving every word. There are some authors who look bashful and shrug off praise at events like this, but Wanda's beaming. She has a childlike attitude to praise, which I quite like. She's holding a glass of champagne in one hand and her clutch bag in the other. Under one arm she has tucked her husband Monty's left hand. He's standing beside her, patiently. Seeing I've finished eating, my snack benefactor hands back my glass.

I look around at the crowd. The current crop of young editors, assistants and publicists are easy to spot; they're the ones necking the champagne like people who barely earn a living wage. Ten years ago, that was me. It's hard to believe. I feel like that's still me, that I should be over there with them, but I realize that to them I am a fossil.

I'm an old person who disappeared off into the bourn from which few travellers return: maternity leave. I remember when I started my job that there was someone on maternity leave. She was spoken of in hushed tones, the way you would if someone had fallen down the gap between the train car and the platform and been horribly killed, and it was sort of their own fault. If they've even heard of me, that's how those girls will regard me.

After the speeches, I turn to thank my saviour, but he's been swept away into the crowd that is building around Wanda. I mean, I assume it's around Wanda, though she's so small I can't see her. Like a whirling eddy, the crowd moves over and the gap in its middle settles around a small table. That's where she'll be signing books. I should make my way over and congratulate her, but I've no need to line up for a signed copy, so instead I cast around for someone I know.

It's been six years since I worked in-house for the publisher, and there's been a lot of turnover. I don't recognize anyone at first. Eventually I spot the boss, Sophie, who I never had much to do with, but who will at least know who I am.

It's been such a long time since I've been to anything like this. Wanda brings out a book every year, but I haven't been to the launches of the last four, I don't think. The last of her launches I came to was when Tim was almost one, and I had thought it would be fine to bring him.

It would have been fine, too, if the launch hadn't been at six o'clock in the evening and if my baby had been a different baby altogether. Tim cried all the way to the event, I couldn't find a parking spot, I missed all the formalities, and once I had him strapped firmly to my front in the baby carrier he unleashed what could only be described as a shituation—a diaper fail of such catastrophic magnitude that there was no way to deal with it in a public place. I had to walk straight out of the bar, back to my car, change the diaper, clean him as best I could using an entire package of wipes, double bag all his clothes and the baby carrier, and drive him home, the front of my dress covered in poo.

That was the last time I saw most of the people I used to work with. Now, understandably, they mostly deal with me only by phone or email.

I'm trying to summon up the courage to walk over to Sophie, when someone taps me on the shoulder. I turn around to see my duck-spring-roll-enabler from earlier. I only saw him from the side before. He's quite handsome, and his eyes are really amazing. My mum would have called him a dish.

'Thanks for the food and drink earlier,' I say. 'I forgot to have lunch and I was about to pass out.'

'Yes, you did seem to be swaying. I thought you might need a bite to eat. If you miss the food at one of these things they're a bit hard to tolerate, I find.'

'Absolutely,' I agree. 'I used to be really good at figuring out which door the waitstaff were coming in from and lurking over there, but I'm a bit out of practice at book launches these days.'

'Have you read this new one yet?' he asks.

'As a matter of fact I have. Many, many times—I edited it.'

'Oh!' His face lights up. 'You must be Emma!'

'Yes,' I say, with some apprehension. Should I know this person? How does he know me? No one knows me.

'I'm a good friend of Wanda's,' he says. 'She thinks you're the bee's knees. She says you're a terrific editor. Very methodical.'

'Well that's nice to hear,' I say. 'I'm looking forward to the new book. It'll be quite a departure from her fiction.'

'Ah, yes.' He suddenly looks intently at his champagne glass.

He knows something about the book. I can tell. 'Are you quite close to Wanda?' I ask.

'I'm staying with her and Monty for a few months.'

'So you know how the book's progressing?' I'm not giving up. Something's going on.

'Look, it's really not my place to report on that,' he insists.

'Fair enough, of course you can't say.' I should stop hassling him, I know. But I'm very curious now. 'How come you're staying with them for so long? Where do you usually live?'

'London, mostly, but my work's pretty portable. And Wanda sometimes finds me useful to have around, when she's working.'

This is all very strange. What is the deal with this guy? Is he Wanda's guru or something?

'So you just hang around her house for months on end providing moral support?' I ask.

'It sounds pretty weird, when you put it like that. I suppose I'm—actually, do you know what I am? Have you heard of emotional support animals? They're a thing in America now. Instead of just having guide dogs for the blind and helper monkeys for the physically disabled, people now have miniature horses and peacocks and all sorts of mad things to provide emotional support.'

I'm laughing now. 'You're Wanda's emotional support peacock?'

'Yes,' he says, puffing his chest out in mock pride, 'I think that's what I am.'

He raises his glass to take a sip and, as he does, Wanda bustles under his arm and hurls herself at me.

'Emma, darling!' she pipes. 'It's magnificent to have you here. A dream! Philip, this is Emma, who is magnificent and a dream. Isn't she gorgeous? I'm the luckiest woman alive to have her to sort out all my wretched scribblings. Emma, have you met Philip? I simply can't do without him.'

'Congratulations, Wanda,' I say. 'You've done it again. The book's going to be a smash.'

'I know,' she sighs happily. Suddenly her smile drops away and her eyes narrow. Philip and I turn and follow her gaze. She's scowling at Carmen, who's raising her glass across the room at Wanda.

'That woman,' she mutters. 'She will not leave me alone. She can't, even for one night, stop bothering me about the new book. Not for one night! I mean, I know it's a bit past the deadline, but that was a soft deadline, surely. It's not as if I'm not working on it.' She looks up at Philip. 'I am, aren't I, Philip? Tell Emma I'm trying my best.'

He looks at me with a twinkle in his eye. 'Wanda,' he says very seriously, 'is really trying.'

'Ha!' she crows. 'See? I'm trying. One can but try. Oh, you must excuse me—that child over there is apparently the new book girl for the Women's Weekly and I have to befriend her.' She shoots off through the crowd like a tipped-over firecracker.

'Wanda is trying, is she?' I say to Philip.

'Extremely trying.'

I laugh. 'She always has been. But I'm sure she'll pull the book together. She always does.'

I'm about to tell him about all the times in the past Wanda has run late and fed us ludicrous excuses, when my phone buzzes in my pocket. Pulling it out, I see Charlotte's number on the screen. It's twenty past eight, which means she's been trying to get the girls to go to bed since I left and now she will have reached the end of her tether.

Unlike Wanda, Charlotte is not a trier. She gives about thirty per cent effort, at best.

'Excuse me,' I say to Philip, 'I have to take this. It's my incompetent babysitter.'

I answer. 'Hello, Charlotte, what's up?'

In the background I can hear crying. Not injured or genuinely sad crying, more the sound of two small girls who are taking immense pleasure in pissing off a fifteen-year-old who wants to be paid for sitting on the sofa, watching TV, texting her friends and eating my chocolate.

'Emma, I'm really sorry, but I might need you to come back. I think Freya and Lola might be coming down with something.'

Yeah, I think. They're coming down with great vengeance and furious anger, on you. I expect they're also coming down from the jelly snakes she will have fed them as soon as I left, since her childcare skills are entirely glucose-based.

'What makes you think they're coming down with something?'

'I don't know. Freya's gone light red in the face and she's quite sweaty. I think she must have a fever.'

'Charlotte, is she by any chance wearing two layers of polyester tiger suit?'

'I don't know. Maybe?'

Philip guffaws. I look at him and roll my eyes.

'Can you check? If she's wearing two, she's going to burst into flames. Take one off, at least.'

I do a quick calculation. I can stay here for another hour or so, during which time the girls will continue to torment Charlotte. They won't go to sleep until at least ten, which means they'll be horrible tomorrow. If I jump in a cab now, I can be home in twenty minutes and have them asleep ten minutes after that, since I can tell from the pitch of their shrieking that they are moving from having-fun-screaming-at-the-babysitter to genuinely overtired misery. Either way, I can tell Charlotte has no hope of getting them to bed.

'Is Tim in bed?' I ask.

'Yep, I think he's asleep.'

'And you really can't get the girls to bed?'

'Nup. They're going a bit mental. They reckon they need you.'

I sigh. 'Fine. I'll be home in twenty minutes. Try reading them a book or something. Just to calm them down a bit. And stick Freya in front of a fan.'

'Yeah, right,' Charlotte says, sounding terribly bored by it all. 'See you soon.'

I end the call. I take a deep breath in and let it out slowly. I love Lola, but she and Freya can wind each other up like you wouldn't believe. If I hadn't let Helen and Troy dump her with me tonight, Freya would have gone to bed as soon as I left. This was a grave miscalculation on my part.

Philip's still standing there, politely looking around.

'Everything okay?' he asks. 'Tiger trouble?'

'You could say that. Do you have kids?'

'No, but we did have a tiger for a while when I was small. I know a bit more about them than I do about kids.'

'You had a real tiger?'

'Only for a few months. My parents bought it from the pet store at Harrods, back when such things were legal. After a little while it became obvious that it was a very bad idea. But you must go—don't let me distract you with tiger tales.'

'I love tiger tales. But I am going to have to head off.'

'Here, did you get a goody bag? They were handing them out earlier.' He passes me a tote bag emblazoned with the cover of *After the Fact.*

I glance inside. There's a copy of the book, a miniature bottle of vodka, a box of chocolates, a red lipstick and a pair of pink fluffy handcuffs. And a voucher for a family visit to the Police Museum. I've never understood how the marketing department of this company thinks.

'Are you sure?' I say. 'Is there another one you can grab?'

'I think I'll be fine without one. I prefer to buy my own red lipstick.'

'Well, it was nice to meet you, Phillip.'

While I'm trying to figure out if shaking hands is the right thing to do here, he hugs me quickly and kisses me on both cheeks. 'Good to meet you too. I'll see you at the next one of these, with any luck.'

'Can you please encourage Wanda to make that sooner rather than later?'

'I'll do my best,' he says. 'Now, go fire that babysitter.'

* * *

I don't fire Charlotte. I don't know how. But I do make it very clear, as I'm paying her, while Freya and Lola leap off the sofa onto the pile they've made of all the pillows and blankets from my bed, that I'm less than impressed with her performance tonight. She doesn't care.

I bundle the girls off to bed, which they do willingly because they have got some sense after all and they can tell I'm not to be trifled with at this point, then I go straight to bed too. It's still early enough that I think I can manage two episodes of *The Devil's Heirs* before I fall asleep.

Tilde still hasn't figured out who is killing the single middle-aged women, and now her boss is concerned she is being distracted from her job by her troublesome ex-boyfriend. I have to say, I'm with the boss on this one. Tilde needs to get her head in the game or she's going to find herself back in uniform and the murderous rampage will continue. It strikes me that her boss looks a lot like Wanda's friend, Philip. I think of his description of himself as an emotional support animal and it makes me laugh again. I could use an emotional support animal. So could Tilde, I suspect.

Chapter Three

Two days later, I'm walking three children to school. Term two has only just started but already it's been chilly in the mornings. Freya's switched from her light summer tiger suit to the fleecy version, and we walk hand in paw. Tim and Lola dawdle behind us, because Lola is insisting on carrying Tim's huge backpack.

We're a good little unit, just the four of us. Lola seems happy enough when she's with her parents, but something's different about her—she's easier and more outgoing when she is with her brother and sister.

'I'll carry it, Tim,' she says. 'I'm the sherpa.'

'Okay, Sherpa Lola,' I tell her, 'if you can let Tim carry one handle, we'll make it to the summit before the bell goes. How does that sound?'

'No, Memma. Sherpas do all the carrying. Tim's a climber.'

Since she learned to speak Lola has called me Memma. It's a mixture of Mummy and Emma, and I like it. I don't know how Helen can stand it. If Tim and Freya ever called her anything even approaching Mum or Mumma, it would destroy me. Helen seems to rise above that sort of thing.

The little sherpa struggles on, up the slight incline of the street the school is on. It's slow going. Tim climbs onto the low front wall of the nearest house and walks carefully along it. He ducks under a low-hanging frangipani branch, and I instinctively move closer in case he overbalances, reaching out to hold his forearm. It's got goosebumps on it.

'Tim, want to put on your sweater?'

He looks at me like I am an oracle. He often reacts like that. As if common sense is some astonishing breakthrough.

'Yes!' He leaps off the wall and darts back to the sherpa. Obligingly, she puts down the bag and Tim rifles through it. A lunchbox, a water bottle and a plastic bag containing various-sized lumps of sandstone tumble onto the grass, but no sweater. He looks up at me.

'I haven't got it,' he says, crestfallen.

It's not the first time this has happened. It's not the tenth time this has happened.

I begin the routine interrogation.

'Did it come home with you yesterday?'

'I don't think so.'

'Do you remember taking it off at school?'

'Maybe? Yes. Yes! I do. I got hot playing handball, so I took it off then.'

'Where did you put it?'

'On the ground, probably.'

I don't shout at him. I'm proud of that. I'm getting good at this. We are five terms into his school career, and so far Tim has lost, permanently, six hats, four sweaters, one entire schoolbag. I've given up counting the drink bottles and lunchbox lids.

Tim resembles a kid who has his act together. His hair is quite tidy and he keeps his clothes reasonably clean, for a six-year-old. He just doesn't have any sense of ownership.

Discarding possessions in his wake, Tim just drifts along happily through life. My dad calls him deciduous, and Laura's take on it is that he keeps losing things because he feels he has lost his father. He feels untethered, so he sets his things adrift in the world. Laura's favourite game is what I call 'Everything Is Troy's Fault' and, much as I appreciate the sentiment, it can get a little wearing.

I take a deep breath and let it out quite loudly. Laura has pulled me up on this many times—she calls it sighing and maintains it is very passive aggressive. I call it practising mindfulness, and a better option than shouting at my kid in the street over a missing sweater. It's probably a form of lung yoga.

Tim loses things because he is a little boy with more important things to think about than stuff. I love that about him. It's why I don't punish him when he consistently comes home without his hat or his schoolbag or, on one memorable and inexplicable occasion, both of his shoelaces. He was as surprised as I was when I pointed it out to him.

And now we have to pick up the pace if we are going to make it to school in time to go to the Lost and Found to find this sweater.

As we approach the school I start seeing more parents—on foot, on adult scooters, and pulling up to unload their offspring from massive shiny cars. I've been walking this route every morning now for more than a year, but I still don't know most of them more than just to say hello.

The mothers in particular all seem to know each other. They call out about swapping pickups from soccer practice, and as they tie their dogs to the fence and hand their kids their saxophone cases and backpacks, their glossy blonde heads bob and glisten in the sunlight.

That's an exaggeration. They're not all blonde. But they are all beautifully groomed, clad in tidy ankle-length jeans and pristine white sneakers or leather boots. They're lean, Pilates-lean, like Helen.

I don't know how they pull it off. I could understand it if they were all housewives with nothing to do but clean the house, get their hair done and tone their muscles for six hours a day, but these women, I've learned, were once lawyers and accountants, stock traders and university professors, and now they are reinvented versions of themselves. Now they are entrepreneurs, corporate coaches, and consultants in their fields of expertise.

In the last three years, while I was leaning over with my head between my knees, waiting for my world to stop spinning around me in quite such a sick-making way, these women were all leaning in. They're the Robocop version of women who have it all. They've been through the fire of early motherhood and have come out the other side like a bunch of very lightly botoxed phoenixes.

I, on the other hand, seem to have come out singed and suffering from smoke inhalation. I have no idea what to say to them, and the feeling seems to be mutual.

I'm unsure how much people around here know about our situation. I've certainly never gone into details with these women, but word gets around in a suburb like Shorewood. It's a tightknit community, its fabric intricately woven from gossip. Without even having many local friends I know all sorts of things about the people who live around here, so I can only assume they know the same about me.

I did try a bit to make friends with the other parents in Tim's class last year, when he started school. But one morning a woman I was standing with outside the gymnasium started talking about how she'd heard about a kindergarten mum who had been left by her husband for a Pilates instructor and now she was raising their baby. I was too mortified to say anything, so I pretended I needed to change Lola's diaper and left.

That was pretty hard to come back from, so now I avoid the school parents as much as possible. Laura tells me I should just own the story, and tell everyone. She reckons people will be on my side. But I don't know. Maybe straight after he left that would have worked. But now I'm pretty sure I just seem like a nutjob.

The Lost and Found is open every morning, but only for ten minutes. The rest of the school buildings have been open for forty-five minutes when Deb, the office manager, turns up at 9:05 a.m. every weekday to unlock the padlock on the door of a small room under the staircase. She returns at 9:15 a.m., five minutes after the bell, to secure the room again.

The pointless and arbitrary nature of this set-up makes less than no sense. It means you have five minutes to search with your child, then another five minutes on your own to find whatever they've lost. If you do happen to be smiled on by the gods and recover your lost property in the second five minutes, you can't just hand it to your kid, because they've gone to class. You have to lurk around outside the classroom trying to get their attention, which is embarrassing for everyone.

Is this set-up in case people wander in off the street to help themselves to mismatched Tupperware boxes and lids, and drink bottles teeming with weeks-old bacteria-infested water? Is it to stop looting? What are the parents who have proper jobs to go to meant to do about lost property? Buy more sweaters, I suppose.

At least Deb is always on time. At exactly 9:05 a.m. she lifts the hinged section of the office countertop and marches along the worn green carpet to where Tim, Freya, Lola and I are lined up at the Lost and Found door, like we're waiting to buy tickets for the world's most disappointing concert.

Deb carries the keys to the school on a short leather strap that she clips each day to the belt of whichever lurid floral dress suits her mood.

We are well known to Deb.

'Good morning, intrepid explorers!' she trills. It is one of the joys of Deb's life to liken the Lost and Found room to an undiscovered treasure trove. Last time it was Tutankhamun's tomb. The time before that it was Angkor Wat.

'What will we find in El Dorado today, Tim, my gallant knight?' she asks.

Tim looks at his feet. 'Sweater, I hope.'

'Right then,' she says as she unclips the bunch of keys and holds them up, squinting at each in turn. 'Aha! Ride, boldly ride, if you seek for El Dorado!'

With a flourish, Deb flings open the door.

'Thanks,' Tim mumbles.

'Remember, in ten minutes the jungle will once again close over the mysterious city of gold, leaving no trace,' she calls over her shoulder, striding back to the office.

The Lost and Found room is no El Dorado. If a tomb raider chanced upon it they would shudder and brick up the doorway. Windowless and poky, its walls are lined with shelves on which stand forgotten drink bottles in rows like the motley recruits of the French Foreign Legion, amid stacks of scarred, faded plastic lunchboxes. Despite a policy of emptying out lost food containers before they are incarcerated here, the remembrance of bananas and sandwich-crusts past lingers in the air.

The clock is ticking. We have just under five minutes until the bell.

'Girls, sit on the floor right there,' I tell them, 'and guard Tim's bag.' There's no point letting that get sucked into the debris. 'Tim, start with that bin: it looks sweater-ish.'

With no discernible urgency, Tim starts plucking pieces of clothing from the bin and holding them up as if they are radioactive. I don't blame him. Everything in here is just kind of gross. Even things that have only been here overnight have acquired a sort of jailhouse stink.

Even if an almost-brand-new sweater comes out, and they often do—it's not the Bermuda Triangle—it is tainted and never feels quite nice again, even if you soak it and wash it and hang it out in the sunshine.

But I'll be damned if I'm paying twenty-eight dollars for yet another sweater.

Tim isn't even looking. 'Come on,' I tell him sternly. 'It's your sweater, buddy. You need to look for it properly.'

I start tossing sweaters over my shoulder so Tim can check their nametags. After six throws I hear a muffled giggle and turn to see him standing motionless, with sweaters caught on his arms and head. He hasn't checked any of them.

Suddenly a man sticks his head around the door. He looks at me, at Tim and the girls, then abruptly disappears.

'Bon,' he calls. 'It's pretty busy in here. Go play and I'll bring it out when I find it.'

Ha, I think. *When* you find it. He must be new here. And did he just call his kid Bon?

The man comes all the way into the room now, and stands with his feet either side of a tub of hats. Two things strike me with a jolt. Firstly, he is very handsome. And secondly, I knew him, once upon a time.

His name is Adam Cunningham. Ten years ago he wrote a book about his backpacking adventures in Europe, and how he ended up living in Amsterdam. It was called *Far Canal.* I was his editor.

For six months we spoke on the phone most days. As we grew closer to the print deadline, we'd spend hours in contemplation of a sentence here, or a tricky paragraph there, together trying to sand this thing he'd written into a form smooth enough that he could bear to let it go to the printer.

His diligence and work ethic had surprised me. Maybe because the Adam in the book was a free-wheeling, devil-may-care fellow, who would wake up one morning and decide that he wanted to be on the other side of the continent by nightfall. His writing made him seem like such a lad, but he worked very hard on that book in its final stages, polishing and refining it until it was as good as it could be. He'd been really funny, and good-humoured under pressure.

We only met in person a couple of times—when he came into the publisher's office once just after his book was contracted, and then again at the book launch in a downtown bar. I'm pretty sure he never knew that I had a complete crush on him. Probably my biggest author crush.

It's an occupational hazard, falling briefly and intensely in love with people whose work you edit, but nothing ever comes of it. There's not enough face-to-face time.

If an author's going to fall in love with someone in the process of their book's publication, it's not going to be the person who asks them difficult questions about why a character is called Jim in chapter one and Steve in chapter three. It's not going to be with the person who tells them that the last third of their book is self-indulgent waffle and recommends that it might benefit from being deleted, and it's not going to be the person who has to politely but firmly suggest they cut five thousand words about a hilarious night out in Stockholm because it's actually not funny if you weren't there.

It's an editor's job to tell an author—diplomatically and while pretending they're doing no such thing—all the places their book could be improved, and you'd be surprised how many writers don't want to hear it. It's unusual for an author to find all that nagging and nitpicking to be a turn-on, and they often react less than graciously.

If authors fall for anyone, it's usually for their publicist. Publicists wear high heels and pencil skirts and sometimes see the daylight. They take the authors on tour, where there are hotel rooms and expense accounts to be used in bars, both things that are more conducive to romance than emails, deadlines, and ultimately snatching away the precious work before the author thinks it is ready. (They never think it is ready.)

Besides, fancying an author you work with is usually more about loving their writing than them as a person. Authors are often their best selves on paper, and not so much in real life.

This makes it easy for a crush to pass without doing much damage, but there was something about Adam Cunningham, in person and on paper, that I felt wistful about for longer than the others.

Maybe because he's so handsome. He was so good looking that the marketing department wanted to override the obligatory travel-lit cover photo of a canal with the title in a whacky typeface, and instead use a picture of Adam looking moodily into a coffee cup. Did I mention he is handsome?

The ten years that have passed appear to have treated him kindly. They have kissed him grey around the temples and sketched a few rather charming crow's feet around his eyes, but other than that he seems unchanged.

Of course it's possible that the years have left him with a noticeable paunch, which he is disguising on a daily basis with the kind of supportive underpants once reserved only for wearing under a very slinky dress to a formal. But I can't see any evidence of it.

I smile at him. He smiles back, without a flicker of recognition. It was a long shot, him remembering me.

Should I say something? Should I remind him who I am? No, people hate being reminded that they've forgotten you. It makes everything awkward. It would get things off on the wrong foot to reprimand him for not recognizing me ten years after he saw me twice, briefly.

'Hello,' I say. 'I haven't seen you in here before.' I immediately realize how strange that sounds. We aren't in a pub. It's the Lost and Found. And I've just made it sound like it's *my* Lost and Found, that I am the queen of the Lost and Found, ruler of the realm of the discarded and the unvalued.

'My son just started last week,' he says.

'And he's already lost something?' I'm genuinely impressed. 'Tim, sounds like you've got competition. You didn't lose anything for at least a month.'

Tim rolls his eyes at me.

'Do you come here often?' Adam says. 'Sorry, that sounds, well you know, like a pickup line. I just meant . . . well, you said your son . . .'

He's getting flustered. What is this about? Is he blushing? He's not. He is. Why would he be? He's probably just embarrassed because I made it sound like I am the troll who lives under a bridge made of lost tennis racquets and he feels like he's treading on my turf.

'Yes, sadly,' I say. 'We're here a lot. Tim has quite a casual relationship with his belongings.' I continue digging through the bucket of sweaters.

Adam smiles at Tim. 'I don't blame you. That's a lot of maroon for one person to wear. If this was my uniform I'd do my best to lose it too.'

'Aha!' I say. 'Sweater!' I hoist it aloft. It's a small victory. 'Tim. Put this on and please don't ever take it off again.'

I turn to Adam just as the bell rings. 'Good luck with . . . what is it yours has lost?'

'His hat.'

'Well, good luck with his hat. If you don't find it, take an unlabelled one from here and wash it on a long cycle in your dishwasher. That'll kill any nits.'

Adam looks faintly disgusted. I must remove myself, because although that is a really valuable tip, for which he might thank me one day, it is possibly the least charming thing anyone's ever said to him.

'Anyway, bye,' I tell him. 'Girls, let's go.'

I'm rusty. Very rusty. Laura might be right about letting my skills become obsolete. I need some sort of retraining program for people re-entering the flirtspace.

* * *

Walking the girls back home, the day seems changed. The light is golden and everything looks sharper. This is very strange. My head is buzzing, and I have butterflies in my stomach. But they can't be butterflies. Not at my age. Moths, perhaps.

I haven't seen that man in a decade. This is not the way you are supposed to feel about someone you barely know, whom you haven't seen in a decade. I've been out of the game for too long and I've lost all perspective. The first inkling that the world may contain someone to whom I'm even slightly attracted and I've come over all Merchant Ivory.

And I can tell from the existence of Bon that Adam is now, at least, distinctly second-hand. He's probably not even single. Despite what happened to me, plenty of people manage to uphold their wedding vows. Betrayal and divorce aren't compulsory.

Adam was lovely, as I remember, and so probably hasn't gone off behind his wife's back and had a secret baby with his girlfriend. He's far more likely to be very happily married, probably to the Dutch girl he fell in love with at the end of his book. The woman who tamed the wild man, who got him to hang up his backpack and settle down for good.

What was her name? Something really Dutch, I remember that much. Elise? No. Ilse! Her name was Ilse and she ticked so many of the boxes of Dutch stereotypes that the publisher and I had to suggest Adam tone her down a bit so she seemed less of a cliché.

Blonde, tall, tanned, with great teeth, Ilse had lived on a houseboat. She was a photographer, and Adam had fallen in love with her at first sight when their bikes had collided in a rainstorm on Adam's first day in the city.

That was a great meet cute, practically rom-com-worthy. I remember working on the book and unfavourably comparing how

I'd met all my past boyfriends. I'd sat next to one in a university lecture, been flirted with by two boys at the next table during a pub trivia night and ultimately picked the wrong one to flirt back with . . . not a European bike collision to be seen.

Troy I'd met at a barbecue. It was my friend's brother's birthday. Troy chatted me up while flipping steaks on the barbecue.

It turns out they weren't even his steaks. It was one of those barbecues people had in their twenties where you had to bring your own meat, and the host would just supply a three-quarters-empty gas bottle for the barbie. Troy had brought a packet of the cheapest supermarket sausages, then he ate the steak someone else had brought.

How that failed to set off alarm bells with me, I'll never really understand. What can I say? I was young. Our meeting was definitely no bolt-of-lightning, hearts-and-bikes-collide moment. He was pretty cute though, and charming. Not to mention sexy. That night, we'd sat side by side on an orange plaid sofa, eating stolen steak off plastic plates, Troy constantly topping up my Jacobs Creek champagne while he told me I was the most amazing woman he'd ever met. I think I was showing off about the people I knew through my job, name-dropping authors I later realized he was only acting impressed by since he had never heard of most of them. It turns out Troy wasn't into books.

I definitely name-dropped Wanda that night to Troy, and I possibly even bragged about working with Adam. A shiver goes through me when I consider how small my life is, how far I haven't come.

So is Ilse, the perfect photographer, the mother of Bon? Is Bon a Dutch name? Is Bon even a name? There's Bon Scott, I suppose. And Bon Iver. But those are nicknames or stage names, surely. Maybe I misheard. Maybe Adam's child is called Ron. Or John.

I'll get Tim to find out.

* * *

It's a week before I see Adam again. Tim has an unprecedented run of responsible behaviour and I have no cause to go to the Lost and Found.

Anyway, he probably hasn't had to go back there. I'll bet that lost hat was a one-off because he has a child who keeps careful track of his belongings. After all, he's grown up on a houseboat, and you'd have to be pretty minimalist and organized to do that.

My week has passed as it always does, in a repeating loop of walks to and from school and kindergarten, trips to the supermarket and ferrying Lola all over the area to her activities, punctuated by long periods sitting at my laptop, at my kitchen table, working, while Lola and Freya rabbit about underfoot.

On Friday afternoon I'm waiting in the playground to pick Tim up. I've already collected the girls from preschool, and they are attempting to climb a jacaranda. They're far too small to reach even the lowest branch, so it's like watching a couple of puppies scrabbling at a table leg.

I sit down on a very low aluminum bench and lean back against the wall of the school. When I was at elementary school there was a bench just like this, but it was called the naughty seat. Naughty seats don't exist any more.

Tim's told me this bench has recently been declared the 'buddy bench'. The idea is that if anyone's feeling lonely, they can sit here and that's an indication to the other kids that they need someone to play with.

That's a lovely sentiment, although it doesn't address the issue of where to put the naughty kids. Perhaps they need two seats, one for the bad and one for the lonely.

There ought be one of these for adults. They could put it outside the pub. It could have one end for the bad and the other for the lonely, with a blurry section in between for those in the middle of that particular Venn diagram.

Though around here, there's probably no great need for a bench for the lonely. I seem to be living right in the heart of happy coupledom.

I close my eyes and the sun warms my face. The burble of gathering parents and the wittering of smaller siblings wash over me.

The bench gives slightly as someone else sits down.

'I thought it was you,' says a voice that with no exaggeration sends a tingle from my toes to my scalp. It's like someone has just played the opening chords of an REM song on the piano, in my soul.

It's Adam Cunningham.

I let my eyes stay closed for probably a fraction too long. I'm sure that seems weird. I open them and get another jolt because he is sitting very close to me.

'You're Emma, right?'

'I wasn't sure you'd remember me.'

'Of course I remember you! If it hadn't been for you, my book would have been forty thousand words too long and the sales figures would have showed it. You saved me from being torn to shreds by reviewers.'

'Oh, that was nothing to do with me,' I say. 'It was all your hard work.'

I wonder how he intends to play this. Are we going to acknowledge that the book sank without trace and sold only about three hundred copies?

Far Canal had come in the last dribble of a wave of armchair travel memoirs, many of which had sold in enormous numbers. The fashion peaked after 9/11, when people were scared to get on a plane and instead wanted to read about exotic locales. But by the time Adam's book came along, the market was oversaturated and everyone just wanted to read about vampires.

And sure, it hadn't been torn apart by reviewers, but that was largely because no one reviewed it.

He grins. 'You know it bombed. I expect it will be rediscovered when I'm dead and considered a classic.'

'Very likely,' I tell him. 'That is often the sales pattern we see with men's travel lit. Have you written any more books?'

'No, I had to get a proper job. As you can see, I have responsibilities now.'

'Ah, yes. What's your responsibility's name?'

'Bon.'

I was right.

'How about yours?' he asks.

'My year-one boy is Tim, and that's my daughter, Freya, with the brown hair. And that's Lola.'

I pause. I'm not sure how to explain Lola. She is with me so often that I've had to do this a lot, but it's always difficult. 'She's my kids' sister' usually leaves the person I'm talking to with a perplexed look. I can see them thinking, 'Does she mean her sister's kid? As in, her niece?'

Sometimes they leave it at that, and sometimes they ask for clarification. If I have to explain more, I try to do it in a no-nonsense fashion that doesn't invite further discussion. 'She's my husband's child with his new wife.' That's what I tell Adam now.

He looks at the girls. They are the same height. They have the same build. There's no mistaking that they are the same age. I use this as a test with new acquaintances. Will they continue asking awkward questions until I am forced to lay out the whole grim tale for them? Or will they guess it and politely move on to another topic?

'They look like they get along well,' he says.

Oh you kind man, I think.

'Bon's an only child. His mum's still living in Amsterdam.'

'Is she the woman from your book? Ilse, the photographer?'

'You have a good memory,' he says. 'She is.' He looks sad. 'I got transferred back here for work, and she's . . . she couldn't come back when we did. She'll be another few months, so we thought it would be best for Bon to get started at school as close to the beginning of the year as he could.'

'That makes sense,' I say. I want to know more about Ilse's absence because that doesn't sound like the whole story. But I can't figure out how not to sound nosy. So instead I say, 'How did you end up in Shorewood? Do you have family round here?'

'My sister,' he says. 'She lives about ten minutes away, and our parents are on the Gold Coast. My new job's in the city and Kit—that's my sister—said this was a good spot.'

Before I can delve any further into his personal life, the bell rings and a sea of maroon-clad children floods from all the doors of the building. It always reminds me of a tipped over glass of Ribena.

Kids run to parents, to trees, and to the gates. Some hurl their bags to the ground and restart games of handball where they left off at the end of lunchtime.

Tim runs to me, pulling a smaller boy by the sleeve.

Adam's face lights up.

'Mum, I have a new kindergarten buddy!' Tim's voice is high and excited. 'He's just started and he's called Ben and I have to look after him and do you know he has been to Legoland? Actual Legoland, Mum? Can he come play at our house? He has Lego Technic but it's in Amsterdam.'

'That's excellent, sweetie. I think he might be called Bon, though, not Ben. This is his dad, Adam.'

Tim turns to Bon. 'Are you? Bon not Ben?'

Bon looks up, shyly. 'I'm called Bon.'

'Oh, sorry,' says Tim. 'Well, can Bon come for a play? Please, Mum, can he? Because he doesn't have all his Lego in Australia yet because he used to live on a boat and his mum has to sail the boat here with the Lego on it.'

'Of course he can, but not today. We have to drop Lola home and go to the supermarket.' I don't add that there's no way Bon or Adam are coming to our house until it has been tidied, cleaned and disinfected to within an inch of its life.

'Bon,' says Adam, 'would you like that? To go play at Tim's house one afternoon?'

'I think so,' says Bon. 'Daddy, will you come too?'

'Oh, I don't know. I think the invitation is for you.'

'Of course you must come,' I say, and my voice sounds slightly hysterical. I lower it and speak deliberately slowly, like a calm person who is not a lunatic. 'Why don't you both come round after school next Friday and we can have an early pizza dinner?'

Adam looks grateful. 'Thanks. We don't really have any friends around here yet. It's been so great to run into you again, Emma. Really.' He takes my hand in both of his and squeezes it quickly. When he lets go, I let my hand fall to my side. I press it against my leg, through the fabric of my skirt.

* * *

That evening, as I boil pasta and grate cheese, rinse lunchboxes, unload and reload the dishwasher, I keep coming back to that word, 'really'. It was quite emphatic. It wasn't required. I am distracted by it. I want to tell someone about it. Mum flickers into my mind and I blink hard to make her disappear. She died more than ten years ago in a way that was so absurdly random and unforeseeable that it still takes my breath away—her first ever bee-sting, at the age of fifty-nine, while hanging out the laundry in her bare feet: an allergy no one knew she had. When will I stop wanting her to be the first person I turn to when I have news?

Laura, I tell myself, firmly. Laura is my option now. I need to get Laura's take on it.

But then again, maybe I need to keep it close. What if it's nothing? It very likely is nothing. He's new in the neighbourhood. He's married. He's just grateful Tim's looking out for Bon, and he hasn't lived here in Australia for a long time.

I rack my brains, trying to remember where he grew up. Melbourne, I think. Or possibly Perth. As soon as the kids are in bed, I'll get online and stalk him. Not stalk him, research him. Just look at what he's been up to since we last met; have a glance to see how locked down he keeps his Facebook profile and his Instagram. A harmless little check. Not stalking at all.

I'm strangely energized. The children notice and feed off it. We play music at dinner, and I make a game out of eating where we each spear a piece of food and feed it to the person on our left, while the person on our right feeds us. It's very funny, until Freya accidentally stabs Tim in the cheek with her fork and I have to shout at them, in the particular, slightly guilty way I have when something that was my idea goes wrong.

Chapter Four

By the time Friday rolls around again I have cleaned my house until it's unrecognizable. The toys are all put away in labelled tubs on shelves and the girls are ill at ease with their new environment. They can't find anything they want, as obviously they are too small to read, and boxes with neat tags that say 'trains' and 'dress-ups' are of no use to them.

Before we leave the house at pickup time I quickly smear on some dark pink lipstick and attempt to organize my hair. It's not that different from Inspector Tilde's hair, really. It's also shoulder-length and a colour best described as 'blonde when I was a kid'. But my hair hasn't been expensively highlighted and it doesn't sit neatly like Tilde's. Mine's more like a disappointing fluffy triangle.

'Why are you wearing *that*?' Freya asks, wrinkling her nose and pointing at my lips. 'Are you going out? Who's going to look after us?'

'What? No, I'm just, I don't know, I just felt like a bit of colour.'

'Can I do colouring in on my face too?'

'It's not really colouring in,' I lie. 'It's just a bit of a pick-me-up.'

'Can you pick me up too?' asks Lola. 'So I can see in the mirror and colour in on my face?'

'Kids aren't allowed to colour in their faces.'

Do we really have to have this conversation right now? One day I will explain to them about how makeup can be just for yourself, not necessarily for the male gaze. I'll explain about the media's portrayal of women and how conflicted you can feel when you want to set an example for your children about how self-love needn't be tied to appearance, but I'll do that on a day when I'm not trying to look hot for someone else's husband.

* * *

We all walk back from the school together, the kids running ahead and mostly failing to stop at driveways to check for cars.

Adam's very easy to talk to. He's still funny and, honestly, I think I'm doing okay. At a glance you wouldn't be able to tell that I haven't flirted with anyone in eight or nine years. It seems to be a skill that stays with you, dormant, until needed. Like riding a bike, as they say, although without any kind of protection so if I crash it will hurt. I have to keep reminding myself he's married. Any flirting I'm doing is strictly practice in case I meet someone who isn't married.

We pass the afternoon drinking tea, separating Lego pieces on request, chatting about this and that, and scrupulously avoiding the topic of my ex-husband and Adam's current wife.

Tim's beyond delighted to have a playmate who isn't a three-year-old girl, and my guilt subsides slightly. I haven't made as much effort as I should to invite his school friends to play. Our afternoons are usually so full of Lola's classes that there isn't enough time.

I mention this to Adam as I'm sprinkling grated mozzarella on the pizzas, and he's confused.

'Why don't her parents take her to the classes, if they're so keen for her to learn all those things?'

'They both work,' I say, knowing already what his next three questions will be because I know how stupid this sounds.

'Don't you work too?'

'I do, but I'm a freelancer and all I need is my laptop. I can work anywhere. I can take her to classes and still get my work done, whereas Troy needs to be in the head office a lot and Helen's a Pilates teacher, which is hard to do via email.'

'You don't feel a bit taken advantage of?'

'No,' I tell him brightly. I put the pizzas into the oven. 'I love being able to make it possible for my kids to spend time with their sister. I'm lucky I have such flexibility. And Helen and Troy don't take advantage, really. They take my two every second weekend, when they're not travelling. They're back from Bali tomorrow, and they'll take all three of them for the next two nights. It's a pretty tidy set-up.'

The doorbell rings and all four children shriek as if they're expecting Santa and the Easter Bunny to be there, arm in arm, ready to announce their engagement.

I hear someone open the door and then 'Mummy!' squeals Lola.

What?

'Hellooo,' comes Helen's voice down the hall. 'Surpri-ise! We came back a day early! There was going to be a problem with volcanic ash, they were saying, so we jumped on the plane today. More time with my baby!'

She appears with Lola in her arms in my kitchen. She looks like Instagram has been attached to a 3D printer. Her tan is perfect, her hair is shiny and falling in waves around her shoulders, and she's wearing a boho Balinese dress with a cashmere sweater.

Instead of looking like she just climbed out of a donation bin, like I would in that outfit, she looks ineffably chic.

Her eyes widen at the sight of Adam.

'Well, hello. I didn't realize you had company, Emma. I hope I'm not interrupting anything?'

'Just a playdate. Helen, this is Adam. Adam, Helen. Adam's son is Tim's new buddy.'

'How lovely. And your wife, Adam? Is she on her way to join you?' Helen doesn't mess around.

'She's overseas.'

'Ah,' says Helen with a little raise of her eyebrow at me.

'Are you planning to take the kids now?' I ask her. It would be very nice if she would go, quickly. 'If I'd known you were coming today I wouldn't have arranged dinner with Adam and Bon.'

I'm not sure what to do. If she takes the kids now, like they're supposed to do the night they return, I'll just be left sitting here eating a huge amount of pizza with Adam and Bon, which I suspect will be as boring for Bon as it will be awkward for Adam.

'The kids haven't eaten yet,' I say. 'Can I drop them over after dinner? I'll need to pack my guys' stuff for the weekend too.'

'Oh, darling,' says Helen. She puts on a serious face now. 'Troy was going to explain but he's just popped into the house to get the heating running. It turns out we can't take Tim and Freya this weekend after all. It's so sad.' She makes a little frowny pout at me.

It turns out. Because this is all just in the lap of the gods, and not at all in your control.

'Ah,' I say. 'You can't. I . . . well, right. How come?'

'It's just that we were going to take them all to Troy's mum and dad's at Whale Beach but Marianne's not been well and it'll be too much for her, having the whole gang, so we thought maybe she could just have some Lola time this weekend. Besides, we're going to be super jet-lagged and it just wouldn't be any fun for the kids.'

It wouldn't be any fun for her and Troy, is what she means. They were planning to dump all three kids on their grandparents all weekend and now they can't. So my kids get the heave-ho and just one kid will be ditched with her sick grandma. Well that's just fucking lovely. I'm not surprised Troy didn't dare come in to share this bit of news.

I can't look at Adam. Suddenly I remember this feeling. It's been a long time since I've experienced it and it very quickly reminds me why this whole fancying-people thing is a mug's game.

This is the feeling you get when someone figures out who you are, when they see through who you've been desperately trying to present yourself as. I've been trying to show him unflappable Emma, tough Emma. Emma, the awesome single mum. In-charge-but-not-bossy Emma. Everybody-loves-Emma Emma. The Emma I was, all those years ago.

I wanted him to think I was the kind of person who, when life gives them lemons, whips up a lemon meringue pie and makes the extra yolks into hollandaise sauce without breaking a sweat.

Right about now he'll be realizing now what a fraud I am. I'm just taking the lemons and sucking them.

He must think I'm the most pathetic wimp.

It strikes me that I'm not used to witnesses. There's not usually anyone here to see how this dynamic works between Troy, Helen and me. I'm used to operating in a shame vacuum.

Honestly, I would fight back about this—I mean, I do absolutely see why it needs fighting back against—but Helen and Troy always pull these stunts when all the kids are right there.

I can't bring myself to stand before my children begging someone else—even if he's their father—to take them away. How damaging would that be? So, as always, I just take it, even though it means looking like a downtrodden loser in front of Adam. 'I'll get Lola's things,' I say.

'Yours won't mind anyway,' she says. 'You've got your lovely friends here this evening and I would hate to drag Tim and Freya away from that just to hang around with boring old Daddy and me! And gosh, doesn't that pizza smell wonderful. I couldn't tear them away before they've had some of that.'

I know what I have to say here and I hate myself as I say it.

'Would you like to take some pizza home? You probably haven't got much in the fridge.'

'You sweet thing! This girl is a complete darling,' she says to Adam. 'Troy and Lola would love some, but *only* if you've got enough and *only* if it's no trouble.'

By the time she trips out the door ten minutes later, Helen has two pizzas, on a tray and ready to be baked, a litre of milk, a few apples and a dozen eggs, and only one child, whose clothes from the past week are all washed and folded neatly in her suitcase.

I close the door behind them and rest my head on the stained glass inlay for a moment. I don't want to go back to the kitchen where Adam is sitting with his glass of wine and his rapidly declining opinion of me. But the pizzas are going to burn.

He's taking the pizzas out of the oven when I come back in.

'More wine?' I offer. If I'm breezy and cool perhaps he won't notice how I was just taken for a complete ride.

'Allow me.' He tops up my glass. I can't meet his eye.

'Does that happen a lot?' he asks.

'What? Helen borrowing milk? No, she's usually very organized, but since they've just got off a plane—'

'I meant more the flaking on taking the kids. That can't be easy. Do you have to explain that to Tim and Freya or will their dad do it? Will they be very disappointed?'

I take a sip of wine so substantial it probably qualifies as a swig.

'Not that often. Maybe once a month. And it's easier on the kids if I tell them. Troy isn't always as tactful as he could be. But honestly, I don't mind.'

'I thought the way you dealt with it was amazing. I don't know how you didn't tell her where to go, but I can see why you didn't.'

I am flooded with relief.

'Thanks,' I tell him. 'I know it looks like I'm being taken terrible advantage of.'

'Which you are,' Adam says, 'but as far as I can see, there isn't very much you can do about it that won't make everything really shit for the kids.'

'Exactly!' Oh my God. He understands. Someone actually understands. There is a very handsome man sitting in my kitchen, drinking wine with me and understanding. And soon we will eat pizza.

I know later things will be bad again, because my kids have been rejected, once more, by their dad, and they're going to figure it out eventually. But selfishly, right now, in this very moment, I'm the happiest I have been in years.

* * *

Tim doesn't say much over dinner. I'm planning how I'll talk to him about it later, when there's no one else around if he needs to have a cry, when Adam asks, 'You right, mate? You a bit disappointed about the weekend?'

'Yep. I'm okay,' Tim says, staring down at his pile of pizza crusts. 'My dad's very busy. Did you know he's the Lord of the Juice? But he's going to make some one-on-one time for him and me soon.'

My moment of happiness is turned to ash by the incinerator that suddenly seems to have taken up residence in my chest. If I look at Tim I will properly cry.

Even worse than me knowing that Troy isn't going to make time for his son is Tim knowing that too. The truth is that Troy is only barely interested in being Lola's dad and he is almost completely not interested in his other two children. This fact is something I had hoped I could keep from my kids.

There is a fashion in modern child-rearing of not lying to children. You know, apart from the Big Three lies—Santa, the Easter Bunny and the Tooth Fairy—that are socially required. Once upon a time I was on board with that theory. I know better now. The people who don't lie to their kids are the people who don't have any real reason to.

I've spent three years lying to myself. I'm exceptionally good at it. Troy doesn't love me. He hasn't for a long time.

And there isn't a lot of evidence that he loves his kids that much either. But I hope I can avoid ever admitting that to them. There are some truths that should not be told.

'That sounds like a good plan,' Adam says to Tim, and I can tell he knows something's up. 'Bon's probably a bit over one-on-one time with me. If you ever want to hang out with us, Tim, we'd be very happy to have you along. Maybe next time we go down to the harbour to fish you could come with us.'

I smile gratefully at Adam and he gives me a little nod. He gets it. I can tell. God, he's hot. What on earth is the story with his wife? Something's not what it seems there. I have to find out more about this situation, but I can't quite figure out how without making my intentions clear.

What I need is to be back in high school. I need a friend to go up to him outside the fish and chip shop after school and suss out who he likes, who he *like* likes and who, if anyone, he loves.

Or I suppose, I could be an adult about this and just enjoy his company, and if it turns out that he and his wife are no longer together, maybe I could, in a totally casual and grown-up way, seduce him some time.

Ha. As if I would have the first clue how to go about that. My three years of single life since Troy left haven't exactly been a riot of passion. Between the children in my bed and my own ridiculous pining for the prick who abandoned me, sex has been fairly close behind exercise as the last thing on my mind.

This evening, however, sex seems to have burst forth from my psyche like a long-dormant bulb in the garden. No, actually it's not as subtle as that. Sex has leapt out of whatever dark shrubbery of my mind I've had it stuffed into, like a flasher, whipping off its raincoat and waving all its bits around for everyone to see. Frankly, it's alarming.

I feel so aflame I'm convinced Adam must be able to tell that although I seem to be participating in a conversation about the upsides and downsides of our suburb (upsides: excellent bakery, low crime rate, good school, many coffee options; downsides: stultifyingly boring after eight in the evening and moderately boring before, painfully middle class, yet no Japanese restaurant), I'm actually thinking only about what his chest might feel like.

All the wine we're drinking is not helping the situation. It's making me think of ways to ask him more about his marriage. Ways that seem subtle to me now, but which may actually just be a function of my thoroughly shiraz-soaked judgment.

Freya's eyes are at half-mast and I realize it's past eight o'clock. Someone has to put this kid to bed. That person, once again, is me. I don't want the evening to end.

'What time's Bon's bedtime?' I ask Adam. 'Shall I put Freya down and we can put a movie on for the boys?'

Christ, I might as well have just taken off my top and jiggled my boobs in his face. As come-ons go, that had all the subtlety of a lap dance.

But he nods! 'Normally he's in bed by now, but what the hell? It's Friday.'

'Okay, will you choose something? Netflix is on my laptop, plugged into the TV. I'm happy with anything G, or PG if you think it's okay for Bon. Tim will try for *Jaws* because he heard about it in the shark talk at the aquarium, but I'm not ready for his childhood to end, so absolutely not. Other than that I will leave it to your discretion.'

'Roger that,' says Adam.

I scoop up Freya and, bypassing a bath, plonk her on the toilet for a pee while I give her teeth a fairly cursory scrub with her beloved Tigger toothbrush. A pull-up, tiger-striped pyjamas, a kiss, and only one reading of *The Tiger Who Came to Tea* later, she is fast asleep.

I return to the kitchen, where Adam is loading the dishwasher. I practically have an orgasm on the spot.

'You don't need to do that,' I tell him.

'It's no trouble,' he says.

There's a pause. The pause turns into a proper silence. What do I say? Is this an uncomfortable silence? It is for me. Is Adam finding it weird? How can I tell? His back is to me and he's scrubbing melted-on cheese from my pizza tray, like something out of a Harlequin romance.

I just stand there and watch, mesmerized by the shape of his back and the way I can see the muscles moving even through his shirt and sweater.

The pause has definitely gone on for too long now for him not to have noticed it. It has to be addressed. One of us is going to say something. Whatever it is, I'm pretty sure it can only lead to him crossing this kitchen in two strides and taking me in his arms.

In movies you can always tell when there's about to be kissing. It's like when you know there's about to be a thunderstorm. You can smell something in the air. I think I've read it's ozone. Is it ozone? I think so. I can smell ozone in this room and there is one hundred per cent about to be kissing.

Adam turns, wiping his hands dry on my mum's old Jenolan Caves tea towel.

'Marriages are really hard,' he says. 'But looking at you and Helen tonight, and how that relationship works, and Troy too, I guess, I can see that not being married any more doesn't necessarily make anything easier.'

I'm sorry, what? That's not how you start a conversation that's going to end in kissing.

'I mean, I'm thinking about Ilse and me . . .'

I'm shutting down all the sex valves in my brain and body as he speaks. I've read this wrong. He's not into me, not like that. He wants to talk to me like I'm his friend. The best thing I can do here is attempt to salvage some dignity.

'Do you mind me talking to you about this stuff?' Adam says. 'I know we don't know each other that well, but I feel like we do, because you worked on the book and you're up on my, well, backstory, for want of a better word.'

'No, no,' I say. 'I'm happy to talk. We're friends. Friends talk.' I sit down before my shaking legs give way.

Adam reaches for the wine bottle to top up my glass but I put my hand over the top. 'I'm cool.'

He fills up his own glass and keeps talking. 'Thanks, Emma. It's really nice to have someone to talk to.'

No problem, I think. I'm delighted to hear all about your marital issues. I'd much rather do that than tear your clothes off and shag on my table.

Aloud, I say, 'So what's going on?' in what I hope sounds like a genuinely concerned voice.

'Ilse's not keen to move here. Her career is in Amsterdam, and she's never lived outside Europe. She's worried that if she commits to Australia, she won't get a job here. She's only prepared to come for a visit late in the northern summer at this stage. She wants us all to go back in September.'

'But you've moved here. You've taken a job here. You've brought Bon and started him in school. That doesn't sound like you're planning to go back to Amsterdam when September comes.'

'I don't know what I'm planning,' Adam says, and he looks miserable. 'My job is only a six-month contract, but they'd make it permanent if I could stay. I think I was trying to force her hand when I came back here. I wanted her to say, "Yes, I love you enough to give up things here for you, and start again in your country".'

'But she hasn't said that?'

'No, she hasn't said that. She's basically said, "I'll come and see how it is." She's not prepared to let me go altogether, but she's not ready to show me she wants me. And I'm sure if I stayed and she didn't, that she wouldn't let Bon stay here with me. God, I wish I was where you are in your relationship. I wish it was three years from now, and there was either a bit of a wobble in my marriage, three years in the past, or I was three years into being on my own again, like you are. Three years into moving on.'

'This isn't going to help much, but although it might look like I'm three years into moving on, I've really only recently realized this isn't a wobble in my marriage.'

He looks confused. 'But you're divorced. He's remarried.'

'Stupid, isn't it?' I say. 'I thought he'd be back. To be fair, that's not just me being a deluded idiot. Back when it happened, when he left, Troy said he didn't know if it was a forever split or not. Helen had just had Lola and he said he needed to look after her. He said he knew I was the strong one so I would be okay, but that he needed to be there for her. And I believed him. You'll believe anything if it makes it hurt less, I've learned. God, I can't believe I'm telling you this.'

Which raises the question, why am I telling Adam all this? I think it's the wine. That and the way I need to reframe this friendship as fast as I can to be just a friendship and not predicated on me wanting to jump into bed with him. Maybe if I talk to him like he's a long-lost girlfriend it will help.

'I don't think it's sad,' Adam says. 'No one wants to give up on love. What if it never comes again?'

'That's a cheering thought,' I say. 'If my marriage to Troy was my one chance at true love, then I don't think love's all it's cracked up to be.'

'I didn't mean you!' Adam laughs. 'You'll be snapped up, Emma. There's no doubt about that. You're gorgeous.'

Just like that the butterflies return to my tummy, and fanned by my total confusion they spontaneously combust. I cannot read this man at all. It's time to call an end to this evening. I don't think my nerves can stand any more of this.

'Yes, I am. And also very tired and a little bit pissed,' I say. 'Do we dare turn that movie off before it's finished?'

'I think we dare,' says Adam.

We walk into the living room and find the boys fast asleep, while *Despicable Me* plays on, disregarded.

'Awww,' we both say.

Adam picks up Bon, slings him over his shoulder, and carries him down the hall to the front door. I dart in front of him to open it.

'Emma,' he says quietly, 'thanks for the pizza. And for everything else.'

He leans in and kisses me softly on the cheek. For a cheek kiss, he lingers longer than I'd expect. He smells like heaven.

'Any time,' I whisper back.

When he reaches the gate he turns and says, 'See you soon? Let's text to plan something.'

'With the kids?' I say, before I can stop myself.

He hesitates, then smiles. 'Sure, with the kids.'

* * *

After I've carried Tim to his bed, I run myself a bath. I climb in and turn off the taps only once the water level has passed the ring of scum on the tub. I don't need to look at that while I lie here.

That was a completely baffling evening. I try to run through it in my head, to make any kind of sense of it.

I'm obviously no expert in judging these things, but Adam was definitely giving off a vibe of fancying me. There was unquestionably flirtation. That last moment, when he said, 'Sure, with the kids,' it seemed like maybe he meant the opposite of that.

But what about all that stuff about his marriage? It sounded like he wants to save it.

And then there was Helen. Adam has seen me being treated like staff by Helen. Adam has, though, also seen me acting like staff to Helen.

Why do I let her treat me like that? It's ridiculous. I spend my life treading softly around Troy and his new family, trying to make things easier for them. I can see it looks bad from the outside—like they have an unpaid child carer and I have unresolved issues with my ex-husband. And honestly, it doesn't feel fantastic from the inside either.

It might be time to turn off the help taps to Helen and Troy. Maybe see how they get on without me there to make everything easy. I'll admit it: I thought Troy would want me back when he realized Helen couldn't handle the challenges of married life. But they haven't had any challenges. Life's been golden since they got together.

What they need are some problems you can't buy your way out of. There must be something I can do. A way to quietly disrupt the perfect existence Helen and Troy have built on the wreckage of my life.

The tap drips and I think.

Maybe I'll stop taking Lola to all her activities. That would make things a bit challenging for them. They might have to think about someone other than themselves for once. It's not the same as actually doing something to them. It's no horse head in their bed. But there's power in going on strike.

Chapter Five

The entire next week, I very seriously consider making good on the threat I have made in my head to stop helping out so much with Lola. I'll admit, as a way of standing up for myself, this mental protest has been entirely ineffective. It has reminded me of the time when I was eighteen and Laura stopped talking to me for an entire month. But she was living in London at the time, and she emailed only sporadically anyway, and since she failed to tell me she wasn't talking to me until she started again, I didn't notice her silent protest.

My week's busy, too—on top of all our usual activities I spend a fair amount of time lurking around the playground hoping to run into Adam. Somehow I fail in that as well.

I make it to Tuesday night before I text him. Lying in bed, watching Tilde wrestle with her burgeoning romantic feelings for a fellow police officer fifteen years younger than she is, I keep one eye on the screen and tap on the message app on my phone.

Adam said to text. That must mean he wants me to text. Surely. You don't just say goodbye to someone with a request that they text you unless you want them to text you.

Christ, he wouldn't want me to text him if he knew how much obsessive thought I was putting into whether or not to text him.

But he hasn't texted. Why hasn't he texted? Stop acting like a fourteen-year-old, I tell myself. Although fourteen-year-olds probably don't even send text messages any more. I expect they use some horrifying platform I've never heard of and communicate entirely in nude selfies.

I'll send the breeziest text ever. There will be no hint of all this *Sturm und Drang* or any other emotionally fraught German terms for things we don't name in English because it's better to just not talk about that sort of business.

Hey, I type.

I delete it. I'm not sure we're on 'hey' terms yet.

Hi Adam, I type. *Pizza night again soon? Kids loved having you guys over.*

How to sign off. An x or not? Maybe just an E.

E.

I tap send quickly, before I can delete it and start again.

Now I'm not going to check my phone until I hear a text alert. I'm just going to nestle into my lovely comfy bed and enjoy my show and if he replies that's great but if he doesn't it's no big deal at all.

* * *

Sixty-eight hours later it's Friday again, and he hasn't texted back.

I check my phone one last time before I get in the car to drive to Dad's house for dinner. There are no new messages. Which is completely fine. The last thing I need is to get involved with someone who's constantly checking his phone. One of those in a relationship is plenty.

Dad would like it if both his daughters came over to his house for dinner once every week, like we used to do when Mum was alive. She had delighted in feeding us while we unloaded our woes and dirty laundry. First it was just Laura and me, from our rentals; then we'd come with boyfriends, then Laura with her husband, then with her babies. I never got to bring my own family home to Mum.

We should have tried even harder after she died to keep up the tradition she loved so much, but it was too sad and difficult. And then there were more babies and more husbands and an untrustworthy dog, and with no Mum there to make it easy, we fell out of the habit.

Now it's a stretch to coordinate our schedules for anything less than Christmas or a funeral.

Out of guilt for last weekend, Troy and Helen have taken Freya and Tim for two whole nights, and Dad texted me this morning to say he was making curry.

Laura's husband and kids are at their house watching some rugby game or other on TV. (The Stingrays versus the Stoats? Does that sound right? I don't pay much attention to these things.) For the first time in I don't know how long, it's just Dad, Laura and me, sitting in the living room of the house we grew up in, eating bowls of chicken curry on our laps.

Dinner on laps in front of the TV was a no-no in this house under Mum's rule, and Dad has tried very hard to keep to her standards, but tonight there has been a special dispensation made, since there are no children to corrupt with our anarchic behaviour and there's a new episode of *Midsomer Murders* on.

Dad hates *Midsomer Murders* so much he can't miss an episode. His objections are threefold and all equally valid: it's too white, it's statistically absurd, and too many characters don't call the police when they should.

Tonight his third objection is bothering him the most. A man has discovered the body of a young woman in his shed. He knows her, and this is apparently why he doesn't call the police for several days. This, as far as Dad is concerned, is complete madness.

'Why?' he splutters through a hail of rice and shards of pappadum. 'You'd call the police. You absolutely would. This just wouldn't happen. Can you imagine, you're a normal, law-abiding farmer and you happen across a dead body—a body you know, the body of your daughter's friend, no less. In what realm would you not call the police at once?'

'Dad, maybe he isn't a normal, law-abiding farmer,' says Laura. 'Perhaps that's why.'

'Then there's even more reason for him to call the authorities at once. If he hangs about like this with a cadaver stinking the place up and putting the cows off their feed, the cops are going to be even more suspicious of him once they do find out. And mark my words, girls, the cops always find out.'

'Well, in police dramas they do,' I say. 'They could hardly make a storyline out of a crime the cops aren't aware of. Things have to happen in stories. That's kind of what stories are.'

'Don't get all up on your narrative high horse with me, Mrs. Emma the Editor. My point is valid. And if you're not going to eat your naan, pass it over here.'

'I'm going to eat it, I just haven't eaten it yet.'

'Dad, there is more naan in the kitchen,' Laura says. 'Feel free to help yourself. Treat the place as your own.'

This is how Mum used to talk to Dad. Despite communicating almost entirely in snide remarks and passive aggressive mutterings, my parents were actually very happily married. It feels weird that Laura's slipped into Mum's role in this respect.

'I didn't father two wonderful healthy daughters in order to miss my show because I'm getting more naan from the kitchen, Laura.'

'Stop pretending to be sexist, Dad. No one's falling for it. We know you're just lazy.'

Laura's got his number. Dad has realized, from his intrepid lurking on Twitter, that he might be from the last generation of men that is going to get away with being sexist oafs and from time to time he has a go at milking it for all it's worth. This wouldn't be half as annoying if he was actually sexist, but he's a bold champion of women's rights. Online, when he's not writing screeds on *Midsomer* forums, he's usually found gallantly attempting to slay trolls on feminists' Twitter feeds. You can imagine how well that goes down.

Sometimes I think it would better if he hadn't ever discovered the internet.

'I am lazy, and I'm not ashamed to say it. I've spent the better part of my life at your beck and call, attending to your whims, dear daughters, and now I don't care which of my children gets me the naan. If I'd been blessed with a son I'd be making him get it for me. I am now in my dotage, and I'm no longer going to leap up all the time like one of those dancing bears in Russia where they heat up the floor so it can't stand still. This bear intends to remain right here in his armchair. If you heat up the floor I will simply put my feet on the coffee table.'

Ignoring Dad works, sort of. It doesn't stop him talking, but you can tune him out because he doesn't care if you're listening or not. I nibble my naan and watch a line of uniformed police officers searching a field for clues.

'And by asking you to get me some naan, I'm also building resilience in you girls. That's a very important thing, you know. I read an article about it on Facebook. By letting your children do more by themselves, they become stronger and more able to face the slings and arrows that life throws their way. Apparently if you are twenty per cent sure your child can do something, you should let them try.'

'Dad,' I say, 'that's for little kids. I don't think they mean you should make your adult daughters get more naan for you from the kitchen. I feel like that's a stretch.'

'No.' He's adamant. 'It's character-building for you, me asking you to do things like this. Think how proud of yourself you'll feel—whichever one of you gets the naan—once you've achieved this, all by yourself.'

Laura gets him some more naan.

'You are a dying breed, Dad,' she tells him, as she drops the bread in his bowl and sits back down.

'Thank you, my treasure.'

'That wasn't a compliment,' she says.

'It may not have been intended as such, but I shall receive it thus anyway. I am a dying breed and you two would do well to heed my example. You both need to teach your kids resilience. Laura, you mollycoddle those boys. By the time I was Harry's age I was getting myself to my soccer games on the bus. Every Saturday. Get them to do more for themselves. You too, Emma.'

'Yeah, Dad,' I say, 'I'll get my three-year-old to do more of the driving, shall I?'

'Don't be facetious, Em. You're in no position. You're even worse than your sister. Not only do you do absolutely everything for your own kids, but you run around like a chicken with its head cut off for someone else's kid! Your Troy's no fool, is he? You're practically raising Lola for him and Helen.'

'Dad!' says Laura. 'Don't say that to poor Emma. And he's not "her Troy" any more. He's Helen's Troy.'

'Well you wouldn't know it, for all the running around Emma does for him,' Dad continues. 'And all the free babysitting she does for that little girl.'

'Dad, she's Tim and Freya's sister. What should I do, ignore her? Not let my kids see her?'

'She's their half-sister, not their sister. Why can't they see her when they are at their father's? You don't need to offer yourself up as a free chauffeur and nanny, that's for sure. Why do you let them take advantage of you like that, Em?'

Suddenly no one is watching the TV. The forensic team continues searching the barn anyway.

'I'm not being taken advantage of. Laura, tell him.'

Laura takes a huge mouthful of curry.

'Really, Laura? You don't agree with him, do you?'

She chews for a long time and then swallows. 'Ah . . . yes. It seemed rude to say it—it was rude to say it, Dad—but yeah. They're taking you for a ride, Em.'

Shit. It's that obvious to everyone.

'How long have you thought that?' I demand.

'Always,' says Laura simply. 'Don't act like you haven't thought it too. You must see that what you're doing isn't normal.'

I don't know what to say. Of course I know this set-up is demented. Now. I'm just a bit mortified to admit how recently it's occurred to me. I can almost hear Mum's voice in my ear telling me to calm down, to listen to what they're saying. But I'm sick of feeling wrong. It's the worst. So I do exactly what I know I shouldn't and go on the attack.

'Mum would have stood up for me. She would have understood that I have to do this for my kids.' How dare she be dead when I need her on my side? 'It's all for their benefit. Kids of divorced parents have better outcomes when their parents get along—that's a fact established by research, I'm pretty sure. And if helping Troy and Helen out with the child care is the way for the family to get along then that's exactly what I'm going to do.'

'See,' Dad says. 'They are taking total advantage of you.'

'I'm not being taken advantage of. I'm setting an example to my children of how to be the bigger person. I'm showing them that just because one of their parents behaved badly, it doesn't mean I have to too. I'm showing them that tit-for-tat is unnecessary. You know, when they go low, we go high. I'm making the best of a less than ideal situation by turning the other cheek.'

Laura and Dad snort in unison.

'There's turning the other cheek,' Laura says, 'and then there's, I don't know, slicing off your own cheek and braising it in red wine in your slow cooker because Helen forgot to get anything for their dinner. You're such a martyr. I know you know, but you're too proud to admit it. You're a cross between an ostrich and a martyr.'

'I'm an ostrich martyr? Laura, what does that even mean?'

'It means you won't admit what everyone else can see. That Helen and Troy treat you like crap, and every time you respond by doing even more for them. What's that about? Are you trying to make them feel bad by being aggressively helpful? I don't know if that's going to work. Is it because of the money? Troy still has to give you money even if you only look after the two kids you had with him. I know he gives you a bit more than he has to, but that isn't enough to be a salary for looking after Lola.'

'Girls, girls,' says Dad. 'This isn't how we talk to each other.

Ostrich and martyr are judging words. And I can't hear the TV so if you're going to continue this, how about popping out to the garden?'

'You started it,' I tell him. 'But you're right. We don't need to continue this,' I say. 'I'm going home. It's pretty clear you both think I'm a useless doormat, even though all I'm trying to do is make my kids' life as calm and stress-free as I can. I don't expect any of you to understand because none of you has the slightest idea what it's been like for me. I'm well aware that mine is the first broken marriage in sixty-five generations of our family, so maybe you should just let me get on with it.' I stand up and grab my bag from the floor beside the sofa.

Laura is rolling her eyes at me. 'All right then, Miss "Nobody Knows The Trouble I've Seen", see you later.'

I pointedly step over her outstretched legs to kiss Dad goodbye. I don't say goodnight to Laura.

I get as far as the front door before I turn around, walk straight back into the living room and give Laura a hug and a kiss on the cheek. 'Love you, bye.'

'Love you.' She knew I'd be back. She knows that since Mum died I never leave anyone I love without telling them that, no matter how grumpy I might be. You just never know when it might be the last time.

* * *

I'm still cross when I wake up the next morning. I'm so cross that I wake up at six and can't get back to sleep. This makes me even crosser, because the children are at Troy's so I am supposed to be able to sleep in.

I roll over and try to force myself back to sleep, but outside I can hear the neighbourhood gearing up for a busy Saturday. My bedroom is at the front of the house, so there's not much between me and the family across the road loading their two Range Rovers, ready to head off for a full day of ferrying their two kids to about as many sports fixtures as the Commonwealth Games.

Along with the rest of Shorewood, in fact this whole city, they seem determined to create as much traffic on weekends as during weekday peak hour. It's worse on the weekend, in fact, because none of the sporting fields seem to be on public transport routes, so everyone drives. Plus all the matches start at different times, which just serves to drag out the traffic chaos until late afternoon. Once you throw in the house-hunters and the people trying to get their shopping done, you have a fully fledged gridlock situation.

'Hockey stick, Georgie!' I hear Julia from across the road yell. 'Hockey stick! Hockey. Stick.'

'God, Julia,' bellows her husband, Ian. 'There's no need to shout. Just go inside and remind her.'

'I have reminded her. I do nothing *but* remind her. This car is leaving this driveway in one minute—and that starts now—and if Georgie is not in this car with her hockey stick and her shin pads and her mouthguard I will simply leave without her.'

'What's the point of that? What are you going to do when you get to hockey without Georgie?'

'I don't know, Ian. Shame her? Tell all her little friends in the team how Georgie has let them down on the field because she is disorganized and lazy? Hmmm? Maybe that's what I'll do.'

I hate Julia and Ian. Quite a lot, but still nowhere near as much as they seem to hate each other. Especially on Saturday mornings.

They're not finished yet.

'Damon,' Ian shouts. 'Damon! Get in the car, Damon. Jesus Christ, Julia, what is that boy *doing* in there?'

'How would I know? Do I look like I can see through walls, Ian? I have just as much idea what Damon is doing in there as you do. Damon! Darling, come on.'

There's the clatter of a hockey stick being turfed with some force into the trunk of a four-wheel drive, and the slam of a car door.

'Georgie! That is a four hundred and fifty dollar piece of premium sporting equipment. If you break it, you are spending your own money on a new one,' Ian says, at top volume. 'I am sick to death of everyone in this family treating their belongings with such a lack of respect.'

'Everyone?' says Julia in a voice that portends danger, if you are Ian.

Uh, oh, Ian. Now you're in for it.

'*Everyone* treats their belongings with a lack of respect, do they, Ian?'

Back down, Ian. You are not going to come out of this well.

'I meant the kids, Jules, obviously.'

'That's not what you said. You said everyone. You meant me. You're talking about the dent in the car again.'

'No I'm not. You said that happened while you were parked at the mall and I accept that. We said we'd say no more about it.'

'But you just can't let it go, can you? I don't think you really believe me, Ian. I think you think I'm lying, and that I just crashed the car willy-nilly because I'm a bad driver.'

This is an interesting tack for Julia to take, going on the offensive, and I'm intrigued how it's going to play out. Because I happen to know she crashed the car right out front of their house, two afternoons ago, doing a very sloppy three-point turn. She reversed it into a crepe myrtle tree. If Ian spent any time at all watching crime dramas he'd figure that out for himself. There's metallic navy paint right there on the tree.

But when Julia goes on the offensive, Ian retreats. I've seen it time and time again in the years I've lived opposite them. Usually, though, when she goes on the attack it's because she hasn't done anything wrong, and she's all self-righteous. This use of attack as defence is new and clever.

His voice is wheedling now, like a dog that has been reprimanded, if that dog were also very conscious of not being late for rugby. 'Jules, love, of course I believe you. You're an awesome driver. You know I think that. Who does your dad let move the Jag when they're away? It's not me, is it? It's you, Jules. Now let's all head off. Here's Damon! Good boy, Damo, you got everything? Mouthguard? Yep? You have a great game, Georgie, and don't let the hockey umpire get distracted by your beautiful, beautiful mother.'

I hear two car doors slam and within seconds he's gone, with a squeal of tires, off up the street.

Julia closes her door, reverses swiftly down the driveway and steams off after him, only very slightly clipping the wing mirror on the Subaru parked next to their drive.

There's no way I'm going back to sleep now. I get up and boil the kettle.

* * *

I get a lot of work done on the weekends when the kids are with Helen and Troy. It's the best distraction I can come up with. If I don't have a book to edit—another person's imaginary world to absorb myself in—the days without them are too long and quiet, and then the loneliness gets me.

Once you've been abandoned by your husband—and I'm going to say this like I'm an expert even though it's only happened to me once—loneliness becomes a big part of life.

Well, it has for me anyway. Oh, I know I should cultivate hobbies and find more friends, but I'm done with that. That was what I did before I was married. I was planning to do it again once the kids were grown and Troy took up some absurdly expensive and time-consuming pastime like jet-skiing, as I assumed he would do. I just thought he would still be married to me when he reached that stage. And I thought all our friends' husbands would be doing it too so I'd have people to hang out with again. I never meant to be thirty-six and having to decide whether to join a hiking group or start taking life-drawing classes.

This was the part of my life where all I was going to do was focus on my family and do some work on the side. Now my family disappears for two days out of every fourteen. That leaves me with work.

When there's work to do, I can just put my head down and get on with it, knowing that every hour I do now is an extra hour I can hang out with them when they're back during the week.

This weekend though, I'm left hanging. The last time she emailed, just after the launch, Carmen assured me Wanda's book would be with me by today.

But the manuscript still hasn't appeared, and this morning when I wake to see yet another email from Carmen in my inbox, I assume it's to tell me of another delay.

I'm correct.

'That bloody woman,' begins her email, in direct contravention of what she taught me about only slagging off your author by phone, and never in writing, 'still isn't ready to deliver. I'm this close to going up to her stupid hippie enclave and hanging her upside down by her ankles until the damn book falls out of her.'

There's another email with the same subject line, only this one is from Wanda's friend Philip. I open it and read:

Dear Emma,

It was delightful to meet you at the book launch. I hope your small tiger has recovered from her heatstroke. It is an occupational hazard for all tigers.

Wanda has asked me to email you, because she does not like to be the bearer of bad news and thought that I would do a better job. She says I should be flattered by this but I do not find her argument watertight.

Anyway, the news, as you can probably guess, is that the manuscript is not finished. Wanda is very sorry, and I am too, only slightly less than she is perhaps because I would not otherwise have had the opportunity to email you and I did very much enjoy our chat the other evening.

We both hope this does not cause you too much inconvenience. Rest assured, work is progressing, just at a slower rate than anticipated.

Please accept Wanda's humble apologies, via your obedient servant,

Philip Albert

I'm very annoyed, but the email mitigates my fury slightly. Philip's quite funny. He writes like he speaks, as if he were raised by Mr. Darcy and Joanna Lumley.

It seems there will be no work this weekend. If I'd had this information on Friday I could have contacted the other publishers I have work lined up with to see if anything they have booked me for has by any miracle come in early, but the emails were sent late Friday night.

That leaves two days of nothing ahead of me.

My heart fills with dread. The weekend stretches out before me in a horrible daunting span of carefree, unstructured time. It's exactly what I used to fantasize about back when Tim was a baby. How can it seem so terrifying to me now?

Troy was just starting his business back then, so for weeks on end I'd barely see him and it would just be the baby and me, together, alone.

Weekends were the hardest, because at least during the week everyone else's husbands were at work too. Monday to Friday, I could hang out with all the women from mothers' group, and all my old university friends and colleagues who experienced the simultaneous explosion of our biological clocks and got knocked up around the same time.

That first year, when most of us were on maternity leave, it was never hard to find people to go to the park with, meet in a café, or just hang out at each other's houses. In those halcyon days before our babies could talk or express their own opinions, I got to have such great conversations with my old friends.

And it was so easy to make new friends. A simple 'How old's your baby?' to a woman waiting at the traffic lights could lead to a coffee and a chat with no awkwardness at all. Babies were such a visible signal of someone who had at least one thing in common with you. It was like the swinging sixties, but instead of sex we'd have banana bread.

It didn't always lead to friendship. I had my fair share of bad mum dates, where I'd get five minutes into a conversation before realizing that the only thing we had in common was that we'd both recently played host to a human parasite, and apart from that I was having a latte with a *Big Bang Theory*-watching racist whose child slept through the night from two days old.

But when the weekends came, back in those days, all the other dads would be around to play with their families, and with Troy still at work I'd be left wandering the suburb with a baby in a stroller, wondering if maybe my dad or my sister were free to hang out with me. Back then, the idea of two whole days to myself, with no small children to look after, seemed like an unattainable dream that I'd have to wait for retirement to experience.

Sometimes the only way I could fall asleep was to imagine that I was alone in the house—or better still, that I was in a hotel—and there was no one who would require my love, attention, or boobs in the small hours. I'd doze off, only to be shocked awake an hour later by Tim's little squawks.

So now, really, I should be beside myself with joy at the uninterrupted time I get as a single mother, on the occasions when Troy and Helen actually do what the custody agreement says and take Tim and Freya every second weekend from Friday afternoon at four until Sunday dinner time. But I'm not.

There's no one around to hang out with now. I could see friends with their husbands and kids, and I know I should because since everyone went back to work after maternity leave those friendships have withered from lack of attention. I still feel like

I know what all my old friends are up to, because I can see it on Facebook and Instagram, but I don't see them in real life much any more.

These are people I once would have called my closest friends, and who in fact I still consider myself close to, but then I realize I haven't met their youngest children, who are one or two years old. That's disgraceful.

And I do have these free weekends, when I could, theoretically, visit said friends. But here's the thing: it feels wrong spending time with other people's kids when my own aren't with me. I've done it a few times, but I always end up talking about them too much. I feel like some weirdo who has an imaginary friend. My friend's child will do something—a handstand, interrupt a conversation, a poo on a potty—and suddenly I find I'm telling everyone how *my* kid does that too.

What I forget, in those instances, is that no one cares about anyone else's kids. At all. They only tolerate them, sometimes, because they provide company for their own children, who they adore. It's human nature, and it means it's just very strange when you hang out without your kids, with other people's kids.

* * *

This weekend, like most of my childfree weekends, I decide to fill my time with household chores. Not so much cleaning or tidying-type chores, more the sort where I take myself to the big shopping centre and walk around putting things in my shopping basket before taking them out again. I can swing between over-consumption and minimalism in the time it takes to do a lap of the mall.

Today I need to replace Tim's handball. We were practising in the backyard earlier this week and it fell down an uncovered drainpipe. The drain bends just beneath the opening, so even with a flashlight we couldn't see the ball once it was lodged in there. We tried poking it with an unwound coathanger, but that, as you would expect, just pushed it further down. God knows what's going to happen next time we get a lot of rain.

I wander around a cheap department store, magnetically drawn to the toy section, past the brightly coloured Fisher-Price farmyards and plastic chainsaws. Toys that were popular when I was little are back, revamped for a new generation of parents trying to buy back some of their own childhood for their offspring. But while the names are similar, it's as if the toys have had a horrible distorting filter applied: the My Little Ponies aren't ponies any more. Now they're teenage girls with pony heads and drag-queen makeup. They confuse me. Do they live in a paddock at the end of a rainbow or are they equine cyberbullies in tartan mini-skirts?

I leave them all on the shelf, where their oversized eyes seem to follow me as I wander down the aisle. At the end of the row I'm distracted by yet more nostalgia in the form of some beautifully packaged games. Snakes and Ladders, marbles, the kind of wholesome, old-fashioned games that kids used to play while their parents ignored them in favour of drinking martinis and smoking. The games are six bucks each, so I stack several in my basket. They'll be good for the present box.

Forty-five minutes and many pairs of kids' pyjamas, handballs, and packets of coloured pencils later, I have had to swap my basket for a trolley, but when I get through the self-checkout and find out the total is forty-seven dollars, I'm so horrified by the low price that I abandon it all. That was a pricing mistake they made there.

They made it so low it alarmed me and reminded me what a lot of mass-produced junk it was, and how it was possibly made by small exploited children in the third world. If the total had been seventy dollars I probably would have bought the lot.

I check my phone to see if Laura has texted me an apology for last night. Nothing. *Martyr.* The word gnaws at me. I feel both unfairly accused and completely exposed.

Can't a person just go about her life being a good person, helping people who need help, without being accused of being a martyr? It's not as if I actively dislike helping out with Lola. I don't go about moaning and complaining, acting all put-upon and big-noting myself for taking her to her activities and having her for the odd sleepover. I love Lola. It's not that much trouble. And it makes my kids' lives better to have her around. And the more I look after Lola, the better an example I am setting to their father. And God knows he needs it. So Laura's wrong and that's that. Now she just needs to text me and say so.

I'm having a coffee when her message finally arrives. It's an apology of sorts.

Sorry I called you a martyr. Can you mind Bledisloe next weekend? Going to the Jacksons' holiday house.

I phone her back immediately. 'I can't take your dog for the weekend, as it happens. Because since you drew it to my attention that I am a martyr, I have stopped doing things for other people when it's not convenient for me.'

'Emma, I didn't mean stop doing things for *me*, I meant stop giving Troy and Helen a free ride.'

'No, I think you're right, I have been too giving and that has to stop. From now on, I am looking out for number one. Which means you'll have to make other arrangements for Bledisloe.'

This is very satisfying. I scrape up the last of the froth from my coffee, and I'm licking my spoon when I hear someone call my name. Except they're more yoo-hooing it than calling it.

'Eeeeee-mmmaaaa?'

Looking up I see, standing by the counter of the coffee shop, her arms festooned with shopping bags, Suze Albion-Davies, the president of the school PTA.

I immediately look down again, letting my hair fall over my face like an invisibility cape. I swivel my body away and through the back of my head I send my strongest ill wishes in Suze's direction, and yet still she comes, barging between the tables like an icebreaker in cropped jeans.

I look around for a cliff to throw myself off or a handful of cyanide pills, but today's safety obsessed culture has left the shopping centre woefully lacking in quick ways to end your life.

'Emma! I am so glad I ran into you! How serendipitous. It's getting close!'

'Hello, Suze. What's getting close?' I ask, as if I don't know. Why am bothering to play dumb? I'm only prolonging the agony.

'Emma! The Shorewood Public Fun Run and Have Fun Day, of course! Social event of the year! We've missed having you on the committee this year. So much. It just hasn't been as much fun without you. But it's not too late to help out. You know, you're in luck—today is the last day I'm finalizing volunteers for the Run-Up-A-Thon. I can count you in for that, yes?'

She tricks people, Suze, by ending her orders with an upward inflection and the word 'yes?'. It fools you into thinking they're questions. Last year when this happened, I fell for it. I was new. It seemed sporting and community-minded to get on board with the school's major fundraiser. I had hoped I might make some friends.

In hindsight, I should have realized that any event with a name like the Shorewood Public Fun Run and Have Fun Day would involve a lot of people who couldn't agree, refused to compromise, and would turn even the easiest decision into a nightmare. It should have been obvious that these people would require months of agonizing meetings that went for two hours when an email would have sufficed. There were subcommittees within subcommittees; motions moved and discussed and seconded and carried just to agree on which of three almost identical quotes for a jumping castle we should accept.

That's why I have been avoiding Suze assiduously for the past term. I thought that since we're only a month out from the event now she'd have finished dragooning people in to help, but now that she mentions the Run-Up-A-Thon it all comes flooding back.

That's the name she gave to the last month of organizing—the run-up, if you will—when all the original volunteers on the committee (except me) had quit in horror and/or sold their homes and moved away in order to avoid ever being involved in this event again.

You'd think word would get around that being on such a committee was a nightmare of epic proportions, but she's a cunning one, old Suze. Last year, a month before the Fun Run, she convinced the principal to implement something called the Be Upstanding Points System, by which the children of people who volunteered would receive special awards in assembly. It was an utter travesty, I thought. Is it not enough that the parents are doing most of the homework? Now the kids are rewarded for the parents doing good deeds in the community. It's a world gone mad and this year I will be having no part of it.

No way. So you think I'm a martyr, eh, sister dearest? A martyr would say yes to this, because this will make my life dreadful but will make me feel smug and worthwhile. This is the perfect test of my new resolution to be less giving.

'Thanks for checking, Suze,' I say. 'But I can't help this year.'

That's it. Plain. To the point. No excuse. No apology. Just no.

Suze cocks her head slightly and stares at me. I'm not sure what I've said is computing. I look back at her. It's agony. This is why people say yes to things—because it is against the laws of society and possibly even nature to cause this level of awkwardness.

But I've started now so I might as well see it through. I mean, it has to end eventually.

Finally Suze seems to snap back into the world and she says, 'Oh, that's all right, I suppose. I'm sure we'll manage without you.' She's obviously spent the last forty seconds hearing in her head the apology I failed to give.

'I'll still be participating,' I assure her. 'Troy and I are both planning to run with Tim on the day, so that's good.' No, I tell myself. Stop. Don't undo your hard work.

'Yes,' says Suze, 'that will be good.' But her gaze is unfocused now and I can tell she's already moved on in her head and is probably running through her mental database of parents to see who else she can rope in. 'See you soon, Emma.'

She walks off, phone in hand, already texting.

Chapter Six

Back home, I lie on my bed, feeling depleted. Standing up for yourself is exhausting. I should be elated, shouldn't I? I'm reclaiming my time. I've said no to something I didn't want to do. But I don't. I feel like I've broken a social contract and I'm waiting for my punishment.

I want to lie here all day, until the sick feeling I get after an adrenalin rush goes away, but I really should do something. Anything. I start to give myself a stern talking to, but then I realize that's Laura's area of special interest, so I phone her instead.

When she answers, I can tell she's at a rugby game.

'What's up now, Em?' she asks. 'Come on! That's a knock-on, surely?!'

'I can't do anything. I'm paralyzed,' I tell her.

'You're bored,' she says. 'Go outside. I know you don't want him for a whole weekend but come get Bledisloe and take him for a walk. He's being a bloody nightmare here.'

'I hate your dog.'

'We all hate him, Emma, that doesn't mean he doesn't need a walk. If you do something for someone else, you'll feel better about yourself.'

This seems to directly contravene what she told me last night about doing too many things for other people. When I mention this she brushes it off.

'Well then, if you won't do it for Bledisloe, do it for yourself. Just get some fresh air, go for a walk. Or a run. Go for a run, Emma.'

'Do you mean a jog? Because I never know any more. When people say "run" they're talking about what used to be called jogging, aren't they?'

'Just put on your sneakers, go out the front door and move your legs until you aren't in the same place any more.'

'Outside is full of neighbours. They're all doing family things. I can hear kids riding bikes and people washing cars. I can't go out there alone. Everyone will feel sorry for me.'

'Call a friend and go for a walk or a run with them.'

'I can't. I don't have any friends, and they're all doing family things. Everyone is doing fun lovely things with their family except me because my family is broken.' I can feel the tears coming.

'Emma,' Laura says in her most serious voice, 'of everyone you know who has kids, at this very moment, at four o'clock on a Saturday, I can guarantee that ninety-five per cent of them would give their left eye to be alone right now.'

I don't say anything for a while. She's right.

'Sneakers on, Em,' she says, more kindly this time.

'All right,' I say. 'Talk later.'

'Bye.'

* * *

Before I leave the house, I neighbour-proof myself. I plug my ears with earbuds and cover my eyes with sunglasses. I pull a baseball cap down over my forehead. I can't think of anything, save a hotel 'do not disturb' sign, that I can add to make it any clearer that I don't want to chat.

I step out my front door, wedge my house key into my bra, and turn left. Left takes me away from Helen and Troy's house. There's no way I'm walking past their place today. It's unlikely I'd see them anyway, because the kids will probably be out the back jumping on the trampoline that's so huge you could bounce a satellite into orbit from it, but I'm taking no chances.

I've been outside for thirty seconds when I realize no one's going to talk to me. No one's even really going to throw a second glance my way. As Mum always said, no one's as interested in you as you think they are. Everyone's only interested in themselves.

On my phone, I open the *Couch to Five K* app. A polite warning flashes on the screen that it's been more than a year since I last logged in. This is not news to me. I've had this app since Tim was a toddler. Every year or so I have a renewed burst of enthusiasm and decide I'm going to start running. I mean, everyone says it's the cheapest way in the world to get fit! You don't need any special equipment! You can do it absolutely anywhere on the planet!

The theory is that you start out walking, then jog for thirty seconds, then walk again. A very smug voice tells you when to run and when not to run. It's basically my sister, only I've paid $4.99 to Apple for the privilege of having her nag me any time I like. This goes on for twenty minutes.

Every time you log in and go for another jog—and you're supposed to run three times a week—the amount of running gradually increases and the walking decreases. You're supposed to not notice that you're getting fitter and it's becoming easier to run for longer periods. Eventually, the idea goes, after nine weeks I'll find myself running for half an hour, or five kilometres.

Yes, well. Every time I've tried this, I get to the stage of running for ten minutes, which is in week six. I am always elated. This must be what people are talking about, I think. This is the runner's high. I mean, it's not a physical feeling of joy and happiness flooding through my body. Obviously it isn't. I'm running. I'm not actually high. I still feel like vomiting, and the underwire from my sports bra is rubbing under my arms and my legs ache and every single step I want to stop, but maybe the high is a mental high that comes from not stopping when every fibre of your being is telling you to knock off whatever this mad activity is. Maybe they mean a feeling of contentedness that comes from knowing there is not an axe-wielding madman chasing you, which is the only other conceivable reason for running for ten minutes without stopping.

The second run in week six has you just plain old running for twenty-two minutes. Twenty-two minutes. Is that not quite a big step up from ten minutes? That doesn't seem like an incremental increase. That's going from your third violin lesson to performing with a symphony orchestra. It is too much for my mind to manage. Run two, week six is where I have stalled in this *Couch to Five K* program, for five years in a row.

The app asks me if I'd like to start again, since it's been so long since I've run. It's polite about it, but reading between the lines, I feel judged. But if I'm going to do this wretched Fun Run with Tim, I'd like to not disgrace myself in front of everyone, so I agree with the app. Yes, *Couch to Five K*, let's start this ridiculous farce all over again.

'Okay!' says the patronizing app voice in my ear. 'Let's warm up.'

So it begins. I head off at a brisk walk towards the park. It's surprisingly warm and there are people out doing Saturday afternoon-type activities everywhere. But Laura, as much as I hate to admit it, was right: no one looks like they're having the time of their lives.

James from number 45 is up a ladder clearing leaves out of the gutters like a man who has been asked more than once to do so. His eight-year-old son is holding the ladder as well as anyone can who is also playing Minecraft on an iPad.

Louise from 49 nods at me as she staggers into the house laden with shopping. Her fingers look like purplish sausages, the circulation is so compromised from the plastic bags cutting into them.

Esther, three doors along from Louise, is weeding around the base of her magnolia tree, and as I approach she turns and lets fly a stream of invective directed at someone in the house. She stops when she spots me.

'Hello, Emma! I was just saying to my mother-in-law what a beautiful day it is!'

I smile back and keep walking. My Farsi isn't up to much, so I can't be sure what was said, but if my mother-in-law, like Esther's, had been visiting for four months and showed no signs of leaving, I imagine we'd have quite a lot of aggressive conversations about the weather too.

'Run now!' my phone orders, and I break into a gentle trot. This isn't as bad as I remember. I can run. Anyone can run. I turn right at the end of the street, dart across the main road and start a lap of the sports field.

Running around the sports field is very dull, but the alternative is to go another kilometre down the road to the patch of woods, and I'm too scared to run there in case I find a dead body. I've watched enough crime shows to know that's what happens to joggers in the woods. You either find a dead body or become one.

It's late enough now that the youth soccer teams have packed up for the day, leaving only the odd chewed orange rind and a large puddle of sausage grease on the sidelines. Apart from a woman flinging a ball for a border collie, I've got the place to myself.

Already my lungs are burning, there's sweat dripping in my eyes and my knees hurt. By halfway around the sports field I'm filled with regret. Why have I come jogging? Why I am alone? Why don't I have any friends? Why did Troy leave me? Why won't Wanda hurry up and finish her book? Why don't I have someone like Philip to do the hard things I don't want to do? Why didn't my parents ever buy me a tiger cub? Why hasn't Adam texted me?

Adam. Thinking about him—even about his probably fine marriage and his probably non-romantic feelings for me—starts to cheer me up a little. At least he's back in my life, in some capacity. Those ever-confused butterflies erupt in my belly and I quicken my pace.

I really haven't felt like this about anyone for years. Maybe not since I felt like this about Adam when I first met him. It's hard to remember if I ever felt this fluttery and romantic about Troy—like I had a proper crush—but I suppose I must have.

I wonder if I'd be three years ahead in my recovery from Troy if I'd had someone like Adam come along sooner. I've been holding on so tightly to the idea that I still love Troy and want him back. Maybe that is what I could be for Adam, someone who shows him that there's no point clinging to the wreckage of a foundering marriage.

Maybe I'll experiment a little with letting the lingering

remains of my love for Troy go properly, and have a try at embracing my crush on Adam. But I have to be careful, I know that. Because essentially, I am on the rebound. I'm no fool. I can see that. And rebound flings are always a disaster. Everyone knows that.

Going right back, I think I was on the rebound when I met Troy. I'd recently been dumped by Patrick, a man I'd been dating for about six months. Patrick and I were just on the verge of getting serious, and I thought that was the direction we were heading.

Patrick took me to his sister's wedding at a winery, introduced me to his whole extended family, then broke up with me the next morning. I never really understood why. I didn't do anything disgraceful at the wedding, he assured me. It was just that he thought we weren't right for each other. Then we had to take the six-hour chartered coach ride back home with his parents, his siblings, all his aunts, uncles, cousins and childhood friends. I haven't been on a long bus trip since.

I think that after Patrick, once I'd started going out with Troy, I was just really happy every time a week went by and he didn't surprise-dump me. That's not setting the bar very high for a relationship.

As I now know from playing a huge amount of handball with Tim, things don't bounce as high on the rebound. A rebound is nothing compared to a serve. So no more rebounds, unless I want my romantic future to be relationships of ever-decreasing quality.

But a tiny voice in my head whispers, 'Maybe not always. Maybe not this time.'

Then through my headphones another, less tiny voice says 'Phew, good job! Let's take a little walk now.'

I open my heart to both voices.

* * *

The end of the weekend drags around and on Sunday at six o'clock on the dot, Troy and Helen bring the kids back. I've tried not to stalk them on Instagram too much, but I've seen they've been at the beach. Helen posted a picture of Lola beside an incredible sandcastle that clearly no children had a hand in making, and a shot of a basket of sandy shells with the caption: 'This is childhood. #childhoodunplugged #roamifyouwantto #seashells #enchantedchildhood #candidchildhood #capturedtreasures #carefreemoments #lettherebedelight'. Candid childhood, my ass. Neither of Lola's siblings are anywhere to be seen on Helen's Instagram feed. To look at it, you would never guess she had a less than perfect nuclear family situation. I mean, I don't want her shoving my kids' faces all over the internet, but I'm a bit offended at the way she just pretends to her many thousands of followers that they don't exist.

After the long drive back from Troy's parents' beach house, Tim and Freya are tired, grumpy and hungry.

'That was so boring,' says Tim. 'That was the worst weekend I've ever had.'

'Oh, really, sweetie?' I say. 'What happened? I thought you got to go to the beach.'

'Well, we did, but Dad went to play golf so it was just us and Helen and she made us sit in a tent on the beach. Why does she bring a tent to the beach? The beach isn't camping. She wouldn't let me go in the water, even though I can swim. Mum, she treats me like a baby.'

'Mummy, see all my shells!' Freya interrupts, and upends a beach bag into the middle of the living room floor. The floor I've just swept and mopped. The beach bag is clearly from the Mary Poppins for Cotton On range, because out of it comes a seemingly impossible quantity of sand and shells.

'Ah,' I say, 'that is a lot of shells. I'm very glad to see you brought back all the shells. Did you leave any shells on the beach for anyone else? Are there a whole lot of little nude hermit crabs scuttling about now? Does Lola have some shells too?'

'Helen said she couldn't take shells home to their house so she put her shells in with my shells. They can live next to her bed here. That one's hers. And this one, and this one . . .'

Freya carefully separates the shells into two piles, examining each one before deciding who it belongs to, acting for all the world like she can tell the difference between any of them.

'That's a bit sad for Lola,' I remark. 'Did Helen say why she couldn't bring home her shells?'

I'll be interested to hear how Helen has spun this to the kids. Obviously she doesn't want shells and sand all through her perfect house. Which is fine, because no one wants shells and sand all through the house. But it's a bit rich to be Instagramming them left, right, and centre and then banning them from her real life. She's such a killjoy.

'I don't know,' says Freya.

'She didn't say why,' says Tim. 'Do you have to keep saying "shells"? It's giving me a headache.'

'Sorry, love,' I say, then I whisper, 'shells.'

'Mum!'

'What? (Shells. Shells.)'

'Stop saying that.'

'Saying what? (Shells shells shells shells.)'

'It's not funny,' he shouts, and rushes out of the room.

I hear his bedroom door slam.

Freya looks up. 'Shells is a funny word, Mummy.'

'Well I think so, Frey-frey, but I don't think your brother agrees.'

Tim's like this more and more when he comes back from weekends with Troy. Usually I can jolly him out of it by being silly—hence all the shells carry-on—but when that doesn't work he needs to be left alone.

I'm still not very good at reading which of his moods require leaving alone and which require jollying-out, so I always try the jolly tactic first. Poor Tim. There's nothing worse than people trying to cheer you up when you are determined not to be cheered. I respect that, I do. Laura does it to me all the time. I hate it when Laura tells me one of her stories when I've got the shits.

It's a waste of a story, usually, and that makes me even crankier. If I'm not miserable and feeling sorry for myself, I'm much more likely to appreciate the tale of when she and her husband Andrew took Bledisloe to the dog park and Andrew loaded someone else's black Labrador into the back of the car when they were leaving. It was getting dark, so when Laura subsequently loaded the correct black Lab in beside it, she didn't see the dog Andrew had basically stolen, and so they arrived home with one more dog than they left with.

They drove Bledisloe's doppelgänger back to the park, where her distraught owner was wandering the sports field shouting 'Pippa! Pippa!' They all had a good laugh and agreed the City needed to upgrade the lighting in the parking lot.

I mean, it's not a hugely funny story, but I would have had a little laugh at it if I hadn't been in a foul mood. Laura wastes her stories because she's always trying to cheer me up. She doesn't have enough good stories to be profligate with them like that. None of us do.

That's why I just use silliness on Tim when he's got the grumps. But tonight he needs peace and quiet. It will take more than some wordplay to mend the wound that I can see growing in his heart every time he tries and fails to spend time with Troy.

Chapter Seven

Troy and Helen's house was identical to my house when they were built, back in the early years of last century. There are ten houses in a row just like them, all down our road. Opposite are ten more. They still all look more or less the same from the street, but once you're through the front door, you start to see the differences.

In my house, the leaded-window front door leads into a dark hallway, with two rooms off each side. Three rooms are bedrooms, and the one with a fireplace is the living room. At the end of the hall is the kitchen, big enough to hold a table and chairs for six, and beyond that still is the bathroom. There's a door off the side of the kitchen into the backyard, and a cracked concrete pathway leads first to the laundry, then on to the Hills Hoist in the middle of what could generously be called the lawn.

Since it was built, very little has changed in this house. That is not the case for the rest of the street.

These days, most of the houses' front doors open to reveal bright, airy, open-plan living spaces with soaring ceilings and glass walls that give onto outdoor entertaining spaces, the sandstone pavers bleached like the cliffs of Dover. Entering these cathedrals of Scandinavian-inspired minimalism, especially on a sunny day, has the tendency to make me feel like I am in the middle of a bomb blast: everything is white and looks like a sharp surface that's about to kill me.

These houses all have staircases that lead up to more bedrooms, bathrooms, walk-in wardrobes, and upstairs decks overlooking back gardens. Helen and Troy's house is a fine example. Half of their new first floor contains what real estate agents like to call 'a parents' retreat'. Because goodness knows, when they are finally at home with her, they need to squirrel themselves away from their one demanding child.

If I sound judgmental about the state of their house compared to the state of mine, it's only because I am. Troy gave me our house in the divorce settlement. He paid it off completely, which I know makes me incredibly fortunate, because I would never be able to keep up the repayments with what I earn these days. And I wouldn't be able to afford to live in Shorewood if I didn't have this house. But with the proceeds of the sale of Helen's home and further funds from the booming sales of bottled juice, they could afford to buy the bells-and-whistles version of our old place. Really, it couldn't be a more obvious sign to the world that Troy upgraded his life, in every sense.

When they moved in, there was nothing they needed to do to the place. Helen immediately abandoned her boho windchimes and crystals and embraced the fashion for white surfaces and pale wood. The appliances in their new kitchen were all top-of-the-line German machines, which emit ten to fifteen self-congratulatory beeps whenever they achieve anything. The backyard was a Tuscan-style dream, framed by neat rows of hedges in descending height order from back to front.

Helen, needing to mark her territory, insisted they have the thousands of dollars worth of travertine paving in the garden torn up and replaced with lush turf, which arrived looking like huge brown and green jelly rolls on the back of a low loader. So Helen could claim she was the one who had nurtured the garden into being, she insisted on rolling the turf into place all by herself.

When I walk into their house late on Monday afternoon to return Lola I'm struck again by the other-worldly tidiness. There is no clutter. There are a few little vignettes set up in homage to clutter, sure. A sort of ironic take on clutter sits in the form of half-a-dozen or so small hand-thrown pottery pieces arranged artfully on an otherwise empty gleaming expanse of engineered stone countertop.

The room is still and quiet.

In my house, there's always movement and sound. A piece of paper will be sliding glacially off the top of a teetering stack. Almost inaudible creaks come from baskets of toys as the Duplo settles in them. The old corrugated iron lean-to that protects me from the rain when I go to the laundry pops and creaks as it stretches and contracts with the weather. The kitchen tap drips. The bathroom taps drip.

If you watched my house through a time-lapse camera it would be like a jungle: growing, steaming, ever changing. Helen's house feels like it's under glass, brightly lit, in a museum.

Helen is running slightly late today, so while the children haul open the glass bi-fold doors and start rolling on the lawn, I find myself with nothing to do.

The kitchen sink is empty and dry, as though it was polished after the dishes went into the dishwasher this morning. It probably was. Helen's tap doesn't drip. Even if I dried my sink, four seconds later it would have drops of water in it again. My tap is old, and though I've taught myself some rudimentary plumbing skills through the wonders of YouTube, no matter how many times I change the washer, it drips with slow determination. Every three seconds. It's a metronome keeping time, waiting for a musician who never comes to play a dirge marked *larghissimo*.

I could make this tap drip. It wouldn't be hard. It would be annoying though, to the people who live here.

Before I can talk myself out of it I open the cupboard that conceals the laundry. Troy's toolbox is on a shelf above the washing machine. Beneath it is a little printed label that reads TOOLS. These little labels are everywhere in this house. Helen is mad for her electric Dymo label maker. I wouldn't be at all surprised if under her activewear her skin is covered in tiny little stickers saying 'boob', 'rib', and 'hip'.

I resist the temptation to peel the TOOLS sticker off the shelf and place it on their bed. Instead I borrow a spanner and a monkey wrench, and set to work, step-by-backwards-step reverse-engineering a leaking tap.

By the time Helen returns half an hour later, the kitchen tap is building a heavy droplet of water that falls about every five seconds. The room is so quiet that I put on some music to disguise it, because the plink of the drip hitting the stainless steel seems to reverberate around like a cell door clanging shut.

I say nothing about it, but as I farewell Lola and Helen, and head off to collect Tim from school, I feel the smallest shiver run through me. I still haven't told them I'm not going to keep taking Lola to all her activities, but at least I've done something. A micro-aggression. I've fired a little warning shot. It's a tiny spark of something that alarms me a bit, as I'm well aware that this feeling is the frisson of misbehaviour, and I rather like it. Sure, it's not setting someone's clothes on fire on the front lawn, and maybe they won't even notice, but maybe it will make their day, or their week, just ever so slightly more irritating, and that can't be a bad thing.

* * *

The next week drags unbearably. Every day before I take Tim to school I spend far more time than usual doing my hair and putting on makeup, in case I run into Adam. Every day, I don't run into Adam. I don't know why. Every day I vary my timing and my route ever so slightly, but we still don't meet.

My efforts seem to please the other parents at school though, and I get so many passing comments about how nice I'm looking that I begin to take offence. How horrible have I been looking until now?

I've never really known how to respond to compliments. When I was young, my mother taught me that the gracious way to accept a compliment is to simply say 'Thank you' and give a pleasant smile. I think this was based on Lady Diana, and what she would do. This approach is utterly at odds with what my mum actually used to do when someone complimented her, which was launch into a flurry of denials, batting away the kind words like she was being attacked by a swarm of mosquitoes.

'No, God no!' she'd scoff if you mentioned her sweater looks nice. 'I look horrendous. This thing? It's so old you can see through it. It's dreadful and I should throw it out. In fact I will, I'll throw it out right now. You've helped me make up my mind. Oh no, I can't because if I take it off you'll see my massive arms. The children will all run in fear! Ha! Here comes your terrible old mum with her horrible smelly old sweater and great big arms and her wrinkles. Have you seen these wrinkles? I suppose the pattern on the sweater distracts the eye from the wrinkles, doesn't it?'

Either that or she'd do a complicated magic trick by which she'd turn the nice comment around and fling it back at you in the form of a suggestion that perhaps you were blind, or thick, or demented. The compliment-to-criticism transformation was as swift as it was brutal.

'I like your lipstick,' I might have said.

'Emma! What on earth's wrong with you? How can you say you like this lipstick? It's a freebie and it's completely the wrong colour for me. It's just awful. Makes me look like I've been dug up. I worry about you sometimes, I really do. Have you had your colour vision checked recently? Because I've read that it can deteriorate with age. It happens.'

I worked very hard not to absorb this attitude to compliments, but when so many people say nice things over the course of a few days, when you've made slightly more effort than usual to put on a bit of mascara and maybe some eyeliner before venturing outside, I can see why it's tempting.

Of course it's lovely that people are thinking I look nice, but I think I'd prefer that it wasn't such a shock to them that they need to remark on it.

By the time Thursday rolls around, I'm starting to remember why I normally don't bother with makeup, because Thursday is the day I take all three kids to swimming lessons after school, and as if that isn't difficult enough without having to deal with mascara dripping down my cheeks and eyebrow pencil smearing across my forehead. I realize this as I'm wrangling three kids and a giant swimming bag through the turnstiles at the local pool.

If I could choose one activity to absolutely never ever do with small children, it would be swimming lessons. Unfortunately, if there's one activity I feel it's really important to do with small children, it's swimming lessons.

I'm paranoid about children drowning—perhaps more so than other people, although maybe other people just manage the fear better. When Tim was born I took him to baby swimming classes as soon as he was six months old—the earliest they would take him. He hated it. Some people just aren't water babies, it seems, or perhaps some babies don't find it relaxing to be joggled about in deep cold water by a clearly nervous mother who keeps saying, 'It's for your own good, it's not as bad as drowning.'

He's better about swimming now; in fact as soon as he was old enough to have a lesson without me in the water with him, infusing the whole pool with my panic like a giant pot of stress tea, his swimming came on in leaps and bounds.

By that stage I'd had Freya, so when Tim had his lesson I'd take her in at the other end to get her used to the water. She loved it from the get-go, and so did Lola, who we started bringing with us when the girls were about eight months old, because Helen always seemed to have a Pilates class scheduled, whichever day or time of the week we had swimming.

Back then, my kids didn't go for overnight visits to Troy's place—it was too much for Helen to deal with, what with having such a little baby—so his offer to feed all three kids dinner at his house once a week, post-swimming, seemed like a good deal. One evening a week to myself—well, two hours really—seemed like the height of luxury to me at that point. It seemed like a fair exchange to take Lola to the pool for the afternoon.

I look back on those days with mixed emotions. There's pride, obviously, because it's an amazing achievement to take one slippery, squirmy baby into deep water, let alone two, and bring them both out alive. There's also astonishment that I agreed to this absurd and hugely unequal arrangement.

But mostly there's horror. The lasting, deeply scarring trauma caused by the dressing rooms at the pool. It wasn't so bad when the girls were babies. Then it was a matter of getting them out of the pool ten minutes before the end of Tim's lesson, wrapping each in a towel and plonking them in the double stroller.

One at a time, I'd take a baby out, peel off her swimsuit, remove her sodden swim diaper, dry her off, put on a fresh diaper and some clothes and replace her in the stroller. And repeat. It took me a few months to realize I should dry and dress myself first, because dressing babies involves a certain amount of holding them against your body while you hold their pants and kind of shake the child in. But the point being that it's no use lowering a baby into dry clothes if you then hold them to your sodden bosom and get them soaked with chlorinated water again. Those were the days.

Once they could walk it was much harder. My fear of the kids drowning turned out to be nothing compared to the very real dangers they faced from cracking their heads open on the tiled change room floors, as they took turns to scamper away, slipping around like two little chubby Bambis on ice.

These days if we make it back from swimming without a cracked open forehead and with even one person wearing underpants that haven't been dropped in a puddle of warm human runoff, it's a very good day in my books.

I have high hopes for today. For once all the kids are well—no one is in the quarantine period post vomiting or diarrhea, there are no fevers, green snot, or stinging open wounds. This is surprisingly rare.

It's five minutes to four when we arrive at the pool. The lessons are at four. Both lessons. It's probably my greatest triumph to date, scheduling the kids' lessons at the same time. It was more good luck than good management, but it's a glorious thing nonetheless.

They're already in their swimsuits, so we just need to make a quick toilet stop and then they're ready.

'I don't need to pee,' Freya declares.

'Me too, I don't need to pee too,' says Lola.

'Well, let's just sit down and try anyway,' I say. 'You don't want to have to get out of the pool once the lesson starts, to come in and pee.'

They look at me as if I'm insane.

'You just pee in the pool if you need to go during a lesson,' Freya explains in a loud, patronizing voice.

A man wrapped in a towel overhears and snorts as he passes us in the corridor outside the change rooms.

Equally loudly, but with more disapproval in my voice I say 'Children, *no*! We never pee in the pool. That's very naughty.'

The man goes into the change room and once we're alone I crouch down and hiss, 'What's the first rule of peeing in the pool, Freya?'

'Oh, don't talk about peeing in the pool. Sorry.'

'That's all right. But really, you shouldn't pee in the pool. We're right at the toilets. Can you go and pee in one of them please?'

Grudgingly all three children enter the ladies' change room and head into the toilet cubicles.

The roar of three very full bladders emptying meets my ears for at least twenty seconds. It sounds like someone's pulling three pints of lager.

'I thought none of you needed to pee?' I say.

'I actually did,' says Tim.

'Mine was keeping a secret,' says Lola.

'I didn't do one,' lies Freya, who will never admit defeat.

* * *

Five minutes later, they're sitting on the edge of the pool under the expert tutelage of a couple of young Brazilian women, and I'm sitting on a bench, trying to decide which lane to swim in.

This is always hard. Generally, I would class myself as a slow swimmer. So I should go in the slow lane. But today the slow lane has two chaps in their seventies, walking side by side up and down it, chatting about their recent hip replacements. I'm not that slow. These guys aren't even creating ripples. They're moving like barges.

But the medium and fast lanes each have one man in them. I've seen them before. They're dads with kids in the same classes as mine. Both in speedos, they are swimming at the same pace. I sit on the edge and watch them for a few laps. Exactly the same pace. And it's not even a constant pace. One lap they'll both swim freestyle as fast as they can, and touch the wall in a photo finish. Then they take a leisurely thrash in the opposite direction, doing what I believe they think to be butterfly, but it's hard to tell with all the splashing. Again, they finish the lap at the same time.

I don't want to get in a lane with either of these guys.

If they were women, they'd notice what was going on, have quick laugh about it together, then one would suggest sharing a lane. One would start and then the other would start when the first one is halfway down the pool. That way they would never finish at the same time, have only minimal contact, and not take up two lanes.

But these two aqua-manspreaders don't do that. I decide to take the medium lane and by swimming at a medium pace—slower than them, faster than the walking rehab team—I will set an example and maybe then they will move over and share the fast lane, like civilized humans.

I kick off my thongs, take off my hoodie and tracksuit pants, and stand for a moment, letting the warm, damp air flow over me. Glancing down I see that one boob is considerably closer to the ground than the other, so I give the right strap a hoick. This bathing suit was rubbish when I bought it five years ago and it hasn't improved with age.

I bought it thinking that having a black, racerback suit would make me look and seem serious about swimming, and also very thin. Neither of those things has happened. It makes me look like a mum, which is fine, because I am a mum, but just occasionally it would be nice to see people looking at me and thinking 'Is she the nanny? I'm not sure. She could be the nanny.' In this saggy suit, with the rough sandpapery patch on the bottom from sitting on the edge of the pool with recalcitrant toddlers while trying to show them that splashing about is fun and it's not scary to get water in your eyes, there's no doubt that I'm not the nanny.

I'm just about to get in, when my phone rings, deep in the swimming bag. My very tenuous resolve to do some laps evaporates instantly and I rummage through the bag, hoping it's a call that might take long enough to excuse me from getting in the pool at all.

I miss the call and it's a number I don't know. Normally that would be grounds to ignore it, but I really don't want to swim, so I call back.

Someone answers immediately. 'Emma!' It's a man's voice.

'Hi, who's this?' I say.

'Philip Albert,' says the voice. 'Wanda Forthwright's—'

'Emotional support animal?' I say.

He laughs. 'You remembered!'

'I don't know many emotional support animals,' I tell him. 'Or former tiger owners. How are you, Philip?'

'I'm very well, Emma. And you?

'I'm fine,' I say.

'Right,' he says, 'good. Now, Emma, as you know, Wanda's hopeless at communicating while she's working, but I just wanted to check in and tell you that there is progress. We're not out of the woods yet, but she's getting there. She's worried, though, that you won't be available to edit once she finally finishes. I imagine you have a pretty full schedule of work, and people mucking around with due dates don't help that.'

It's surprisingly thoughtful of Wanda to be concerned about my schedule. It's quite flattering.

'Tell Wanda not to worry. I can move things around so I'll be able to do her edit, but it would be good if she delivered soon, you know, from a not-annoying-the-publisher perspective.'

'Understood,' he replies. There's a pause. 'Right. Well then,' he says.

'Philip,' I say. 'What else do you do, apart from Wanda's dirty work? I mean for a job.'

'I work for an aid organization. We work in a lot of areas, but especially child and maternal health, and water sanitation, which obviously go hand in hand.'

'That's a very cool job.' I'm momentarily overcome with envy. I wish I were helping to save the world.

'We can never do as much as we want to, of course,' Philip says, 'but it does feel good to try.'

I'm about to ask him more, when the phone buzzes in my hand. It's a text from Adam. Finally!

'Philip, I have to run,' I say. 'I'm at swimming with the kids.'

'Of course, of course,' he says. 'I won't keep you. I'll let you know when I know more about the delivery date.'

'Great, thanks,' I say. 'See you.'

'Goodbye,' he says, very formally. I feel bad for rushing him off the phone but it's a text from Adam! He's still alive! His texting fingers still work! My patience has paid off.

Hey Emma, it reads. *Thanks for the pizza the other night. Let's definitely do it again. A.* There's not much to it. But it's better than no text at all.

By the time I've spent ten minutes analyzing Adam's text in painstaking detail—there's no 'x' at the end but abbreviating his name to 'A' shows a certain familiarity, as does the 'Hey' salutation—there's no point swimming, so I change back into my clothes. After the kids' lessons end we have forty-five minutes to get home before Dad arrives to mind Tim and Freya during parent–teacher night, and I have to drop Lola home before that.

I hustle the kids into the ladies' change room. Trying to foster independence, I tell them they all have to dry themselves, so they dab at their skin in a desultory fashion, removing none of the moisture. Then they try to put their clothes on and complain when it's like trying to get dressed in rubber bands.

In the car I try to think about Adam, and how I can see more of him without making it massively obvious how much I fancy him, but it's not easy with the girls wittering on to each other about something in an episode of *Peter Rabbit*, and some early 1980s Michael Jackson playing on the stereo.

My phone buzzes with another text and I reach for it.

'Whooooo,' comes an uncanny impression of a police car from the back seat. It scares the daylights out of me.

'Tim! Don't do that. It's very realistic.'

'Don't use your phone when you're driving.'

'I wasn't. I was just checking the texts.'

'Do you want to go to jail?'

I make a great show of putting on the indicator and pull over into a bus stop. The message is from Dad.

Please confirm parent–teacher thing is next Thursday, not tonight. Calendar on my phone is not to be trusted. If tonight, no can do: Widowers Anonymous twilight driving range outing.

Shit. I text back: *It is tonight but it's early. I'll be back by 6:30.*

Bloody Widowers Anonymous. It's not even a real group. It's Dad and his old friends Keith and Pete. They all lost their wives and when their kids were harassing them to get some counselling they invented this support group, which is mostly just them getting together for Thai food or golf.

I wait.

Sorry love, can Helen take them? I have to pick up Keith on the way to Wid Anon.

Bugger. Helen. I hate asking Helen to watch them.

No probs! I text. *Love to Keith and Pete.*

I consider calling Helen to ask if she minds me dropping off my kids for an hour when I drop off Lola, but that will give her the opportunity to say no, so I decide I'll just dump and run. I hardly ever do this.

Back when the situation was all new, Troy used to discourage me from dropping by. 'I just think we need to give this time to settle,' he said. 'Helen's new at motherhood, and she'll feel more confident if you aren't always there showing her how good you are at it.' So I kept away, except when they wanted me to mind the baby—then I was always right there for them.

Simple flattery. How did it get him so far? How did I not see it for so long?

It's mortifying, really, how blind I was, that I didn't see that he was playing off what I thought was my point of strength. Being a good mother was the one thing I thought I had over Helen. And it's remained that way. I've been a terrible show-off about being able to manage two small kids on my own with no trouble whatsoever. And then I added a third for much of the time. It's like I was saying, 'Hey, check me out! I can manage all the kids! Your kids, my kids—can't have too many kids!' I thought that would impress Troy enough that he'd want me back. What a dickhead I've been.

When people in books and films have epiphanies, it's always as if they really, really couldn't see what everyone else around them could see as plain as the nose on their face. Dramatic irony, that's called. But I'm not convinced that really exists.

Looking back, I knew what was happening. I knew I was being taken for a ride. Sure I wasn't prepared to admit it, and I was determined to cloak it under layers and layers of denial. But deep down, I can't really say I didn't know I was being exploited. On some level I must have wanted it, or liked it. And that's pretty shame-inducing. I mean, what sort of person likes being treated that way?

I think I've known all along, on some level, that Troy wasn't ever coming back to me. I mean honestly, when has that ever happened? When has a husband ever left his wife, remarried, for heaven's sake, and then come back to the first wife? Not even Elizabeth Taylor pulled that off, and I'm no Elizabeth Taylor.

Now, it's time to even things up. Only a tiny bit, because there's the small issue of Helen and Troy being selfish shits who I don't actually want to spend too much time around my kids, but tonight at least, I'm going to drop my two off there with Helen, and head off to parent–teacher night without a backwards glance.

This would have more dramatic impact if I were swanning off on a hot date with some gorgeous man like, oh, I don't know, Adam, for instance, and not going to sit on a very small chair next to Troy, across a small desk from Tim's teacher, but a win is a win.

* * *

Helen wasn't pleased to be lumped with three kids, but I didn't leave her a lot of wiggle room to get out of it. Grudgingly, she went to thaw out a few more lentil patties and wash some more baby spinach as I mouthed 'Sorry' to my horrified-looking kids and beat a hasty retreat.

It's strange, being at the school in the evening. I always think being somewhere out of hours feels like intruding. Buildings emit a certain off-putting vibe after their usual closing time. Like the school probably wants to have its bra off and its sweatpants on at this point in the day and isn't pleased about having to be on show for a bunch of parents so they can flit from classroom to classroom, judging the teachers and raising their eyebrows about the quality of the children's art projects.

In fact, I'd go so far as to say that schools feel unwelcoming to parents at night because parents don't really belong in schools at any time of the day. Oh, I mean it's fine every now and then—you go in and help the kindergarten classes with reading groups, you might do a shift at the canteen—but in general, what happens at school is the business of the teachers and the kids.

I'm sure the teachers don't want us getting involved, and honestly, if I can put my kids in at one end of this elementary school when they're five and they come out at the age of eleven able to read, do a bit of maths and name a few places on the map, then I'm going to be quite content.

Outside Tim's classroom is a display of self-portraits the kids have done in crayon. Some of them are quite good, though its now clear to me what Tim was going on about recently when he was telling me about the sharing crayon. Apparently the art lesson when they did these took an unexpectedly long time because there was only one peach-coloured crayon to be found and a class of twenty-three children who all have more or less the same peach-shade of skin. Plus Gaurav, who used the brown crayon, finished early, and got to have Personal Reading Time until the rest of the pale-faced ones had managed to colour themselves in.

Troy is supposed to meet me outside the classroom. I'm about eight per cent sure he knows where it is. Our appointment is at six o'clock, and it's only a ten-minute window so he'd better not be late. He has three minutes to go. He always cuts it fine and he thinks it's charming, but it really isn't. It's disrespectful, and it's annoying, and at this point in my life it's very boring.

The door of 1M opens and out come Gaurav's parents, Vihaan and Ellie Darsha. They're leaving early—it's only 5:58 p.m. I'm not surprised though. How much can there be to talk about when you have the cleverest, and possibly the nicest, kid in the class?

Gaurav is my top choice of friend in this class for Tim, and I can't figure out why they haven't become friends.

'Hello, Emma,' Ellie says warmly. 'How's Tim?'

'He's just great, thanks Ellie. And Gaurav?'

'He's good too. Spends too much time on the computer, but don't they all?'

I think Ellie and I could be friends. I wish the boys would hit it off. It's awkward otherwise. Maybe I should invite them round to play.

Mrs. Mayall sticks her head round the door and spots me. 'Ah, Emma, come on in. Is Tim's dad . . . ?'

'On his way, I believe. I'm sure he'll be here in just a minute.'

'Good, lovely. Have a seat.' Mrs. Mayall lowers herself into a small plastic chair, designed to accommodate a six-year-old bottom, and I do the same.

Mrs. Mayall and I each have roughly two six-year-old-bottoms' worth of bottom, so we aren't comfortable. I shift about on the tiny furniture and clasp my hands around my knees, which are up under my chin.

Mrs. Mayall smiles at me, with her lips pursed together. 'Shall we . . . get started, or . . . ?'

'I don't know,' I tell her honestly. I hate to bring honesty into situations like this because it's very uncomfortable for people, but I don't know if Troy's on his way, or he's caught in traffic, or he's dead under a bus. I should be so lucky.

Suddenly my phone rings in my bag. 'Aha! That'll be him. Will you excuse me for a second? Then I'll know if we should start or . . .'

Mrs. Mayall waves me on to get the phone, her lips pursing even tighter.

Troy's name is on the screen, and I answer as I'm hoisting myself out of the chair and leaving the classroom.

'Where are you?' I ask.

'Em, I'm so sorry,' he says. 'I'm not going to make it.'

I bloody knew it.

'Why?'

'Lola's sick and I think Helen's coming down with it too. I'd better stay here and keep an eye on them. I'm really sorry. Can you write down everything Mrs. Miles says and we can discuss it tomorrow, or whenever everyone's better?'

'Mayall.'

'What?'

'Mayall, the teacher is Mrs. Mayall, not Mrs. Miles.'

'Oh, right.'

'What's Lola got? She was fine at swimming. Are Tim and Freya all right?'

There's a pause. 'What? Tim and Freya?'

I can almost hear the gears cranking in his head. He's breathing faster now.

'Yes, your other two children. Since you're at home I presume you've noticed that they are also there, with Lola and Helen.'

Nothing.

'Troy? Are you there?'

I hear a quiet shaky breath.

'You're not at home, are you?'

'What? Sorry, the phone keeps cutting out.'

'No it doesn't, I can hear you breathing. I said, you're not at home, are you? If you were home you would know that all the kids are there because my dad cancelled on babysitting Tim and Freya. And as of about fifteen minutes ago everyone in that house was perfectly healthy. So what the fuck is going on?'

All I hear is more quiet breathing. A familiar feeling shoots through me. It's nausea. It's the feeling I had when Troy confessed his affair with Helen. It's the feeling I get when I'm between six and twenty weeks pregnant. I'm fairly certain I know which of the two situations is being repeated here. It strikes me as unfair that my body is reacting in the same way to Helen being cheated on as it did when I was the one being wronged. I wonder who's he's shagging this time.

'I'm not home, no. No one's sick. I just can't make it to parent–teacher night. Sorry. I shouldn't have lied.'

'Why can't you come? What's so important? Is there some sort of juice crisis?' It all comes flooding back: all the calls like this I had from him when I was pregnant with Freya; all the delivery drivers who went AWOL; the catastrophes with labelling that only Troy could solve.

'Emma, I'm at a doctor's appointment. She is running very late.'

Now a jolt of worry surges through me. He never sees doctors. This must be serious. I don't want Troy back but I don't want him to die. On the other hand, this could easily be another lie, the cover for another affair. 'A doctor?' I say. 'What kind of doctor? Are you all right?'

He doesn't reply and in the background I hear a woman's voice say, 'Sir? You can't use your phone in here.'

Either his new lover is very strict about phone etiquette, or he really is in a medical establishment.

'Troy?' I ask again. 'What is the matter? Why are you seeing a doctor?'

'Look, I really don't want to talk about it.'

It clicks. He's not sick. He's seeing a therapist. Finally.

'Is the doctor a psychologist? A therapist? Are you finally seeing someone?'

'Yes!' he almost shouts. He sounds relieved I have guessed. 'Yes, that's it, I'm at my therapist's and she is running late. Shit, Emma, I just wanted this to be private. Can't a guy have any bloody privacy?'

I speak more gently now. 'Sure, Troy, of course. Sorry. Don't worry about tonight. I'll fill you in on what she says about Tim. Tim's great. He's a wonderful little boy and everyone knows that. And for what it's worth, I'm really proud of you for doing this. It's a healthy thing to do. I wish you'd done it a long time ago.'

'Thanks, Emsie,' he says. That's what he used to call me. Emsie. Hearing it now makes me feel a very confusing mix of sorrow, love, and rage.

So I tell him, 'Next time, don't bloody lie about everything. That might be something your therapist will tell you too, but don't disregard it automatically just because it's also something I've suggested.'

I hang up. I take a deep breath and stare at my phone. I've just wasted three of my ten minutes.

'Have you been sent out of class for having your phone on?'

I look up. Adam. Of course. Right now.

'Hey, no, I'm just . . . I was just talking to my ex-husband, who is, as you can see—' I gesture around me '—not here where he is supposed to be.'

'Oh, that's shit. I'm sorry.'

'Thanks. I'd better get back in and explain to the teacher. I don't think she approves of divorced parents.'

'I don't think Bon's teacher approves of absent mothers. I just got eight minutes of questioning about my wife's whereabouts and two minutes of telling me Bon's fine.'

I'll bet you did, I think. I know Bon's teacher, Miss Fairley. She's very fond of the dads, or so I've heard. Maybe I should pick her brains.

'Text me, though, or call, you know, if you want to chat or anything,' he says awkwardly.

'Yeah, I will, thanks,' I say. I'm still distracted by Troy's nonsense, but a spark of joy flashes inside me nonetheless. And sure, our conversations are awkward, but so were Elizabeth Bennett and Mr. Darcy's to start with.

* * *

On my way to pick up the kids, I mull over whether I'll have to explain to Helen why Troy isn't with me. I'm not going to lie to his wife for him, even if he is getting some therapy, finally.

But he's thought ahead, it seems.

'Poor Troy!' she says as soon as she opens the door to me. 'I can't believe the new driver would just not show up like that for his shift. I mean, who does that? So irresponsible. Now Troy has to miss parent–teacher night and spend the next however many hours doing deliveries? That's so unfair.'

'Isn't it?' I agree. 'So unfair. Poor Troy.' It's not a bad excuse, as they go. It's not original, by any means, but it's effective. There were constantly delivery drivers failing to show up for shifts in the last year of Troy's and my marriage. I'm just not entirely sure why he's lying about going to a therapist. Stubborn pride, I expect.

It's nothing to be embarrassed about, but maybe that's the

issue. Maybe even admitting he needs help is so mortifying for Troy that he can't bring himself to be honest about it. I don't know, and frankly it's not really my business any more, thank God. And there is, obviously, still the other possibility—that Troy is not seeing a therapist but having it off with someone else, again—but I don't think that's it.

Tim and Freya are lying on the sofa, still in their school uniforms, still stinking of chlorine. Beside them, Lola is in her pyjamas, her freshly washed hair damp and neatly combed. They all look exhausted, and they're staring at the huge TV on the wall. It's not switched on, because Helen doesn't believe in screen time, but that doesn't seem to worry the kids. They are resigned to their fate.

'Sorry,' Helen says. 'They didn't want a bath here. They said they'd wait and have one at home.'

'That's fine,' I tell her. 'Thanks for having them. I was really stuck.'

'My pleasure,' she says. 'I'm always happy to help.'

I know she doesn't mean it, but still, it's a nice thing to say. I'm torn between hoping Troy's having an affair and hoping he's not. That wasn't really the sort of problem I was wishing on her.

'Come on, gang,' I tell Tim and Freya. 'Let's head off.'

'Will you carry me?' asks Freya.

'No, you're a big girl, you can walk. It's so close.'

'But I can't walk because my legs hurt and they are too tired,' she moans.

'Well, I suppose I could carry you, but if you're too tired to walk then you're probably too tired for books when you get to bed.'

She knows this trick and scowls at me. 'I'll walk. But I need extra books.'

'Deal,' I say. 'Timbo, say "goodnight and thank you for having me" to Helen.'

'Goodnight and thank you for having me,' he mumbles.

'You're welcome, sweetie,' she says. 'Any time.'

Yeah, right.

* * *

When we're all washed, de-chlorinated, and tucked up in our beds, I pick up my phone. Text me, he said. Or call. I'm obviously not going to call. Calling is awful. No one likes talking on the phone. Even Jane Austen never wrote anything approaching as awkward as a phone call between two people who may or may not fancy the pants off each other. Especially when one of them is me.

I hate phone calls. Always have. If I could have a phone that does everything else—internet, texts, email, Instagram, Facebook, and the *What Bird Is That* app—with no actual phone? It would be a dream come true.

I put an episode of *The Devil's Heirs* on my laptop. I go back about fifteen minutes because I fell asleep watching it last night. Tilde is arguing with the forensic pathologist during an autopsy. She knows not to take anything at face value, that one. She's always questioning.

Chapter Eight

The dripping tap has had precisely no impact on Helen and Troy's life. The next time I visited their house, it wasn't dripping any more, which meant one of them simply went to the cupboard, took the appropriately labelled tools and repaired it, with no fuss.

That's quite disheartening. I was sure it would just drip away, causing an almost imperceptible irritation in their days that would, slowly but surely, infect other parts of their lives until the whole relationship imploded, but apparently that was not the case. To be honest, I don't even know if it made a blip on their radar.

It's Tuesday—ballet day for Lola—so after I drop Tim at school, Freya and I stop in at Helen and Troy's house to collect their daughter.

The front door is open, so we knock and walk straight in. Helen is standing at the gleaming kitchen island, her laptop open in front of her. She's standing on one leg, with the other foot tucked neatly into the top of her toned thigh. Balanced there, like a Lorna-Jane-clad blonde flamingo, she scrolls with the trackpad.

'Hello, hello,' she says, not looking up from the screen. 'Isn't this a funny thing? I think I might have just gone viral!'

'What?' I ask. 'What have you done that's gone viral?'

'Well, I just popped up a little video on my Instagram last night—did you know you can do videos on Insta, by the way? I always thought it was just photos. Anyway, Troy's new social media girl at work showed him, and he showed me, and he filmed me doing, like, a four-minute routine, just on the mat, and he sped some parts of it up, and this morning I've got nine thousand new followers.'

'That's good,' I say pleasantly. 'Is that a lot?' As if I don't know. As if I don't realize that's an enormous number of followers to jump on after one video. There must be a lot of shots of her Lycra-clad bum in the video.

'I sort of think it might be a lot of followers,' Helen tells me. 'How funny is that? I didn't even try! I mean, I already had seven thousand-ish, so that's almost double.'

'Funny, yes.'

'And just now I've had five messages from PRs, wanting to work with me on some, gosh, I don't even quite understand it, but I guess you'd call them sponsorship deals? Like, they'll pay me to wear their clients' activewear in my videos, and then I just have to tag them or mention them or something. Isn't that amazing?'

'Where's Lola?' I ask. I've heard enough about this viral business.

'She's just in her room. Lola!'

'Oh good,' I say, 'you've had that tap fixed. I saw it was leaking last week.'

'What tap?'

'The kitchen tap, just there. It was dripping. It's so annoying when they do that.'

Helen furrows her brow slightly. 'Was it? Troy must have just fixed it. He's great like that. I never even have to ask him to do those types of little jobs. He just seems to notice what needs doing and does it.'

It takes an inner strength I didn't know I had not to shout 'He fucking *what*?' at Helen's perfect face.

When he was married to me, Troy never lifted a finger until I had asked him at least twenty times to fix anything around the house. He'd look at me like I was the fussiest, naggiest shrew if I ever mentioned anything about how perhaps he could nail back down the floorboards he left unattached to the joists after he prised them up to see if he could find what was causing the rotting dead animal smell coming from under the house.

For as long as I've known Troy, he's been a world class unfinisher. He'll start anything you suggest, after about six requests, but completing the task? That's too boring, too pedestrian. He's moved on to bigger and better things. Every cupboard he's ever opened would still be open if it hadn't been for me. His bath water was always still there in the morning, and if the police had ever needed to retrace his steps, their job would be have been made simple by a quick walk through our house. Keys and wallet dumped on the table; shoes in front of the couch; beer bottle top on the coffee table, next to the empty beer bottle; dirty clothes on the bathroom floor; damp towel on the carpet in front of his chest of drawers, which would be open to reveal he had taken out a T-shirt, shorts, and undies. If they had gone on to discover his body, bludgeoned to death by his wife, driven to her wits' end, I think the jury would have been sympathetic.

What has Helen done to turn him into such a Stepford husband?

Maybe it's sexual. It must have started that way, at least. I try very hard not to think about Helen's Pilatified body and how slim and bendy and leggy she is. Isn't it remarkable how calling someone 'leggy' is always a compliment, but venture slightly further up the body and you get hippy, which is never a positive thing. I'm hippy; she's leggy. So she's the winner.

Before I can fall deeper into my rage spiral, Lola appears, kitted out in the palest pink tights, leotard, gauzy skirt and little wrap cardigan.

'Hello, gorgeous!' trills Helen. 'You look perfect! What a beautiful ballerina you are.'

'Memma, can you do my bun, please?' asks Lola.

Helen finally puts her other leg on the ground and darts over to her daughter. 'I'll do your bun, my sweet, no need to bother Emma.'

'It's no bother,' I say, secretly thrilled to be asked. 'I've got a little trick, haven't I, Lols, that helps it stay up when you do all that twirling?'

'Yes, Mummy, can Memma do it?'

I catch a flicker of hurt crossing Helen's face, but she almost instantly replaces it with a convincing smile.

'Of course she can—we can't have your hair falling down during the twirls, can we?'

'Right, I'll do it when we get to ballet, Lola, so it isn't uncomfortable in the car seat. Let's all go hop in the car now.'

It's probably best if I don't reveal here that my 'secret' to the stay-up ballet bun is around ninety seconds of spraying very cheap and almost certainly toxic hair lacquer all over Helen's child's head, while telling her not to breathe too deeply. The girls love it—they say it makes their hair crunchy and they spend an hour or so after Lola's ballet class scraping the hairspray out with their fingernails, like little chimps in a beauty pageant.

Freya, of course, doesn't do the ballet class, but she does like me to put her hair in a crunchy bun too. I did once take her in for a trial class, but when she realized ballet lessons involve a lot of being told what to do while standing still holding onto a barre and bending your knees a hundred times in a row, and very little leaping around in free-form interpretive dance pretending to be a tiger, she decided she'd rather just hang out in the foyer with me during Lola's lessons. I respect that.

Helen's back on one leg in front of the computer again, which I take as my cue to remove her child.

'We'll see you later then,' I say. 'I'll bring Lola back about twelve, shall I?'

'Oh there's no rush. Keep her as long as you like. I'm going to be flat out here on the phone, by the looks of all these crazy offers that just won't stop flooding my inbox! She'll have more fun with you and Freya. She can even stay for the afternoon and dinner, if she wants.'

Oh, can she? I think. How very generous of you to offer. I should say no. I should say, 'How about you look after your own kid, Helen? How about you stop using me as a free nanny?' Next time she does this, I promise myself, I'll say something. We'll see how much time she has to go viral and get clothing sponsorships when she's got a bored three-year-old underfoot all day long.

In the car, I mull over how this would work. If I tell Helen I'm not going to look after Lola any more, I have a horrible suspicion the only ones who are going to suffer are Lola and Freya. Helen will just get Lola a real nanny. It will be slightly inconvenient, for a few days, but they'll throw money at the problem, and then Lola and Freya will be separated and bereft. Because they're almost like twins, these two. Sisters from the same mister, but other mothers.

Even though it'll look to the rest of the world—and by that I mean my judgmental, unsupportive sister and dad—like I'm being a martyr, to use their own delightful word, I think I'm just going to have to go on with this set-up, for the moment, being the best stepmother to Lola that I can be. Except that's not the word. I'm not her stepmother. I'm her out-of-stepmother.

* * *

Lola's ballet class is held in a church hall two suburbs away. It's too far for the girls to walk, so each week we drive there, and each week we do battle with the parking gods on the street outside.

We've been doing this for close to a year now, and I'm yet to understand what causes the extraordinary demand for parking spaces within walking distance of this church hall, at precisely this time every week. There are only twelve kids in the class, and none of them come with motorcades or extra security vehicles in their convoys.

It's mostly residential, and none of the houses appear to have garages, but surely some of these people must drive their cars away from their houses during the day? Do none of them have jobs to go to? There are a few stores nearby, which would account for some of the demand, but not to the level of difficulty that we have every week when we spend upwards of twenty minutes cruising around, trying to wedge the car into spaces that are too small or too illegal.

Every week it gets more and more stressful as ten-thirty approaches. The ballet teacher, Miss Annabelinda, does not take kindly to latecomers. Even three-year-olds need to be on time, she has stressed to me on more than one occasion. It's how they learn respect and discipline, which are the cornerstones of a dancer's practice. Miss Annabelinda is a twenty-three-year-old who has clearly failed to become a professional ballerina and has been reduced to creating a hybrid of her real first and middle names in order to assume the appropriately la-di-da persona of a ballet teacher. She likes nothing more than telling off women almost twice her age who bring children late to class and don't seem to even care.

This morning it's no different. Round and round the same three or four blocks we go, willing people to come out of wherever they are hiding and get in their cars. 'Come on, come on,' I mutter. 'Leave your houses, you mad shut-ins. Go for a drive. Surely you need milk. Don't you have packages to collect from the post office? Where are you, people of this street?' It has no effect.

The class begins at ten-thirty, and by ten-thirty-five, I still haven't found a parking spot.

That's it. That's enough, I think. I have one life to live. I am not spending any more of it trying to telepathically convince suburbanites behind picket fences to come outside and drive off in their cars. We will not be going to ballet today.

'Girls,' I announce. 'Today, I cannot find anywhere to park this car, so we are not going to ballet. Miss Annabelinda will have to manage without Lola today. We're going to have an adventure.'

'Can we still have crunchy buns?' asks Freya.

'Yes you can.'

'Where are we going for our adventure?' asks Lola. It's a valid question, and not one for which I have a ready answer.

'It's a surprise,' I tell her.

'But we're still having crunchy buns,' she says to Freya, 'your mum says.' I love the way kids talk about adults like we aren't there. It's very fair payback for all the talking over their heads we do.

All this talk of crunchy buns gives me an idea and I turn onto the expressway. We're going to go to the promised land, where the cinnamon buns are plentiful, the coffee is cheap, and the child care and wi-fi are free. We'll be spending the morning at Ikea.

* * *

A lot of people hate going to Ikea. They say there are too many people, they feel trapped, the food is bad, and they always spend more than they plan to and come home with things they don't need. Such people just don't know how to do it properly. It's like drug-taking, or alcohol: you have to know what you're doing, what your limits are, and most importantly, you have to be with the right people. And, like getting drunk or high, first thing Saturday morning isn't the best time.

Once you know the secrets, once you've embraced the Swedish way, there's really no downside to Ikea. The key is to go early on a weekday, and to take a minimum of two children, and no significant others. Never take only one child. They won't want to be parked in the playroom, and they'll insist on tagging along through the furniture display area. You'll find them attempting to scale bunk beds using the ladders that have Plexiglas nailed on them to stop exactly that behaviour.

Turn up early, delight in the microscopically subversive act of feeding the children a one-dollar hot dog, embracing the mystery and wonder of what might be in the pasty-looking meat tubes, then deposit them in Småland. The older the kids get, the less likely they are to lick the balls in the ball pit, so the chances of coming home with hand, foot, and mouth disease or stomach flu diminish with every visit, which always feels like a win.

Then, and this is the good bit, I get to go sit in the cafeteria, alone, and drink coffee. I can eat meatballs or cinnamon buns. Hell, there's nothing to stop me eating both. In that hour, I can be anyone or no one. Nobody's mother, nobody's ex-wife, nobody's editor, nobody's daughter, and nobody's sister.

One coffee in, I usually start to unwind. One and a half coffees in, I feel edgy and a bit morose, like I'm a detective in a Swedish crime show. I like to sit with this feeling for as long as I can. All around me people are doing the same thing, so I like to exercise my imagination and surreptitiously watch them, trying to figure out what crime they are planning or concealing. Once I start freaking out that someone's baby carrier is actually a bomb, I know it's time to leave the cafeteria.

Next I wander through the furniture display, to walk off the worst of the caffeine jitters, and imagine for myself a life where the people I live with would adhere to the organizational systems I implement. A life where I would not only buy the storage solutions from Ikea, but once I got them home I'd actually get around to explaining to everyone what is supposed to go in which square basket in which pigeonhole of the Kallax shelves. In a life like that, I wouldn't end up marching around on Sunday evening, swearing under my breath about how I don't know why I even fucking bother because clearly no one cares about their possessions in this house at all and how if this ever happens again I'll just be putting all the neatly labelled toy boxes into the car and driving them to the donation bin.

I find it very meditative, the Ikea stroll. Gentle Euro-pop plays through the sound system, and little arrows are projected onto the floor, telling me where to go next, removing all the options from my life except which microfibre bathmat I'm going to take home today to add to the already excessive number of microfibre bathmats I've brought home from previous trips to Ikea.

Eventually I have to snap out of this reverie because the little buzzer they've given me at Småland pulses. That means it's time to float back to earth, collect the small people, and go about my day. After an hour at Ikea like this, the feeling is not dissimilar to what it used to be like, before kids, to spend four or five hours at a day spa.

* * *

On the way home from Ikea, I try to nut out how I'm going to get Lola to keep this little excursion from her mother. I can't tell her to keep it just our little secret. That phrase has been comprehensively ruined by child molesters. Which is a shame for many reasons—obviously the child molesting first and foremost, but also because having secrets from your parents is enormous fun when you're a kid.

I need Lola to just lie by omission. I need to give her something better than Ikea, something that Helen and Troy will approve of, that she can tell them about. Or I could just rely on the natural disinclination of small children to talk about their day.

In the end I do nothing. If Lola tells her parents, so be it. If I can stand up to Suze Albion-Davies I can stand up to Helen.

Chapter Nine

The next morning Tim and I are headed back to the Lost and Found again. This time it's his hat that's disappeared. I've got the girls with me, again, because although it's normally not a day I have Lola, Helen's going to a meeting in the city with some people who call themselves branding specialists.

There aren't as many red-hot pokers involved with this business as the name suggests, more's the pity.

According to Helen, they're going to talk about her social media presence and which brands they should be connecting her with. The company is called LikeLike. It sounds to me like a lot of BullshitBullshit.

Helen was planning to take Lola with her, because apparently Lola, as Helen and Troy's child, could become a social media influencer too, with a bit of judicious product placement. I think they are overestimating how cooperative a child they have on their hands, possibly because they so rarely actually have her on their hands. I'm not going to pretend I understand the first thing about social media and how this influencing business works, but I can't imagine Lola getting on board with any of it, especially if it's Helen suggesting it. Helen must have had a last-minute flash of insight into the true nature of her child, because she called me at eight-thirty to say that on second thought Lola might rather spend the day with Freya and me.

So Helen has swanned off in an Uber, and Tim, Lola, Freya, and I are returning to where we belong: the Lost and Found.

I'm not altogether sure that the recent loss of the hat is legitimate. Tim has started saying he wants to wear the baseball-style school cap, which I am not keen on because it offers about as much in the way of sun protection as a flyswatter.

Tim thinks this sun-protection obsession of mine is just a ruse for making him look like a baby, because according to him, broad-brimmed hats are babyish. No amount of me pointing out adults wearing broad-brimmed hats has convinced him otherwise. 'Look,' I've said, 'the postman's wearing one! Look, the parking attendant has a broad-brimmed hat.'

'Babies,' is always Tim's reply. 'They look like babies.'

'Does that roofer look like a baby?'

'Yes. He does. A big dumb baby in a dumb hat.'

'. . . on a roof, without a rope, with his shirt off, doing a very dangerous job? Doesn't look very babyish to me.'

This argument never gets me very far and now I suspect he has taken matters into his own hands and ditched the broad-brimmed hat altogether, in the hopes that I'll replace it with a cap to stop the whingeing.

But I can handle a lot of whingeing. I've tried explaining to him about skin cancer, and how, yes, sunscreen is helpful in protecting the skin but the more layers of protection the better, but it means nothing. If he'd ever had a really nasty sunburn I feel like he'd take my warnings a lot more seriously, but of course he hasn't ever had a sunburn. From birth he's been in a muslin-draped stroller, or smothered in SPF 50 sunscreen for sensitive skin. I don't think he actually has sensitive skin but it's always felt more caring to buy that one. And he's been wearing a babyish broad-brimmed hat. Which I intend he will continue to wear. As we amble up the sidewalk towards the school, I wonder how this has turned into such a big deal.

Until recently, whenever I asked Tim to do something, he by and large just did it. There were times he did it slowly, or with some reminding, and perhaps with more daydreaming along the way than other kids, but generally, Tim's always been such an amenable person.

This new-found stance on hats is unlike my easygoing boy. Maybe it's not about the hat at all. Is he trying to gain a tiny bit of control in a life where he basically has none? I mean, he's six, he shouldn't be in charge of his own life, but I feel like his mood has been getting worse and worse over the past few months.

What I fear is that as he's started to grow up, he's begun picking up on Troy's lack of interest in him and Freya. Troy never does anything with Tim. Even when he has them for visits, he's on his phone all the time, dealing with work issues, and it's Helen—and I'm loath to give her credit for anything—who talks to him and takes care of him. She treats him like a baby, sure, but at least she pays him a tiny bit of attention.

It's bang on 9:05 a.m. when we roll up outside the Lost and Found. Deb is there, unlocking the door. Today she is a symphony of red and orange. She looks like she is going straight from work to play the part of a wildfire in an eisteddfod.

'Good morning, Indiana Jones,' she says to Tim with a wink. 'Have you lost your Ark? I hope it had your name on it. Lots and lots of Arks in here today!'

This is utterly lost on Tim, referring as it does to a movie made over thirty-five years ago, which is too scary for him to see. He gives me a baffled look.

'In you go,' I tell him. 'I want you to find that hat.' I'm using my most serious voice. The one that implies there will be Serious Consequences if the hat is not found. Of course I have no serious consequences, which he well knows, but he's mostly a good boy so he pretends to be daunted. He turns to the first bucket of hats that time forgot, and starts checking nametags.

I start in on the second bucket, while the girls take turns climbing a set of shelves that I quickly assess will probably not fall on them.

The first hat I check belongs to someone called Matilda Makepeace. The second hat I pick up is Bon's. Bon Cunningham, the tag says. I recognize Adam's handwriting. That's a bit weird, really. I don't know if I'd recognize Troy's handwriting. I haven't seen Adam's handwriting for many years, not since he returned his edited manuscript with manual mark-ups. But it's unmistakeable. He has really nice handwriting. It looks sort of French.

'Tim,' I say, 'this is Bon's hat. Did you know he'd lost his hat too?'

Tim doesn't look at me. 'Um, nup.'

Tim lies to me very rarely and very badly. He's lying to me now. You don't have to be Hercule Poirot to figure out what's happened here. The two of them have decided they're too grown up—at five and six years old—to wear broad-brimmed hats and they've made an executive decision to jettison them. But because they're five and six, they didn't think to hide them where they wouldn't be found, like in the bin. They probably just abandoned them in a part of the playground where they don't often go and assumed that was the last they'd see of them. Sometimes the dumbest criminals are the cutest.

If I deduce correctly, Tim's hat will be the next one down in this bucket. I flip over another hat and there it is. Tim Lawson. And people say watching endless crime shows is a waste of time.

'Did you guys chuck away your hats so Adam and I would buy you caps?' I ask him.

He cracks immediately. 'Yes.'

'That's pretty naughty.'

'I know.'

'Hats cost money, Tim. You don't just throw them away because you want a new sort of hat.'

'But I just really wanted a cap.'

He looks so dejected, it's all I can do not to grab five of the nearest caps and give them all to him—after we boil them for a few days, obviously. He's so sad his terrible plan failed.

And he's right. All the big boys at the school, and all the cool ones, they all wear caps. It's the little ones who go about looking like a bunch of mushrooms in their stiff-brimmed hats with a chin-strap. It's the chinstrap that really adds insult to injury, I think. How grown-up can you feel when your hat is held on with a toggle?

'You have to get to class—the bell's about to go. We'll talk about this after school.'

'I'm sorry, Mummy,' he says, and he looks so little. I scoop him up off the ground and cradle him in my arms like he's a baby. He doesn't resist.

'It's all right, Timbo. We'll figure something out with the hat. I love you.'

'I love you.'

I put him down, glance into his hat, giving it a quick once over for obvious signs of head lice, and finding none I cram it down over his hair. He grabs his bag and scoots out of the room, up the corridor towards his classroom, as the bell rings.

* * *

With the girls at kindergarten, I head home. I drop Bon's hat on the floor by the front door so I don't forget to take it to school this afternoon, and sit down to work on the edit of an autobiography of a recently retired cricketer, which Carmen has flicked to me by way of apology for the lateness of Wanda's book. As apologies go, it's quite punishing. I keep having to google terms that sound like they can't possibly be correct. Each time they turn out to be totally legitimate expressions from the cricketing world. I struggle to keep my biffers and my blockers straight. Someone chops on, someone else farms the strike and someone else delivers fruit salad bowling.

In between paragraphs, I stare at my phone, willing it to ring. Surely someone, somewhere needs me, urgently, to do something that is not this. Anything but this.

Astonishingly, this works and the phone rings. It's Wanda's friend Philip.

'Philip,' I say, thrilled to hear from anyone, 'you couldn't have called at a better time.'

'Hello, Emma. I'm glad to hear it. I'm not interrupting anything?'

'You are interrupting me trying to edit a book about cricket and I can't thank you enough. Do you know anything about cricket? You're an Englishman, you're probably an expert.'

'It's never been my thing, I'm afraid. We did have to play it at school, but I was always twelfth man.

'Aha. I know what that means. If you'd called me an hour ago I would have had to just laugh politely, but I now know it means you were a sort of back-up guy who plays when required but mostly gets the tea. Oh!' Something occurs to me. 'The twelfth man is the cricket version of an emotional support animal, isn't it?'

He laughs. 'Yes, I think that's more or less it. You're quite taken with that emotional support animal concept, aren't you?'

'I really am. It's such a great idea. I read recently that an airline in America now has a long list of animals you can't take on board a flight as emotional support. Apparently you can't take a hawk, but a falcon is fine. And they've banned hedgehogs. Sorry, Philip,' I say, remembering suddenly that this isn't just a friend calling for a chat. 'You didn't ring to talk about cricket or hedgehogs. What can I do for you?'

'I wish I were calling to say Wanda's finished and I can deliver you from the torments of your cricket book, but she's not quite done. She has written another chapter though; that's what I wanted to tell you.'

'That's good news. Progress is good. How many more does she think she has to write before it's finished?'

'That I don't know. She's being a bit cagey. I'm leaving here tomorrow, but I've given her a huge pep talk, and she knows what she has to do to get to the end.'

'Have you threatened her with Carmen if she doesn't hurry up?' I say. 'I think she's getting pretty antsy.'

'I haven't but I will. That's a good idea.'

'Thanks for keeping me in the loop, Philip.' I should get back to work but I want to keep talking to him. 'Where are you heading on your travels?' I ask.

'Back to London, to begin with. Then I'm not sure. Could be one of a few places.'

Wanderlust sweeps over me like morning sickness. Travel. I wonder if I'll ever get to go overseas again. Or even somewhere else in Australia. It doesn't seem likely. Imagine just jetting off to London, and not knowing where you'll go next.

I must have gone oddly quiet, as I try to breathe my way through the envy and the sudden panic that this is it, that I'll never leave Shorewood again, because Philip says, 'Emma, I'm sorry, I really am distracting you from your work. I'll let you get back to it.'

Reluctantly I agree. 'I suppose I had better figure out if a trundler is a person or a type of bowling. Maybe I'll see you at Wanda's book launch, if we ever get there?'

'It will happen,' he says confidently. 'She will pull it all together in the end. And I think a trundler is an old, slow bowler. Someone who's a bit past it.'

The call leaves me a bit dejected. I think I'm a trundler. I'm certainly not getting through the cricket book at any great speed, and I can't stop thinking about all the places in the world I haven't travelled and probably never will.

I give in to all distractions now, and by two-thirty I have done three loads of laundry and hung them out, made a chicken pie, stalked Helen on Instagram and Adam's wife, Ilse, on Facebook. I've not edited nearly enough pages.

As I go to leave the house to pick up the kids, my phone buzzes with a text. It's Adam. I get a crazy little jolt of joy.

Hey Emma, do you know Suze Someone-Someone at the school? She has got me involved in a Fun Run thing. Are you helping too? It would be more fun if you were. A.

Well shit, I think. No sooner have I escaped Suze's clutches than I need to find a way back into them. I realize two things: I'm going to have to execute a human version of a reverse swing bowl, and I've learned more about cricket in one day than I have in thirty-six years.

* * *

After school, I spot Adam in the playground. I head over and hand him Bon's hat.

'Bloody hell, where did you find that? Bon said he looked everywhere for it.'

'He didn't look in the Lost and Found.'

'I've already bought him a new cap, but I suppose it's good to have a back-up.'

A cap. Bon's got a cap. He's a whole year younger than Tim but he has a parent who hasn't taken a lunatic stance against caps and so now he's going to be a cool kid.

Tim, on the other hand, is being raised by me, and for some reason I've decided that this is the parenting hill I want to die on. I don't know why I get my mind so set on things like this. Maybe it's in my DNA. Dad's been known to drive to three different supermarkets if they don't have the brand of spreadable butter he likes.

But it's not too late to change, is it?

'Yeah,' I say to Adam, very casually. 'I think I might get Tim a cap too. I'll just have to get him to learn to reapply sunscreen to the back of his neck before recess and lunchtime. And really properly rub it into his ears. I think the boys might have won this round.'

'What round? What do you mean "they've won"?'

'They chucked their uncool hats away so we'd have to buy them new ones, because they decided they both wanted caps.'

'Did they?' Adam sounds quite delighted. 'The little pair of shits!'

'It's not really a laughing matter. This may be the start of a slippery criminal slope,' I say.

'It might be. From here they might start not giving back all the change from their lunch orders.'

'Or deliberately leaving the caps off pens.'

'Or swapping sandwiches with kids who have white bread.'

'Now you're just being silly. Nobody brings white bread to this school. I think it's banned, like nuts and weapons.'

He laughs and I engage in a little internal air-punching.

'Oh,' I tell him. 'I got your text about Suze Albion-Davies. She's pretty ferocious. I think I'm helping out too, with the Fun Run.'

'Excellent,' he says. 'Sounds like it will be more fun with a friend. And I've also been meaning to ask you—are you guys going on this family camping thing? Is that something worth doing?'

The family camping thing is something I've been mulling over. It's a completely optional camping trip that's vaguely organized under the auspices of the school. The school doesn't really have much to do with it but it's advertised through the newsletter and it's just families from the school who go.

The venue is a bit of woodland on a river, several hours' drive west. We didn't go last year, but Tim's been asking about it a lot lately. A few kids from his class are going, and some families from our street. It takes place on a weekend when I'll have the kids. There's no real reason why we shouldn't do it. Unless you count the fact that camping with children is completely awful as a reason. And that I would be, I think, the only single mother going.

From what I can gather, last year several dads went with their kids while their wives went on a spa weekend to the wine country a little bit past the campsite, but I haven't heard of any women doing it sans husband.

Even thinking like this makes me want to give myself a swift kick up the butt. I am better than this. I can absolutely take my kids camping without a man. You don't need a penis to erect a tent. And my kids deserve to experience the great Australian outdoors. They're too cooped up where we live. Their eyes are probably damaged from never seeing faraway vistas—they will have developed suburban myopia from never being more than two metres from the next object they need to focus on. Wide open spaces are what they need, and a bit more freedom.

I'm always with them. They never get a chance to really be independent and make their own choices about what to play with and how close to go to murky waterways and whether to put their hands into dark rotting logs or whether that is a stick or a snake and oh God this a terrible idea. No way are we going camping.

'I'm considering it,' I say to Adam, my desire to seem cool once again overriding every ounce of sense I possess. 'It looks like it could be fun. How about you?'

'I thought we might go if you guys were going. You're kind of my only parent friend, so far.' He looks a little bit sheepish.

'I know some people who are going, but not many. They're mostly not terrible. Shall we brave it? I think they close the bookings in a couple of days.'

'Why not?' Adam looks excited. 'I'll need to buy a tent. Do you have camping gear?'

Do we have camping gear? The answer to this is yes, in spades.

When Tim was two, just before I got pregnant with Freya, we all went camping. It was a two-night trip, and what Troy spent on equipment would have paid for a week at a five-star resort in Fiji. But it was an investment, he kept saying. He pictured us becoming one of those families who went camping all the time, at the drop of a hat. Because once you have the gear, it's so easy! You just toss it in the back of the car, and off you go.

Unless, that is, you've bought so much gear that it doesn't fit in your car. Then you have to spend a couple of thousand bucks having roof racks installed so you can strap a sort of fibreglass coffin to the top of your stuffed car, which you fill with more camping paraphernalia.

Because the camping gear was a year old when Troy left me, and no longer bright and shiny, he gave it to me as part of the settlement. Well, he just ditched it and moved on, really. It's all still in the Spidery Shed of Doom that lurks in the weedy corner of my back garden. From memory, there's a two-room, eight-man tent. I don't know how many kids Troy thought he and I were going to have, but we certainly never discussed more than two, so the size of this nylon McMansion was and is something of a mystery to me.

There's also a set of camping bunk beds. Yes, camping bunk beds. They weigh about forty-five kilograms, and you have to build them when you want to use them and then disassemble them afterwards. They're not unlike an actual set of bunk beds, except they have an uncomfortable fabric sling to lie on instead of slats and a mattress. That's pretty much the only concession to them being camping bunk beds and not just bunk beds. They are absurd. They are under no circumstances coming on another camping trip with me, ever. I'd sooner pack the sofa.

Then there is a four-burner camping stove, some collapsible chairs, a few tables, a galvanized tin washtub and a huge quantity of clattery enamelware plates and mugs, because plastic ones, while sure, you can do the washing up without sounding like you are practising the carillon, didn't fit in with the lumberjack-shirt-wearing, neat-whisky-from-a-tin-mug, sling-up-a-hammock-between-two-trees sort of vibe Troy had envisioned. So there's also a pair of hammocks, because when you take a two-year-old camping there's so much chance of you both getting to lie in a hammock and gaze up at the gum leaves.

Troy did manage to put in some hammock time, the one occasion we actually went camping and used all this stuff. He spent an hour putting it up, and then was so cranky he retired to it for the rest of the afternoon, while I scuttled around after Tim, who was going through a particularly suicidal phase, as many two-year-olds do, where he wanted to run with sharp sticks, trip over guy wires, choke on small rocks, fall into fires and drown in rivers, preferably all at once.

But that was a long time ago. My current situation has three distinct advantages over my life back then: Tim is six and very sensible; Freya is three and not at all like Tim was at two; and Troy won't be coming. I think it might be time to reclaim camping, starting with getting a much, much smaller tent.

'I have some camping gear,' I tell Adam. 'But I'll need to get a new tent. Apart from that, I'm pretty much set. How about you?'

'We don't have any of our stuff with us, but I'll get a little tent, and a couple of sleeping bags and I reckon that'll do,' he says. 'If you've got a stove, maybe we can join up and split the catering? I mean, it's only one night. A few cans of baked beans and some weiners, a box of cereal and some long-life milk, that's basically it, right? Oh, and that pancake mix where you just add water.'

He makes it sound easy. And fun. This is not the camping preparation I remember. Where are the elaborate braised meat dishes to be cooked over coals for hours and hours in a cast-iron camp oven? What about lugging separate containers of flour, baking powder and eggs to make waffles in a vintage campfire waffle-iron Troy sourced from www.insufferablehipsters.com?

I can do this. A small tent that I can put up easily by myself, and a selection of the least ridiculous items from the Spidery Shed, and we'll be on our way. Without the car roof coffin.

It's not a date, I remind myself. Of course it isn't. He's married. But the idiot butterflies in my stomach won't be told. Sometimes I think those butterflies are only interested in one thing.

* * *

In one of those weird moments of synchronicity that come along every so often and make you wonder if perhaps there isn't a force other than chaos arranging things here on earth, when I drop Lola home that evening after her gymnastics class, Troy asks me about our camping gear.

'Is that all still in the shed?' he asks, sipping a foul khaki-coloured juice as he stirs a barley risotto on the stove. 'Oh, and do you want to try this? It's a new smoothie combo we're trialling: pineapple and pea. We're going to call it Peanapple.'

That is a terrible name. Who is in charge of marketing in that place?

'No, I'm okay, thanks,' I say. 'Do you mean is it all still in my shed? Because yes, it is, on account of how it's now my camping gear.' Troy brings out the very pettiest part of me, every time.

'I know it's yours, I was just wondering, if you aren't going to be using it, if we could borrow it—not this weekend, and not the next one, but the one after that.'

For a second I'm sure that's the school camping weekend. Surely he's not planning to go on the school camping weekend? But then I do the maths and realize that's a week earlier. He's talking about the weekend of the Fun Run.

'Where are you going camping?'

'There's this amazing festival on down south,' he says, and takes another sip of juice. There's the smallest grimace as he swallows. 'I'm a sponsor, so we thought we'd take the kids and camp there.'

I'm suspicious. 'What kind of festival? Like a music festival? That doesn't sound very child-friendly.' The last time I went to a festival the image I was left with was a girl leaning over to vomit, her skirt accidentally hitched up into her G-string, while her friends used her back to spread out their map of the festival grounds. It's not quite what I had in mind for my kids just yet.

'It's amazing—totally family-friendly. In fact it's designed for kids. You'll have heard of it—it's called Yeah Baby Yeah Festival?'

I have not heard of it.

'Is it new?'

'No, they ran it last year, and it was huge. It totally blew up on Instagram.'

Oh, that's where it's famous.

'I don't know,' I say. 'Tell me more about it.'

'Well it's just like the festivals we used to go to, but there are no drugs, the booze is really good quality—like there are about nine artisanal gin companies coming, and all these microbreweries—amazing food trucks, mass yoga classes, cool bands, and then all this brilliant stuff for the kids, like jumping castles and face-painting, and everyone dresses up and you camp in a big field beside it. It's just overnight.'

'Sounds right up your alley. How does Helen feel about taking care of three kids for the weekend, because presumably you'll be networking and selling juice to people a lot, won't you?'

'She's looking forward to it. She loves the kids, you know that. And I won't really be working—I'll be there to help. So, can I grab the camping stuff for it?'

'Knock yourself out,' I say. 'The kids will be experts by then, because as a matter of fact I'm taking them actual camping, in the woods, the weekend before that. With no food trucks. You'll have to wait until after the Fun Run, though, before you head off.'

'Oh shit, is the Fun Run *that* weekend?'

'Yes it is. Tim's really excited to run it with you.'

'Right, cool, yeah we'll go after the run. Wouldn't miss running that with my boy. And thanks for the loan of the camping gear. You're the best.'

'Well, second best,' I say.

Troy's smile fades and he gives me a look I suspect he means to be longing and wistful. 'Hey, don't be like that. You know how hard this has been for me.'

A few months ago, I would have, if not melted, then at least defrosted a little at this sort of thing. But those days are over.

'No it hasn't. You can knock off that bullshit, Troy. You moved on. End of story. Don't try and string me along, and don't try to get my sympathy. I'm done with that.'

He looks genuinely surprised. 'But you know I love you, right? Nothing's ever going to change that.'

'Are you insane?' I ask him. 'You divorced me and married Helen. That changed it.'

'Not for me,' he says softly. 'Part of my heart will always belong to you, Emma.'

I feel a bit sick. I don't think he's right in the head. Thank God he's finally started seeing a counsellor.

'That's a weird and wrong thing to say to your ex-wife, Troy. If that's really how you feel, and I actually doubt it is, it's something you need to discuss with your therapist. It's not something you can mention to me, ever again.'

'Love is never wrong, Emma.'

I have to get out of here. He's just going to keep saying things like that until I do.

'Tim, Freya! We're going,' I call.

Helen walks into the kitchen, carrying her laptop. 'Emma, I didn't know you were still here.'

'I'm just heading off. I was hearing about the festival.'

Troy interrupts, 'Hellie, Em's cool with us taking the camping gear. She's going camping the weekend before the festival too, so she can troubleshoot any tent issues or whatever.'

'Are you?' says Helen. She raises an eyebrow. 'Who with?'

This rankles. Why assume I'm going with anyone?

'The school,' I say. 'A bunch of families from school.'

'Including Adam?'

'Who's Adam?' Troy asks.

'Adam's Emma's new friend,' says Helen, in the tone of a person who is quite close to chanting something about being in a tree and K-I-S-S-I-N-G.

'Adam Cunningham,' I say. 'You won't remember him, Troy. I edited his book years ago.'

'Why are you going camping with one of your old authors?' Troy asks.

'I think he's a little bit more than an old author, right, Emma?' Helen says.

What is this woman trying to do?

'He's now a parent at Tim's school and his son is a friend of Tim's. And yes, they are also going on the school camping trip, along with about forty other families.'

'They, as in he and his wife and their kids, or . . . ?' Troy is trying to look casual.

'He seems pretty footloose and fancy-free to me,' says Helen. 'And he seems to really like you, Emma.'

Why is she acting like we're best friends? Having Helen comment on my potential love life is unnerving.

'*Tim*, *Freya*, I am leaving right now.' I don't think I can handle much more of this.

I turn to Helen. 'As I was just saying to Troy, you're welcome to the camping gear the weekend after that, but you can't go until after the Fun Run on the Saturday. I'd better get the kids home now—they're always starving after watching the gymnastics class. Goodnight, everyone.'

* * *

My kids are starving when we get home, but not because they've been watching Lola's gymnastics class. We didn't go to Lola's gymnastics class. In fact since we skipped ballet yesterday, we've gone on a bit of a hooky bender.

Today we didn't go to her French class in the morning, and that didn't seem fair to Tim, who was at school and missed out on the good times, so we bunked off gymnastics this afternoon too.

The girls and I spent the morning in a graveyard. I love a good graveyard, and after we dropped Tim at school and collected Lola, I said to Freya, 'What do you want to do today? What would you do, if you could do anything?'

'Climb up the outside of a castle,' she replied, immediately and with odd specificity.

Living where we do, in a country where people of castle-building origins only showed up around the time that castle-building was falling out of fashion, Freya's not had a lot of exposure to real-life castles.

But we do live in a country where church-going types have been dying for over two hundred years now, and for a while back in the day it was very popular to build small monuments to the dead out of stone. The sort of monuments that could reasonably fool a three-year-old, who has only seen her architectural dreams in books, into thinking they are actual castles. And while real castles are generally unsafe for climbing by small children, stone obelisks are a fairly good height and have been unpopular for over a hundred years. This means they are often in parts of graveyards where people rarely venture, and their inhabitants died so long ago that you're unlikely to have an irate relative happen upon you when you're scaling them.

So I drove the girls to a disused cemetery—a term I love for its honesty—and they passed a happy few hours scrambling up and down monuments to Captain R. Carlysle, Mr. George E. Robinson, and the gloriously named Admiral Bertrand Beaverstock.

Those chaps resided in a corner of the graveyard almost

entirely overgrown with ancient thorny roses and wildflowers, and the lesser graves—those marked with low stone walls and ordinary headstones—had all fallen into such staggering disrepair that it was clearly impossible for the municipal workers to get along the paths with their ride-on lawnmowers any more. It was just like a secret garden.

The whole morning we only saw two other people—a teenage girl and boy in the local high school's uniform who stumbled, giggling, through the bushes, with all sorts of non-school-related business clearly in mind. They were very disappointed to find me there, working away on the laptop, while Freya and Lola squealed and threw rainbow handfuls of lantana flowers in each other's hair.

We ate our sandwiches on top of the relatively unbroken grave of one Agatha Gordon. Well, Freya and I ate our sandwiches and Lola dutifully shovelled down some sort of quinoa-lentil business that Helen had packed in a stainless steel box for her. Afterwards we all shared a Kit-Kat, and the girls played more while I texted Suze to casually ask if there was now anything I could do to help with the Fun Run.

Annoyingly, she phoned me back. I don't understand why people do that. There's almost never any need to talk on the phone any more.

'That is brilliant,' she shrieked, as soon as I answered. 'I knew you'd change your mind. No one wants to miss out on all the fun! Do you know, of the six mums from last year's kindergarten class who all helped out with the last Shorewood Public Fun Run and Have Fun Day, none of them has been able to help out this year? Can you believe that? It's like they think they've done one thing for this school and that entitles them to a free ride for the next six years! I can tell you, the senior schools won't be looking very fondly on that as a service record, come year six.'

'No!' I say. 'Suze, that is shocking. Well I've had a few things move around so now I can help. Just give me a job.'

'I have the perfect position for you,' she says in a low voice, like I am a hot commodity and she doesn't want any other committees to hear of my availability and head-hunt me to work in the canteen or the uniform store. 'You can be the new Head of the Prize Donations Subcommittee! Hana Ito and Gillian Phipps were co-heads until last week when they both had to resign because of sudden important work commitments. It was so sad.'

'It sounds sad,' I agree. 'But awesome for me!' I sound twelve, and very unconvincing. 'I can't wait to get started!' All I want to know is what job Adam has, but if I ask Suze she'll see right through me.

'Right,' she continues importantly, 'I'll email you all the details, and you can report back at the next meeting.'

Head of Donations. This is what I am reduced to. I am charged with going round to the stores and begging the local small business owners to hand over vouchers for facials and free dinners. Being a scab, that's what it was called when I was at school. I don't even have anyone to do it with. What have I done?

I hope Suze won't be too disappointed if every single prize this year is a bottle of Lord of the Juice's most unpopular variety, Viscount Capsicum of Kale.

* * *

Only when my laptop ran out of power did we pack up and head home. They need more power outlets in graveyards.

All in all, we had a much happier day than we would have if Lola had been stuck in a classroom naming animals in French for an hour while I worked in the foyer and Freya played with a sticker book at my feet.

Eventually Troy and Helen are going to figure out what's happening, and they are really not going to be happy about it. I'll cross that bridge when I come to it. I'm slowly crawling out from under their spell and I rather like it. Not being in love with Troy is one of the nicest feelings I can remember.

After I've fed them, I bathe the kids, and carefully comb the lantana flowers out of Freya's hair. They're a bit withered, but she asks me to put them in water beside her bed, so I fill a soy-sauce dish and float them in it. She falls asleep smiling.

When I get into bed I text Adam.

Camping is a go, and I've just been informed I am the head of donations subcommittee for Fun Run. Flowers and champagne acceptable as congrats for my appointment.

I spend ages scrolling through the emojis on my phone to find the one that best expresses self-deprecating humour but is also kind of cute.

I promise myself I won't check the phone until it pings, and settle down with *The Devil's Heirs* to see if Tilde has also found herself volunteering for a stupid Fun Run to try to impress a guy. She hasn't. She has to fight her boss to stop him scaling back the search for another missing woman. We all have our struggles.

An hour later Adam replies with emojis of a tiny bunch of flowers, two champagne glasses clinking, and a thumbs-up.

Chapter Ten

In the morning, I take my time getting the girls to preschool after we drop off Tim. I would rather do pretty much anything else in the world than what I have to do afterwards. Suze Albion-Davies has emailed me a list of businesses in the area that I am supposed to approach for donations of raffle prizes. Quite why we're having a raffle as part of a Fun Run, I don't understand. Maybe there's a minimum raffle requirement for any fundraising event. Sorry, no, it's not a raffle; it's a guessing competition. I think once upon a time you needed a permit for a raffle, but you didn't if it was a guessing competition, so that's what the school has always done. It means the tickets are all printed with the name of the event, missing most of the vowels. SH_R_W__D P_BL_C F_N R_N _ND H_VE F_N D_Y. It looks incomprehensible and no one ever fills the vowels in on their tickets anyway. The whole thing is a F_CKING W_STE _F T_ME, if you ask me.

But I think of Adam, who has no doubt been roped into something similarly mortifying, and I think of Philip, who saves the lives of women and children by giving them access to clean water. Come on, Emma, I tell myself. Step up. Be the change you want to see in the world. It takes a village. Think global, act local. Life, be in it.

The most annoying thing about begging for prizes for the guessing competition is that the local business owners I am being sent to today are all, to a person, parents at the school and thus probably also coming to the Fun Run and paying their entry fees, and buying sausages at the cookout and paying for their kids to go on the jumping castle and have their faces painted and so on and so forth. And these people are small business owners in an increasingly retail-hostile world. It hardly seems fair to hit them up for a fifty-dollar voucher for their business too.

But today that's exactly what I'm going to do, because Suze is a terrifying person and I don't dare show up to the meeting tonight not having done my homework. The bakery, the drycleaner, two cafés, the Thai restaurant, the pizzeria, the pharmacy, the butcher, the auto-repair—all on my list. The auto-repair, seriously? What kind of a raffle prize is a voucher for fifty bucks off your next bodywork, which expires in three months? It's a prize some lucky winner will be getting, because I'm going there first.

Mechanics' workshops are weird. They always seem unattended for the first five minutes. This one is no different. I wander in through the open garage doors at the front. It's cavernous. There's room for fours cars on the floor and a couple more are suspended in the air. The cars on the floor are in various states of disrepair, and one of the ones in mid-flight is practically a skeleton. It's like a natural history museum exhibit, except with vehicles instead of prehistoric creatures.

I can't see anyone. A radio is playing nineties George Michael, so I can't hear anyone either. I shuffle around near a green Range Rover, trying to make my footsteps loud, but since I'm wearing sneakers that's a bust. I move on to some light key-jangling, and venture a little cough. Gradually my eyes adjust and I catch some movement beneath the Subaru Forester behind the Range Rover. Then I see another overalled body, half inside the hood of another large four-wheel drive. Once I get my eye in, it's like being in a jungle—I start to see grease monkeys everywhere. They're just very well camouflaged. They know I'm here though.

'Be with you shortly, love,' comes a voice from somewhere.

'Thanks!' I call back. 'No rush.'

Five minutes later, an older man in a blue jumpsuit scoots himself out from under a car on a giant skateboard. He gets up and, giving his hands a cursory wipe on a grease-blackened rag, ambles over to me.

'What can I do you for?'

'Are you Murray?' I ask.

'Depends who's asking.'

'Hi Murray, I'm Emma. I'm collecting donations for the school fundraising raffle,' I tell him, sticking to the script Suze has given me. 'Since you gave so generously last year, we were hoping you might be able to do it again?'

'Yep. No worries. Voucher for fifty bucks off bodywork do you again?'

'Whatever you can spare. Only, and I realize how cheeky it is to ask when you're being so generous, but is there any way it could have an expiration date longer than three months? It's just, bodywork isn't one of those regular expenses people generally have and the last couple of years the people who've won them actually didn't get to use them before they were out of date. Sorry.'

He looks at me with a twinkle in his eye. 'Only the last two years they've said that, eh? I've been donating these every year for—geez, it'd be fifteen or so years now, since my kids were at the school—and I've *never* had one of these vouchers redeemed.'

'Really?'

'Really, so between you and me, this costs me nothing and I look like a top guy. I think I'll leave the expiry at three months.'

Well, clearly that's the way to run a small business. I thank him, collect the voucher that will never be used, and head off on my begging tour.

Everyone gives what they can. A twenty-five dollar voucher from the bakery and two kilos of thin sausages from the butcher. A few free pizzas. A very decent voucher for dinner for two from the Thai place. The beauty consultant at the pharmacy promises to put together a hamper of luxury skincare—'Only it'll be the sort of hamper they'll want to use pretty sharpish,' she advises. 'We'll be sailing close to some expiry dates.' That seems a common theme.

By lunchtime I've finished my list. Suze said I was to supplement her list with my own ideas for potential donors, but no. I'm done. I'm not asking anyone else. I'll ask Troy, but no. Then tonight at the committee meeting, where I'll hopefully get to see Adam again, I can hand over the vouchers I've collected and then have nothing more to do with the wretched Fun Run until the day itself, when I will be running . . . if I ever go for another practice jog. So far I'm still on week one of the *Couch to Five K* program, and the race is in three weeks.

* * *

For the second week in a row I'm back at school at night. The Fun Run committee meeting starts at eight o'clock, which is later than ideal, but Suze has another committee meeting before it, and that finished at seven forty-five. Listening to Suze talk about how she manages to be on so many committees is like watching a very accomplished juggler: it stops being interesting when she gets past three or four.

At one minute past eight, Suze looks brightly around the staffroom at the five of us who have assembled. Adam's not here. I don't know any of the others well, but I recognize in them the look of people who were too slow, either physically or mentally, to get away from Suze in time. We are all sitting on Department of Education-issue, vinyl-covered foam easy chairs in assorted shades of turquoise, brown and orange. The floor is covered in the same rough square carpet tiles that I remember from schools in my childhood.

I read the passive-aggressive notes on the fridge and signs stuck to the cupboard doors, reminding people to clean the toasted-sandwich maker and to respect other people's yogurt. It's really just every office kitchen I've ever been in, but with better grammar and correct use of apostrophes.

'Shall we get started?' says Suze. 'I'm sure there are some others coming but they must have been held up, certainly for very good reasons, I'm sure.'

She carefully opens a giant ring-binder to a yellow tab.

'Let's start with sponsors. How are we going with sponsors? Well, as Head of the Sponsorship Subcommittee, I think I can speak to that. We are going very well. Geoff Lang is back on board as our major sponsor.'

No surprise there. As one of the two local real estate agents, Geoff Lang is never far from a community event.

The door opens and Adam's there, late, smiling, and forgiven by Suze before he even sits down.

'Adam, hello! Everyone, this is Adam. He's a kindergarten father and a new member of the school community, having just moved back from the Netherlands, or Holland, as it's sometimes known.'

Oh Suze. Be cool.

'Sorry I'm late,' says Adam, and he sits beside me and gives me a quick eyebrow raise.

I catch Suze narrowing her eyes at us, just for an instant, before she collects herself again. 'That's absolutely fine, Adam, I was just saying that our major sponsor this year is once again the terrific Geoff Lang. He's a real estate agent and just a stalwart of the community.

'And this year we have a new sponsor, who is also a father at the school! The Lord of the Juice, aka Troy Lawson, has kindly come on board and will be donating a bottle of juice to each and every competitor who finishes the race.'

Shit. Then he's probably not also going to donate heaps of raffle prizes. I should have thought of that. There goes my slightly-more-than-the-bare-minimum effort.

'Related to that, though not strictly concerning sponsorship so perhaps I should wait until we get to the "running order of the day" point in the meeting—No, no, I'll tell you now: Troy's lovely wife, Helen, who owns Studio H Pilates, will be running a warm-up session for us before the run begins. Do you all know Helen? She's absolutely gorgeous and so personable. Well, obviously Emma knows her. Isn't she divine, Emma? Will you tell them how divine she is?'

'She's . . . just great,' I say, with moderate enthusiasm.

Suze waits, still looking at me.

'She's divine!' I say. 'Divine.'

Adam stifles a laugh, the other three people in the room have the good grace to look extremely uncomfortable, and Suze is happy now to continue the meeting.

'Now,' she says, breathlessly, 'Adam has come to our rescue and has taken over the organization of the barbecue, which is *such* a relief, I can't tell you.' She pauses, and smiles beatifically at Adam, like he's come from heaven to post a sign-up sheet on a noticeboard so parents can volunteer to cook sausages and bacon and egg rolls on race day. He looks embarrassed when she requests a round of applause for him.

After that, Suze goes back to her agenda and starts working through her binder, which has many coloured tabs. Each committee head reports on their work, and Suze behaves as if each of them has taken the organizing back a step or two, steps that she'll personally have to make up.

I tune out after the first one, and instead let my mind wander in Adam's direction. Maybe by the time the Fun Run comes around he will have fallen in love with me, properly and forsaking all others. I picture him gazing at me, unable to peel his eyes from my loveliness, even when Helen is prancing around in front of the crowd in tights and a crop top, showing them all how to stretch out their hip flexors before the run. Where Adam's wife is in this fantasy is anyone's guess. I wish I knew what the story was there. I wish he knew. She's quite a fly in the ointment and I do my best not to think about her when I'm picturing spending the rest of my life with her husband.

It's nine o'clock by the time it's my turn. Suze is very unimpressed with my efforts. 'Three months again, for the car repair voucher, Emma, really?' She shakes her head as if I personally donated this.

'Suze, I tried, but Murray was very firm.'

'Murray is a swindler,' she tells me. 'The amount of time that man *allegedly* took to install the DVD players in the back seat of my car, well . . . let's just say I was very tempted to make a report to consumer affairs.'

'At least we have a voucher.'

'I suppose,' she says.

When the meeting finally wraps up, Adam and I are the first out the door.

In the cool night air I shiver and it feels, for the first time in ages, like my life contains possibility.

Adam seems to feel it too. 'Right, it's Friday night! Shall we kick on to the pub?' he suggests. 'Maybe cab into town, hit up a few clubs?'

'Oh definitely,' I say. 'Let's buy loads of drugs and get completely smashed.'

'Would you even know where to go these days?' he asks.

'Nope. Not a clue. And I wouldn't know how to buy drugs either.'

'Are we old?' he asks.

'I think we might be,' I say sadly.

'Anyway, I've got to collect Bon from my sister,' he says. 'Another time?'

'Definitely,' I tell him.

* * *

Walking home in the dark after the meeting, I'm struck by how rarely I do this. I almost never leave my house after sunset any more. Back before I had kids, Troy and I went out all the time. We saw movies and went to gigs, and we ate out far more than we ate in. After Tim was born I still went out with friends from mothers' group once in a while for a dinner, and then there was all the night stroller-walking.

Now I can't even pop out for a litre of milk once the kids are asleep. The night has become a strange and foreign place to me.

Even when the kids aren't with me I rarely go out at night. It's just habit now that I'm almost always tucked up by half past eight.

I have to remedy this. I feel like this is not an attractive character trait, this reclusive thing I've got going. If I were Adam, and I were possibly looking for someone to replace my (hopefully) estranged wife, I wouldn't be turned on by someone who is so out of practice at leaving the house at night that she keeps dashing between the pools of darkness on the sidewalk where the trees block the streetlights and the well-lit middle of the deserted street. I can't decide if it's safer to walk in the dark where no potential attackers can see me, or in the light, where all the potential attackers but also perhaps witnesses can see me. I'm very glad I only live five blocks from the school.

* * *

I lie in bed, scrolling through Instagram while keeping one eye on the laptop screen, on which a reindeer herder is making the gruesome discovery of nine severed arms trapped under a frozen lake. It's going to fall under Tilde's jurisdiction and it's exactly what she doesn't need right now.

Idly, I switch to Facebook and see a notification. I click on it and read, with horror, that Ilse Cunningham has accepted my friend request. Ilse, Adam's wife. What the fuck have I done? I looked up her profile a few days ago, but it was all locked down so I couldn't see anything other than her name and picture. I must have clicked the wrong button and sent her a friend request and now she's accepted it and what on earth am I supposed to do? Why has she accepted? That's odd. We don't have any mutual friends. Adam isn't even on Facebook.

Oh God. What if they're one of those couples who *share* a

Facebook profile? No, surely they can't be. Only the over-seventies do that. And they always have a hybrid name: LynnGraham Page, or something like that. This must be just Ilse.

I breathe slowly and try to think rationally. I know. I'll write her a message introducing myself and say that our kids have made friends with each other at school and I just wanted to say hello, and tell her what a nice son she has. That's all right, isn't it? It's the best I can do. Or I could just unfriend her and hope she never realizes I have any connection with her husband or her child.

That's probably a better plan. But before I do, I might as well have a look at her profile. If I look for two minutes, then unfriend her, she'll never know I was here.

My hand shaking, I scroll through her timeline. She's a vegetarian—maybe even a vegan—that much is immediately apparent from the stories of animal cruelty she's shared. There are a few pictures of her posted recently, in bars, with other hot Dutch people.

Then I see a message someone called Stijn has posted that mentions Sydney. I can't read the rest because it's in Dutch, but I press the translate button beneath it and it now reads, *Hello Ilse, your mother says in a few weeks you are going to Sydney to live. I hope you have a lot of rooms for your aunt and I!*

God bless uncles who don't understand the difference between direct messages and wall posts, I think. But what's this 'in a few weeks' business? Adam has definitely not mentioned that.

I scroll a bit more, before losing my nerve. I click 'unfriend' and close the app as fast as I can, as if that will make this all go away.

My phone buzzes in my hand and my heart leaps in fear, as if it's going to be Ilse, demanding to know who I am and what I want from her. But it's only a message from Helen, thank God.

Hey hun, sorry for late notice but having a little bday bbq for Troy tomorrow 1 p.m. Do come. +1 welcome. Then there's a sausage emoji and a winking face emoji.

For a hundred reasons this text gives me the shits. Starting with 'hun'. Editors have pet hates, and we are generally pernickety about language to a degree that makes normal folk never want to open their mouths around us, never mind send us anything in written form. But the abbreviation of the word 'honey' to 'hun'? For me that's a crime up there with putting an apostrophe before an s in a surname to signify a plural.

If you have to call anyone honey at all—and I'd argue fiercely that you don't, and certainly not your husband's ex-wife—surely the shortened form is 'hon'. The Huns were warlike Asiatic nomads. I am a very white middle-class Australian who never leaves her suburb and says yes to everything. I am about as far from a warlike Asiatic nomad as it's possible to get. You should never steal an editor's husband. You'll be judged on your spelling, vocabulary, and grammar for the rest of your life.

Who else is going to this barbecue? Text message invitations are awful because you can't see who else has been asked. That's why all good and right-thinking people use Facebook, so that their guests can judge the quality of other invited guests before making up their mind. I was well brought up, I promise, but who can resist the lure of waiting to see if anyone good is going before saying they'll attend an event? Not me, that's who.

The chances are this barbecue will be full of Troy's old friends. Who used to be my old friends. People who came to our wedding. We went on overseas holidays with some of them. I've been on more weekends away with them than I have with my own family. Every single one of these people dropped straight off my radar screen very shortly after the Helenpocalypse occurred, mostly without so much as a voicemail to explain themselves.

They don't need to explain themselves, really. I know that. Generally speaking, you take out of a relationship the people you brought into the relationship. The lawyers divide up most of your assets, but the friends sort themselves out.

For the most part, I don't miss them. With one or two exceptions. There were a couple of old university friends of Troy's, both called Dave, funnily enough, who married women I really liked, Kate and Sofia. Those relationships began just before Troy and I got together, so I suppose I thought the rules might be different with them, since they knew me for almost as long as they knew Troy.

Sadly, both Kate and Sofia remained loyal to Troy, and I haven't seen or heard from them since, which was a bit of a blow. I didn't think that much about it at the time, because after being dumped by Troy, losing a couple of friends was like getting a paper cut when you've just been shot in the stomach.

I imagine they'll be at his birthday barbecue though, and I imagine it will be quite awkward to sit around in Troy and Helen's garden with them drinking boutique beers and eating grilled snapper, which is what Helen serves at barbecues. Poor old Troy can't even steal someone else's steak any more.

That fact makes the sausage emoji, and the smutty wink, even more troubling. Plus-one welcome, indeed. She's obviously referring to Adam, and I'm about as likely to invite Adam to this nightmare as I am to get back together with Troy. Even if I did, for some mad reason, invite Adam, I wouldn't get to talk to him because I'm pretty sure I'll be expected to be on kid duty the whole time. That's why they want me, really. As a free babysitter, just like always.

But then there's the extreme lateness of the invitation. Who sends an invitation fourteen hours before an event? Someone who doesn't want you to come. That's enough reason for me to say yes.

For etiquette reasons alone, this invitation should be declined. It should also be declined because the last place I want to go is Troy's birthday barbecue. It's not like he's turning a milestone age or anything. He'll be forty-four. It's intriguing, though, that I'm being invited at all, and so late. What are they playing at?

Perhaps Troy wants to show everyone his 'before' and 'after' wives? Or maybe it's something to do with his therapy? An attempted reconciliation of parts of his old and new lives? Is that a thing?

I think I'll go. If it's completely horrible I can make my excuses and leave. But this is too intriguing to pass up.

I text back: *Thanks! Sounds great. What can I bring? A dessert?*

She replies, *Just bring yourself!* which everyone knows is code for 'I hate your cooking'.

Fuck you, Helen. I hate your cooking too.

* * *

I can't get to sleep once I know what tomorrow holds. I need to figure out what I'm going to wear.

Casual, cool, and relaxed, but better than Helen—that's the look I'm going for. Quite how I'm going to achieve that is anyone's guess, given that Helen is a Pilates-toned sylph and I am an editing-toned . . . well, I don't know what I am any more. I was never a sylph. I suppose I'm just person-shaped. There's nothing ethereal about me. I'm the sort of person whom Dove might use in a campaign about 'real women'.

I hop out of bed and stand in front of the full-length mirror. God, it's filthy. When did I last clean this? Come to think of it, when did I last look in it?

After giving the mirror a quick once-over with a wet cloth, I look again. It's hard to assess my figure though my pyjamas. I take them off and stand, chilly and feeling foolish, in only my socks.

I don't like what I see. Actually, it's more that I don't recognize what I see. I suppose what is reflected is all right, you know, if it were someone else's body. It's just not what I remember as my body. There are extra handfuls of me that didn't used to be there. My breasts have the distinct look of empty IV fluid bags. There's something approaching a belly overhang that I look away from very swiftly. Unless I stand like I just got off a horse, there is no fashionable thigh gap. I venture a small jump and it's a while before everything stops moving.

The phrase 'let yourself go' leaps unbidden into my head. It's a phrase that's only acceptable in relaxation classes. It makes me cross to think about it. 'Just let yourself go,' yoga teachers say, but in real life, under no circumstances should you let yourself go.

I suppose I have let myself go. I've had good reason for that. I've been too busy keeping two children alive and scrabbling around trying to gather up all the shattered pieces of my heart and life to be worried about bouncing back to my pre-baby body.

Be kind, I tell myself. Beating yourself up isn't going to make your ass any smaller before one o'clock tomorrow. Nevertheless, I lie down on my bedroom carpet, naked except for my bedsocks, and do twenty penitent stomach crunches. Then I roll over and hold myself in a plank position for thirty seconds.

That's enough of that. Opening my wardrobe, I survey my options. Back in my old life, I had work clothes, casual clothes, and going out clothes—roughly equal quantities of each. Now I'd say my wardrobe is thirty per cent easily washable T-shirts, sixty per cent jeans with a high stretch factor, and ten per cent historical clothing artifacts that I rarely wear, probably can't fit into any more, yet can't bring myself to part with.

Nothing in here will convey to anyone that they are a fool to have let me go.

It's time for a panicky text to Laura: *Need a smart casual outfit to make men want me and women want to be me etc.*

Why? is her response.

I don't want to tell her. She will disapprove. *None of your business.*

You're not going to something for Troy's birthday, are you?

Laura has an astonishing gift for reading my mind. She can put fragments of information together and come up with the truth in a way that would make Sherlock Holmes look like Forrest Gump. There is no point lying to her.

Yes, BBQ, don't ask any more please. Just help re clothes.

There's a thirty second pause, then: *Weather will be 24 degrees and partly cloudy. Wear floral ASOS midi-dress you ordered at Christmas when you were pissed, denim jacket, black ankle boots. Hair down but blow dry it properly. Plenty of makeup. No red lippie.*

She's a terrifying force, my sister.

There's one more text: *No sucky-in undies, they make you too cranky. Go for a run in the morning. And remember he is a fuckwit who doesn't deserve to like your boots.*

I think that's a typo, that she means he doesn't deserve to lick my boots. But neither does he deserve to like my boots.

My heart warmed by Laura's righteous indignation, I can rest now.

Chapter Eleven

I always assume it's the kids who make me late for things, but when I ring the doorbell of Helen and Troy's house at a quarter to two the next day, I have no one to blame but myself. I've just forgotten how long it takes to make yourself look really nice.

I got up at a reasonable time this morning, went for a jog, as per Laura's orders, but by the time I'd done the grocery shopping, unpacked it all, showered, dressed, blow-dried my hair, and applied a quantity of makeup that would have been adequate for the whole cast of a Broadway musical, I was running very late. Whatever effort I've been making lately to look good in case I run into Adam pales in comparison to this. If I did this regularly my children would never get to school. How do people do this every single morning? Maybe they get faster with practice.

I definitely used to be quicker at the makeup. But this morning I made the mistake of having a look at the internet to see if how I was doing my makeup was still within the realms of fashion. I was absolutely not expecting to discover that makeup application has changed utterly in the past seven years.

When did this happen? And why? The last time I learned anything new about applying makeup was when I was about twenty-five and I read in a magazine that a little bit of shiny white eyeshadow on the inner corners of your eyes makes you appear more awake. So that's what I've been doing. It seems to look all right. I didn't realize people had moved on.

Apparently now everyone draws on their own cheekbones using some sort of brown cream or powder. And then the shiny white business, which it seems is called highlighter, goes in various other spots to provide contrast. I watched three YouTube tutorials this morning and I could not have felt more like someone emerging from a decade living in a cave.

I wasn't confident enough to try any of this newfangled contouring business, for that is its name, putting on brown and white stuff so you look like a topographical map. I just stuck to the old foundation, mascara, blush on the cheeks, rosy lipstick combo I've been wearing my whole life. Perhaps everyone will think I look refreshingly retro.

* * *

I ring the doorbell even though the door is open, because I am painfully nervous. I'm not at all sure this is a good idea. The reasons for coming that seemed clear last night, and that even stayed with me as I left my house, now seem to have flung themselves into the bushes and under the neighbours' cars and are no longer evident. Traitors.

Helen comes darting down the hall, barefoot, in jeans of a cut that should look atrocious but of course don't. She's wearing no makeup at all and an oversized grey T-shirt that is slipping charmingly off one bony shoulder. She looks like she's just jumped up from an Annie Leibovitz shoot to answer the door.

'Emma, come on in!'

'Hi Helen,' I say and awkwardly thrust at her the peanut butter chocolate cheesecake that is the other reason I am late. The one she said I shouldn't bother bringing. 'I had all the ingredients, so I thought why not?'

'You really shouldn't have,' says Helen, and we both know she means it.

This cheesecake is Troy's favourite dessert in the world. It might even be his favourite thing in the word, present company included. It is not a food of which Helen approves. Between the crust—melted butter processed with store-bought chocolate cookies—and the filling of cream cheese, sour cream, eggs, peanut butter, and sugar, this recipe ticks every box on the list of foods Helen has banned from her family's diet.

To be honest, it's pretty over the top and makes me feel sick after about two bites, but it's Troy's birthday and given all the chia and coconut-based nonsense he and Helen eat these days, he deserves a treat.

Helen carries the cake into the kitchen as if it's a landmine, and I follow. The house and garden are full of exactly the people I thought would be here.

About ten kids are playing in the family room, including mine. Tim is poring over a Minecraft book with two little boys who look familiar but who I can't quite name, and he breaks away and comes over for a cuddle when he spots me.

Freya and Lola are being dressed up in princess costumes by two older girls, one of whom is the spitting image of Kate-Who-I-Thought-Was-My-Friend. Freya's wearing a Snow White dress, but she's put a tiger's tail over the top, like a belt. There are a couple of rather beautiful young women with them. I don't recognize them, but they're speaking French to each other while they plait the hair of two other kids. My little girls see me but they don't come over. They are powerless in the thrall of bigger girls.

Outside, lunch is in full swing around Helen's extendable teak outdoor table, which has been extended for the event.

Holding court at the barbecue, a beer in hand, gesturing with tongs at a huge fish-shaped foil parcel on the grill, is Troy, resplendent in light chinos and a pale pink linen shirt. His trousers are fashionably rolled up and he's barefoot. In spite of itself, my heart flutters. I ignore it, because I have long reconciled myself to the fact that Troy is, and will forever be, my idea of pretty hot. His looks aren't a million miles away from Adam's, come to think of it. It doesn't make him less of a bad person, though, and I would do well to remember that.

He spots me. 'Emma!'

'Hey,' I call back.

'I'm so glad you made it!' He comes over and kisses me on the cheek. 'Helen said yesterday she wasn't sure if you were going to come but I'm so glad you did.'

Yesterday? She only invited me last night. What's going on? Did Helen pretend to Troy that she had invited me and that I'd said I wasn't coming, and then panic at the last minute? Why? Why would Troy want me here?

Is he trying to prove to his friends that he's not the bad guy? That has to be it. He wants them all to see that he, Helen and I are one big happy family. He really is clueless. I mean, it's fine to tell everyone we get along and that the split is amicable, but seriously, no one wants to see it put to the test over lunch.

But for all his flaws, and he has plenty, Troy isn't like that. He's held on to this idea that all this happened *to* him—this new love, this new life. I can see now this is pathological, but he believes it.

The animated conversations that were taking place around the table subside when people see me. It was a terrible idea to come. It's as awkward as a stripper jumping out of a cake, if the stripper is also your ex-wife. I just have to hope everyone here feels the awkwardness too and decides we should all pretend everything is absolutely fine and there is nothing at all excruciating about this.

One of the Daves—Sofia's Dave—leaps to his feet. 'Emma, mate! It's been ages. We were just saying.'

'Dave, good to see you too.' We do a sort of will-we-hug-or-will-we-kiss dance that ends with him crushing me to his chest and kissing me on the top of my head. I feel like a five-year-old.

Troy shoves a glass of champagne into my hand, Sofia scoots over so a chair can be brought out from the kitchen for me, and then suddenly, bizarrely, I'm back in the fold. The conversation resumes, wine flows, and I'm laughing with my old friends—our old friends.

Three glasses of champagne later, the awkwardness has completely drowned in the bubbles and it feels like I've never been away. Everyone is being so lovely to me, filling me in on what's been happening in their lives and asking about mine.

No one else from this gang has split up. Almost all of them coupled up during or shortly after university, and until their mid thirties they regarded Troy as the wild singleton of the group. I was the first person he settled down with, and so they welcomed me with open arms. After all, people were getting engaged and Troy having a different girl on his arm each week was starting to get a bit awkward for them, socially.

Now they've reached their forties and they're all homeowners with two cars, two kids, and an au pair each.

I look around and everyone seems so happy. Troy looks happy. Helen looks happy, now that her snapper has been a triumph and everyone's praised and eaten the five different salads. Even I feel happy. Maybe that's why Troy invited me—to show me and to show his friends that happiness can take different forms, that even if we aren't the traditional structure of a family we are still able to find joy and contentment in our lives.

The children, having already been fed barbecued organic chicken skewers and grilled sweet potato slices, are nowhere to be seen, and when I inquire after them, Kate explains they have gone to the park with the au pairs she and Sofia have brought to lunch.

'How long have you had the au pair?' Helen asks Kate.

'Well, Clara is our second, and we've had her for a month, so I suppose for about seven months altogether. It's the best thing we've ever done, isn't it, darling?'

Her Dave momentarily breaks off from a conversation about superannuation to agree that having a nineteen-year-old French girl sharing their house has indeed been life-changing. 'Can't walk around in the nude any more though, can we, love? Ha!'

Kate ignores him and turns back to Helen. 'Really though, it's excellent. You guys should try it.'

'Helen doesn't need an au pair,' I say. 'She's got me! I mean, I'm no French babe, but at least I'm not subject to a six-month working visa.'

Kate looks confused. 'Sorry, Em, what do you mean?'

'Just that I do the work of an au pair for Helen and Troy, so they don't have to get a French girl and then have to wear dressing gowns around the house.' I think I'm sounding a tiny bit pissed.

'You look after Lola?'

'Yeah! Didn't you know that? I've looked after Lola since . . . well, basically since forever. We're friends, me and Lols.'

'I didn't realize. How often do you look after her?'

'Oh a few days a week—three, really. And then I pick her up on her two kindergarten mornings and drop her and Freya off, and bring her home after. I take her to all the classes she does, except the weekend ones.'

The look on Kate's face is of polite bemusement, but it's nothing compared to what's happening over on Helen's face. If I didn't know better, I'd think she was embarrassed. No, ashamed. Ashamed? Of what? Of me? Of our arrangement?

It occurs to me that it's odd that Helen and Troy's friends don't seem to know that I look after Lola. What's that about? Has Helen been making out like she's able to run a Pilates studio and be a growing Instagram star with a toddler underfoot? Why, I believe she has! The fucking cheek.

Someone opens another bottle of wine—something special they brought back from France, because they thought of Troy for some reason when they tasted it. At this point all the wine is delicious to me. I've stopped counting drinks because why should I? I have no kids to look after this weekend, so I am free to indulge and free to waste the day tomorrow in hungover misery if I choose. I finish the last of my champagne and hold out my glass for a refill.

'No, no,' says the other Dave, looking quite offended. 'Not in your champagne glass, Emma,' and he replaces my slim flute with a goldfish bowl on a stem, which he generously fills. It's so big I have to hold it with two hands, bring it up to my mouth like I'm taking communion.

'Anyway,' I say loudly, in case the conversation has moved on, 'so, yeah, I am basically Lola's nanny, most of the week. It's fantastic. My kids love her, and she loves us. I can work anywhere, and the girls entertain each other most of the time.'

'Wow,' says Kate. 'That's generous of you.'

'No!' I tell her. 'It works for everyone. It makes the kids feel like they're all one big, weird family, which we are, aren't we, Helen?'

Helen gives me a tight smile and starts stacking people's plates. 'Who's ready for dessert?' she asks the table.

'Hang on, hang on,' says Troy's friend Luke, who has an uncanny ability to draw awkwardness out into the public realm like a splinter from a toe. 'Emma, you take care of your kids and the child of your ex and his new wife, basically full-time? While you work freelance? Is that what you said? And you take Lola to loads of activities and classes? Does Freya do the classes?' Luke worked briefly as a journalist before moving into insurance, but he still knows how to ask the hard questions.

Helen's watching me. 'No,' I say, 'Freya doesn't do the classes because, well you know, she's only little and when else can you just play? I mean, no disrespect to Helen, because everyone does things the way that works for them and their kid, right? I'm totally happy to take Lola to her stuff. And I mostly do.'

'You mostly do what?' asks Helen.

Oh shit. Why did I say that?

'You're mostly happy or you mostly take Lola to her classes?'

Well, she was going to find out sooner or later.

'Sometimes—not often, just in the last week or so—we don't go to the classes,' I say. I hold my hands up. 'Arrest me! Cuff me and lead me away! We've skipped ballet. And gym. And French.'

They're all laughing now, even Troy. Everyone except Helen. She's plainly furious, but Helen won't make a scene. Not in front of everyone.

'How dare you?' she says, in a voice white-hot with rage.

I stand corrected. Maybe she will make a scene.

'How dare you show such disrespect to me, as a mother? We had an arrangement, Emma. If you weren't happy with it, you should have told me. Who are you to decide what's best for my child?'

A few people get up from their seats, suddenly very interested in clearing the table.

'Dave, shall we . . . er, maybe head down to the park, see how the kids are doing?' says Luke.

One by one they find reasons to leave, until it's just Helen, Troy, and me.

'Helen,' I say. 'It's only been a few times. Just when Lola's not been that into it.'

'You don't get to make that decision,' she says. 'I'm her mother, not you. If you agree to help out by taking her to classes, then you need to take her to classes. Where on earth have you been taking her instead, by the way? What's she been doing?'

'Nothing, nowhere.' I'm pretty flustered. 'We haven't gone anywhere. Well, Ikea, once. Other than that we've just been hanging out, you know in the park and the graveyard and stuff.'

'*The graveyard*? We've been paying for ballet and French and God knows what else you've skipped and you've been dumping our child in a *graveyard*? God, Emma, how you raise your children is up to you and Troy, and if Troy's happy for you to give them absolutely no developmental advantages in life then that's between you and him. But Lola is my daughter and she will go where I say.'

'Will she? Then maybe you'd better start taking her yourself. I don't need this shit. I was doing you a favour, Helen, and I was trying to help Lola bond with her sister and brother, but if that means nothing to you then I am more than happy to let you take over.'

'Hang on, hang on,' says Troy, 'let's not say anything we might regret.'

Helen turns on him. 'I regret ever letting your ex-wife get her hands on our daughter.'

'I have done nothing to your daughter except love her and care for her—and actually spend some time with her, which is more than I can say for you.'

'I spend plenty of time with Lola,' Helen says scathingly. 'And when I am with her, I'm actually paying attention to her. You're never giving the kids your full attention when they're with you, are you, Emma? You're always trying to work too, so they get the worst of both worlds.'

'Now, now . . .' says Troy, but he trails off as if he doesn't know what to say beyond that.

I can't quite believe I'm hearing this. She's having a go at me for looking after her daughter for free, for years, and telling me I've been doing a bad job.

'If you really thought that, why haven't you taken Lola back before now?'

'Because Troy wanted the kids to be siblings and spend time together, that's why.'

'Yes,' says Troy, 'I think it's impor—' but Helen cuts him off.

'And you're right, I should have said something before now because it's been clear for a long time that you are not up to the job.'

I reach for my glass but it's empty. There's another glass beside it, that's mercifully still about half full, so I drain that.

'Oh, nice,' Helen says. 'Just keep drinking, Emma, that'll fix your life.'

'There's nothing wrong with my life, and thank you, I will keep drinking.'

'I think you'd better go home.'

'That's the first sensible thing you've said all day,' I spit back at her.

I stand up, the world does a magnificent spin around me like I'm in *The Matrix*, and the next thing I know I'm lying on the patio looking up at the bougainvilleas growing over the pergola.

Troy leans over me. 'Are you all right?'

'Oh for fuck's sake,' says Helen. 'I'm going to get people back from the park. We need to serve dessert so they can fuck off home.' She turns and marches off through the house, towards the front door.

I think it's the first time I've heard her swear.

I'm all right. I haven't broken anything. I think all the alcohol made me floppy, like a baby, so I didn't get hurt when I fell. I don't mean babies don't get hurt when they fall because they're drunk, obviously, just that I seem to have very little control over my limbs right now.

'Let's get you up,' Troy says. He leans over, grabs my hands and pulls me into a sitting position. 'Can you stand?'

'Of course I can stand.' I haul myself to my feet, and sway dangerously. Troy grabs me, putting one arm around my waist.

'How about I walk you home?' he says.

'Home? But we haven't had dessert yet!' I say. 'I made the chocolate peanut butter thing, the one you used to love, remember?' My legs feel shaky. 'Can I have a little lie-down?'

He looks worried. 'Can't you lie down at your house?'

'I won't be sick,' I tell him.

'Let me just have a piss,' he says, 'then I'll take you home.' He trots off towards the downstairs bathroom, giving me a concerned glance over his shoulder.

I need to pee too. I'll go up to their ensuite, I decide. It feels like it's taking me forever to get up the polished wooden stairwell. I have a rest halfway, then haul myself the rest of the way up to Troy and Helen's room.

It's really beautiful. It's like a room in a smart hotel. There are no piles of laundry, children's books or stacks of newspapers. The bed cover is so smooth it looks like fondant icing. The walls are covered by pale oak panels, and behind one of them, somewhere, must be the bathroom. I'm about to randomly start opening doors when I hear Troy behind me. I turn to ask him where the bathroom is, but I trip. There's nothing to trip on, only acres of smooth cream carpet, but I manage it nonetheless.

Troy catches me before I hit the floor this time, and suddenly I'm in his arms. I wrap my arms around his neck and push my face into his shirt and breathe in his scent.

I look up and say, 'Thank you. You're being lovely to me.'

He moves one hand up my spine and cups the back of my head. There's going to be kissing.

I can't remember the last time Troy and I properly kissed. I mean apart from accidental lip-brushes. It might have been the day Freya was born, but I was so high on oxytocin and other, less natural drugs, that my recollections are hazy. Or maybe it was four days later, when we had our photograph taken by a nurse as we left the hospital, Freya in the car seat and Tim standing over her like a little bodyguard in a Mickey Mouse T-shirt.

Lasts are funny like that—you rarely know they're the last so you rarely know to remember them.

So whatever this is—our last kiss after the last kiss, or our next first kiss—this is a kiss I pay special attention to. It's at once familiar and strange, and ridiculously erotically charged. I'm completely lost in it, and all I can think is that the only reason I want this to stop is so we can take our clothes off and go to bed. That is, until I'm distracted by the urgent need to vomit.

I tear away from Troy and, gagging, turn every which way, realizing I still don't know which of the seemingly dozens of doors leads to their bathroom.

'Emma. Shit. Wow,' he says. 'What are we doing?' He moves towards me and leans in for another kiss.

In desperation I shove him aside and make for the stairs, and from the top step watch as a tsunami of champagne, red wine, snapper, and five kinds of salad sails to the bottom.

'Oh my God,' says Troy.

'Sorry,' I say. 'There's a tummy bug going round at school. There was a note about it in the newsletter yesterday.'

He just stares.

'Sorry,' I say again.

'You'd better go, I'll take care of this.'

'Yes, yes, I'll go. Say bye to the kids for me? What time will you be dropping them back tomorrow evening?'

Troy looks at me like I've lost my mind. 'Maybe I'll just text in the morning to let you know. Seriously, Emma, you need to go now.'

I pick my way down the stairs, avoiding my splattered lunch as best I can.

* * *

My walk of shame is mercifully short. As I close my front door behind me I hear the rest of the lunch party approaching up the street. They've retrieved the kids and the au pairs and they're heading back to eat my peanut butter chocolate cheesecake and whatever sugar-free concoction Helen had planned before I dessert-bombed her lunch.

I rinse my mouth from the bathroom tap, pee, then flop face-down on my bed. I feel wretched. What have I done?

Reaching for my phone, I find a text from Laura, sent a few hours ago.

How's the bbq?

Where do I begin?

Disgraced myself in front of everyone. That's just the tip of the iceberg.

NO. Really? Pub in a bit? I must hear this.

Oh yeah, the pub. That's definitely the right place for me. They probably wouldn't even let me in.

Sure, I text back. *Give me an hour.*

Now that I've ejected several hundred dollars' worth of champagne from my body, I feel considerably better. I'm still drunk, I'm not denying it, but I don't feel like I'm going to fall over or be sick again, so that's something.

The mirror tells a different story. My skin has a greenish hue, all my mascara has migrated south under my eyes and my lips look cracked and bloodless. My hair probably doesn't have any sick in it, but I don't think 'probably' is good enough in these circumstances, so I strip, climb gingerly into the shower and wash every part of me.

Forty-five minutes later, I'm clean, my hair's once again blow-dried, I'm dressed in jeans and a sweater, and ready to face the world again. Four slices of buttered toast and a cup of tea complete the transformation.

I'm ready to go, but before I can there's something I need to check. I pull my bedroom curtains open a tiny crack, just enough to see what's going on in the street. Suddenly half a dozen kids from Helen and Troy's party, one of them my own son, thunder past having a running race.

Shit, they're all still there. And what's worse, I think they're in the phase of leaving that involves everyone standing around out the front for half an hour making hollow promises to have each other round more often. Then there will be another fifteen minutes of strapping children into car seats and one parent going back inside four or five times for forgotten sweaters, insulated wine carry-bags and sunglasses that have been left on the table.

It's not a kind thought, but the best-case scenario would be if one of the kids—preferably not one of mine—trips on the sidewalk and skins his or her knee quite badly. That would wrap things up far more quickly, because all the crying will ruin the parents' chat.

More quickly than I expected, I hear car doors opening and slamming, engines being started—though only one or two, as this lot mostly drive hybrid vehicles—and pretty soon I see them all drive off, almost in convoy. My guess is that Helen made it very clear that the party had ended, probably through the never-fail parental method of picking up your smallest child and pretending they've just asked to start their bedtime routine. Everyone knows they haven't, but in polite society we understand these codes and know it's time to end the long boozy lunch and remember our parental responsibilities, making noises about 'warming up some leftover pasta and running a nice bath' all the while knowing the vehicle is going straight to the McDonald's drive-through and the kids are going to bed in their clothes.

I feel a pang of longing. I want that. I want to host a lunch and have someone to go back inside with, once the guests have gone. Someone who will hand wash the good glasses while I wrap up leftovers and cover up the outdoor furniture.

And then I remember what Helen and Troy are actually going to be cleaning up this evening, and my sadness washes away on a river of slightly maniacal laughter, as I picture Troy on his hands and knees, scrubbing my vomit from his staircase.

I grab my bag and head out the door.

Chapter Twelve

The Feathers is the only pub in this suburb, and it's pretty much pub perfection. Well over a hundred years old, all the good bits have been preserved beautifully by the current owners, who have added a beer garden and—best of all—no play area for children. It's only a small pub, with one bar and a side room, but they've resisted the temptation to make it kid-friendly, which I think most of the parents in the area appreciate.

Entering The Feathers is like time travel for me, back twenty years to the pubs of my young adulthood, just without all the smoke. This pub is, in fact, one of the main reasons Troy and I moved to the area. We came here one night for my friend's twenty-seventh birthday, fell in love with the art-deco tiled exterior, the shining brass bar-rails, and we never wanted to leave. So when I was pregnant with Tim and we were house-hunting and stumbled across what is now my house, the worst house in the best street in the suburb, a mere three blocks from The Feathers, it seemed predestined.

Of course I hardly ever come here any more. It's really only to have a drink with Laura every few months. Pubs now seem like the past to me, and I look back fondly at the me who thought I'd be here every weekend once I had kids. I think I pictured myself nursing a leisurely glass of wine or a gin and tonic while I bounced a happy baby on my lap, surrounded by other, like-minded parents—mums and dads—as we nurtured new friendships and discussed world events and what fringe theatre we'd seen lately.

I knew nothing. I had no idea that once I had a baby, I would be considered a marked woman. There would be no friendly socializing with dads. Mums hang out with mums, and dads hang out with dads—those are the rules in these parts. And around here mums don't hang out casually in pubs. It's only acceptable to be at the pub with your husband, or your sister, or bi-annually with a gaggle of six or more other mums, as long as it's described as a Girls' Night Out.

Of course as a single mother the rules have somewhat changed. I'm allowed to be here now. But still, when I'm here I invariably see several dads I know from the school, who will nod nervously at me or say hello if we happen to be standing at the bar together, but they certainly wouldn't venture a chat. Word might get back to their wives.

Tonight The Feathers is pretty quiet. Sitting on a bar stool at a high table near the window is Laura, her face uplit by her phone in the comparative gloom of the dim pub lighting. Two other tables are occupied: one with four older men, who are dressed like they've come from the golf course, and the other with two men and a woman. One of those men is Adam.

He sees me and his face lights up in delight. Equal parts of confusion and desire race through me. They're followed by a guilt chaser, because of the Facebook-wife-stalking episode of last night.

'Hi!' he calls.

I go over.

'Emma, this is Maria and Jake. They're kindergarten parents too. Guys, this is Emma. Her son's in year one.'

We all say pleasant hellos, and I note a slight tone of desperation in Adam's voice when he asks, 'Please, join us?'

I'm torn. All I want to do is sit down with Adam and, I suppose, whoever these people are. Actually I want them to leave so I can somehow find out more about when Ilse is coming and what that situation is. But Laura won't take kindly to me pretending not to know her. And I really do need to download to her about my day.

'I'd love to,' I say, 'but I'm meeting my sister. Thanks, though. Have a great evening.'

Adam looks crestfallen. My heart leaps.

Laura has a bottle of wine and two glasses before her, so I bypass the bar. Astonishingly, given my state just a couple of hours ago, I quite fancy a glass of cold white wine.

'What did you do?' Laura asks, by way of a hello. She pours my wine so generously I'm forced to lean over and slurp some before it's safe to lift it to my lips.

'Oh man, what didn't I do?' I'm not sure where to start.

'Why were you even at Troy's birthday party?'

'Helen asked, and do you know what? I have no idea why. I think maybe Troy really wanted me there. Maybe it was to show off to all his old friends that we're still on good terms? It was the Daves and all that lot from university.'

'You don't really see any of them any more, do you?'

'Nope, not since we split. They all ran away. Anyway, so last night Helen texts me and asks me to come. I said yes, I went, and then I got pissed.'

'How pissed?'

'Quite pissed. I told Helen I've been skipping all Lola's classes for the past week, then I fell off a chair, then I spewed on the stairs.'

Laura is laughing so hard she has tears in her eyes.

'And I may have made out with Troy,' I add in a whisper.

'You may have *what*?'

'You heard me. I don't know what happened. I went upstairs for a pee after I fell over in the garden, and everyone else was at the park, and he came up after me and then we were just kissing. And I don't know what would have happened if I hadn't had to throw up.'

'Jesus, Emma. There's a lot to unpack there. We're going to need some potato chips.'

* * *

We end up eating three packets of chips—all salt and vinegar, tipped into small woven wooden bowls because this pub is old school. The chips form something of a defence against the two bottles of white wine we take care of while we unpack, to use Laura's phrase, all the things I did this afternoon.

As we talk, things that happened come back to me, things that I didn't quite take in at the time. Like the fact that Helen more or less fired me from my position as Lola's default carer.

I wasn't expecting that. I know I shouldn't have skipped taking her to all those classes—I should have been upfront with Helen—but it wasn't that big a deal. And to tell me I can't see her any more? That's a bit of an overreaction, surely.

'What did you say to that?' Laura wants to know.

I try to remember. 'I think I may have said something along

the lines of "You can't fire me because I quit", you know, like people in movies say when they get the sack.'

'Nice,' Laura says approvingly. 'Good comeback.'

'Yes, I thought so. I was very restrained, I think. Even when she said I was a shit mother because I work while I look after the kids. Apparently, according to Saint Helen, you can only do work or mothering at one time—never both. Which is fine for her because she's always had me to do the mothering bit while she works. But I was very grown-up and I didn't say anything terrible back to her because, Laura, I am better than that. However, I may have undermined my position by falling over straight after.'

'Oh, you complete fool.' Laura is loving this. She grabs my hands and gets very serious. 'Those *assholes* don't deserve you, Em. They don't. You have been a fairy stepmother to their little girl, who is so, so lucky to have you.'

'No,' I say, 'I wasn't even that. I'm not her stepmother, I'm like the reverse of that. We don't even have a name for what I am to her, which is probably because anyone with half a brain stays the hell away from their ex-husband's new kids, which is what I should have done.'

We sit and drink for a few minutes in silence.

Laura licks her finger and cleans the remaining chip shards and loose salt from the bowl. 'Emma, you do realize that Helen's pissed off with you because she's threatened by you?'

This doesn't seem right.

'How? There's nothing threatening about me. She won. She has everything. She has the perfect house and the body and the well-behaved hair, oh, and let's not forget, she has Troy. He picked her, remember.'

'Then why is he making out with you when his wife's just stepped out for a minute?'

I steal a look at Adam to make sure he didn't hear what Laura's just foghorned across the whole pub. He seems engrossed in whatever Maria is saying. He doesn't even seem to be trying to eavesdrop on our conversation, which is disappointing.

'That was nothing. That was the booze. I think he was as pissed as I was. Anyway, I can't be sure who kissed who, to be honest. I might have initiated it.'

'You might have, but personally, I think it was Troy being Troy, and keeping you dangling, just like he always has. And no wonder Helen feels on the back foot in her own marriage, with you always right there, being all helpful and making those kids into a little family. Do you see the position that's put her in?'

'Are you defending Helen?'

'I think I am. Helen's pissed off with you because she can't just have her own marriage, her own go at being a mum, without you there doing everything better. She wants her kid to do all these classes and lessons, but she also wants to be a Pilates guru, or whatever it's called. She thought she had it all set up with you being so ready and willing to take over that side of parenting for her, but she didn't realize that maybe now you know her daughter a whole lot better than she does. And that's got to suck. I'm not surprised she sacked you from Lola duty. I imagine she's just been waiting for a good enough reason to convince Troy you should get off the scene.'

I think about that. It makes some sense. I mean, when you marry someone who had an affair with you behind his wife's back, there are going to be some trust issues. And if he had me feeling for so long that there was a chance for us one day, then she must have seen that too. That's got to have been quite unnerving.

'But what about Lola?' I ask. 'What about what's best for her? Like you said, she's closer to me than she is to her own parents. What's it going to do to her if I'm suddenly ripped away? And poor Freya and Tim. They love her.'

'They're still going to see her, Em. It's just you who isn't.'

I can't help it. I start to cry.

'Em, I'm really sorry.'

This makes me cry harder. Laura speaking so kindly to me is a sign that something is really wrong.

'I've lost my job as a doormat. I wasn't even a good doormat,' I weep into my wine.

'No! You were a brilliant doormat. You were too good at being a doormat, that's all,' my sister consoles me. Then she adds, 'There's a very handsome man over there who keeps looking at us. Which of us do you think he's giving the eye to?'

She must mean Adam. 'Me,' I say, without turning around.

'Well you're very sure of yourself, for a sacked doormat, I must say,' Laura says huffily.

'No, it's not that, it's just that I know who you're talking about. He's a friend of mine.'

'A friend? He's having a hard time taking his eyes off you. Wish I had friends like that.'

'It's not like that. He's married. I used to know him through work, that's all. He's coming on the camping trip we're going on.'

I don't know why I bother lying to Laura. It never works. She's a human polygraph.

'You *like* him,' she says, in a voice filled with wonder. 'Emma, I'm shocked! A married man?'

'Keep your voice down,' I hiss. I reach into my bag for a tissue and attempt to wipe away my tears without removing all my makeup. I feel like an art conservator trying not to destroy an ancient painting. 'There's nothing going on,' I repeat.

'Not yet, maybe. But you'd like there to be—hey, his friends are leaving. Ooh, he's coming over!'

I barely have time to tuck my snotty, mascara-blackened tissue into my pocket when Adam's hand is on my shoulder.

'Hello,' he says.

'Hello to you. I'm Laura. Emma's big sister.' Laura thrusts her hand across the table at him, almost taking out her empty wineglass in the process.

'Adam,' he replies. 'Emma was my editor, long ago, and now our kids are friends.'

'Is that right? What a small world! Now, Emma tells me you guys are going camping together.'

'I didn't say together—' I attempt, vainly, but there's no stopping Laura.

'That sounds awesome,' she gushes. 'Camping is so great for kids. I haven't been camping with my lot for ages. Not since the incident down in the Mungo National Park with Bledisloe—he's our Labrador—and some birds that just look like any old pigeons but turned out to be an endangered species called a plains-wanderer. They were considerably more endangered after Bledisloe got hold of them and there was a bit of a to-do with a ranger. It was very educational for the boys. They ended up doing a presentation on the plains-wanderer at school that term. But you'll have a great time camping, as long as you don't bring any dogs that are bred to retrieve ground birds. In fact I'd recommend not taking any dogs at all. Apparently it's against the law.'

'Good tip,' Adam says. 'Well, I just came over to say goodnight—I'm heading home.'

'Where's Bon tonight?' I ask. 'How have you managed a leave pass?'

'Sleepover with the cousins,' he says. 'I came in for a quiet beer but I sort of got stuck with Maria and Jake.'

'With the cousins? And where's Mrs. Adam tonight?' asks Laura.

'Amsterdam,' he replies. 'Bon and I have just moved back to Sydney and my wife's not sure when she'll be able to join us.'

Well now, I think. That's a curious lie. If Uncle Stijn is to be believed, Ilse's coming here soon. And if it's on her Facebook page then it's not a secret. Unless she was going to surprise them and Uncle Stijn has blown it on Facebook. No, Adam must know. Maybe they really are on the rocks though, maybe she's only coming back because of Bon. That's totally plausible.

'Actually,' Laura almost shrieks, 'I'm leaving now. Right now. In an Uber which I called and which is here'—she pretends to check her phone—'so Adam, could you do me an enormous favour and have a seat right here and help Emma finish off this bottle of wine?'

'Oh, I think I might have had enough,' I say, giving Adam the chance to go. 'I should probably head home too.'

'Oh.' He looks disappointed. 'I'm up for another drink if you are. Or you can just keep me company while I finish your wine.'

'Bye, Ems,' Laura says, and she smooches my cheek. 'Have a good night. Love you.' She leers at me with a wink that Benny Hill would be proud of and, giving walking straight her very best shot, zigzags out of the pub, only lightly clipping the doorframe as she leaves.

'One more?' says Adam.

'Why not,' I reply, because when has drinking too much white wine and eating only salt and vinegar chips ever been the wrong decision?

Over the last two glasses in the bottle, Adam regales me with stories of Maria and Jake, who have, over the last week, latched on to him like social barnacles. He has no idea why, but he reckons they're either swingers or involved in a multi-level marketing scheme.

'If it's pyramid selling, they're not very good at it. Or they're selling lots of different things,' he says. 'Tonight alone they told me about their Thermomix, some smoothies they love that caused them both to lose fifteen kilos, and they talked a lot about essential oils.'

'Maybe they're not pyramid sellers,' I suggest. 'Maybe they just like buying all the products from those schemes. They might be the reason for other people's success at selling Thermomixes and protein shakes. They could just be wildly enthusiastic consumers.'

The barman comes over to tell us that it's ten o'clock and last call, and I realize I don't want to go home. Adam's so easy to talk to. After the day I've had, it feels simple and uncomplicated to sit and chat with him. Which it obviously isn't, because he's married and I might be in love with him. I push to the back of my mind the thought that wine is known for making people's moral compasses go a bit funny.

And I'm full of energy, all of a sudden. I want to go somewhere where the pub doesn't shut at ten o'clock on a Saturday, where everyone I see isn't a parent from school. I'm momentarily overwhelmed with the feeling that I live in a Lego village, with Lego people. And not many Lego people, either, like it's a Lego village built by my children, who are known for losing all the mini figures in the garden and sewer drains, down the back of the car seats and very occasionally, into the vacuum cleaner, on the odd occasion I press it into service.

I'm in a Lego town, with Lego people, and there's only about five places for those people to go. God, you'd think we were in a country village, miles and miles from anywhere, not in a suburb a fifteen-minute cab ride from a buzzing metropolis that is consistently voted one of the best places in the world to live. But no one here seems to ever leave this suburb.

We all moved here because it has everything you need, but now we seem to be trapped. We go to the one pub, the six restaurants, the three cafés, the one gym, the two Pilates studios, the doctor, the dentist, the optometrist, and the chiropractor. And the school. Only the people with real jobs get to leave here, and they have to rush straight back at six o'clock in time to pick up kids from after-school care and daycare.

'Adam, don't you sometimes feel like you need to get out of here?' I ask. 'It's so stifling. The same people, going the same places.' I realize he probably doesn't know what I mean. He hasn't been here long enough.

'Where do you want to go?'

'Fuck, I don't know. Anywhere. Just somewhere that isn't here. I have a kid-free night, I'm still young. Why aren't I out? Like, out out?'

'There's no reason,' he says, sounding only slightly alarmed by my sudden wild enthusiasm. 'Let's go out out.'

'Only I don't know where to go. I never go out out. Where do you think we should go?'

'I'm new around here. I work in the city, but apart from that I'm as housebound as you are these days. We could ring someone cooler than us and ask them, but it's getting a bit late.'

'Where do the young people go, Emma?' I ask myself aloud. 'Come on, think!'

I scrabble around in my bag until I find my phone. There are three missed calls from Troy but he hasn't left a message. I don't want to deal with whatever he has to say. Certainly not right now.

Instead I begin mashing the keys. I'm trying to Google things like 'cool places to go out', but I'm all thumbs and even my iPhone, who knows my wants and needs better than almost anyone, can't figure out what I'm asking. I know I have an app on here somewhere that tells you where to go that's trendy and hip. I downloaded it by accident and I've kept meaning to delete it. I stab away at every icon that looks like the one I think I want, but the one for ordering lunch from the school canteen and the one that tracks my period both look very similar. Someone needs to invent an app that when you've done this much random opening and shutting of other apps and typing of words that even autocorrect can't figure out, would kick in and disable all apps except Uber. It would flash up a screen that reads: That's enough. Go home, you're drunk.

Finally I give up. 'You know where there is booze to be had? My house. It's still open.'

'Then let's go to your house,' Adam says. 'Do you think you can find it?'

'It's not guaranteed,' I tell him. 'It looks very like many other houses around here.'

We head off down the road together, and when my foot catches on a piece of broken curb and I stumble, Adam grabs me by the elbow. He tucks his arm though mine and says, 'There,' like something has been fixed up satisfactorily.

The streets are very quiet. One taxi passes, heading back towards the city with its light on. An old man walking a pair of corgis nods to me and I smile back. I try to say 'nice evening' but it doesn't come out sounding anything like that.

It's dawning on me that I'm really quite, quite drunk. I thought after I was sick at Troy's that I'd purged all the alcohol from my system, and that I was starting again at the pub with a blood alcohol level of zero, but in hindsight that was the kind of theory a very drunk person comes up with. I feel great though. It's a good level of drunk.

I feel like I'm wrapped in a warm blanket, and the soft fuzziness is muffling any questions I should be asking myself, like why I'm taking a married man back to my empty house in the middle of the night. Although I think both me and my drunk self know the answer to that and to ask it would be disingenuous. We both know where this is heading, and right at this moment the fact that Adam is married to someone else is not my problem.

I push open my rusty front gate and it makes the hideous screech it always does.

'You need to get a bit of WD-40 on that,' Adam says.

'*You* need to get a bit of WD-40 on that,' I say, before I can stop myself, and before I realize how poor an attempt at innuendo that is, and how if he even recognizes it as an attempt at innuendo he is going to think I'm referring to my vagina, which I seem to be suggesting is rusted shut.

Yet he's still holding my arm. Getting the key into the lock proves more of a challenge than it should, and when the door finally gives, we stumble in over the doormat. I think I trip Adam with my foot, or I trip over his foot, because suddenly we're falling, arms still linked, onto the floor of my hallway.

'Ow, fuck!' he says. He lets me go and rolls onto his back, his leg pulled up to his chest, rubbing his knee where he has smacked it into the umbrella stand, which contains two hobby horses that neigh when you bump them.

The neighing doesn't stop for a full minute, because the hobby horses are from a discount store and are beginning to malfunction. We lie on the floor, dazed, listening to the just-out-of-synch mechanical whinnying. As romantic soundtracks go, it's a long way behind Barry White.

Once the horses fall silent again, I prop myself up on my elbow to look at Adam, and almost without realizing I am about to do it, I kiss him. Adam Cunningham. My old author. Bon's dad. Ilse's husband, for God's sake. My drunken brain catches up and for a moment I am flooded with panic, but then he puts his arms around me and returns my kiss and there is nothing but skin and breath and feelings of plain desire such as I had forgotten I could feel. The kissing seems to anaesthetize the part of my mind that houses any remaining inhibitions, and we lie down on the hard floorboards, and kiss with an increasing urgency.

There's no way to tell how long this has been going on when we pause to catch our breath. Five minutes? An hour? I need to pee, but I fear that if we stop for any real length of time we'll lose our nerve or come to our senses. Adam seems to feel the same because he gets to his feet, and pulls me up. He holds me close and whispers, 'Shall we go to your room?'

'That is such a good idea,' I whisper. He pulls my hair back, kisses my neck and my knees almost buckle.

Then something happens that is so rare, so unlikely, that it takes me a moment to figure out what it is. The home phone starts to ring.

Chapter Thirteen

My home phone never rings. I don't even know why I still have a home phone. I think maybe the number came with my internet deal and I haven't bothered to get rid of it. I'm never more than about two feet from my mobile phone. I suppose the home phone could be useful if I had a heart attack while sitting on the toilet looking at Facebook and I dropped my phone in. The kids could call an ambulance on the home phone. Though I feel like my iPhone preservation skills are so instinctive now that I'd manage to place it on a safe, dry surface before I collapsed and tumbled, dead, onto the bathroom tiles.

But my home phone, which sits, utterly neglected, on a small table just inside the living room, is now indisputably ringing. Adam and I spring apart like the adultery warning siren has just gone off.

I lurch into the living room and, fumbling mightily, I grab the handset. I don't even know if you have to press the on button to answer it.

'Hello? Hello?' I say loudly into the receiver.

'Emma?'

It's Troy. Something terrible has happened. I know it in my soul. Why else would he be ringing me at this time of night, using the phone that is only for terrible emergencies?

'Troy? What's wrong? What's happened?'

'Where the fuck are you?'

I'm very confused. Obviously I'm at home. This is my home phone.

'Who is it? Who's hurt? Troy, tell me.'

I hear him sigh. 'Well Emma, it's nice that you've finally answered your phone. I'm at the hospital.' He pauses and years are stripped from my life. 'It's Freya.'

Oh no. Not my baby. My heads begins to buzz in fear. I don't think I can listen to what he's about to say.

'She's been vomiting all evening.'

Relief floods through me. She's vomiting. Vomiting means alive.

'She started just after you left, and we couldn't get her to keep any liquid down. Then she went all floppy and tired and so I brought her to emergency about an hour ago.'

'She's all right though? It's just stomach flu?'

'Well, no, she's not really all right,' he says, sounding profoundly irritated. 'She's not feeling well at all, Emma, and she's been asking for you. I tried calling your mobile sixteen times. Sixteen times, Emma. And I've been calling the home number. Where the hell have you been?'

Now is not the time for this. 'Troy, has she stopped vomiting? Can she talk to me?'

'Yes, she's stopped now. They gave her an injection. She's keeping down some Gastrolyte. But you need to get up here. You're supposed to be her mother, for God's sake.'

I start to cry. 'I'm sorry, I'm so sorry. I'll get in a cab straightaway.'

'Well that would be great, if it's not too much trouble. You know, if you've finished whatever it was that was so important you couldn't answer the phone—'

I cut him off. He can berate me when I get there. 'Troy, I'm hanging up and getting a cab.'

He keeps talking. 'You know, Emma, you make such a big deal about being the primary parent, but where are you when things get hard? Nowhere to be found.'

'Troy, stop talking, please. This isn't my mobile. Call me back on the mobile if you have to keep yelling at me. I need to get in the car.'

With that, I hang up. I feel completely sober, but I know I'm not. It's just adrenalin, I'm aware of that. The same adrenalin that just nearly convinced me to shag someone else's husband is now doing its best to convince me I'm fine to drive my car to the hospital, which I'm very much not.

Adam is leaning against the wall in the hallway. He's cradling his phone with his shoulder and buttoning his shirt back up, while he phones for a cab for me.

He hangs up and asks, 'Do you want me to come?'

'No, God no,' I say, horrified at the thought. 'The last thing I need is Troy knowing why I wasn't answering the phone. He'll have social services round here before I know it.'

'Emma, that's absurd. You're single. He's married to someone else.'

'So are you.' I almost tell him I know Ilse is coming back. But something stops me.

His expression hardens. 'Right. I'll go. I'll suppose I'll see you round then.'

'Oh shit, Adam, I'm sorry, I didn't mean . . . well, I don't know how it is with your wife. I'm sorry, we shouldn't have . . .'

He sighs. 'No, probably not.'

A beep from the street stops us. This can wait.

* * *

We don't live very far from the hospital. This has come in handy over the past few years, as Tim, in particular, is something of a strife magnet. Since he was four he's broken his arm falling out of a tree, knocked out two baby teeth sliding down a slippery dip on a friend's skateboard, and had his foot stitched up after a run-in with some oyster shells on rocks at the beach. He's not a daredevil as such, he's more just got an avid curiosity that is unmatched by any sort of physical prowess or judgment. He has tested the limits of his body by weaving his arm through stair bannisters, and the limits of nature by wrongly assessing which variety of hedge can bear his full weight.

Freya, on the other hand, has never been in hospital. The poor little thing will be freaked out. She thinks injections and operations are the same thing and I can't imagine she's being a particularly good patient.

It's half past eleven by the time the taxi drops me off at emergency, and I rush through the waiting room, which is filled with the typical Saturday night assortment of people who've fallen over pissed, taken something they shouldn't, and the ones who thought their sports injuries from earlier in the day were okay until they tried to go to sleep. There are also several parents holding small children and sick bags.

The triage nurse waves me through to the paediatric emergency ward, which is much quieter than the waiting room. Fewer sports injuries and drug-taking mishaps, I suppose. The nurse on the desk here directs me to bed nine, where I pull aside the cubicle curtain to reveal a tiny wilted Freya, fast asleep on the bed, and a rumpled-looking Troy.

'Nice of you to make an appearance,' he says, running a hand through his hair and rubbing the back of his neck. 'Sorry to drag you away from whatever you were doing that was so much more important than your child.' There is no sign of the man who kissed me earlier today.

'I'm so sorry,' I say, sincerely. 'Has she been very upset without me? I'm sure you did a great job.'

'Of course I did a great job, I'm her father. That's not the problem, Emma. I was fine with her here, but that's left Helen at home alone with Tim and Lola.'

The penny drops. Of course. They've probably all got whatever this bug is. How horrendous.

'Shit, are they all vomiting? Oh, poor Helen.'

'No. They're not. But that's not the point. They could start spewing at any moment, and how's Helen meant to handle that by herself, with me stuck up here, dealing with a sick little girl, and doctors who don't even bloody speak English? One of them asked if she wanted an ice lolly, and I didn't know what that was.'

For a moment I pause, confused. So, everyone at home is fine, he is fine, Freya's on the mend, but I'm a bad person because I wasn't here to relieve him *just in case* Helen had to deal with a bit of vomit at home? Seriously? I deal with the only part I understand.

'It's a Popsicle, Troy. An ice lolly is what the English call a Popsicle.'

'Well if English doctors are going to come here and take jobs from our doctors the least they can do is call a damn Popsicle a Popsicle.'

'Right,' I say, wanting to get back to the matter at hand. 'But what were you saying about Helen and the kids? Are they sick or not?'

'Not yet, Emma, but stomach flu is very contagious. Extremely. Freya was sick all over our sofa, before we moved her to the bathroom. After that it was pretty contained because I kept her in there with me and the others went to bed, but they've all been exposed. I don't know how long the incubation period is. What happens if all three of them get sick while I'm not there to help? Helen needs me there. I don't know what you're playing at, Emma. Is this about this afternoon? Is this your way of trying to sabotage my marriage? First you kiss me, and now you try to make me look bad by leaving Helen at home to deal with this by herself? Because if that is what you're trying to do, ignoring your own sick child is a pretty disgusting way to go about it.'

'Deal with *what* by herself?' I shout, losing my calm completely. 'There's nothing to deal with—you just said that. Everyone's fine there. I honestly do not understand what the *fuck* you are talking about.'

Troy looks alarmed.

'I was out, Troy. My phone was on silent. I wasn't ignoring anyone. And do you know what? If one of the other kids had been sick, or if Helen had, she would have dealt with it the same way I have dealt with it every time our two kids have been sick for the past three years. She would deal with it by putting them in one bed so there aren't as many sheet changes, and using lots of buckets, and bleach, and giving them Gastrolyte. But the difference, Troy, is that Helen would only have to deal with that alone for about two hours, until you get home. Unlike me, who has to deal with it alone, every single fucking time, Troy, because you fucked off.'

He tries to interrupt me but I'm in full furious flight.

'And, Troy, let's not forget that right now Tim and Lola are not sick. They are fine, you just said so. They are probably fast asleep, and so is Helen. You're just pissed off because you aren't, and that, you utter shit, is just one of so many reasons you are such a bloody weapons-grade dickhead.'

I'm sure the whole children's ward can hear me. But I'm so far past caring. I move away from the bed, and stand outside the cubicle, gathering myself. The nurses are watching me, but no one says a word. I'm fully expecting to be told off at any moment, but although the staff are all clearly listening, they continue to type, and shuffle papers together, and one gets up and writes on a whiteboard. Two young doctors bury their heads in clipboards of patient notes.

I hear a little voice say, 'Mummy?' and turning round, I see Freya's awake. She's very pale, with dark circles under her eyes, and her fine hair is matted into a bird's nest at the back. With the most impeccable timing and aim, she rolls onto her side and vomits all over Troy's shoes. I can see the nurses have been giving her Gastrolyte, probably the lemon-lime flavour.

'Good girl,' I tell her, and reach for a tissue to wipe her mouth. 'Troy, go get her nurse.'

* * *

Three hours later, in the darkest, quietest hour of the night, I take Freya home. A rehydration IV and some more anti-nausea medication, along with a few Popsicles, have done the trick and she's exhausted but all right. She'll need a day or two on the sofa, with a high dose of *Peppa Pig*, but she will be fine.

Troy's at his house, having left the hospital shortly after the spewy shoes incident. He didn't quite storm out, because he cares too much about his image for that. He put on a show of good humour for the nurses, and accepted a pair of elasticated blue surgical shoe covers to wear home. He carried his soiled Converses in a red plastic bag emblazoned with warnings of biohazardous waste contained within.

Before he left, he informed me—as if it were some massive favour—that he would keep Tim until Sunday night, as agreed, unless he also started vomiting.

At home I tuck Freya into my bed, then set about covering the floor in old towels, in case this is merely a lull in the vomiting. If there's one thing parenting has taught me, it's never to trust a stomach bug. The moment you let your guard down is the moment it rears up. I crack open the window in the hope that the fresh air will blow away the contagion, and collapse onto the bed beside her. She curls her little body into mine and together we try to sleep off the illness, the shame, the guilt, and the anger. And all the wine.

* * *

Three hours. That's how long the quiet lasts.

At six-thirty, a car door slams outside my window.

'Back it into the driveway, Julia!' comes Ian's voice at top volume in through my open window.

'What do you think I'm doing? I have to start the car before I can back it into the driveway,' Julia yells back. 'And I still think it will be easier to attach the trailer if it's in the street behind the car.'

'I know you think that, you've told me six times. But which one of us has done this before? Me.'

'You haven't. Your father hooked it up last time.'

'We did it together.'

They have a trailer now? What the hell for? I wonder idly as I gingerly attempt to move my head. It bursts into throbbing agony, which is nothing less than I deserve, seeing as I drank the world dry of white wine last night. Freya is still asleep, her face pressed into the crook of my neck, and not covered in sick. I consider this a very promising start to the day.

'If we're going to make it to the guy's house in time to pick it up—and he is expecting us at eight—load it and then get to the beach, we need to get a move on, so back the car up, Julia.'

'If you'll stop ordering me around for five seconds, I will,' she snaps. 'This bloody Jet Ski is more trouble than it's worth. I don't see why you can't just rent one, like everyone else.'

They've bought a Jet Ski? Of course they have.

'Because, Julia, the amount I plan to use it, it doesn't make economic sense to rent one.'

'You'll use it twice then hurt yourself and lose interest. We both know that. It'll be dressage all over again.'

'That's not fair. You know Boadicea wasn't right in the head. That horse had a mean streak a mile wide. My back issues were entirely separate.'

I hear Julia rev the engine twice, then back her car around and into her driveway, where she obviously almost hits Ian, judging by his panicked yelps. If she ever does run him over, and I do feel like it's just a matter of time, I would not feel comfortable giving evidence for the defence.

While it's definitely irritating to be woken so often by Julia and Ian carrying on like a pair of upper-middle-class Jerry Springer guests, I do have a sort of grudging respect for their lack of self-consciousness. In a suburb where people mostly keep to themselves, airing all your dirty laundry on the street is a surprisingly effective way of avoiding being the subject of gossip. No one ever talks about Julia and Ian, because they are an open book. Sure, they're a boring, aggressive audiobook that comes on far too early and you can't make them stop, but I rather admire the way they live their lives out loud.

When my stomach flops over alarmingly, and I know I'm about to be sick, it's not a great surprise. When it comes to spreading the stomach flu, all the hand-washing in the world is no match for a toddler who sleeps more or less in your mouth. I carefully extract myself from Freya's pestilent embrace and with grim resignation pad quickly down the hall to the bathroom.

* * *

The next forty-eight hours are endurance parenting at its finest. Freya doesn't get sick again, but at ten o'clock that morning the doorbell rings and I open the front door to find a very green Tim being returned by Troy. He doesn't quite hand his son over using a pair of tongs, but he doesn't even come in the front gate.

'Poor kid wants you, Em,' he calls from the sidewalk. 'Think he's about to come down with it. You look rough.'

'Yep,' I say, and bring Tim in. I barely have the energy to stand. There's nothing left for talking to Troy about anything.

Tim only just makes it to the bathroom. I hand the room over to him for the afternoon and I sit in the hall with a bucket, emptying it as necessary. Freya lies in my bed limply gazing as the iPad plays episode after episode of *Peppa Pig* and *Ben and Holly* and the endless stream of cheery British voices fails to drown out the disgusting sounds Tim and I are making.

On Sunday evening Freya manages to nibble on some dry toast, but Tim and I are still on the Gastrolyte. Mercifully, late that night the vomiting comes to a halt.

I shift a sleeping Freya back to her bed, now that she's twenty-four hours clear of throwing up, and tonight Tim and I lie in my bed in an exhausted heap, sucking our Popsicles and watching *The NeverEnding Story*.

'I'm glad I came home early,' Tim says.

'Me too, matey. It's better to be together when we're sick.'

'Dad's not very good at looking after people,' he says.

'No, well, everyone has different strengths. Dad's better at . . .' I have to think.

'Juice?' offers Tim. 'He's really good at making up new juices.'

'He is,' I agree. 'Very good at juice, your dad.' I kiss Tim on the head and we return our attention to the boy-warrior Atreyu as he is knocked into the Sea of Possibilities.

Chapter Fourteen

None of us wakes until after nine o'clock on Monday morning. It is the latest I have slept in six years. We are all groggy and tired, and starting to regain our appetites, so I prescribe us another day of TV and whatever snacks we so desire.

I make that grand proclamation before considering the fact that we don't have any good snacks in the house, and the idea of taking the kids to the supermarket makes my body threaten to restart the vomiting. So I send an SOS text message to my dad.

Since I've been single, I've made a point of not asking Dad for help every time I'd like to. He would help, that's not the issue. I just feel like I should reserve the mayday calls for when things are really impossible.

This isn't one of those times. I could put the kids in the car, drive to the shopping centre, drag them around the supermarket with me as I fill the cart, wait in line, load it all in the car, and drive back home. But frankly, I'm totally drained and I'd just rather not. I could order a home delivery of shopping but that won't come until four, and we all have a post–stomach flu hunger that won't wait.

Dad is thrilled to be asked. Within an hour he's at the front door, loaded up with bags of raisin toast, chocolate cookies, packets of fish fingers, two-minute noodles, oven fries, and cans of lemonade.

'The cavalry has arrived!' he says, beaming.

'Don't come in,' I say. 'You'll probably catch it too.'

'I don't catch stomach flu,' he says. 'I haven't thrown up since the night before Uncle Jeremy's wedding in 1981.'

This isn't true. To be fair, he's probably only thrown up a handful of times since then, but every time he tells us it's the first time since the night before Uncle Jeremy's wedding in 1981.

'Thanks, Dad,' I say, following him down the hall to the kitchen. 'It was really nice of you to do this.'

'That's all right, Emma, my love. That's what dads are for.'

The kindness of this sentiment, the genuine belief that it's a father's responsibility to bring his daughter junk food when she's well over thirty, just because she's tired and she's been sick and can't be bothered to go get it herself—that's what undoes me. I start to cry.

Dad puts his arms around me and just makes it worse. I stand and sob into the front of his shirt, while the kids look uncomfortable and nudge the plastic bags with their feet, trying to see which one contains the mini Milky Ways they have requested.

Eventually Dad extricates himself and locates the Milky Ways. He opens the back door, tears open the bag, flings the chocolates into the garden and shoos the kids out after them like puppies. Then he puts on the kettle, unpacks the groceries, and makes me four slices of buttered raisin toast and a strong cup of tea. I start to calm down.

'No Lola today?' he asks.

I start crying again. 'No Lola any more at all. Helen told me I can't have her again.'

'Did she now?' Dad says calmly. 'Why was that?'

I hate telling him when I've done the wrong thing. But he can always tell anyway, so I might as well fess up.

'I sort of stopped taking her to her activities last week. And I didn't tell Helen. Then I did tell Helen, but I did it when I was pissed, in her garden, in front of all Troy's old friends. And I think I may have humiliated her.'

'Emma.' That's all he needs to say and I am five years old again, and so ashamed. In one word it's clear that I've let him down, I've let the family down, but most of all I've let myself down. I don't think I've ever had that much power with my kids. Then again they're not really in the business of doing things that bring shame on our family, at least not to this level.

'You know why this happened, don't you, love? You were showing off—trying to be the best at everything and in control of everything.'

'I wasn't!' I'm outraged. 'I was, as I have explained to everyone a thousand times, trying to do the right thing by my family.'

'. . . while also showing Helen how you can manage three kids more easily than she can manage one.'

'Maybe there was a bit of that initially, after Troy left me, but not any more, Dad. I know you think I shouldn't have been looking after Lola so much, but I love her. I know that's really twisted, but I do.'

'I know you do, Ems. You've got so much love. They don't know how lucky they've been, having you to help with their child. It's an unorthodox arrangement, and I don't think it's a bad thing if it's over, because I think you need to get on with other things now. But I'm sorry you're so sad.'

'What other things am I going to get on with?' I ask. 'All I am is a mother now, and not a very good one at that.'

'That isn't true. You're still a person. You have friends. Maybe you could find a boyfriend. You have a job; you're a very good editor.'

'I'm not. I don't even really work that much any more, Dad. I earn bugger all. Financially I'm completely reliant on Troy, still.'

'Well, maybe you can move towards changing that,' he says gently.

'What, you mean go back to a publishing company job?'

'Maybe, or just increase your freelance workload a bit, and look at working somewhere more professional than the park or your kitchen. There are lots of co-working thingummy places now. Keith's son runs his business from one.'

'What about Freya and Tim? Freya's only at preschool a couple of days.'

'I could help you look after her another day or two. I'm retired. What else am I going to do? I think Twitter can manage itself all right without me a couple of days a week. I'd like to help more. Maybe I could even take her to a ballet lesson or two.' He's got a little smile on his face.

Outside I hear Freya squeal with laughter, followed by a low noise that tells me Tim is doing his impersonation of a grumpy fish. It's the first time they've played or laughed in days. Once again my eyes fill with tears.

'I don't know, Dad. Even without Lola I think I have enough on my plate. I'm helping organize this awful Fun Run at the school again, and I'm taking the kids camping on the weekend, if we can manage to continue to not throw up. And that's probably a terrible idea. I can't manage camping with two kids by myself. I'm only doing it because bloody Troy is taking them to some fancy camping festival thing and I want them to think I'm better.

So I think it would be a mistake to try to take on more work. Everything I do at the moment is a mistake. I'm trying my best but I keep mucking everything up.'

'Give yourself a break, love.' Dad tears open a packet of chocolate cookies, takes two, and slides the pack across the table to me. 'Stop trying to be the best and do your best at everything. I know Mum always told you and Laura that it's important to do your best, but I've always thought doing your best all the time is a bit of a tiring proposition. Maybe try doing your second best for a bit.'

I think about it, while I eat three cookies. Doing my second best. Not trying as hard all the time. It's an idea. A terrifying idea, but maybe I could consider it. But things and people would suffer. That's what Dad doesn't understand.

'Dad,' I say, 'if I ease up and stop trying so hard, like if I don't try to sort out this—I don't know, maybe you'd call it a feud, no, this dispute—with Helen and Troy, and I don't start looking after Lola again, then it won't be fair to the kids. I'm the only reliable parent they have. Me going to Troy's house to get Lola and then take her back, it's at least a chance for my kids to see their father sometimes. You know how often he cancels his weekends with them. At least this way he can't avoid them completely.'

'Yes, it would be hard for Tim and Freya if you gave up the Lola-sitting, I understand that,' Dad says. 'But if Troy is really determined to be a shit dad, and not give them the time they deserve, well, they're going to figure that out eventually. That outcome isn't up to you. You can't keep juggling all the balls for everyone. Let Troy and Helen's balls drop, love. Let them deal with that. And maybe you could pick up some other balls, more interesting, fulfilling balls.'

At this point the conversation seems to be veering

dangerously into double entendre territory, so before I end up discussing which specific other balls I would consider handling, I decide it's time to move on.

'And as for my work, Dad, I don't know if I should still be an editor. The pay is terrible, the scheduling is unreliable, and I'm not even that good at it.'

'Do something else then.'

'But that's all I know how to do!' I wail. I know as it comes out that I've pushed Dad's sympathy to its limit.

'Emma,' he says, exasperated. 'Come on. You are a bright capable girl. There are many things you can do, but you can't do any of them unless you stop feeling so sorry for yourself. You are fine. You have two healthy children, a very nice house, and a lovely family, even if you are trying their patience at bit at the moment.'

'It's not that nice a house,' I say sulkily. 'It's a complete mess. My children never, ever put anything away.'

'Well, no, your perfectionist tendencies don't appear to stretch to housekeeping,' he agrees. 'But that's all right. I mean you're not a hoarder. It's not dangerous to live here.'

'You're too kind,' I say.

From outside I hear shrieks of sugared delight.

'I shouldn't let them eat that whole bag of Milky Ways,' I say. 'I mean, I'm not obsessed with sugar, like Helen. But surely eighteen mini Milky Ways are too many.'

'Oh leave them alone, Em,' Dad scolds me. 'They'll stop eating when they've had enough. Kids need to work out their limits for themselves. How are they going to do that if you're always hovering around, doing all their thinking for them? Mum and I always thought that was important, letting you two learn to figure things out for yourselves.'

'I don't do that,' I say, realizing as the words come out that I absolutely do. 'And I don't know what Mum did or didn't do with us because she's not here to tell me. Dad, it's so unfair. How can I be a mum when I've forgotten so much about what Mum did for me?'

'You haven't forgotten. You might think you have, but you know, deep down. You're doing it fine, Ems. Mum would say the same thing.' His voice thickens. 'She'd be very proud of you, but I think she'd say it's time to let Troy and Helen and Lola do their own thing.'

He's right. I do need to step away from my kids, and Lola, a bit more. The very thought fills me with panic, but I sit with the panic for a moment, and when it settles I realize I'm panicking because I don't know who to be without them. It's a very big thought and one that, for me to process, requires more cookies.

'Dad,' I say, casually, 'maybe you could help me out with the kids. I mean, not right away, because we're going camping and I haven't got much work right now, but maybe next week? I've been booked for an edit that's running really late, so when it finally lands I'm going to need to turn it round fast. I always work with the kids here, but I could do it quicker if I had some help with them.'

'It would be a pleasure, love. Just say the word. And say the word, too, if you want any help with plans for the camping trip. I've still got my checklists from when we used to take you and Laura down to Kosciuszko. I can't imagine anything much has changed since then.'

Dad stays for dinner, which is a joyous fish finger and two-minute noodle feast, and we all celebrate the fact that no one is being fed Gastrolyte through a syringe.

As I see him to the door, he turns suddenly and says, 'Oh—Em, I nearly forgot. Laura says she wants to talk to you. She said she's texted you but maybe you haven't been getting them? I told her you were all sick and she said to call when you have time. She said to say she needs to hear more about your author. Is that the one writing the book you're expecting?'

'Ah, no,' I say, 'I think she means a different author.'

'Righto then, call her and tell her about that author because she says she is keen to hear. She's a very good sister. She seems more interested in your job than you are, Em!'

'Yes, yes she does,' I agree. He kisses me hard on the cheek, hugs me tightly, and heads home to watch *Midsomer Murders*.

My very good sister is not interested in my work. She only wants to know about what I did with Adam once she'd left the pub. I'm not sure I want to tell her. I've been receiving and studiously ignoring her texts, with the excuse that we have all been knee-deep in vomit, but I can't put her off forever.

And I know what she'll say.

* * *

The next morning Dad comes back bright and early to collect Freya. He thinks they should start hanging out together even before I have more work to do. They're going to go to the beach, he tells me, and maybe the hardware store too.

I take Tim back to school, still a bit pale but otherwise recovered. I keep my eye out for Adam in the playground, but I don't see him anywhere. He's probably hiding from me. I can't even quite remember what I said as I hurtled out of the house and into a cab on Saturday night, but I definitely remember him looking hurt, and I haven't had so much as a text message from him since, so I think I can safely assume I've buggered that up, whatever it even was.

Probably for the best, really. I need to focus on other things.

After dropping Tim off, I head to a café. I see lots of school mums and dads doing this. I've never quite managed to crack the scene though, because as much as Freya and Lola are excellent playmates for each other, they're not exactly what you would call café-friendly.

I've given it a few tries, in several different local establishments, but never with any real degree of success. First we always have to have an argument about whether they will or won't be sitting in highchairs. (Spoiler: they won't; never have.) I order coffee for me and babyccinos for them, which they always manage to up-end on themselves. The espresso cups the babyccinos come in are designed on Tardis principles, because although they are small enough to be clutched in chubby toddler hands, they seem to contain enough warm milk to irrigate the Murray–Darling. It's certainly enough to course off the table and run directly over to whichever is the most expensive handbag another customer has placed by her feet. That's one outcome.

Or the girls will spot another child who has a milkshake and then they set up a two-kid lobby group to be allowed to upgrade their babyccinos to chocolate shakes. That's always successful because by the time I've ordered my long black I will do almost anything to remain sitting down until I've drunk it. Maybe if I drank lattes I would have more power in this equation, because you can knock back a latte in eight seconds, if required. But try that with a long black and you end up with a scalded esophagus.

So in the past I've found myself sitting at a table, with two toddlers armed with chocolate milkshakes as big as themselves, who then ask for toast, which is a build-up to asking for Nutella on toast, and before I know it I've spent twenty-five dollars and the two of them are laughing maniacally, drunk on a heady cocktail of sugar and power.

No thank you. Milk Arrowroot biscuits and mandarins in the park is more my style.

But today, for the first time in ages, I enter the nicest-looking of the three cafés in the strip mall. All three have had a hipster-makeover in the past five years, so they've been thoroughly subway-tiled and visible-filament-lightbulbed. The one I like the best has succulents growing in Spanish tomato tins as table decorations.

More than half of the tables are occupied by parents I recognize from the school. There are a couple of babies and toddlers, but they're all sitting in high chairs and behaving like civilized humans, mostly clutching a parent's phone that they have handed over in return for some peace and quiet.

See, that's where my problem has been—I didn't succumb to the lure of plugging the kids into a screen in a café. Not because I'm above that. Oh no, I'm not Screen-Free-Until-They're-Three Helen. It's just that I only have one phone. That's the real reason to stay in a marriage: you need to keep the number of phones and children equal. Handing my phone to either Freya or Lola would not have made for a calm coffee hour.

Today I am alone. I'm not sure where to sit. I don't want anyone to join me, so I don't want to sit at a table for two, facing the door. If I sit facing away from the door I won't be able to see anything interesting. There is a bar-height table along the front window, and I could sit there, but I'd have to sit on one of the high bar stools, which are slippery vinyl, not super comfortable, and always make be worry that my bottom is spilling over the edges. My bottom isn't huge, but in a seated position it's definitely wider than one of those stools.

A man who has been sitting at the very end of the window bar table stands up, closes his magazine and puts it back on a pile of other magazines the café has provided. He calls out a goodbye to the barista, who gives him a cool nod.

This is a win for me. I can now sit on a barstool, thus giving me a view of the street, but also lean against the wall, so if my bum on the stool looks like a denim beret atop a small bald man's head, no one will be the wiser.

The waitress comes over and I order a long black, while marvelling at how and why someone with such perfect, plump, unlined skin could possibly feel she needs to slather on as much makeup as this girl has. Nothing makes me feel older than wanting to tell girls in their teens that they should wear less makeup. 'Heed me,' I want to beseech her. 'Believe me when I tell you your face is perfection and it's only downhill from here. Your skin will never look better than it does now. Even with the odd zit.'

While I wait for my coffee, I take out a notebook. It's time to make a list. Quickly I jot down: camping, Fun Run, work, Laura, Adam, Helen, Troy. It occurs to me I've ordered it from 'task it will be easiest to deal with' to 'task I really, truly, deeply do not want to address. At all. Ever.'

I stare into my coffee instead. Suddenly there is a loud rapping on the window. My heads snaps up and there, inches from my face, outside the café, is the third-most difficult entry on my list: Adam. The butterflies erupt. Stop it, I think. He's married and confused at best, but certainly not available. Let it go. He's smiling. He doesn't look like he hates me. How about that?

Maybe we can pretend that what happened on Saturday night, on my floor, didn't happen. That's possible, surely. It was just a very drunken fumble between friends. No big deal. Certainly not a big enough deal for him to tell his wife about. Probably not even a big enough deal to ever mention again. Right?

Wrong. He comes inside. The stool beside me is empty and he sits down. He looks very intense.

'Hello,' he says.

'Hello to you,' I reply.

'We need to talk.'

'About camping?' I say hopefully.

'Well, yes, that too. But more about, you know—Saturday.'

I'm going to play it down, see how that goes.

'Saturday? Oh, that. That was nothing. Don't even worry about it.'

'Really?' He looks a tiny bit forlorn. 'Oh. Right. Okay. Well. Good, I guess.'

'It shouldn't have happened, I totally get that you were probably just a bit pissed, and missing Ilse and there was nothing more to it than that. I was smashed too. We're friends. Just friends.'

'Oh. Yes, friends.'

I peer at him. 'Aren't we? Or have I got this wrong? You are married?'

He straightens up. 'Absolutely. I'm married, we're friends. Shall we say no more about it?'

'Say no more about what?' I ask.

'Ha!'

We are both being too jolly now.

'So, camping,' he says, and smacks the table firmly with both hands. 'Let's plan this.'

'Just so you know,' I say, wanting to be up-front. 'If we go camping together, there is going to be talk. Even with separate tents. We're likely to be the only single parents there and the fact that we know each other, that we are friends—well, that's going to be some serious grist for the rumour mill.'

'Is it?' He looks perturbed.

'It doesn't bother me,' I tell him. 'I've been through that mill before. I'm already regarded as a bit worrying around here. I don't have a lot of women friends around this area. I had a few sort of acquaintances back when we first moved in, but I don't think people here quite know how to cope with me being a single mother and with my weird situation with my ex. It makes them uncomfortable.'

'Surely not,' Adam says. 'Why would they care?'

'I don't know. But people seem to think you're safer in a couple. Like I'm going to try to steal their husbands or something.'

We're both quiet for a second.

'Which obviously you're not,' he says.

'Obviously. But lots of the parents act strangely towards me anyway. They have ever since Troy and I split up. I don't know if they will on the camping trip, but I thought I'd better give you the heads up, just in case.'

'I think I'll cope,' he says. 'In any case, I'm not doing this camping thing on my own, so they can just think what they want to think.'

'That's the spirit,' I tell him.

* * *

I leave the café an hour later feeling surprisingly on top of things. I've dealt with the Adam issue. That is sorted. We are just friends.

A small voice in me tries to speak up and ask what kind of friend doesn't ask about your kid who was in the hospital last time they heard, but I tell it to pipe down. He's just a new friend. He doesn't have to be interested in my kids.

Walking home I think about the weird warning I just gave Adam. It's true, what I said about people around here not being very friendly to me since Troy and I split up. I mean, they're not out and out rude, but there are definitely a few couples who were neighbourhood friends who stopped contacting me once I was single. The sort of people you meet in the park, on a Saturday morning, and get chatting to while you push your kids on the swings and drink your takeout coffee. There were a few people like that, who we progressed to having a dinner with, at either our house or theirs. We only moved in here when Tim was born, so there were only a couple of years in which we built these kinds of relationships, but it's long enough to see the general direction a friendship is going, and it was definitely strange the way those people dropped off the radar once Troy left me.

I suppose I can't really blame them. They probably didn't know what to say. And then when Troy and Helen moved into my street, that was just the icing on the freak show cake. I guess that's why I've worked so hard to be cool about it. I think I thought that if I acted like it was no big deal that my ex-husband and his mistress-turned-wife decided to live three doors up from me, then other people would be admiring and chilled about it too.

But now I suspect that's made us look more like a freak show. And it's probably why I'm clinging so much to the idea of having Adam in my life. He's a nice fellow. Normal. A friend.

As I turn the corner into my street, a car passes me. A big, white Range Rover. It's Helen's. I deliberately slow down so that she'll have parked and gone inside before I have to walk past her house, but she pulls into a space in front of her house and lingers in the driver's seat.

Has she seen me? Can I walk past and pretend I don't know she's in the car?

I don't know what to say. What if Troy's told her about our kiss? That's the sort of dick move he would pull. It's what he's been doing to me ever since he told me about Helen and Lola: trying to involve me in his emotional quagmire. His attitude seems to be 'Why bother having an emotional crisis if you can't bring someone else down with you?'

I speed up, ready to charge past her car, and just as I reach her rear bumper she leaps out. She walks around the front of the car and stands in the middle of the sidewalk, blocking my way.

I come to an abrupt stop.

'Oh!' I say, feigning surprise. 'Helen. Hi.'

She looks me straight in the eye. 'I'm only going to say this to you once. Stay the fuck away from my family.'

It feels like the air has been sucked from my lungs.

She continues, in a clear but quiet voice. 'I know you kissed Troy. He told me. You were drunk and disgusting, but that is the reason—not an excuse. You are pathetic, Emma. He's not interested in you. He never really was. You think it was me who destroyed your marriage, Emma, but it wasn't. It was you.'

I'm rooted to the spot, and she's not finished.

'We tried to be nice to you. That was what Troy wanted, because he wanted to think that you were capable of rising above the break-up. And we genuinely thought you loved Lola. It's clear we were wrong. You couldn't even respect us enough to take her to her classes.'

I still haven't moved. I can't believe we are having this conversation in the street. To a passer-by it would look like we're coordinating a soccer pickup carpool. Instead I'm enduring a blow-by-blow character assassination.

There's a tapping sound from the car and I turn. Right beside me, in the back seat, strapped into her car seat, is Lola, wearing her pale pink ballet cardigan, wrap skirt, and tights. She's smiling at me and tapping her little fingernails against the window to get my attention.

I move to open the car door but Helen pushes straight past me to get there first. She unbuckles Lola and picks her up.

'Hi Memma,' Lola says, and my heart almost breaks.

'Emma,' Helen corrects her. 'Emma, not Memma.'

Lola looks confused.

'How was ballet, sweetie?' I ask.

'A bit boring. I wanted to go to the ball room again. But Mummy said no.'

Helen looks at me with nothing but loathing.

'Time to go in for some lunch, my darling,' she says, and opens the front gate. As she walks up the path Lola watches me over her mother's shoulder.

'Bye-bye, Memma.'

'Bye-bye, Lola.'

I stand for a moment, my chest feeling like it's about to explode. Then I hear my voice, calling, 'Helen.'

She stops, about to close the door behind her. She puts Lola down, sends her into the hall, opens the door fully and looks at me.

'Helen,' I say. 'You were fucking my husband. Before I was pregnant and then all through my pregnancy. You will never be in a position to criticize me.'

I turn away. Then I stop. I look back and she's still at the door.

'And we both know I'm not the one you're really angry with.'

* * *

Inside my house I push the door closed behind me and realize I'm shaking. My hands are trembling and my knees are so wobbly I feel like I could collapse. I don't know what just happened. Obviously some of it's pretty clear—Troy told Helen I kissed him—but what was all that stuff about me destroying my marriage? That doesn't make any sense.

The kiss was a mistake, although I still don't know who initiated it, so I can't say with any authority whose mistake it was. I guess it doesn't really matter. What matters is it won't happen again.

And if Troy and Helen want to destroy the happy co-parenting relationship we've built together, there isn't much I can do about that. Let's see how they like it when there's no flexibility in the care arrangements, when I'm not at their beck and call when they want to have a week in Bali.

I feel like I'm on fire. I want to sort this life out. I want my independence from them. For that I'm going to need a hell of a lot more money. A bit of freelance work here and there—fitting it in around the kids—that's got to stop. I don't want to need the money I get from Troy every month. Work needs to become a serious business.

And it's got to start now. The first thing I need to do is figure out when this ridiculously late book of Wanda's is going to show up—if it is even still coming—and then fill in the gaps around it with other work. Preferably not cricket-related.

In the kitchen I pour myself a huge glass of water, which I drink with shaking hands. Then I sit at the table, open my laptop and check for emails from Carmen. I want to call Philip, who for some reason seems to be the only person who understands Wanda's schedule and cares enough to keep me in the loop, but he'll have left Wanda's by now. Anyway, it's Carmen's job to keep me informed, not Philip's. She can sort this out.

Surprise, surprise . . . there's no email from her. Well that's not good enough. If they want me to edit this book, I'm going to have to insist on having a manuscript. I know how this works: they'll keep putting me off and putting me off, and then all of a sudden the manuscript will arrive and they'll want me to turn the whole edit around in about three days. And it'll be when I have the kids, or when we're camping or the weekend of the Fun Run. I need to be more proactive about this.

It's time to do the thing I hate most. I pick up my phone and place a call to Carmen's office phone number.

She answers immediately.

'Hi Carmen, it's Emma Baker,' I say.

'Emma Baker!' she cries. 'That is just the weirdest thing. I was just about to call you.'

Highly unlikely, I think, but I let her continue.

'I've finally managed to get Wanda on the phone and we've had a very good talk.'

'You've spoken to Wanda herself, or Wanda via Philip?' I ask.

'Philip who?'

'Philip her friend, the one who's been staying and helping her.'

'Why would I talk to him?'

'Never mind,' I say, wanting to keep her on track. 'Is the manuscript ready?'

'Nowhere near,' she replies. 'Miles and miles from ready. So not ready. Apparently she has writer's block. She says she's written eighty per cent of it but she is now stuck. How anyone can have writer's block when they've been give a six-figure advance is beyond me. I think I'd find that much money to be very unblocking. But that's what she's claiming, and frankly I now need to do whatever it takes to unblock her.'

'How will you do that?'

'She wants me to come up to her house in fucking Woop Woop and sit with her while she writes, but that's not going to happen because the bigwigs from the UK office are out for two weeks and if I'm not at my desk here it's not going to be a good look. What I can do is be there for her in a virtual sense. I'll Skype her every day, and if she wants me to sit there with her for twelve hours at a time, talking it through while she types, then that's what I'll do. Surely that will work.'

'I hope so,' I say. 'When shall I expect the manuscript then?'

'Let's see . . .' I can hear her clicking away with her mouse, no doubt confronting the full horror of the state of her calendar. 'It's Tuesday now . . . and if she really puts her head down I would say that if you put aside next week and the week after, we should be good.'

I'm not going to hold my breath. This book is so late now that it would be a miracle if it were suddenly completed in the next five days. I'll have to line up some other jobs.

The adrenalin from my run-in with Helen is still coursing through me so I harness the energy and fire off half a dozen emails to other publishing contacts, advising that I'm available and ready for whatever editing or proofreading they want to send my way.

I've relied on Troy for too long. Inspector Tilde would never do that. Sure, she's got exes too—many of them are her police colleagues, in fact, and one was even a suspect she had to investigate for a while there—but she lets them go and moves on. She just gets on with her job, and keeps taking steps up the ladder of success, and doesn't spend half her life waiting for them to text her or wishing they weren't married. I need to remind myself to do what Tilde would do, and to that end I take a sticky note, write 'WWTD?' on it, and stick it to the screen of my phone.

It's a small step, and it makes using the phone quite hard, but it feels significant.

Chapter Fifteen

I don't hear another word from Helen or Troy the whole rest of the week. I'm focused, sharp. The days go by quickly—several small editing jobs come in and I turn them around in record time. I'm reminded of why I like my job, something I seem to have forgotten while attempting to do it with two or three small children for company. Dad minds Freya again on Wednesday, and then on Thursday and Friday she is at preschool.

I fob off her questions about where Lola is as best I can, but when I see her run through the preschool gate and straight into her half-sister's open arms I feel another wave of anger at Helen and Troy. How dare they try to destroy this bond? These kids are practically twins, and two short preschool days plus every second weekend is not going to be anywhere near enough time for them together.

Tim can tell something's amiss with Lola. At dinner time on Thursday, after swimming lessons from which Lola is conspicuously absent, he confronts me about it.

'Mum, is Lola still sick?'

'Still sick? I don't think she has been sick at all, love. What do you mean?'

'I thought she must have got the vomits like we did.'

'Oh, sweetheart. No, I think she's okay. Dad and Helen are just . . . trying some different childcare arrangements for her for a while, that's all.'

Tim twirls his spaghetti around his fork for so long that his meal looks like a ball of wool. 'Okay. Are we still going to see Dad sometimes?'

'Mate, of course you are. The new arrangements are just for Lola. It's not going to affect how much time you guys spend with Daddy.' Except as I say the words I realize it's not true. Legally, Troy has the kids two nights out of fourteen. But the way we've operated until now, he has seen the kids almost every day, either when we have picked up Lola in the morning or dropped her off in the evening. He's always been distracted, and never spent time actually playing with my kids during those brief interactions, but it's clear to me now they have meant something to Tim. And now they've stopped.

I know from reading books about divorce and kids that what I really ought to do now is encourage Tim to talk about how this makes him feel. We should sit together with the bad feeling, and name it, and acknowledge it. This will reduce the power the bad feeling has. This seems to me, in this moment, to be a horrendous idea. Instead I offer him a bowl of ice cream and try to change the subject.

'Who's excited about camping?'

'Me!' squeals Freya. 'I'm going to sleep in a bag. Can I have my own handlamp?'

'I don't know what that is, but maybe,' I tell her.

'She means flashlight, like one you hold,' Tim translates. 'You know how she has a headlamp for her head? She thinks that means a headlamp in your hand is a handlamp.'

'Huh,' I say. 'Not a flashlight?'

Tim gives me a look that suggests I am asking too much of a three-year-old.

'Yes!' I say. 'We will have so many lamps. On our heads and in our hands and up our noses and hanging inside the tent. It's going to be excellent. And there might even be a campfire.'

'No there won't,' Tim corrects me. 'It's in a national park. No fires.'

'Really?' I'm quite disappointed. 'Not even in a rock circle? How do you know these sorts of things?'

He absorbs information like this and I'm constantly surprised. He's usually right.

Tim's little factoid about there being no campfires is the first chip in my camping confidence. Why didn't I know that? What else don't I know about this camping expedition?

That night, once the kids are in bed, I scan the information the school emailed when I signed us up for this.

It's a camp for all the school community. It's for one or two nights. We've gone for the one-night option, just to see how we go. Campsites are unpowered, up to a ten-minute walk from the parking area and an amenities block with toilets and cold showers. As it is in a national park there are no open fires. Oh. Tim was right.

But that's okay—we have a little gas camping stove. We can sit around that and toast marshmallows. It'll be great. This will be great.

As I fall asleep, I hear rain start falling lightly on the roof.

* * *

It rains all night, and when we wake up on Friday it's still tipping down. Camping with two kids is one thing, but camping in the rain with two kids is something else entirely. But I will not let my kids down.

After all, there's a saying I've read on a website for eye-wateringly expensive Scandinavian raincoats that there's no such thing as bad weather, only the wrong clothing. All I need to do is make sure we are appropriately outfitted for the rain. It's not terribly cold, so really, who cares about a bit of water?

On Friday, after I drop Tim at school and Freya at preschool, I scurry out through the rain to the shed. The water is ankle deep in parts of the garden because of the handball that's still trapped in the drain. The camping gear is sealed in several big plastic tubs, which is good because that means with a bit of luck it won't have perished along with my marriage.

I drag the tubs through the muddy garden and up to the back door, then return and haul the tent back too. I wanted to get a smaller tent, but now that I'm hoping to become more financially independent I shouldn't go buying a tent when I already have a perfectly good one, even if it is embarrassingly big.

I was hoping to put the tent up today to make sure I can do it by myself, and that it's in working order, but the damn thing is bigger than any single room in my house so there's no way I can do it inside. It's pointless doing it out here in the rain, because then I'll have to put it away wet and we'll be sleeping in a damp, mouldy tent tomorrow night. I'll have to take my chances.

Once the kids are asleep, I pack the car. It's raining still, but more lightly than it has all day. Maybe it will clear.

I'm hoping to get an early start. I don't generally consider myself a vengeful person, but I can't deny there's an element of that in my plan to leave, loudly, at six o'clock tomorrow morning. Julia and Ian, the shouters from across the street, might be the ones getting a rude awakening, for once.

* * *

In the morning, I wake to the sound of more rain. Harder rain. But that's all right because I have the right clothes for everyone. Well, I have a lot of clothes for everyone, and surely that's the same thing. The car is crammed with at least six changes of outfit for each kid, and a few for me. We have a raincoat each, gumboots that sort of fit, and I've thrown in a pile of our oldest towels—all fresh from a hot wash after the stomach flu of last week.

For the first time I can remember, I have to wake my kids up. Every other day of their lives they are awake before six, but not today.

'Wakey wakey, campers!' I say cheerfully before switching on their lights, but suddenly it's as if I have two teenagers. They are disoriented and grumpy.

'No, Mummy, it's cold. I don't want to go,' Tim moans.

Freya doesn't say anything, but sits up in bed looking like a surly and baffled tiger.

I dress them, make them go to the toilet and, putting on my jolliest front, herd them out through the rain and into the car. They're furious.

Two kids yelling out the front of your house at dawn on a Saturday? Take that, Ian and Julia, I think. But I look across the road and their driveway is empty. Their car and trailer are nowhere to be seen. They must have gone away for the weekend. How disappointing.

I cram the kids into the small spaces left in between the tent, cooler, camping stove, foldable table, chairs, bags of clothes, blow-up mattresses, pillows, and sleeping bags. I refuse to attach the roof coffin, so whatever fits in the boot and under the kids' feet is what's coming camping. At the last minute I run back into the shed and return with the beach umbrella, hoping I can use it to shelter the butane camping stove from the rain.

At seven o'clock, we finally get on the road. For reasons I can't fathom, the campground that's been chosen is four hours' drive away, on the other side of the mountains. It's not as if there aren't closer national parks for us to camp in. There will be some reason for this, like the parents organizing it have a holiday house nearby and want to be able to decamp if the weather gets too bad. A theory they may get to test this weekend.

The drive is meant to be four hours, but that's in good weather, with more synchronized bladders than ours. This is not good weather, and we stop six times for toilet breaks, and twice for french fries. With every minute that passes, the feeling that this is a very bad idea grows, and it's in directly inverse proportion to how great I tell the kids the camping is going to be. By the time we arrive I've practically shrieked at them a hysterical list of all the wondrous things about living at one with nature.

They continue to just stare at me in the rearview mirror. I'm fooling no one.

But as if by magic, when we pull into the campground the rain eases, and then stops altogether. A tiny patch of blue appears in the sky above the clearing where the rest of the school families have set up camp—right beside their cars, thank God.

I park beside a Land Cruiser with a snorkel and a bumper sticker for our local soccer club, and get out.

Looking around, I can see there is some next-level camping equipment here. These people are serious. There are lots of large tents, similar to mine, but there are also some techie-looking geodesic domes.

Tucked way over on the edge of the clearing is something that resembles a bluebottle and when I move closer to check it out, I realize it's a transparent plastic bubble tent. It's been inflated by a small fan, and from the sounds of it, the fan has to keep running or the thing will collapse, like a commercial jumping castle. Whoever owns this is running the power leads from the fan straight to their Prius, which is idling gently. I'm not sure this is going to work for as long as they need it to.

'Emma!' I hear Adam calling me and I turn around and see him emerging from the trees. 'You made it!'

'We did. Somehow. Not sure how good an idea it was, but we're here now!'

'It'll be great,' he says. 'It's meant to clear up this afternoon. But the ground is pretty mushy. We're setting up over here.' He points to a secluded nook off to one side of the clearing. There's a neat little pod-like tent there, a cooler, and a couple of bags.

I'm suddenly mortified by how much I've packed. But looking around I see I have nothing to be ashamed of. People have set up whole kitchens under canopies, complete with plumbed sinks and battery-operated refrigerators. We are not camping among minimalists.

'Can I go play with Bon?' Tim asks, tugging on my sweater.

'Sure,' I say. 'Go, be in nature. Only first, here are the rules: stay together, stay where you can see or hear the campsite, and what do you do if you see a snake?'

'Hit it with a sharp stick.'

'Tim!'

He rolls his eyes at me. 'Walk away and come tell a grown-up. I know all this. You told me the rules the whole way here in the car.'

'All right then. And remember Bon is littler than you. You need to take care of him.'

'I'm all right,' chirps Bon.

'Can we go?' asks Tim.

'You can go.'

They squelch off through the mud to where a gang of other kids are dragging fallen tree branches and piling them up. They're either building a campfire that we aren't allowed to light, or it's an attempt at a shelter.

Adam helps me haul all our gear out of the car, and together we start to set up my tent. The one time Troy and I came camping, erecting the tent took us over an hour—longer if you count the breaks where one or the other of us had to go for a walk and take deep breaths until he or she could trust themselves to resume. That was one reason I wanted to do a test run with the tent before I came, but because we follow the steps as laid out in the instruction manual, which still bears the scars of having been thrown in the dirt and stomped on, Adam and I have the thing up in no time.

'That's a good tent,' he says, admiringly. 'It's big, but it's quite straightforward to put together.'

'It is ridiculous. It's a silly big show-off of a tent. I'm embarrassed to have anything to do with it. If it had been up to me, I'd have gone for something more understated, like yours—but the man who chose it was into grand gestures. Go big or go home, that's how he rolls.'

'Yes, well, sometimes we just end up with the tent we end up with,' he says. 'It could be worse. You could have a clear plastic igloo.' He jerks his head over towards the *Grand Designs: Camping Edition* set-up. 'Are they really going to leave their car running the whole time so they can keep it inflated? That seems to defeat the purpose of driving a hybrid.'

'I'd say so.' I look around the campground. It's pretty full. There's only one spot left—a bit behind us. I'm hopeful that no one will take it and we can have a bit more quiet. From what I can see, Freya is the youngest child here, and not being next to a rowdy tent full of year four kids would be quite useful, on the sleep front.

But just as I'm thinking that, I hear a familiar shout from where the cars are parked.

'Ian, you can't leave it there. How's Karen supposed to get her car out if you've wedged her between our trailer and that bloody great tree?'

'I'm not planning to leave it there, Julia. Of course I'm not planning to leave it there. That would be a very inconsiderate place to leave the car and honestly, it worries me that it would even occur to you to think anyone *would* leave their car there. Good grief.'

Excellent. They're going to be my neighbours here as well.

Adam looks horrified as he sees Julia and Ian striding towards us. Ian has four fluorescent orange traffic cones under his arm.

'Hello!' shouts Ian. 'We know you, don't we?'

'I live opposite you. I'm Emma,' I tell him.

'Of course we know her, Ian. Emma has lived across the road from us for years. Years. Sometimes I wonder if you ever look out the windows of your own house, Ian.' Julia shakes her head. 'Hi, Emma.'

'Hi, Julia.'

This is the longest conversation I've had with them. I truly wasn't sure they knew my name, or that I live ten metres from them, but it turns out they do.

'Hello, mate.' Ian offers his hand to Adam. 'You must be Emma's other half. Haven't seen you around the street much. Work odd hours, do you?'

Julia looks mortified. 'Ian,' she hisses.

'What?'

'This is not Emma's husband. She was married to the . . . you know, *at number twenty-four*.' She says this while trying not to open her mouth at all, but the volume is still high. She looks like a demented ventriloquist.

Comprehension slides over Ian's face. 'Oh. Right, yes of course. Troy. He was . . . yes, and now he's, er . . .'

'This is Adam,' I say. 'He has a son in kindergarten. We're old friends from work.'

'Are you? That's good,' Julia says, but she has lost interest. She's got her eye on Ian, who is marking out their space with the traffic cones.

'Ian, is that really necessary?'

'Yes, I think it is. It makes it easier for people.'

'How does it?'

'Well, it's easier if they know not to walk through other people's areas, that way they won't, well . . . walk through our area.'

'Jesus, Ian, it's not a battlefield. What are you planning to do if someone walks through our area?'

'I'm not planning anything, Julia. You see, I don't have to plan anything because people aren't going to walk through our area because I've marked it out with the cones.'

'I might get some lunch started,' I say, by way of excusing myself. We stopped at two different McDonald's on the way but I need something to do.

Adam and I move as far away from them as we can and begin to make sandwiches while Julia and Ian continue their skirmish.

'Are they always like that?' Adam asks.

'Yes, always. They're pretty awful.'

'What he said about Troy, does that sort of thing happen much to you?'

'Not as much as it did to start with, but until something more scandalous happens around here I think it will continue, to some extent.' I try to sound sanguine.

'I'd hate it if people were gossiping about me,' Adam says, wrestling with a packet of ham that is determined to remain unopened.

'You get used to it.'

'I guess.'

'There are ways to avoid it.'

'Really? What?'

'Don't have your husband run off with his Pilates instructor and move three doors up the street. That's the main way I can think of.'

* * *

After lunch several of the more gung-ho camping parents, Harvey, Sarah, and Steve, round up the kids for a wilderness skills workshop. It's a great idea, except between the fire ban and the reluctance of the parents to allow their children near anything bladed, quite a lot of activities are out.

They manage to divide the kids into groups and take turns teaching them to tie some knots, pull paperbark off a tree and draw on it with charcoal they have sourced from an art supply store, and how to navigate using the sun, although the dense cloud cover makes this more of a challenge and the kids mostly end up looking at pictures of animal poo on Harvey's iPhone.

The afternoon passes peacefully. It's really quite remarkable. The kids stay more or less entertained by the wilderness workshop, and when that's over they all seem to know each other well enough that they break off and play in exactly the way that I dream of. No one is on an iPad, they've hardly any toys—they're like kids in the 1970s, just running around pretending to massacre each other with sticks, and getting extremely muddy.

Around four-thirty people begin to make dinner preparations, firing up the propane stoves, grilling sausages and heating cans of baked beans. By dusk the children are all fed, and beginning to fade.

When I suggest bed to Tim, he begs me to let him sleep in the tent with Bon.

'Me too, me too!' Freya joins in the lobbying.

I look at Adam. 'Maybe we could let them all go to sleep in your tent,' I suggest, 'and then I'll move them back once we're ready for bed. I mean, once we both, separately, are ready for bed.' I'm blushing.

Adam looks at me with a distinct twinkle in his eye.

'Good plan,' he agrees.

The kids are beyond excited, and Freya and Tim drag their sleeping bags into Adam's tent. As I climb in to kiss them goodnight, they all babble to me about how they are going to stay awake and have a midnight feast. Apparently the talk all over the camp this afternoon has been midnight-feast related, and they're definitely going to stay awake and have one.

'I don't know if you will,' I say. 'I don't want to burst your bubble, but no child ever in the history of children has stayed awake for a midnight feast. It's a myth.'

'Mum!' Tim is horrified. 'It isn't a myth. James and Lachlan have done it. They told us this afternoon.'

'Maybe they think it was midnight, but it was probably about eight o'clock. How about this? If you all go to sleep now, when you wake up, once it's light, you can all sneak out and have some chocolate. I'll put it near the front of our tent, so you can find it first thing in the morning. Deal?'

That placates them, and about eight minutes later they are all fast asleep.

It's a bit of an odd set-up, this camp. Now that the kids are in bed, I'm not sure what's going to happen in the absence of a communal campfire to sit around. But it's only seven o'clock.

Adam and I do the washing-up and put away the food. We're suddenly a bit quiet around each other. Despite what we agreed in the café, it still feels like there's something more between us. Maybe it's just me. It probably is. I still fancy him, so I'm feeling awkward. He'll be feeling strange because I'm acting oddly around him. We're caught in a vicious circle.

'Do you think the others are going to hang out?' he asks. 'It looks like some of them are putting their camping stoves in a circle. I think they might be trying to replicate the campfire experience.'

'Oh, that's weird,' I say. 'That isn't going to work, is it? It's just going to be a bunch of people sitting on chairs around ten two-burner stoves. They're all going to run out of propane. And they don't give off much light.'

'But look, Ian's added his flashlight, so that's helping.' He's right. Others put their flashlights on the ground too, and although there's nothing authentic about this, it's quite a sweet attempt to create a central space for congregating.

'Shall we?' Adam asks, holding up a bottle of whisky in one hand and a Dolphin lantern in the other. Oh God, I'd forgotten how people drink whisky when they go camping. It's some sort of rule. Even people who wouldn't touch it with a ten-foot pole under normal circumstances will drink whisky from a tin mug if they are camping. I suppose they realize they'll be having a terrible night's sleep anyway, so why not throw a whisky headache into the mix?

I grab two mugs and we head over.

* * *

Over at the fireless campfire, people are gathering. It's very dark, and the flashlights don't quite work like ambient firelight would. There's a lot of discussion over how to angle the flashlights so they aren't shining into people's eyes, and the final consensus is that they should point up. People give up on the propane stoves pretty quickly, once they realize they won't have any fuel left to fry their eggs in the morning.

We're left with a circle of a dozen or so yellow and red plastic flashlights, pointed skywards, illuminating only the gum tree branches above our heads.

People gather with their bottles of whisky and bottles of wine. One or two people declare themselves the designated drivers, in case a child takes ill in the night or someone falls drunkenly over the flashlight heap and breaks their arm. Everyone else gratefully raises a toast to the drivers. The drivers, both women, respond with pinched smiles, and retire to a tent within half an hour to play *Bananagrams.*

Most of the other mums decline the whisky, but when I notice Sarah, who I think is beautiful and cool, is having some I decide to align myself with her, and hold out my mug for a slug of Chivas Regal from Steve who can't navigate by the sun or the stars, or, I'll wager, by the GPS.

'Drinking with the boys, eh?' he says admiringly. 'Good girl. No nasty spumante for you.'

Good girl. Good girl? What am I, a beagle? How dare he? The fire of righteousness ignites in my belly. Lifting my mug, I clink it against the bottle, and I drink deeply. The fire of righteousness ignites the whisky and almost blows my face off.

A shiver runs through my whole body, and I feel the alcohol warming every part of me. Its effect is instant. I can almost see my inhibitions flying up into the night like cinders from the fire we aren't allowed to light. It was quite a big slug of whisky.

I'll say this for socializing with parents, they're highly efficient at getting pissed. Parents realize that there is no time to waste. Anyone's kid could wake at any moment, so the time for fun is right now.

The conversation sparks so quickly it's almost unreal. It seems we go in minutes from being near strangers, politely helping each other with tent pegs and guy wires, to a band of merrymakers, laughing and carrying on, arms around each other's shoulders, and very soon I hear someone strumming a guitar. I look over the torch heap and see, to my surprise, that it's Ian.

'Ian, Ian, play "More Than Words"!' calls Steve.

'No, Ian, Ian, play "Wonderwall",' someone else requests.

'Don't encourage him,' says Julia.

But Ian doesn't need any encouragement. He strums a few chords, twiddles the tuning pegs a bit, then without further ado plays the most glorious version of 'Throw Your Arms Around Me'. His voice, which I've only ever really heard shouting at Julia and their children, is rich and strong, and it cracks and wobbles with true feeling.

No one utters a sound.

When the song ends everyone sits in silence. The notes seem to float in the air around us.

Then Steve pipes up. 'That wasn't "More Than Words", you dickhead. Play "More Than Words".'

Ian plays five more songs, including 'More Than Words' twice.

Bon wakes up at around nine o'clock, which feels like 3 a.m. to those of us who started drinking neat whisky at seven. Adam takes him back to the tent, whispering to me that he might be a while.

I fill my mug with water and drink it straight down. I refill it and sit back down in my camping chair. Around me, little groups of two and three have formed, and people are having the intense conversations of the quite drunk.

'. . . and I said to her that unless we were guaranteed a place, that I was going to send them to Doug's old school . . .'

'We're supposed to be going to Canada skiing but we can't now because *someone's* mother has decided it's going to be her last Christmas and now we all have to go to them in Melbourne. No, she's absolutely fine. Too mean to die, if you want to know the truth . . .'

'No, well, you see she couldn't, could she? Because her husband was already having it off with her personal trainer—'

The woman who says that is hurriedly shushed by her friend, and they both look over at me, worried that I've overheard. I pretend I haven't and they make relieved faces at each other.

I wish Adam would come back.

Just as I'm about to go find him—what if all three kids are awake and he's trying to get mine back to sleep as well as Bon?—Ian plonks himself down in Adam's chair.

'That was beautiful,' I tell him. 'Your playing before. I liked the Hunters and Collectors one a lot.'

He smiles. 'One of my favourites. Jules and I had our first dance to it at our wedding.'

My surprise obviously registers on my face.

'What's that look for? Oh, you think we don't get along.'

'Well, I—'

'I can see how you'd think that, but that's just how we are. I've been arguing with Jules since the day I met her. I hope we never stop.'

'Really?'

'Really. We always make up afterwards.' He winks at me and I burst out laughing.

'So what's your story, Emma?'

'Don't you know my story? I thought everyone here knew.'

'I know the nuts and bolts of it. Husband, Pilates teacher, two babies on the go at once, that about it?'

'More or less. There's also the bit where I looked after their baby for about three years, until they recently gave me the heave-ho.'

'That's pretty rough. Why did they do that?'

'I didn't do what I was told, Ian.'

'Got a new guy? That Adam seems pretty keen on you.'

'He does, doesn't he?' I say. 'But he's married, Ian. And the sad thing is, I knew him long before I married Troy, so I guess I missed my chance.'

'Look, Emma, I don't know you well, but can I give you some advice?'

'Why not?'

'I'm going to use a watersport metaphor here. Now, I don't know if you know, but recently, I bought a Jet Ski.'

'I am aware of your Jet Ski.'

'And, Emma, if you've never been on a Jet Ski, let me tell you, it is the most magnificent thing in the world. It's as close as you can get to flying. You cannot be more free, more wild, more independent, than when you are on a Jet Ski, on open water, going full throttle.'

I can't see where he's going with this analogy.

'If you've never driven your own Jet Ski, you can't understand how wonderful it is. And even better is when someone you love is on a Jet Ski too, and they are right beside you—a safe distance away, obviously, you don't want to collide and kill each other. There's no greater feeling.'

I'm not sure if I'm meant to respond. 'That's sounds great,' I venture.

'Before I had a Jet Ski, do you know what I used to do?'

'Dressage?'

'Water-skiing. I thought water-skiing was the greatest. But now that I've known jet-skiing, I realize that on water skis, you're not free. You're at the mercy of the boat driver. And they might be good and steady and they'll help you get up on the skis and zoom along a bit, but eventually they'll make a funny turn or slow down too quickly and you'll be ass-over-tit in the water. And then you're just a guy being dragged along on the end of a rope.

It strikes me, Emma, that you haven't quite managed to let go of the rope.'

I sit and think about it, sipping my faintly whisky-flavoured water. I'm about to reply, to ask Ian to clarify a few things for me about how his water-skiing parable works, when Adam returns.

He rests his hands on my shoulders and squeezes, then crouches down between Ian and me.

'Everyone's back to sleep,' he says. 'What did I miss?'

'We were just talking about jet-skiing and water-skiing,' I tell him.

'Yes, and more,' adds Ian, in what I'm sure he thinks is an enigmatic way.

'I think it's time for me to turn in,' I tell them. 'If we're doing this hike in the morning, I need—' I check my watch, imagining it will be past midnight. It's nine fifty. 'At least eight hours' sleep.'

'Goodnight, Emma. It was lovely to talk with you.'

'The pleasure was all mine, Ian,' I tell him, and I mean it.

Adam doesn't say goodnight to anyone, but he walks back to the tents with me.

'I've got to get the chocolate out for the kids to find in the morning,' I tell him. 'I'm so impressed that I remembered that.' I take the bar of chocolate out of the cooler and put it in Tim's right gumboot, which is just inside the door of my tent. There's no way he'll miss it.

'I'll get my two out of your tent,' I tell Adam.

There's a pause.

'You don't have to,' he says.

'It'll be very squeezy in there with four of— Oh.' The penny drops.

Adam pulls me to him. He cradles my head in his hand and

kisses me. This time no phones are going to ring to interrupt. The only thing that might stop this is me. And I'm not going to stop this.

We kiss, more urgently now, and still kissing, somehow I manage to unzip both layers of my gargantuan tent. We both trip over the small door sill left at the bottom. I've never wondered before why a tent has a door sill but it must be to trip adulterous campers. As I stumble, my thoughts momentarily straighten out and I wonder if this is a good idea. We tripped over the first time we kissed too. What if the universe is trying to tell me something? What if Adam doesn't want anything more than a night? Am I all right with that? Second best is okay, isn't that what Dad's been trying to tell me? I might not be Adam's first choice overall, but right now I'm the winner. Fuck it, I think. It's good enough tonight.

We crawl through the first room of the tent and into the back, where my blow-up mattress is waiting. It's completely dark and we both sit for a moment, fumbling with our shoelaces.

'We're going to need a light,' says Adam. I find my phone and illuminate the tent. I hold the light down over his shoes while he unties his laces, and then he does the same for me.

Adam heaves himself backwards onto the mattress, pulling me with him, and the bed begins to hiss, slowly but surely, from a leak that has sprung in protest at such rough treatment.

I sit up and pull off my parka and my sweater.

'Shit it's cold,' I say, my teeth chattering. My teeth are chattering from nerves, not cold.

'Come here,' he says. 'I'm warm.'

Chapter Sixteen

Afterwards we lie on the now uncomfortably soft air mattress, wedged into my single sleeping bag. I'm in a post-coital daze, delighted in equal parts by the sex itself and the fact that I remember how to do it. Because I didn't tell Adam this, obviously, but that was my first time since Troy left.

It seems weird, but the months just kept creeping by and I never went out and sought anyone to have sex with. And no one asked me. Three years can go quite quickly when you spend the first in a complete daze of abandonment and survival mode, and the next two throwing yourself body and soul into motherhood.

In hindsight, it probably would have been healthy to get on Tinder and have a few one-night stands, but I've never been any good at sleeping around. Turns out I'm not bad at seducing married men though.

A wave of shame washes over me. I've done to Ilse what Helen did to me.

I roll away from Adam, which is a challenge in a single sleeping bag.

'Are you all right?' he whispers.

'I don't know,' I say. 'What have we done?'

He's silent.

'I think you should tell me the truth about your wife.' I'm not sure why I'm doing this. I know what he's going to tell me isn't what I want to hear.

There's a long pause. Outside a night bird hoots, in judgment, probably.

'I'm not sure what to tell you,' he says. 'Things have been bad with Ilse for a while. I don't know if she wants to continue our marriage. She is still in Amsterdam for work, but she could have left early, come over when Bon and I did.'

'And you don't know if she's coming here at all?' I want him to tell me the truth. Please Adam, just say it.

'I don't know,' he says. 'I just don't know. Whenever I ask her she won't commit. It's very hard on Bon.'

That is a lie. It's in his voice. He knows when Ilse is coming. How on earth is this what I'm having to wrestle with after I've just had excellent sex with a man I've fancied for years? It doesn't seem fair.

In the past after I've had sex with someone, we've either gone to sleep or had sex again. Either of those would be preferable to this.

Adam raises himself on his elbow and I can feel his face close to mine in the dark. My heart races in spite of itself.

'I'm not sure she still loves me.' His voice cracks a little.

'Do you still love her?'

'Yeah,' he says, without a moment's hesitation. 'I love her.'

I want to ask why he's just spent several weeks getting close to me and has now just fucked me in a tent if he loves his wife so much, but I don't know if I can manage that in a quiet voice.

I take a deep breath. 'So you and me? That's just . . . sex?'

'I don't think there was anything "just" about that sex,' he says, attempting levity.

This is not the time.

'I mean it, Emma,' he says. 'You're amazing. I've always thought that. And now, being thrown together like this, well, it's hard to believe something wasn't meant to happen.'

'But you love your wife.'

'Yeah.'

'And you're not sure if she still loves you, so you thought you'd have a bet each way. I'm your back-up plan.'

'No! It's not like that. I genuinely have feelings for you.'

I've heard this line before. This is Troy all over again. Wanting Helen but not prepared to fully let me go. That's what Adam's doing. Christ, what the hell attracts me to these people? I should have a slogan: Emma Baker—she's what happens when you're busy making other plans.

Maybe Ian was right. I need to let go of the tow rope. I think I've had enough of being dragged through the water at high speed.

'Adam, you need to go back to your own tent now. I'll move my kids.'

I feel around for my clothes and dress clumsily in the dark. It's even colder now.

Unzipping the tent, I clamber out. Inside Adam and Bon's tent, the three kids are curled around each other like kittens. None of them has remained in their sleeping bags. Carefully moving heavy little arms and legs, I untangle my children and haul first Tim, and then Freya back to our tent, tucking their sleeping bags around them.

Adam is standing awkwardly outside, waiting for me to finish.

It's a petty move, but once I've brought Freya in I don't go back out. I zip the tent up behind me and climb into my sleeping bag, with a child tucked under each arm.

I hear Adam, in the darkness, waiting. After a few minutes he must figure out that I'm not coming out to say goodnight, and I hear him get into his tent.

I'm so tired now, but sleep isn't coming. The heady cocktail of whisky, anger, and guilt see to that. The air mattress has now almost fully deflated and I can feel the rocks on the ground digging into my back. It's no less than I deserve. I hope Adam's air mattress is flat too, and there are rocks under his back.

What was I thinking, going to bed with Adam? Of course he wasn't seriously interested in me. He's been so sweet and attentive, but also so vague about Ilse. Looking back, it's perfectly clear he was just trying to make himself feel better. That's what you do when you love someone and you think you've lost them. You do whatever it takes to make yourself feel better. For Adam it was flirting with me. For me it's been inserting myself into Troy and Helen's relationship. How could I have been so foolish, for so long? Well I'll be buggered if I'm going to hang around on the reserve bench of yet another marriage.

Something rustles in the leaf litter outside my tent. It's something small. Probably a mouse. But it's quite close to my head. I whack the canvas and the thing scurries away.

All is quiet for a moment, and then I hear it come back. This time it's come along the side of the tent, near where my feet are. It's scratching at the canvas. I kick the tent wall and it stops.

Then it runs up the side of the tent, mercifully still on the outside, and across the roof, which sags alarmingly. Whatever it is isn't that small. It's not a mouse. It runs back down the other side.

This needs to stop. I've no idea how to make it stop. I don't know what it wants.

'Go away,' I whisper. 'Please.'

The rustling stops. I lie for several minutes, listening. Nothing. Slowly, my eyelids droop and I fall into the deep sleep of the emotionally exhausted.

I wake in utter confusion, what could be moments or hours later, when something furry runs across my head. What the fuck?

Flailing madly, I leap upright, but there's just enough air left in the mattress for it to behave like a waterbed and I immediately tumble over again. I feel for the flashlight, which I know I left near where my head was, even though I fear that's where the creature is. But I need light.

Flicking the flashlight on, I see there is a hole in the tent; something has eaten its way in. And now it's in here somewhere. What does it want? Food. It must want food. But I don't have any food in here. I'm not an idiot. I know you don't keep food in your tent.

Except the chocolate. There's a bar of chocolate in a boot. Inside the tent. That's what the animal wants. A midnight feast.

I put the boot outside the tent, with the chocolate still inside. Maybe if I leave the tent flaps open the animal will follow the chocolate outside. That's the extent of my problem-solving capabilities right now.

I don't know what else to do. I really just don't know. And I'm so tired. I start to cry.

I'm tired of doing the hard things by myself. I know that's pathetic, and that I'm a capable grown woman who doesn't need someone to help me get this probably very small and not in any way dangerous native animal out of my tent, but I wish I weren't alone.

It turns out that sitting down on the bed and crying for a while isn't the worst idea. While I'm still, a little furry brown face ventures out from behind a backpack in the corner. I think it's some sort of bush rat.

Neither of us moves.

'Hey, rat,' I whisper. 'Could you go? Outside? There's chocolate out there.'

It stares at me for a few more seconds, before turning and burrowing back into the corner of the tent. There's more scrabbling and a tearing sound, and then everything's quiet again. It's eaten its way back out. I sigh.

I zip the tent up again, switch off the light, and lie back down between the kids, who, astonishingly, have slept through the whole rodent incursion and mother meltdown.

Of course that doesn't last. No sooner have I closed my eyes than Tim nudges me.

'Mum, I need to pee.'

'Mmmm . . . just go out and pee on a tree,' is the best I can offer.

'It's too dark. I need you to come.'

Trying my very best to keep my muttered 'fuck's sake' inaudible, I stagger outside and while Tim relieves himself of what sounds like about twelve litres of pee, I stand in the freezing air and realize I can see the faintest glow of morning in the sky.

* * *

Freya's the first camper awake, properly, for the day. I make no effort to keep her quiet. Fuck you all, I think. It's hugely uncharitable, but I haven't slept. Kids only grow when they sleep, and adults only regenerate goodwill when they sleep. I'm all tapped out.

Ian and Julia, aggressively early risers themselves, decide to come over to our camp with their bowls of cereal. I'm actually pretty pleased to have their company, but maybe I'm delirious from lack of sleep.

By the time Adam emerges, I've had three cups of coffee and two sachets of toffee-apple-flavoured instant porridge. I'm nevertheless still a bit drunk.

'Morning,' he says cheerfully. 'Good sleep?'

'Not really,' I reply. 'I had a rat in my tent.'

'Hah!' Ian snorts. 'Is that what they're calling it these days?'

'Ian!' Julia thumps him on the arm, but she's trying to conceal a smile.

Everyone heard us last night. Oh God. I thought we were so quiet. But realistically, how quiet can two drunk people shagging in a tent really be? My embarrassment is so strong I feel I could actually dematerialize and vanish. That would be the absolute best-case scenario right now.

'No,' I say, pretending not to know what he means. 'An actual rat ate through my tent.'

'Shit, really?' Adam looks astonished.

'Really.'

'How did you get it out?' asks Julia.

'I suggested we start a relationship and it ran screaming into the night. It's my signature move.'

Julia and Ian roar with laughter and Adam looks suitably mortified. Good.

* * *

By nine o'clock, I've packed up our tent and loaded the car. I want, with every fibre of my being, to drive home at once, get into a hot bath and then sleep for twelve hours, but Tim is determined to go on the hike everyone's been talking about.

'It's not super long,' Julia tells me. 'About six kilometres, round-trip. The kids love it.'

'Fine,' I say. 'Let's do it.' My ears are ringing with tiredness, but I just can't ruin this for Tim. He's having such a nice time.

Everyone's faffing about packing their rucksacks and filling their water bottles, so I head off down the track with Freya and Tim. We're going to be slow, going at Freya's pace, so we might as well get a head start.

Julia's right—it's a beautiful walk. The sky is finally clear and blue, but we're protected by the canopy, so we walk in dappled sunlight. The path is an access track, wide enough to get a vehicle down if you needed to, so it's a pretty smooth walk for Freya. I'm sure I'll end up carrying her for much of the hike, but for now at least, she and Tim seem happy to walk together.

I take huge breaths of the fresh cool air and, as I put one foot in front of the other, I start to feel human again. Maybe there's something to this whole 'getting out in nature' idea. It does seem pretty restorative. The kids want to chat, and we have one of those aimless, fascinating conversations you can only have when there are no other distractions.

They ask me dozens of questions, and I do my best to respond, even though I don't know the answers most of the time. A combination of guessing and distraction works well.

'What's that tree for, Mummy?' asks Freya.

'It's for measuring the distance between the ground and the sky.'

'Really?' Tim is skeptical.

'No, probably not really. It's for birds and animals to live in, and to shade the ground so smaller plants can grow. It was also food for dinosaurs, originally.'

'Not T-Rex.' Freya is very sure of herself in this department.

'No, not T-Rex,' I agree. 'He ate meat, didn't he.'

'Yes, but Charlie at my preschool is like an ankylosaurus.'

'Is he? How's that?'

'He only eats plants.'

'Oh. With people that's called being vegetarian.'

'Sometimes he eats the plants in the gardens at preschool and the teachers have to stop him.'

'Maybe he's actually an ankylosaurus then,' I suggest.

Freya looks at me like I'm insane. 'No, he has really soft feet.'

We've been walking for an hour when I realize no one has overtaken us, which is very strange because a herd is only as fast as its slowest buffalo, and Freya is really a staggeringly slow buffalo. Maybe we've gone the wrong way, or maybe everyone else sensibly decided that hiking with a hangover is a terrible idea. We turn and head back to the campground.

There are two cars left: ours and Ian and Julia's. They are sitting on the hood of their car, and when they see us they cheer.

'Hooray! You're back! Everyone else decided to give it a miss, but we thought we'd wait for you.'

'Everyone?' I ask.

Ian gives me a wry smile. 'Afraid so,' he says. 'A bunch of them decided they would rather visit those caves on the way back than do a hike.'

I'm so touched they didn't go as well. I feel like crying. 'You didn't have to wait,' I say.

'Nonsense,' Julia says. 'We weren't going to leave you alone out here.'

'Well, thanks. That was really kind.'

'Now,' Ian says, peering at me, 'are you all right to drive back?'

'Oh, totally fine,' I say, opening my eyes as widely as I can and trying to look alert.

'You're completely exhausted,' Julia tells me. 'I'll drive you home.'

'Really, I'm fine, there's no need—'

'Excellent!' Ian looks thrilled. 'She never lets me drive.'

'Daaaad,' comes a moan from the back seat of Ian and Julia's car. I peer in and see Georgie and Damon sitting, seatbelts fastened, ready to go.

'Emma, give me your keys,' Julia orders. 'Ian, get those kids on the road. They've had enough of you fooling around.'

Looking delighted, Ian jumps into the driver's seat and starts the engine. He makes a wide victory circle around the campsite, with his window down, waving merrily at us the whole way.

'Good grief, Ian, just go!' Julia shouts.

She turns to me. 'You need a sleep. Are you any good at sleeping in cars? I can never sleep in a moving vehicle.'

'I could probably sleep standing right here,' I admit. 'Thanks, Julia. This is so nice of you.'

'Don't be silly. This is what friends do. We can't have you falling asleep and crashing into a tree.'

I put Tim and Freya into their seats and then we are away.

We bump along the track and tears start to fall down my face. I pretend to look out the window at the trees. I'm so disappointed—in Adam, but also in myself. I don't know what I was expecting to happen with Adam today, but not only is it clear that he doesn't want to go out with me, now I don't think I even want him as a friend.

Against my will, my mind drifts back to the sex last night, and I realize with a shock that we didn't use a condom. It never even crossed my mind. I'll need to get the morning-after pill, like some stupid teenager.

I close my eyes and lean my head against the window. Long before we get to the main road, I am asleep.

Chapter Seventeen

Thanks to Sunday traffic, it's late afternoon before we get home. Both children and my mobile phone are completely lifeless on arrival, but perk up significantly with some wi-fi and electricity for the phone, and a couple of hours of TV for the kids. I'm slightly alarmed at how intent Freya and Tim are on absorbing the screen's rays. I thought being outside in nature was supposed to recharge them, but instead I think it just wore them out.

After almost complete silence the whole way home, fifteen minutes glued to the TV and they start to make sounds again. Likewise the phone. Once it gets enough power to switch back on, it emits a volley of notification pings and buzzes and bleats.

When I've loaded the washing machine and stuffed away the camping gear in the shed—temporarily, of course; I know I need to open the tent and let it dry properly or it will turn into a mouldy horror show—I sit down with my phone. I have five voicemail messages from Carmen. I check my email: eight emails from Carmen. Where to begin?

The doorbell rings, immediately followed by the sound of a key in the lock. Laura. I don't really know why she bothers with the doorbell when she only gives you approximately eight milliseconds to respond before she lets herself in. It's not enough time to stop doing anything, should I have been doing anything I didn't want her to see.

'Hi, Laura,' I call.

She comes in carrying a steaming dish of lasagna and I want to fall to the ground and kiss her besneakered feet.

'Thought you might need some dinner,' she says. 'Camping's exhausting. How was it? Did you have an amazing time? Also, I still don't know what happened with that hot man after I left you at the pub last Saturday. Presumably nothing, because Dad said you all had the stomach flu on Sunday.'

'Do you even need me in this conversation or are you happy to answer all your questions yourself?' I ask her.

'Sorry,' she says. 'Well?'

'In a nutshell, last Saturday night Adam came home with me and we kissed and then Troy rang from the hospital where he had taken Freya because he is a massive overreactor. Then there was the stomach flu. Then we went camping and I got pissed again and this time no one called to interrupt so Adam and I slept together, not as quietly as we thought, either, but that's another story. Then he told me he loves his wife. Then a rat ate its way into my tent and eventually back out again. Then the kids and I went on a hike, while everyone else, including Adam, bailed and left early, and my shouty neighbours drove me home because I was so tired I would have crashed the car. So, no, I wouldn't say we had an amazing time.'

Laura is looking at me, slack-jawed. 'Right. Well. Shit. That's quite an impressive effort for your first game back after injury, so to speak.'

'Indeed,' I say. 'And on top of that, last week Dad gave me a lecture about being less of a perfectionist and less helicoptery and letting the kids go more and focusing on my career.'

'He's right about that,' Laura says, matter-of-factly. 'You do need to ease up on the perfect mother and ex-wife act.'

'That's what he said. But I don't understand. I'm not a perfect mother. I'm not trying to be. That's Helen. I'm trying to give my kids a normal childhood. I let them watch TV and they don't do any extracurricular activities and they always have stuff on their faces. They eat sugar. One of them dresses as a tiger every day, which is probably not psychologically healthy, because I can't be bothered to talk her out of it. And I'm not allowed to even see Lola any more.'

My phone rings. I can see it's Carmen. I ignore it.

'Do you need to get that?' asks Laura.

'I can't answer it until I've listened to her five voicemails. I need to know the backstory.'

'Maybe you should listen to them now then, because now there are six voicemails to catch up on.'

'Fine.' I dial up my voicemail and put it on speakerphone while I get on with making a salad.

'Emma!' comes Carmen's immediately hysterical voice from the tinny phone speaker. 'Tiny hitch with the manuscript. Might need to pull you in on this one. Call me ASAP.'

That's a bit vague. I play the second message.

'Emma, what I said before about the tiny hitch. It's not a tiny hitch. I was in the room with Wanda before and I couldn't talk but things have gone fucking tits-up here. I ended up coming up to Woop Woop to help her and now she's got the holy furies with me. Some rubbish about negative energy. The mad witch reckons I'm harshing her vibe and she can't write with me here. Like, not even with me in the house. It's beyond unprofessional. She wants me to leave. You'll have to take over. Call me immediately, if not sooner.'

Take over? As in, go up to wherever Wanda's house is? That's well above my pay grade.

Message three starts: 'All right, Emma. I don't know what this silent treatment is about but frankly it's not okay. I called you an hour ago. You need to ring me back or I'll go to the next editor on my list. Maybe I wasn't clear in my earlier messages. Wanda can't finish the book alone. She needs someone, and she would like that someone to be you, to come up here and help her. I have tried, but we aren't really seeing eye to eye on a few issues and we've decided it's best if I take a step back. So I need you to call me to say you can be on a flight up here first thing tomorrow morning. Okay? It will take her three days once you're here. She's so close, but there are a few people she hasn't managed to write about who quite frankly are the ones we want to hear about, so she needs someone to sit with her all softly softly and pat her back and get her to fucking write those chapters. Otherwise the book's not worth publishing, and if the book's not worth publishing . . . well, I don't want to sound dramatic, Emma, but my life won't be worth living.' With that entirely non-dramatic statement she hangs up.

Messages four and five are just the sound of Carmen sighing and hanging up.

The emails are more of the same.

This is not a normal situation. Editors never get to go anywhere. Especially not freelance editors.

If I look at it one way, this is an incredible opportunity. For whatever reason—probably just to annoy Carmen—Wanda has decided my presence is necessary to the completion of her book. And for Carmen to capitulate to that demand means Carmen is utterly backed into a corner. She is out of options. She's emailed to offer me my normal hourly rate for every hour—day or night—that I am away from home. This is unheard of. They are completely panicking. I'd be a fool to say no.

But there are two small reasons to say no, and they are slumped against each other on the sofa, munching cashews and staring unblinkingly at an episode of *Bananas in Pyjamas*, a show they would ordinarily consider so babyish they would actually rather play a game than watch it. These kids are exhausted.

I've never left them. Sure, they leave me every second week for two nights with Troy and Helen, but I've never left them. I'm not sure why that feels like a distinction worth making.

'Where is Wanda's place? Isn't it up near Noosa? That sounds awesome,' says Laura, interrupting my trip down Maternal Panic Lane. 'Why are you even hesitating?'

'I can't possibly go.'

'Why not? The kids?'

'Of course the kids. I've never even left them to go work in an office in the city. I can't just abandon them and disappear for God knows how long.'

'No one's suggesting you abandon them,' Laura says mildly. 'They have a father and stepmother three doors away, Mark and the boys and me five minutes away, and Dad. Any of us could look after them for a few days.'

'But what if something happened?'

'You'd be a couple of hours away. You would come back.'

I look into the living room at Freya and Tim and it feels like my heart and my stomach are inching towards each other, trying to either snuggle the other for comfort or squeeze the life out of them.

'Won't they feel abandoned?' I ask Laura. 'Don't you think it will feel like now I've left them too, just like Troy did?'

'No, I don't think they will, because they aren't massive catastrophists like you—who reads too much into everything—and because they will have a nice time and won't miss you nearly as much as you think they will. And trust me, you won't miss them as much as you think you will either, and that will give you a whole other avenue of things to feel guilty about, which I think you'll love.'

I think about this while I take cucumbers and lettuce from the fridge and wash them in the sink.

'Also, Em, if you ever want to be anywhere even approaching financially independent of Troy, you need get back in the work game properly. You've been lucky you haven't had to do much paid work since your kids were born, but I think that hasn't been the best thing for you, as a person. You've always been a bit all or nothing about stuff, and I think you've sort of disappeared into motherhood in a way that's okay for a while, but long term, it's not ideal.'

I wonder if Freya will lecture Tim about his life choices when they're grown up. Or if it will be the other way around. Laura's never been shy about telling me how she thinks I should run my life, but since Mum died she's really taken it on as a serious enterprise. I'm sure she thinks she's channelling Mum.

I suppose I could ask Dad to come stay here and look after them. He'd be pleased to see me doing something with what remains of my career. And while I don't think Laura's point about disappearing into motherhood is valid at all, she's right about the issue of money. Troy doesn't have to support me to the extent he does. He might not always be willing or able to. I would be much happier not relying on the vagaries of the juice market to keep my kids in school shoes and cookies.

'Mum!' shouts Tim from the sofa. 'We're hungry. We need some cookies.'

'We're about to have dinner.'

'But we need some cookies.'

'We're eating in five minutes.'

'But we really need some cookies now.'

'Are you hesitating because you're scared you're not up to the task professionally?' Laura isn't going to let this go.

'*Mum! Cookies!*'

And just like that, my mind is made up.

'Stop yelling at me, Tim. You're not having any cookies, because it is dinnertime. And even if it weren't, you haven't once said please. I'm not your cookie slave. And Laura, stop hassling me. You aren't Mum. It isn't your job. If Troy and you and Dad can mind the kids, I'll go.'

Laura looks satisfied. 'Good. That's the right decision.'

Her smugness is too much. 'You don't know that,' I say. 'Stop pretending you know what's right and what's wrong. Anything could happen at any time, for any reason. I might go to Wanda's place and get bitten by a snake and die, or be electrocuted by a faulty toaster. You just don't know and you never can.'

A tear breaks free from Laura's welling eyes and she rubs it angrily away.

'I miss her too, Emma. Just as much as you do.'

'She never got to see me be a mum,' I say quietly. 'She got to see you do it and you knew she thought you were good at it. I don't know if I'm doing it right and I never will.'

Laura puts her arms around me. My tears drip off the end of my nose and soak into the back of her sweater.

'You're doing it right,' she whispers. 'Mum would think you're an amazing mother, Em. You just need to make sure you're an amazing Emma as well.'

The children, sensing a hug all the way from the other room, come in and put their arms around us too.

'Are you sad, Mummy?' asks Freya.

'A little bit,' I admit.

'Me too,' she tells me, because misery loves company. 'We should all have a cookie.'

* * *

After we feed the kids lasagna, which they devour in spite of their amuse-bouche of Chips Ahoy, Laura scrubs the camping filth off them with a long, hot bath, while I quickly head to the pharmacy to make sure this situation doesn't get any worse. I text Troy and explain my trip. I want him to be able to discuss it with Helen before he says yes or no to having the kids for at least three days.

He calls me when I get back five minutes later, sounding delighted and a little relieved.

'Of course we'll have them. That would be terrific. I'll be pretty flat out at work, but Helen's very happy to help out. To be honest, Em,' he drops his voice a little, 'Lola's been a complete shit this week. I don't know what is wrong with her but she's saying no to everything and chucking massive tantrums all the time.'

'Maybe she's missing us,' I suggest.

'Oh,' he says, as if this is the first time such a thought has occurred to him, and maybe it is. 'Yeah, that could be it. I suppose she's used to spending a fair bit of time with you guys, isn't she?'

How can someone be this thick?

'Sometimes I wonder if it's easier to look after several children at a time than just one,' he tells me, as if he's discovered gravity.

We arrange that Dad will come here in the morning, get Tim to school, then he, Troy and Helen will figure out the rest of the childcare arrangements between them. I won't be at all surprised if that means Dad ends up looking after both girls while Tim's at school, but when I call him to explain, he seems cheerful enough about that possibility.

'And Dad,' I say, 'if Helen asks you to take Lola somewhere, tell her to bugger off.'

* * *

I wake the next morning at six on the dot, the first person up in the house. Whenever this happens I can't stop myself thinking it's because my children have died or been abducted during the night. Instead of being able to enjoy the peace and quiet, I'm always compelled to rush into their bedrooms to check they are present and breathing. In doing so I always wake them up.

But this morning there is no time for me to even consider lying in bed. I need to be out of the house and in a cab to the airport at seven o'clock. I haven't packed for me. I packed for the kids last night, in case they stay at Troy and Helen's, but now that it's my turn I'm rather at a loss.

I haven't packed just for myself in so long that once I've thrown some clothes, shoes, my laptop and toiletries into a bag, it still feels like I must have forgotten a dozen things. No night nappies? No wipes? No snacks, drink bottles, sippy cups, stuffed animals, battered copy of *The Tiger Who Came to Tea*, extra changes of clothes for the flight for when a pressure-packed orange juice is opened onto my lap, resealable bags for orange-juice-soaked clothes, an iPad loaded with so many episodes of *Dinosaur Train* that it can't open a single other app? No giant over-the-ear headphones shaped like tigers? No stroller?

My small bag, with everything I think I'll need for three days, contains less than I would take out with me for a walk to the playground with my children. It's a marvel. I start to feel the tiniest twinges of excitement.

At six fifteen Dad arrives, and the doorbell wakes the children. They both bound down the hallway to meet him and neither exhibits even the slightest hint of apprehension over me leaving them for the first time.

Tim just wants to show his grandad the sticks he's brought back from camping yesterday, and Freya won't stop telling him that they should pick up Lola soon and go to the park.

Before I know it the taxi is beeping in the street and I have to go. The kids are eating bran cereal in the kitchen, and they both give me a fairly cursory hug and submit to a kiss. I sniff Freya's soft hair, trying to absorb her back into my body, but she gives me a shove.

And with that I am away. In a taxi, bound for the airport. The strings that bind my children to my heart unwind further and further and get thinner and thinner. I cry and tell the completely uninterested cabbie that I've never left my kids before.

'Really?' He is astonished. 'In six years? Mate, that's no good for anyone. I've left three wives in six years and they're way harder to outrun than a couple of kids.'

I think he's trying to be nice but it's such an odd comment that for the rest of the trip I busy myself with my phone, and there's plenty to do because Carmen has sent me ten emails overnight, explaining in minute detail where the project is up to and what still needs to be done.

The impression I get is that Wanda has tried to be a bit coy with some of her exploits, and that's absolutely not what Carmen signed her up for. She wants all the gory details of all the affairs and, reading between the lines, if Wanda's not prepared to disclose them then I am to make them up myself.

Getting through the airport is so easy I feel like I might be a ghost. I'm unencumbered by small bodies and excess baggage, and when I need to stand in a lineup I just . . . stand in a lineup, quietly, without anyone swinging on the stanchions and kicking other passengers in the legs. Getting through security is almost a pleasure, not having to wrench a stuffed tiger out of anyone's arms and later convince them that it wasn't replaced with an exact replica when it went through the X-ray machine.

On the flight, which is only an hour and a half, I don't read or watch a movie or listen to music. I stare out the window, first at the vanishing city, then at the clouds, and finally at the landscape as we approach our destination. It's green and lush, squares of fields interspersed with darker forested areas, and all along the edge is the ocean, which looks from here like a pretty scalloped ribbon trimming the coast.

I marvel at where I am. It's ten-thirty in the morning, on a Monday. I should be sitting in a waiting room while Lola attends a French lesson, reading children's books in French I don't understand to Freya because I rarely remember to bring anything for her to do.

I get off the plane and look around. The arrivals area is small. I asked Carmen if I should rent a car to get out to Wanda's place but she assured me that Wanda would send someone to pick me up.

To my great surprise, standing front and centre and holding a handwritten sign that reads *Emma Baker?* is Philip. I've never seen anyone put a question mark after the name on a sign like that, but it makes immediate sense to me. Of course there should be a question mark. The sign is asking 'Are you Emma Baker?' But why he's holding a sign with my name on it when he's already met me is a bit mysterious.

He smiles when he spots me. I smile back. It's like seeing an old friend. Quite an old friend, really. He's really handsome—I'd forgotten that. I don't know exactly how old he is, but he'd have to be about fifty. Too old for me. Although all the actors I had a crush on when I was a teenager are in their fifties now, I realize. As a seventeen-year-old it seemed quite plausible that I would grow up to marry Colin Firth. I suppose I just thought I would catch up to him in age.

I walk up to Philip and he hugs me, slightly awkwardly. It is, after all, only our second meeting in person, but I feel like we've always known each other. 'I'm still Emma Baker,' I tell him. 'Did you think you wouldn't recognize me after three months?'

'I was worried you wouldn't recognize me!' he replies. 'Silly of me, probably, but I never think people will remember me. Was your flight excellent? I love that flight. I think this is one of the most beautiful places to approach from the air. I hope you had a window seat?'

'It was a fine flight, and I did have a window seat,' I say.

'Oh that's good. I'm very pleased to hear it. I always think it's so much better to be the climber overer than the climbed over.'

'I thought you had left,' I say.

'I did go, but then I came back—as you can see,' he says. 'One of my projects in the South Pacific was delayed by bad weather, and I didn't think it was worth going all the way back to Europe when I could just continue to make a nuisance of myself here. Hopefully I'll be off again soon.'

He reaches for my bag and gestures with his other arm. 'Car's just out here. I love little airports like this, don't you? The parking is always free, and about six steps from the gate. And you're always going somewhere fun when you arrive at a one-room airport, I find.'

'Well I'm here to work,' I remind him, 'but it's certainly a beautiful spot.'

'Yes, of course you are. Wanda's very excited you're coming. Almost more excited than she was when Carmen agreed to leave.'

With no warning that we've reached the car, Philip suddenly slings my bag into the back of an open-top sports car. It's a Mercedes, an old-looking one—candy-apple red and very beautiful. Philip opens the passenger door for me, and waits while I settle myself into the leather seat before gently closing the heavy door and darting around to the driver's side.

'What did happen with Carmen?' I ask as Philip reverses out of the parking space and we head for the exit. 'She said something about not seeing eye to eye with Wanda.'

He laughs. 'That's putting it mildly. Carmen was in a flap when she got here, and she seemed determined to infect Wanda with that same sense of urgency. Of course that just made Wanda panic and get cross, and I suppose you could say she then went on an even slower go-slow with the book.'

'I know that move,' I say. 'It's what my three-year-old does when I try to rush her into putting on her shoes when we have to leave the house.'

'There is something of the three-year-old about Wanda,' he agrees. 'Maybe you can bring whatever techniques you use on—what's your three-year-old's name?'

'Freya.'

'Whatever you do to get Freya to put her shoes on, maybe you can try that on Wanda.'

'All right,' I tell him. 'We're going to need a lot of chocolate cookies.'

He laughs and I look out at the lush fields and feel, for the first time in a long, long time, that maybe the old me isn't entirely gone. Maybe there's a chance for me after all.

Half an hour later Philip turns off the main road, guiding the car between two stone pillars from which two white gates have swung open at our approach. From there we drive for another five minutes up and over gently rolling hills until we reach a second set of gates. We rumble over the cattle grid and make our final approach to the house along a palm-lined driveway.

Chapter Eighteen

Philip swings the car around the gravel driveway and comes to a stop in front of the house, which looks like a vast Hamptons-style plantation house, only with two medieval-style round stone towers. It's absurd.

'Ta-da,' he says, switching off the engine. 'Welcome to Wandaland.'

'That's not really its name, is it?' I ask, astonished.

'If it's not, then Monty will have to redo the driveway,' he says, and points towards the front of the house. On top of the dark red gravel, someone has sprinkled tiny white stones to spell out 'Wandaland' in script. 'He does it every day. No one cares if it gets messed up, which obviously it does because it's right in front of the door, but it's a little labour of love for him. He started doing it after they visited Nepal and he saw the sand mandalas the monks make.'

I consider my own marriage. Troy never did anything even close to as romantic as this. Sometimes he used to draw a heart on the steamed-up shower screen, but he'd always ruin the moment by pressing his bum up against it straight away.

Philip leads me inside. It's like walking into a luxury hotel. The air smells like a duty-free store, and when I close my eyes and try to figure out why, I identify the fragrance of expensive leather upholstery and Chanel No. 5.

The source of the Chanel perfume is reclining on the leather sofa in the huge living room we enter, and she springs up with remarkable agility.

'Hello, Emma!' she calls, and scurries over to hug me around my waist. Wanda Forthwright is elfin, with a dark pixie haircut and small, sharp features. She doesn't look like she'd be as loud as she is. The quietest she can make her voice would still have the downstairs neighbours banging on the ceiling with a broom, should she ever have to live anywhere as downmarket as an apartment. She doesn't shout; it's more that she projects her voice to the back rows of a theatre, even when she's standing two feet away from you.

'You are the most wonderful darling for coming,' she booms. 'I can never thank you enough for agreeing to do it. Getting Carmen out of my house and back to the office where she belongs was the only way this book was ever going to get finished and I'm sorry it meant you had to be dragged up here.'

'It's my pleasure, Wanda,' I say. 'I hope I can help. Carmen said you were getting a bit stuck on a few chapters. Maybe we can unstick them together.'

'Of course we can. Let's get started straight away, as soon as you've seen your room and had some lunch and maybe a nap and a swim. Shall we say, three o'clock?'

That's over three hours away. I need to get started so I can get finished and back to my children.

'I'm fine to start now,' I suggest. 'No time like the present.'

'Absolutely not,' she says, with great certainly. 'You must eat, rest and swim. And then you may rejoin me and we can look at the manuscript. I'll be working on it in the meantime, don't you worry about that.'

'Oh, well, all right,' I say, a bit confused. 'Carmen made it sound like you weren't really able to get on with it at the moment. She said you were stalled.'

'No no,' she says. 'I'm getting on beautifully now. I had some trouble remembering some stories but it's all coming back to me. Now, darling Philip will show you to the guesthouse. I like to make him earn his keep.'

My phone rings and Wanda says, 'I'll bet you one hundred thousand dollars that's Carmen, ringing to check up on us.'

I glance at the phone. She's right.

'I'd better get this,' I say.

'You better had,' she replies.

'Hello?' I say.

'How's it going?' demands Carmen. 'Have you unblocked her yet? Remember, I want you to think of her as a toilet. You are the plunger. Go at her with whatever force is required until there is a Word document containing ninety-thousand unputdownable words about all the people she's fucked.'

'Hi, Carmen. Thanks, I had a very good flight. I found the place okay.'

'I'm not paying you to have a good flight,' she says. 'Have you started work?'

In mock fear, Wanda has done an exaggerated scuttle over to a great mahogany desk on which stands a computer. She sits down and begins to type.

'Hold up the phone,' says Carmen. 'Wanda,' she yells so loudly that she can be heard across the room. 'I want to hear typing.'

'I'm typing,' Wanda shouts back. 'But I will stop if you keep calling and harassing poor Emma.'

'All right, all right,' Carmen says. 'I'll leave her to you. Good luck.'

'Thanks, see you.'

I hang up and sit down on one of the large sofas. Philip nods to me and leaves. The room is quiet, except for the sound of Wanda's nails clicking against the keys. With a slightly furrowed brow she stares at the screen and types furiously.

For fifteen minutes I sit there until she stops, looks up and seems surprised to see me.

'Emma! Why haven't you gone for lunch and a rest? You don't need to just sit there. I'm not a flight risk.'

'Sorry, sorry, I just thought you seemed like you were on a roll and I didn't want to disturb you. Are you sure you don't want me here on hand? I'm very happy to just sit quietly in case you need me.'

'Go to your guesthouse, Emma.' She waves imperiously in the direction of some French doors leading to a verandah. 'Philip? Philip! Come rescue Emma.'

Philip must have been just outside, like a secret service agent, because he appears instantly.

'Ready?' he asks me.

'Sure,' I say.

'Follow me.'

Philip has retrieved my bag from the car and carries it for me. We walk around the side of the house, along the wide cool verandah. The day is hot but there are ceiling fans out here to keep the air moving. A flight of stairs leads down to a gravel path—this one without any love messages spelled out in contrasting stones. Bay hedges tower over us on each side, and it's like walking through a maze.

Eventually we emerge onto the flagstones surrounding a huge swimming pool. Under a pergola covered in vines are six sun lounges, on three of which are draped lithe golden young women. They're all wearing bikini bottoms, large sunglasses, and that's all.

'Edie, Clara and Kate, please meet Emma Baker, Wanda's editor. Emma, this is Edie, Wanda's goddaughter, and her friends, Clara and Kate.'

The girls greet me in a languid fashion. They look as though they've been in a sun for a while. They ought to be wearing hats and rashguards. A sudden urge to make them all have a big drink of water and generously apply SPF 50 sunscreen comes over me. Instead I politely say hello, trying not to look at their small pert breasts, which is difficult because they are all pointed at me like the eyes of three little owls.

I feel a hundred years old.

One girl, who might be Edie, says, 'Come have a swim with us. The water's amazing.'

'Oh, thanks,' I stutter back. 'I didn't actually bring my bathing suit, and I'm probably mostly going to be working pretty hard with Wanda while I'm here, so I might not . . . but thanks.'

'Cool, no worries. We've got loads of bathing suits, you know, if you want to borrow something.'

'Yeah,' says one of the others, 'Edie got a huge box of samples today, so there's plenty of stuff to try on.'

'Great,' I say, trying to sound as if I have the faintest idea what they mean by samples and why Edie, who appears to be about twenty, would have just received a huge box of them. 'I might see you later.'

Philip sets off towards a building at the far end of the pool and I trot after him. It looks like a miniature version of the main house, but without the towers.

Opening the doors from the verandah and gesturing for me to go inside, Philip announces, 'Voila! The guesthouse. Well, a guesthouse. There are three more down the hill. I'm in one, and the girls have the other two at the moment. You get top billing so you can get to the house quickly if Wanda needs you.'

I look around. This is the nicest place I have ever stayed. It's far more luxurious than the hotel Troy and I went to after our wedding, which until now was my absolute benchmark for elegant places. My little house has a living room, a bedroom with a king-sized bed, a bathroom with a sunken bathtub beside its own set of doors opening onto a lush tropical garden, and even a kitchen. Everywhere are vases of fresh frangipanis and gardenias, and all the upholstery is cream.

Instinctively my body tenses up and I mentally start moving all the vases to high shelves. Then I remember, with a jolt, that my tiny interior decimators aren't here. No one's going to knock over vases and spill milk on the Moroccan rug. There's a bottle of red wine on the counter in the kitchen, and the only person who's likely to knock a glass of it onto the pale couch is me.

Philip reads my silence as disappointment. 'Is something wrong?' he asks sincerely. 'If there's a problem you can move down the hill. Is it the girls? Do you want to be further from the pool? I can assure you they aren't loud. They're like a bunch of cats. They just lie in the sun all day and then have a brief flurry of activity as the sun goes down. Then they don't trouble anyone until a very late breakfast time.'

'It's lovely, Philip,' I say. 'It's the nicest place I've ever stayed.'

'I'm so pleased,' he says, beaming. 'It is nice, isn't it? I've been known to outstay my welcome here, it's so hard to leave. Shall I make you a cup of tea? Coffee?'

'Tea, please.'

'Tea it is.'

'How did you meet Wanda, originally? Have you been friends for a long time?'

He switches on the kettle.

'Once upon a time I was married to Wanda's little sister, Jean. It didn't last very long. We weren't a good match and after a few months she met someone she liked better and moved to Jamaica.'

I can't help myself. 'Jamaica?'

He smiles at me. 'No, she went of her own accord.' He hands me my tea. 'Jean and I didn't stay in touch, but Wanda sort of kept me in the divorce. We got on, and she was never close to Jean. And then of course years later, I introduced Wanda to Monty—that was all my doing. My first and only successful experience as a matchmaker. That was ten years ago. I think your boss Carmen was quite cross when she found out I was responsible for that. I think she thought Wanda would be having dangerous liaisons with unsuitable men to this day if I hadn't ruined everything by putting Monty in her path. Carmen seemed to think there might have been enough material for a second volume of *Affairs in Order* if it hadn't been for me. But hey ho. The heart wants what it wants.'

'That's what they say,' I agree.

He gestures to the kitchen. 'There's lots of lunchy things in the fridge there—would you like me to put something together for you? A sandwich? An omelette?'

'I'm sure I can manage. Thank you,' I tell him. 'You've been very kind. I should probably get to work. Do you happen to know if Wanda's printed out the chapters she's done so far?'

'I do! She has. I was meant to mention that. They're on the desk there by the window. She's printed them out in Times New Roman, but I'm to tell you that if there's a font you prefer, we can reprint them with no trouble at all.'

'That's great,' I tell him. 'I have everything I need. I might get started.' I'm keen to call home and see how everyone's getting on, and I wonder if Philip is going to stay here all day, anticipating my every need and making me tea.

He takes the hint. 'I'll get out of your hair then. I'm going to be back up at the main house, and when Wanda's ready we'll give you a call.' He gives a little wave, followed by a strange sort of awkward bow as he backs out of the room, closing the French doors behind him. I watch as he bounds back around the pool. He moves beautifully. He's fit and strong, probably because he hasn't had his body destroyed by childrearing. I can't think of anyone who has had a kid and not come away with a bad back or a busted shoulder or something similarly debilitating. Lugging well-fed toddlers around and wrangling them in and out of car seats is not good for your spine.

Sitting down at the desk with my tea, I try calling Dad. It goes to voicemail. I leave him a quick message, letting him know I've arrived safely and asking for an update, then I turn my attention to the manuscript.

I read for about a minute and a half before I can't concentrate any more. It's too quiet. All I can hear are trees moving in the breeze and the odd birdcall.

My usual soundtrack of gently or sometimes violently squabbling toddlers is conspicuously absent and it's really throwing me. That's ridiculous, I tell myself. This is how people work. This is an utter luxury: uninterrupted, peaceful editing time. This is what I long for when I'm attacking my work in five-minute bursts at home, getting up constantly to cut up carrots or attempt to glue broken Milk Arrowroot biscuits back together with peanut butter.

It's good that I'm not having to decide whether it will be more distracting to be asked for the scissors every thirty seconds or hand over the scissors and worry about what's being done with them in the next room, and whether the sound of the curtains being opened and shut is in any way related.

Refocusing, I manage about three more pages before I have to get up. On a bookshelf in the corner, along with every book Wanda's ever written, is a CD player. I haven't seen a CD player for years. I switch it on and press play. It's *The Best of David Bowie 1969/1974*. Perfect.

I sit back down and work for an hour, solidly, without getting up.

The chapters Wanda's written so far are, mercifully, excellent. She's done just what she said she would do, which is dish the dirt on everyone she's ever been with. And because it's in chronological order, the book has a natural flow. She's captured her own character development too—from the fearless but naive teenager, fresh off the farm in 1961, through her time as a lover and muse to some of the biggest names in rock and roll history, to the point where she embraced the fledgling feminist movement and began to exert a new kind of power, taking charge of her career and her future, and in doing so becoming an icon to a whole new generation.

But there are some unexplained gaps: two years in the late 1960s are unaccounted for, eighteen months in the mid seventies, and four years from 1987 to 1991. These are the gaps that have been causing Carmen so much distress.

Once I finish a quick first read through of the chapters, I check my phone. There's a brief text from Dad—*All good here*—and several from Carmen. At least she's easing up on the voicemails. The first text says, *Any luck? If not, try standing behind her and Heimlich manoeuvring the chapters out of her.*

Her second text says, *Update please.*

I write back: *Progressing. Will update again tomorrow.*

I make and eat a sandwich, and then I'm not sure what to do. There's no point working on the edit any further until I have the missing chapters. I consider heading back up to the house but Philip was pretty adamant that I'd be called when I was required.

I lie down on the couch, close my eyes, and Adam pops unbidden into my head, like a sexy, dishonest jack-in-the-box. Bloody Adam. Thinking about him makes me feel a bit sick. What's causing that, I wonder. Guilt? Shame? No, it's embarrassment. I misjudged him. I feel foolish. I was seeing who Adam once was—or who he once presented himself as, in his book. I should have known that wasn't the whole story. People in books aren't real. Not even in memoirs. It's like I've tried to have an affair with a fictional character. I might as well have tried to date Heathcliff, or The Cat in the Hat, or some other distinctive Man of Literature.

I open my eyes and check my phone.

Three o'clock. Dad will be collecting Tim from school soon. I hope he's got something for their afternoon tea. I probably should have left some instructions about that, and about what they'll want for dinner. I hope Freya's not missing me too much. She's awfully little to be left. Guilt begins to bubble away in my gut. I'm clearly not even needed up here. Wanda seems fine. Who abandons their kids so they can swan off on a junket like this? This is the kind of thing Troy does. The kind of thing Helen would do. I'm as bad as they are. My poor children don't stand a chance. They have two parents who are incapable of putting their needs first.

I begin envisioning a future where my children—lacking the ability to love because I haven't shown them enough of it, devoid of empathy because they realize their mother doesn't value their feelings sufficiently to stay at home with them and raise them—become terrible adults, blithely crashing through life with complete disregard for others. They'll probably become conservative politicians, or property developers, or business efficiency experts. Deeply engrossed in this awful spiral of guilt and shame, I almost don't hear my phone ping with another text alert.

It's from Laura. *OMG IS THIS WHERE YOU ARE?*

I click on the link she's attached and it takes me to a photo essay about Wandaland on an architectural website. The photos are beautiful, but they don't do the real thing justice. This really is an amazing place.

Affirmative, I text back.

Have you swum in that pool yet? she replies instantly. *Do not come home until you have. Mum would have LOVED that place.*

She's right. She's always bloody right. Our mother would have been in that pool faster than you can say 'I didn't bring a bathing suit'. She wouldn't have cared. She'd have bowled up to those terrifying girls and borrowed one, or she'd have gone swimming in her bra and undies.

When did I get so scared of everything? This is no way to live. No one seems to need me to do any work right now, so I might as well be in the pool. I'll go and ask Edie and her friends if I can borrow a bathing suit.

* * *

I find the girls right where I left them a few hours ago. But they've swapped sunloungers and are now all looking at iPads and phones.

'Hey,' Edie greets me. 'What's happening?'

'I was wondering if I might be able to take you up on your offer of a bathing suit,' I say. 'If it still stands.'

She raises her sunglasses and props them on the top of her head. 'Absolutely. Come down to my guesthouse and I'll sort you out.'

She grabs a white caftan that's draped over a nearly table and drops it over her head. It floats down and she starts walking, surprisingly quickly, although I suppose she does have extremely long legs. I follow her down a path that weaves from the pool through the gardens to another guesthouse, very like mine.

'Come on in,' she says, so I follow her inside. The living room is awash in Express Post bags and courier satchels. There are unopened boxes from expensive makeup brands all over the coffee table, and piles of clothing with tags heaped on the couch.

'I know I've got something in here that will work for you,' she says, narrowing her eyes and scanning the room.

'What is all this stuff?' I ask her.

Edie turns to me and somewhat shamefacedly says, 'I'm an "influencer". Apparently. Basically, I have a lot of Instagram followers and companies send me stuff that I might like and then mention. Some brands I have partnerships with, where I advertise things for them, you know, for money, but others just send me things on spec, and if I think they're good I show them and if I don't, I don't. Wanda thinks it's ridiculous. She's probably right. But it's kind of fun.'

'It would be,' I agree. This must be what Helen's been banging on about recently. Is everyone an influencer now? Does anyone have a real job?

'Anyway, I know I got a whole lot of bikinis the other day from a new brand called Tanline. You're welcome to any of them.'

'That's really nice of you,' I say, 'but if they're all your size they might be a bit small for me.' That's putting it mildly. Edie's waist is the size of one of my thighs.

'Nah,' she says, dismissing my worries. 'They're all string bikinis so they can be let out to fit anyone. You might not get a massive amount of coverage in the ass, or the boobs, but as long as you don't try to go jogging you'll be fine.'

Jesus.

'Aha!' She holds up a handful of strings and triangles. 'I've got them! Blush, hot pink or black?'

'Black,' I say at once. Then she tosses me the black bikini and I realize this won't have a hope of being slimming. It will be slimming only in the way that the black boxes over people's faces or genitals in photographs are slimming, which is to say not at all.

'Try it on,' she says.

'Here?'

She looks at me as if this is a strange thing to ask. Why wouldn't I get naked in front of a complete stranger fifteen years younger than me?

I think of Laura, and of Mum. What would they do? I think of how little privacy I've had for the past six years and it seems absurd to balk at this. From the first time an obstetrician inserted her gloved hand where no gloved hand had been before, my body ceased being mine alone. I suppose you could argue that the loss of physical autonomy began nine months earlier, when I started sharing my body with another human, but Tim was a reasonable bodymate and didn't bother me nearly as much as the two fingers of the obstetrician.

So right there in the guesthouse of a famous author, I get nude in front of a girl I've only just met. She doesn't bat an eyelid. The bikini, with some adjustment of straps and ties, goes on.

'Is there a full-length mirror anywhere?' I ask Edie with trepidation.

'No,' she says. 'It's one of Wanda's weird ideas. She says we aren't the best judges of how we look, and we should only see ourselves reflected in the eyes of those around us.'

I've never heard anything so absurd. All I'm going to see reflected in these girls' eyes is horror and a terrible fear of the future.

I take a deep breath. I won't see any of these people again. Who cares if I look less than perfect? I'm heading towards forty and I've grown two children, which is more than any of these girls' bodies have done. I think about Freya and Tim, and Lola, and how I want them to feel about their bodies. Proud would be fine. Completely indifferent would be ideal.

I stride out of the guesthouse and back up the path and dive into the water. Both parts of the bikini immediately migrate north. When I surface the top has become a necklace and the bottom has almost completely disappeared between my buttocks. I'm wearing no sunscreen, no rashguard, and now no longer even a bathing suit. It's the wildest thing I've done in years, and the girls on the side give me an only slightly patronizing round of applause.

* * *

Wanda doesn't call for me all afternoon, and by sunset I start wondering if I should force my way in to see what she's doing. After swimming for a while I've showered and dressed, and when Philip knocks on the door I decide to see what he thinks I should do. He seems to understand how things work in this very odd place.

'Oh no,' he says. 'Probably best to leave Wanda to it, at least for the night. If she hasn't come out of the study by now, it means she's actually writing, and we don't want to interfere with that. Come have some dinner with Monty and the girls and me. Monty's been cooking all afternoon.'

'All right,' I say, 'but maybe I'll just stick my head in to let Wanda know I'm here if she wants to run anything by me.'

'If you feel you ought,' he says, in a tone that strongly suggests I oughtn't.

And so, even though I'm being paid to be here helping Wanda, and have nothing to report back to the persistent nagging emails and text messages from Carmen, I take Philip's advice and spend the evening with him, Wanda's husband, and three teenage girls.

Monty greets me when I enter his kitchen by handing me a glass of champagne and kissing me on both cheeks. We eat sitting on stools around a kitchen island slightly smaller than Tasmania.

In addition to writing his wife's name in gravel every day, Monty is an enthusiastic amateur chef and horticulturalist. He plies us with plate after plate of delicious morsels: oysters, local crab, tiny lamb cutlets, and many curious and small vegetables. He seems particularly fond of miniature things, so we eat baby zucchini, carrots, and artichokes. None of these is in season, but he grows them in his greenhouse, apparently, where he controls the climate year round.

Every time he puts a small plate of food in front of us, I'm the first to finish. The first few times it's not such a big deal, since each dish is only a bite or two. Then I start to get self-conscious. Maybe no one else will notice. I inhale a dish of homemade angel hair pasta with scampi.

'Wow,' Clara says, 'you eat really, really fast.' She's staring at me, wide-eyed. She's twiddling a fork around in her own, still full pasta bowl.

I blush. 'Sorry, I know I do. I never ate particularly quickly until I had kids. It started when they were babies. Did you know babies have this uncanny ability to sense when their mother lifts a fork to her lips? It causes them to either become roaringly hungry, even if you've just fed them, or unleash their bowels. I think it's just a habit I have now—eat fast before someone needs a glass of water or a different fork, or their bottom wiped.'

The girls laugh, but they also look faintly disgusted. I realize I'm the only parent here. Monty and Wanda never had kids, nor did Philip, and these girls are too young. For the first time in about six years, I'm conversing with a bunch of other adults, and none of them are parents. I feel like an alien.

I've forgotten what it's like to be in company where people don't discuss bodily fluids and recipes in the same breath. The girls and Monty seem to be regarding me in the way I would if I met someone at a dinner party who was a lion tamer, or a taxidermist: they're curious and appear to regard what I do as quite exotic. Me, with my boring, repetitive, stay-at-home, freelance life. With the children and the grocery shopping and the park and, until recently, the tragic lack of romance.

'Is being a parent the joyous, life-changing experience they say it is?' asks Monty jovially.

'Yes and no,' I tell him. 'I mean, if you get off on constant, low-level terror and guilt, it's a delight. I can honestly say my children are the greatest things that have ever happened to me, and they are the bane of my existence. I lost my identity, my body, and my ability to sleep past 5 a.m., but I can't imagine my life without them. It would be about ninety-six per cent less snotty. I had no idea that children are born with unblemished and unchallenged immune systems, which means they spend their first five or so winters failing to fend off pretty much any virus they encounter, and coating themselves and everyone around them with a thin film of mucus.'

Edie grimaces and puts down her fork.

God, Emma. Stop talking about snot and poo.

'I remember my sister saying something similar when her children were small,' Philip says. 'They seemed incapable of blowing their noses. She used to say they were knights of the order of the shining sleeve.'

That makes me laugh, and I drink some wine and start to relax.

The conversation moves on, and this too is like a new world—a whole discussion that not only doesn't centre on babies or toddlers, it doesn't even skirt the periphery of parentland. No one mentions schools, after-school activities, screen time, or whether Kmart or Target has the better range of kids' clothes at the moment.

It's not like when parents try to have a conversation about something other than our children, when inevitably, no matter how hard everyone tries, the talk always returns to kids in some way. Because children are like the moon—even when you can't see them, their pull is constant and affects the way everything else works.

But sitting here, around this granite island covered in delicious things to eat and drink, surrounded by interesting people, I realize that what I thought was a permanent state of affairs might be changing. I mean, I wouldn't say my repartee is sparkling, but I'm holding my own, more or less, in a conversation that's not about milestones and reading levels.

We sit for hours, eating and talking. Wanda never joins us. A few times I ask Monty if I should go into her study to see how she's getting on, but he tells me she's fine.

'She says she'll see you in the morning,' he reassures me. 'She says to say she's blazing along and you'll be very pleased.'

Mellowed by the champagne, I agree we should leave her to it.

On the stroke of midnight, Monty announces it's bedtime, and I feel a pang of sadness that the evening's come to a close. I haven't felt that in years. Normally, if I do manage to leave the house, I'm dying for it to be a socially acceptable time to scurry home to my bed and my Nordic murder shows. What have I become, under the influence of these people and this new freedom?

Philip walks with me to my guesthouse. At the door, he reaches out and pats me on the shoulder. It's an awkward gesture.

'Well, goodnight, Emma,' he says. 'Sleep well. What a fun evening that was.'

'It was a brilliant night,' I say. 'Really, I haven't enjoyed myself so much in ages. I can't believe I'm being paid for this.'

He grins. 'I must say, having you here is an absolute tonic, after three days with Carmen.'

He turns to leave, then suddenly spins around, as if he's decided something, and kisses me on the cheek.

'Sorry,' he says. 'That was probably inappropriate. You're here for work. I just, well, better head to bed. Night.'

He heads off down the path, stopping after a few steps to turn back to me. 'Night!' he says again.

'Night!' I reply.

I stand at my door. I hear his footsteps resume, and then stop again. 'Night!' he calls again.

'Goodnight!' I say.

I wonder if he'll keep this up until he's inside, but I hear the door to his guesthouse open and close.

After a few minutes, I realize I'm still standing in the garden, with my hand on my cheek. I look up at the sky, but I can't see any stars. The moonlight glowing through the clouds is just as beautiful as the stars would have been.

* * *

Lying in bed, I realize I didn't call the kids at bedtime. There are no missed calls on my phone though, so I feel better knowing that they haven't missed me enough to ask Troy or Helen to help them call me. I'm glad they're all right.

I feel so far away from them, but strangely I don't feel lonely. I feel like I exist again, as a separate entity from my children, and my ex, and all the things that tether me to my normal life. It's not an unpleasant feeling, but it is slightly overwhelming, so I get my laptop out and lull myself to sleep to the familiar sounds of Swedish police officers unsuccessfully trying to liaise with their Finnish counterparts.

Chapter Nineteen

I jolt awake the next morning, disoriented. There is sunlight streaming in through the huge windows, and all I can hear is birdsong and rustling foliage. I'm ill at ease at once. This is not how I wake up. My body does not awaken naturally after a full night's sleep. My body is now accustomed to a small warm form snuggling up to me, or a patter of feet dashing over the floorboards to kiss my nose, or Julia and Ian having a loud set-to outside the house.

This just feels weird, and I don't like it. How can that be? This is paradise, for all intents and purposes, but it feels six kinds of wrong to me. I make myself a cup of tea and some toast.

It's eight o'clock. Last night Monty said I shouldn't bother Wanda before nine, but I don't think I can wait that long. What on earth am I supposed to do here, alone, for an hour? I've read what I have of the manuscript. I did my relaxing by the pool yesterday. That was very pleasant, but it's time to get on with things now, otherwise what's the point of me being here?

I consider calling the kids, but Helen will be trying to get everyone up, dressed, fed, and Tim off to school, while Troy, if their household is anything like ours was, gets in her way, distracts the kids, and slows everyone down. I know it won't be helpful if I interrupt that. Laura will be in the same boat with her lot.

Staring out the window, I catch sight of the top of Philip's head above the bay hedge outside. He's heading down the path.

I dash out. 'Morning!' I shout.

He turns around, with such a pleased look on his face that I can't help but smile too. His feelings show so openly.

'Hello!' he says. 'Did you sleep well? I've just had a swim and I was going to go for a little walk through the rainforest. Would you like to come? It's about an hour, round trip.'

'I'll get dressed,' I say, without even thinking about it. 'Give me three minutes.'

* * *

The walk takes exactly an hour. We move through some fields into the cool shadows of the rainforest and along a path through the undergrowth. We pass two waterfalls, balance on stepping stones across the same creek in four different places, and emerge, somehow, back at the bottom of Wanda's garden again.

The whole time we chat companionably, in the way you can when you aren't looking at someone. Philip is very easy to talk to. I tell him about Tim and Freya, about her tiger obsession, and he tells me more about his real tiger.

'What was his name?' I ask.

'His real name was Hyrcan,' he says, holding aside a lantana branch and allowing me to pass along the track ahead of him. 'It's a reference to a line from Macbeth, but I always called him Stripe. Drove my mother mad, especially when the cub started to respond to Stripe and not to Hyrcan. But I was the one who spent the most time with Stripe, in the few months we owned him. I was heartbroken when they sent him to live at an animal sanctuary.'

'It was probably the right thing to do,' I say.

'Oh, undoubtedly. But it didn't make it easier. It did make sense though. My parents liked to travel a lot and there weren't a lot of housesitters who would mind a tiger.'

'What did your parents do, for work?' I ask.

'They were . . . they did . . .' He seems to struggle to answer. Finally, in an embarrassed tone, he says, 'They did nothing. They were very wealthy because my father's father had made a fortune in ice.'

'Ice?' I say.

'Frozen water,' he clarifies. 'I'm not even sure the other variety was invented back then.'

'How do you make an ice fortune?' I ask, intrigued. All I know about the ice business I learned from *Frozen*, and it didn't seem like the sort of endeavour that could make you rich.

'Like many fortunes, it was made quite unethically. My father was always a bit vague about it but there was quite likely some patent theft involved, or at least some funny business about how much a patent was acquired for, and my grandfather ended up building the biggest commercial ice-manufacturing plant in Great Britain.'

He goes on to tell me that his mother died when he was in his twenties and, upon his father's death, five years later, he took his third of the ice fortune and started a small non-profit aid organization. He worked away at that, while also making investments in the burgeoning tech start-up scene.

When Google eventually bought one of them, he found himself richer than God and with significantly more concern about the state of the world. He massively increased the scale of his non-profit work and now spends his time flying around the world, visiting countries where he is funding aid projects.

'Doesn't it overwhelm you?' I ask. 'All the poverty you must see, and knowing you can't fix it all?'

Philip turns back to look at me. 'I didn't come by my wealth through my own hard work. I don't really feel like it's mine. I've found that difficult, actually, but over the years I've discovered I'm good at organizing ways to use that money so that it makes as much of a difference as it can. And yes, it can be very overwhelming, but I try to focus on the positive effects my work can have, and the positive effects the positive effects can have, you know, as it ripples out through the world.'

I don't know if the things I've been doing to help other people have had any positive effects. I haven't created ripples of goodness.

'It sounds like you're achieving a lot,' I say. 'I'd like to achieve something big like that, one day. I just seem to create small amounts of strife. At least they're not large amounts of strife.'

'You're being too hard on yourself,' Philip says kindly. 'Maybe you just need to reframe what you're achieving. I'll bet you're doing better than you think.'

We finish our walk in companionable silence, and his words stay with me.

When we get back, I head up to the main house in search of Wanda.

Monty's leaving her study as I approach the door.

'Oh, Emma, good,' he says. 'I was just coming to fetch you. She's ready.'

* * *

Wanda's lying on the sofa. She has one hand across her forehead, like she's trying to take her own temperature.

'It's very hard, you know,' she says without any preamble. 'Writing what I'm writing. I'm dredging up a lot of memories. Not all of them are pleasant.'

'It's brave of you,' I tell her.

'I don't like who I am in some of these memories. I don't suppose it's all right if I just change them so I'm a better person in them than I really was?'

'You could do that,' I say, 'but it might not read as authentic. I think your readers might be on to you. They want the truth, if you can bear it.'

'Oh, I can bear it, I just regret it, that's all,' she says. 'The parts that are missing from the manuscript, you've probably figured out that those are the parts of my life where I really did not behave at all well. In fact I'm quite ashamed of myself.'

'Maybe we can find a way of reframing those things,' I say, 'to a degree, anyway. But honestly, Wanda, if you can stand to tell it like it was, I don't think anyone's going to judge you.'

'Of course they'll judge me!' she says, and she sits up and looks fiercely at me. 'And so they should. I ruined several marriages. I caused children to become estranged from fathers. I'm not claiming sole responsibility for any of that, by the way, because all those men made choices when they did what they did with me, and to their families, but I'm not proud of those interludes.'

She's right. People might judge her harshly when they read the book. But part of my job is to help her shape what she is prepared to reveal into a form that will have her coming off in the best possible light. The way I'll edit the book will be equivalent to gentle Photoshopping of a photograph. No one will notice it, but she'll look a hell of a lot less imperfect once I'm done.

I explain this to Wanda, who is remarkably surprised,

considering how many books she has written and has had edited previously.

'I suppose you're right, Emma,' she says in wonderment. 'I just hadn't thought of editing like that before. I mean I know how it works with fictional characters, but I suppose you'll just treat me, in the memoir, like you would any of the characters in my novels? I mean, we can't change what I did, but we could put in a nicer way.'

I hesitate. 'Sort of,' I say. 'But I can't edit what you haven't written. So if you get the stories down on paper, warts and all, we can tackle them like we would if it were fiction. I promise I won't let you come across as too awful.'

She thinks for a moment. 'You can let me come across as a bit awful. Not irredeemably dreadful, but mildly shit. Because of course I do come around in the end, don't I? When I fall in love with Monty and we live happily ever after? But there needs to be punishment before that, doesn't there? It won't look good if I get no comeuppance at all before my happy ending.'

'I don't think you need comeuppance, necessarily. What do you think was motivating your behaviour, at those times in your life? Was there something making you sad, something you were using these relationships to compensate for?'

'Like what?' she says.

Something occurs to me. 'What about children?' I ask. 'Was motherhood something you ever wanted? If it was, and it never happened for you, then it could work to weave through the later chapters the idea that for all the taking of what you wanted, you never got the one thing you truly desired. It could play as a mitigating circumstance.'

Wanda looks at me straight-faced for a few seconds before erupting into gales of laughter. 'No! I can't think of anything worse! No offence, darling, but being a mother looks like a mug's game to me. I never wanted babies, but if I write that people really will think I'm a terrible villain. Because, Emma, darling, if there's one thing I've learned, it's that if you're a woman who doesn't want to have a baby, people think you are a wicked witch.'

'Then let's not worry about finding a punishment for you in the narrative,' I tell her. 'Just tell the stories how they happened. They'll be enough.'

'Hmm,' she says thoughtfully. 'Leave it with me.'

She settles back at the computer and works away quietly. I sit and look at pictures of the kids on my phone.

After half an hour, she stops typing, looks up, and says, 'I think I'll be all right now for a while. You can go find some fun.'

'Are you sure?' I ask.

'Absolutely. I'm getting it all down. I'm sure I'll have a few more chapters for you by dinnertime.'

* * *

Back in my guesthouse, I check to see if any of my other editing jobs have come in, but there's nothing. It's making no sense, me being here. Wanda clearly doesn't need any help. The interactions I've had with her could have easily been done on the phone. I'm reasonably sure now that she has dragged me up here just to annoy Carmen.

I want to text Helen for an update, but I'm nervous. I haven't spoken directly to her since our conversation in the street. I could try Troy, but he'll be at work and won't have a clue what's happening with the kids.

It's Tuesday morning and Helen will be at ballet with Lola.

Freya will, I hope, be off doing something fun with Dad, not kicking around in the foyer while her half-sister twirls and dances. With a bit of distance, the arrangement up until now looks absurd: one kid in a class, one kid bored outside the class. I can't really remember why we've been operating like that for so long. Laura used to badger me about it, and say that Freya should just join in. She wasn't very impressed with my argument that Freya had tried ballet and not really been into it. Maybe Laura was right. Maybe I should have persisted and just stuck Freya in with Lola each week. I just wanted Freya to have a free and unscheduled childhood, but from here it looks like sheer bloody-mindedness and I'm slightly embarrassed by it.

I'm at a loose end. I email Suze to make sure there's nothing I can do from up here to help with the Fun Run, and she replies immediately to say that everything is under control.

It's only eleven o'clock. What am I supposed to do for the rest of the day? Lie by the pool and try to stay out of the girls' Instagram shots? Listen to *The Best of David Bowie* again? Watch the midday movie? Does that even exist any more? I'd quite like to go find Philip and see what he's up to, but I don't want him to think I'm latching on to him. I'm very bad at having nothing to do.

Given the lack of alternatives, I let my mind wander back to Adam. Thinking of Saturday night, my first feeling, once again, is a flood of embarrassment. But I prod around my emotions gingerly for a bit and realize that although I'm mortified over his rejection, and angry at how he led me on, I'm not heartsore over him. Hmm. That's not what I expected. I thought I really had feelings for him.

If what I felt for Adam had been more than lust, surely now I'd be feeling more devastated that he doesn't feel the same for me. Maybe it was just plain old lust. God, I'm thirty-six years old. You'd think I'd be able to tell the difference between lust and something more serious by now. Maybe Troy was my only chance at love, and now all that remains for me is lust. I wonder if that's such a bad thing.

I'm sitting on the sofa, staring out into space. I'm also considering that inside me where my soul should be is an abyss no longer capable of love, when there's a knock and I look up to see Philip on the verandah.

'Am I disturbing you?' he asks.

'No. I'm at a completely loose end for the first time in about six years,' I say.

'Well, that's good timing for me, isn't it? I'm heading into town. Do you want to come?'

'Why not?' As soon as I say it, I feel guilty. I have not come up here, and left my children for days on end, in order to swan about with Philip. That was not the deal. I'm supposed to be working.

If it's going to take Wanda a few days to write the rest of the chapters, I could fly home. I could spend two days with the kids, have the weekend with them and do the Fun Run, then come back on Monday to go through what she's written—if it's even necessary for me to do that in person. Then Carmen wouldn't have to pay me for doing nothing, and my children wouldn't be at home wondering what on earth's happened to me.

I push the guilt aside. Guilt and shame are useless emotions, Mum always said. When else am I going to get a chance like this, to be away from the kids, with a lovely man offering to drive me around and entertain me? Never, that's when. And I've had so many years of charging publishers for way fewer hours than I actually work. I might just even up the ledger a bit by slacking off on the publisher's dime.

* * *

For the next two days, Philip and I drive into the town and wander about, stopping whenever we feel like it to eat amazing food. I keep the receipts, though I don't feel like I'll be brave enough to claim them back from Carmen. It's like being on a honeymoon, but with an almost-stranger. In fact, it's better than my honeymoon, because Philip is a much easier companion than Troy was. Philip isn't constantly on his phone, negotiating prices for boxes of fruit and vegetables, and when, on our second afternoon sightseeing, I wander into a store full of white organza dresses and hand-thrown pottery in various shades of mud, he comes in and browses too, looking for presents for his nieces and sister.

I try on a couple of *Picnic at Hanging Rock*-style outfits and come very close to convincing myself that I would wear these wafty creations back home, before acknowledging that I would slam the handkerchief hems in the car door and the crisp white fabric would stay that way only until I walked past the first avocado-smeared child.

The salesgirl gushes over me when I emerge from the changing room. 'Oh my God,' she says, 'that looks like it was made for you. You should absolutely have that dress. I can't imagine any dress suiting anyone any better.'

Steady on, I think. It's a nice dress, but I recognize someone working on commission when I see her. Philip must see my sceptical glance, because he picks up a necklace and says, 'Have you any more like these?'

'Out the back,' she says. 'Just hang on a sec and I'll go find them.' She bustles off into the back room and Philip says quietly, 'There, now you can try on the other one in peace. I'll be outside.'

Gratefully I change into another dress, and I don't even come out of the change room in it. It's beautiful and I wish I could pull it off in real life.

I hear the salesgirl outside the curtain. 'Knock knock!' She says. 'You all right for sizes? I've got those other two necklaces your husband was interested in. Is he coming back?'

My husband? I guess we're pulling off the honeymooners act pretty convincingly.

I get dressed and come out. I'm about to tell her we're not married when Philip walks back in. I go to return the dresses to the racks and he seems surprised. 'They looked lovely, Emma,' he says. 'Why don't you buy one?'

'They are beautiful,' I agree, 'but they won't work in my real life. I'm more a jeans and T-shirt person. Well, maybe not, but I have a jeans and T-shirt life right now. And besides, buying this sort of thing, in this sort of town? My mum used to call it the turquoise coyote effect, after she and Dad went to New Mexico and brought home all sorts of serapes and Native American-styled homewares that looked ridiculous in their art deco bungalow in Sydney. It wouldn't fit in at home.'

'I know what you mean,' Philip says, 'but I don't think these are turquoise coyotes. You looked so happy in this one.' He holds out a broderie-anglaise dress with a pie-crust collar.

I know I would look silly in this dress, swanning around Shorewood. The place for this dress is here, with the beach and wholefoods cafés. Not grocery shopping and playing Lego on my grubby floors.

But there's something in Philip's hopeful face that makes me pause.

'You know what?' I say. 'Fitting in is overrated.'

The salesgirl looks delighted. I put the dress on the counter and get out my credit card. Even if it never sees the light of day back home, this silly dress might remind me to take a chance every now and then.

As the salesgirl wraps it she gives Philip what is unmistakably a flirty smile. 'You have excellent taste,' she tells him. 'Your wife is a lucky woman.'

Philip turns scarlet. 'Goodness,' he stammers. 'I should be so lucky. No no no, Emma and I aren't married. God, I'm old enough to be her—'

'Emotional support peacock?' I say.

* * *

By Thursday afternoon, I'm starting to get nervous about time. I have to leave here on Friday evening. If Wanda doesn't hurry up and finish these chapters, I won't be able to look over them before I go. If there are any problems, I'll be back in the city and we'll need to work through them remotely, which I don't imagine Wanda will be thrilled about. But I truly can't stay away any longer. I don't want to miss the Fun Run.

The pebbles spelling 'Wandaland' are immaculate this afternoon. Either no one's been in or out of the front door today or Monty's had nothing to do but tidy his handiwork repeatedly.

On the door of my guesthouse, which is really beginning to feel like home, there's a note. *Emma, new chapters will be with you tonight! W.* Great. I will work on them through the night and that gives us all day tomorrow to iron out any last issues. I go inside and drop the note on the counter.

Edie sticks her perfectly tousled ombré locks through the French doors.

'Philip's going to make caipirinhas by the pool. You want in?'

I haven't heard anyone mention a caipirinha since about 2002. I do need to keep a clear head so I can edit the chapters tonight. But one drink can't hurt.

* * *

When Wanda sends Monty down to the guesthouse to deliver her new chapters to me it is five o'clock.

I have had four strong cocktails in the sun and without quite meaning to, regaled the girls with the whole sad sorry tale of my love life so far. Philip, whose idea it was to have caipirinhas in the first place, has listened to it all too.

It came about because one of the girls made the mistake of asking me what my husband does. I gave an answer that was probably more than they needed. I didn't stop talking for about fifteen minutes.

When I'd brought them up to speed on the situation with Helen and Troy, I paused. No one spoke for a few seconds.

Edie fished an ice-cube out of her tumbler, crunched it in her mouth and said, 'Troy sounds like a dickhead.'

'Yeah,' I admitted. 'He is a dickhead. I wish I hadn't picked a dickhead to father my kids. I hope being a dickhead is a recessive gene. Maybe it'll skip my children.'

'I know lots of people who have dickheads for fathers,' Philip said encouragingly. 'Some of the nicest people I know, in fact. Your children will turn out beautifully.' He holds my gaze and the demented moths erupt again in my stomach.

I smiled gratefully at him, but then I thought of Adam. 'They won't have much hope if I continue to date dickheads though,'

I said, 'and they have a constant stream of dickhead input into their upbringing.'

'Oh dear,' said Philip. 'And do you?'

'Possibly,' I said. 'I had a near miss recently. I thought he wasn't a dickhead, but it turned out he might actually be one. Maybe that's too harsh. He probably just wasn't that into me.'

'That sucks,' said Clara. 'What was the story there?'

I wasn't sure if I wanted to tell these people what a fool I had been to pursue a married man, who I thought I knew and loved from the way he wrote about himself in a book a decade ago. I hardly know them. But then again, I hardly know them.

'It's embarrassing,' I said, 'but he was a guy I used to know, from way back, and I was really into him then, but nothing happened for various reasons. Now he has a kid at my kid's school, he's separated—well, he sort of implied he was separated—and we've been getting close recently. And we got, you know, really close, and then straight after he said he's still in love with his wife. Mortifying. I think I was just a bit of fun for him, which I don't like, because it's not as if I'm desperate to get married again or anything, but I do feel I deserve to be something more than someone's back-up plan. And I also knew his wife was coming back, but I couldn't tell him how I knew because it made me look insane, so I just waited for him to tell me and he never did. So maybe I'm the dickhead for sleeping with him when I knew, on some level at least, that he wasn't available. I don't know why I'm telling you all this. I'm sure it makes no sense. Sorry. You must think I'm an idiot.'

'It's all right,' says Edie. 'We've all been there.'

* * *

We've all been there. I don't know why, but somehow those words, from a random drunk twenty-year-old, in a bikini, on a sunlounger, who probably hasn't actually 'been there', suddenly made things seem a bit less dire. Now, lying on my bed, drinking water and trying to sober up enough to read the new chapters, the knot of shame in my stomach has unravelled.

A bit of distance from home has been a remarkable thing. I feel like I can see more clearly what matters more and what matters less. Maybe by obsessing over the kids and Troy and Helen so much, I've been trying to ignore myself, my own thoughts and feelings. It's probably time to look at the shape of my own life.

Things are never going to go back to how they were before Troy left me and, really, I probably don't want them to. If I stand back now and look at my life, I can see that there are some perfectly fine parts, and some not too terrible parts that will be good foundations for building new parts.

When my phone rings, I get a shock. No one has called me for several days. Carmen has retreated to email and no one at home seems interested in talking to me.

I look at the screen. It's Troy.

'Hello?'

From his first words, I can tell he's furious about something. But there's so much wailing in the background, it's hard to figure out what's he's saying.

'Emma? Freya, just stop crying. Take a deep breath, it's going to be all right, but you need to stop crying. I can't hear myself think. Emma? Are you there? Freya. *Freya.* Seriously, mate, I don't know what the problem is. You need to calm down and—' he interrupts himself. 'Emma? What is the deal with this bloody tiger book?'

'Which tiger book? *The Tiger Who Came to Tea*?' I say. 'It's her favourite book. I packed it in her bag. She has to have it read to her every night. She has done so for a year. You know this, Troy. How is this news? What have you been reading to her for the last three nights?'

'I don't know. I haven't been home for bedtime. I am now though, and Helen's gone out for dinner and I couldn't find the book.'

'Oh no,' I whisper. I can see where this is going.

'I put all three of them in the car and drove all the way to the bookstore and bought her another copy—'

'And you read the whole thing to her,' I say, deflated.

'What? What have I done wrong now? That's what you do with a book. I read it to her and she's totally lost it. I have no idea why. I can't make any sense of what she's saying.'

The wailing has given way to sobs now. Poor Freya.

'She's never heard the last page,' I explain. 'I glued it to the one after so she never knew the tiger didn't come back. It's the worst ending ever otherwise. There's no hope. No wonder she's upset. She feels like her favourite book is a lie.'

Troy is quiet for a moment. All I can hear is sniffling from Freya.

'Emma, that is completely insane. Who does that to a kids' book? Of course she feels like the book is a lie. You've lied to her!'

'I was protecting her! She's three, she doesn't need to know how shit the world is. She doesn't need to know what a let-down life can be, that people sometimes just leave and never come back.'

'Jesus, Emma,' he says with a sigh. 'It wouldn't have been that big a deal, if you'd just left it how it was. You don't get to decide how a book turns out. It's not a choose-your-own-adventure. And you should have told me, if it was that important. How am I meant to tell the right lies if you don't tell me what I'm supposed to be lying about?'

'I'd have thought you would just lie about everything as a matter of default,' I hurl back. It's not a mature response. But good God, who is he to lecture me about lying?

'Can you put Freya on?' I say. 'I need to explain.'

'I don't think she needs that right now,' he says imperiously. 'She's tired and disappointed. She needs to sleep. I'll call you in the morning if she wants to discuss it.'

He ends the call. I'm shaking with anger. What in God's name has been going on? Where is Freya's proper copy of *The Tiger Who Came to Tea*? That poor kid. I can't believe Troy's buggered this up. I open the doors to breathe the cool night air.

On the doorstep is a bundle of paper. It's Wanda's final chapters.

* * *

An hour later, my mood has gone from bad to worse.

Wanda's new chapters cover the period of her life when she had a long, torrid affair with a very famous man whom the world, including his wife, thought was happily married. She has filled it with not at all subtle hints about her unhappiness at not having a baby. This was when Wanda was forty-two. The ship for having kids had sailed and she was sad, she writes.

She uses it to justify what she did.

When I see what she's done, I feel a bit pissed off. It's exactly what I advised her against. I was stupid to have given her the idea.

She could have just accepted some culpability for her behaviour without bringing the idea of motherhood into it. I don't think her readers would have turned on her. Her fans think she's fabulous. They won't care if she slept with one or two people's husbands.

And even if they do think what she did is a bit questionable, morally, everyone knows it takes two to tango. I never blamed Helen for what happened with her and Troy. Well, maybe I did at first, but not once I really thought about it. Because Helen isn't the one who cheated on me. That was all down to Troy. He's the one who broke a promise, not Helen. My problem with Helen has been her behaviour *since* she wrecked my marriage.

I realize this line of thinking is being influenced by both the Brazilian sugarcane spirit pumping through my body and my own guilt at having recently slept with someone else's husband, so I try hard to be measured in my analysis of what Wanda has written.

But fuck it. I didn't force Adam to cheat on his wife, Helen didn't force Troy to cheat on me, and Wanda didn't force the Pulitzer prize-winning war correspondent who is the subject of these chapters.

She needn't make excuses.

When dinnertime comes around, and Philip pops his cheery head over the hedge, I send him up to the house with a note for Monty, declining dinner, and a message for Wanda. I tell her I'll have a report on the chapters ready to go through with her first thing in the morning. I want to go have it out with her now, but there's enough sobriety left in me—only about six per cent, but enough—to make me realize it's better to confront her in the morning. This is my job, after all, and I'm a firm believer that you should do your job, when possible, not shit-faced on caipirinhas.

What I can do in this state is call Laura. She may not quite understand the nuances of what's making me so cross, but that doesn't mean she can't sympathize with me.

'That sounds crappy,' she announces, once I've finished outlining the situation.

'It is,' I say. 'It's wrong of her, and I just want to talk her out of it and make her see that she has a duty to be honest, because there is power in honesty. I'm going to rewrite it. Well, not rewrite it, but suggest some really serious edits. She'll thank me for it, ultimately. I know she will.'

Laura pauses for a second. 'This reminds me of a book,' she says thoughtfully. 'A book or a movie. Or maybe both. I can't quite put my finger on what it is. Oh wait, yes I can. I know who you're reminding me of right now.'

'Who?' I have no idea what she's talking about.

'*Misery*,' she says triumphantly. 'You're behaving like Kathy Bates's character in *Misery*. What are you going to do, chop off Wanda's foot if she won't write what you tell her? Remove her thumb? For fuck's sake, Emma. Get a grip. It's not your book. It's not your story. Let Wanda write it however she bloody wants to. Stop being such a mental control freak. It's time for you to come home.'

And with that, she hangs up. She actually hangs up on me.

* * *

On Friday morning at nine o'clock on the dot, I am sitting on a hard chair in Wanda's study. No buttery soft leather sofas for me this morning. I mean business.

In the cold light of morning, what Laura said last night stings. That means she is at least a little bit right. But I'm determined to tell Wanda how disappointed I am, even if she won't change a word.

When she finally ambles in at about half past nine, carrying a giant cappuccino, Wanda smiles at me. 'I like my coffee how I like my men—wearing a little cap made of chocolate,' she says with a wink.

I don't smile back.

'Do I take it from your expression, Emma, that you didn't love the chapters?' she asks me lightly.

'Wanda, we talked about this. You said you wouldn't carry on with that business about how you slept with other people's husbands because you couldn't have a baby. It's just not true.'

'No, it isn't,' she says, and spoons the froth into her mouth. 'And with all due respect, darling Emma, that's my decision to make. Not yours. The chapters are great. Who cares whether they're true or not? As far as I'm concerned, the only truth that matters here is the actual, factual questions of what happened between me and my lovers. That has to be true so we don't all get ourselves sued. But as to my motivations and my interior life, well, it's my story and I'm at liberty to make up anything I like. And what I'd like is for my many fans to still think I'm a delight, and that my womanly grief over not being a mother led me to misbehave.'

'Why be dishonest?' I ask. 'Why not just say that you did what you did because you loved these men? Don't you want to be a voice for people like you, who didn't want to go down the road of having kids? You've been bold and brave in your actions. Don't rewrite history now.'

'Emma, my mind is made up. This is how I choose to tell the story.'

'I think you're making a mistake,' I say, though I know it's in vain.

'I'm very aware of that,' she replies. 'Carmen doesn't agree with you. I ran the chapters by her last night too and she's delighted with them. She's currently delighted with you, as well, but I don't imagine she'll stay that way if she hears you've been trying to convince me to undo all my hard work, and delay the book even further.'

So that's how it's going to be. Well, enough is enough. She's right: it's her story, she can tell it how she likes. All I can do is make suggestions. I'm supposed to do invisible mending and hemming of people's stories, not tell them they should make their dress into a pair of shorts. It doesn't make me wrong though. I'm sure the book would be loads better if she took my advice, but this is where I have to stop. It honestly feels like there was no need for me to be here in the first place. I've accomplished nothing except inspire her to lie to her readers.

'I'll tell Carmen how hard you've worked,' Wanda says, and it's clear that this lie is also a dismissal.

'Thank you,' I say. 'I'll head back today, then, if I can get a flight. Would it be possible for Philip to drive me to the airport?'

'Darling, that's what I was supposed to tell you! I knew I was forgetting something. Philip's had to leave already. He took the first flight this morning. He said to say goodbye to you.'

'Oh. Where's he gone?'

'I want to say the Solomon Islands? Or is it Samoa? Somewhere like that. He flew to Sydney this morning, because obviously there aren't direct flights from here to the Solomons. Or Samoa. Or was it the Marshall Islands? Somewhere Pacific, either way.'

I feel bereft. How silly. But he is so nice, and he gave me hope that maybe good men do exist. It would help if such good men existed anywhere near where I live, and didn't spend their lives jetting from one third-world trouble spot to the next. We live in completely different worlds. But I still wish I'd been able to say goodbye.

* * *

The first flight I can get a seat on isn't until four o'clock this afternoon. The sky is cloudy, and the estate is quiet. The girls aren't by the pool. I spend the day in my room, editing the chapters. They're well written, even if I think they aren't written how they should be.

I leave Wandaland in a taxi. Wanda's retreated to her study, and there's no sign of Monty, so in the end it's just Edie who sees me off.

As the cab pulls up, Edie says, 'Emma? You should try and see Philip again. He's a good guy.'

'I agree,' I say. 'He's very nice.'

Edie makes an awkward face. 'I've known him since I was a little kid and he's a really, really great person. I'd like something good to happen for him.'

She looks me in the eye for a quarter of a second, not nearly long enough to get a handle on why she's telling me this. Then she grabs her phone and starts scrolling through. 'See you,' she says.

'Bye, Edie.'

I drag my wheeled bag straight through the stones spelling out Wanda's name and they scatter every which way.

* * *

At the airport, the clouds have lowered. There are rumbles of thunder and the sky feels like it's about to break open.

I check in, and sit down to wait for the boarding call.

When the storm breaks, it sounds and feels like the end of days. Rain pounds on the airport's tin roof, and everyone moves to the picture windows to watch the lightning shattering the sky.

'Tropical thunderstorms are quick,' says the woman sitting beside me in the waiting area. She's drinking from a coconut and her sandals look homemade. She seems like a person who would know about tropical storms. 'Won't delay the flights. It'll be all over in twenty minutes.'

Three hours after the flight was meant to leave, the airline's ground staff announce that the rest of the day's flights are cancelled. All the chilled-out travellers, who have been coping with the delay by taking moody photos of the storm and eating paleo muffins from the café, suddenly realize they aren't going home tonight and there's an unseemly stampede for the service desk.

Tomorrow is the Fun Run. I need to get back in time for that or my name will be mud.

Fired up with righteous indignation, I join the lineup of everyone else who is determined to be on the first flight out of here, ready to plead my case and pull the single-mother-desperate-to-get-back-to-my-kids card. But it turns out I don't need to. Everyone has a similar tale of woe and the airline only cares who paid the most for their seat. Because the publisher bought me a full-fare ticket, I get priority in the rebooking process and, weather permitting, I will be on the first flight out, at six-thirty tomorrow morning.

* * *

I spend the night in a cheap local motel. For a few minutes I consider going back to Wandaland, but having left with my tail between my legs, I feel like it's probably better if I don't do that.

My room is musty and damp, but the sheets seem clean enough and the toilet is reassuringly sealed with a paper wrapper. There's a small pool, but it's not appealing in the pouring rain. I order room service for dinner, and eat my lukewarm club sandwich in front of the TV. It's a far cry from life at Wanda and Monty's, but it reminds me of the motels we used to stay at when I was a kid, when Mum and Dad would take us on road trips to the far west of the state to visit their old school friends.

I set my alarm for five o'clock for the six-thirty flight. That should get me to Sydney by seven-thirty, which leaves me an hour to get from the plane to the Fun Run. It will be cutting it fine, but I can do it, I'm sure. Whether I can run for any distance when all I've done for training is loll by a pool for five days, eating and drinking, is another question entirely.

Chapter Twenty

At the airport at half past five, the weather's looking promising, and the flight leaves on time.

Once we get to Sydney though, it's a different story.

'Ladies and gentlemen,' announces the captain, 'it's a busy morning here at the airport, and as anyone who lives in Sydney knows, parking is at a premium. We currently don't have a gate, so we're just going to be a few minutes longer. We appreciate your patience.'

I don't have time for this. I can't miss the race. And I have to get home first to get some running gear, unless I'm going to do the Fun Run in my new bikini and sandals.

Although the staff haven't said we can, everyone around me has switched on their phones, so I ring Laura.

'Hello, jetsetter,' she says.

'I'm stuck on the tarmac in Sydney, Laura,' I say. 'The Fun Run is at eight-thirty and I don't have any running clothes with me. Can you meet me at the sports field with sneakers and leggings and a sports bra?'

'Sorry, matey, no can do. I've got to have three kids in three different parts of the city playing three different sports. I may be Wonder Woman but I can't clone myself,' says Laura.

'Well, do you think Dad can?'

'Possibly, but he's going away for the weekend. He said he was leaving late morning.'

This seems unlikely. Dad never goes away. 'What?' I say. 'Where? Who with?'

'With someone called Penny, apparently.'

'Who on earth is Penny?'

Laura is drip-feeding this information in the most annoying fashion.

'Well,' she says, 'from the way he stammered and repeatedly called her "my friend, Penny, who's just a friend", I'd say she's Dad's girlfriend.'

Dad has a girlfriend? He can't. He's never had a girlfriend. Not in all the years since Mum died. I can't think what to say.

'And get this, Em,' says Laura. 'Penny's a beekeeper.'

'She isn't,' I say. 'You're lying.'

Laura bursts out laughing. 'Of course I'm lying. That would be all kinds of fucked up. She's a bookkeeper.'

'Laura, I can't deal with this information right now. I just need some runners and a pair of leggings. I'll ring Dad.'

'Look,' she says, 'if you're still on the plane now, you're going to miss the race anyway. You can just go in what you're wearing and cheer them on at the finish line. Troy can run the race with Tim.'

Yes. Yes he bloody can.

I ring Troy next. It's not too early. He's sharing a house with Freya, who's up early enough to wake the early birds.

'Emma,' he says blearily. 'You back?'

'Not exactly. I'm stuck on the ground at the airport. We might be on the tarmac for a while longer and I don't think I'm going to make it in time for the start of the race. Or maybe the whole race. You're fine to run it with Tim, though, aren't you?'

There's a pause.

'Well, actually I thought I might not because you were going to do it. I think I'm down for a shift on the bacon and egg roll stall during the race. And I'll need to keep an eye on Lola and now Freya too, if you're not going to make it back.'

'You have to,' I tell him. 'You've cancelled on Tim enough times. This is not negotiable. It's not even the five K. The kids' race is two kilometres, and all the other kids will have a parent running alongside them. There is no reason on earth you cannot run two kilometres with your son.'

'Em, I'm not feeling crash hot, if I'm honest.'

'I imagine that's what's called a hangover, Troy. Drink some of your bullshit juice and harden up. If you disappoint Tim today, you will have me to reckon with and I really don't think you want that.'

'Fine. Jesus,' he says. 'I'll run it. Hopefully Helen won't mind looking after both the girls, even though she's done it all week and she's leading the warm-up for the runners today.'

I don't even address that. Of course he's dumped all the kids on Helen and Dad all week. Of course he has.

'I'll see you when I get there. Tell Tim I love him and I hope he has an awesome race.'

I hang up and let out a huge sigh.

The man in the next seat looks at me. 'I'd do it, if I was him,' he tells me. 'I wouldn't cross you.' He moves his arm. 'Here,' he says. 'You have the middle armrest; I think we're going to be on the plane for a while.'

* * *

When the starter gun goes for the two-kilometre Fun Run, I'm still in a taxi, on the expressway. I'm wearing jeans, but it doesn't matter now, because I've missed the race I vaguely helped organize, the race I was going to run with Tim. The race I've been failing to train for.

The taxi pulls up near the gates of the sports field, and I leap out, flinging a fifty-dollar note at the driver and not waiting for a receipt, even though I need it for my expenses. I can see a crowd gathering at the finish line.

I have to admit, the whole set-up looks super professional. There's an inflatable arch over the ribbon, balloons everywhere, and everyone I pass seems to be wearing the same hat: a bright yellow cap provided by Geoff Lang Real Estate bearing the slogan 'Shorewood? Sure Would!'

I can smell sausages on the barbecue, and bacon and eggs, and one of the Lord of the Juice's hideous chartreuse trucks is parked beside a Mr. Whippy. I know who'll be getting more customers. There's a jumping castle doing brisk business, and two St. John Ambulance workers standing beside their vehicle, looking bored.

The crowd is starting to get louder, which must mean they can see the runners approaching. Picking up the pace as much as I can while carrying my bags, I jog to the arch.

I'm stuck behind several rows of spectators, but I jump and peer around shoulders until I spot Helen. Resplendent in cobalt blue activewear from head to toe, she is in prime position, right beside the finish line at the front of the crowd. I force my way through, the insincerity of my apologies matched only by the sharpness of my elbows.

A tall blonde woman cries out when I give her a slightly hard shove with my laptop bag, and she scowls at me as I barge past. When I reach Helen, I see Freya and Lola are standing in front of her, bouncing up and down with excitement as they watch the runners coming up the home straight.

I crouch down and pull them into a hug. They hug me back for about two seconds, before pulling away and returning their attention to the runners. 'Go Tim! Come on Daddy!' they shriek, even though they can't see them yet. 'Run faster!'

Helen looks at me. 'You made it,' she says, in a tone that suggests this is too little, too late.

'Any sign of them?' I say.

'Not yet, but they're probably not going to be in the first bunch of finishers. Troy's actually feeling pretty ill.'

'Did he have to work late?' I ask, and don't even try to disguise my sarcasm.

Helen stares straight ahead and says nothing. She runs her hands through Lola's hair and Lola bats her away.

The race is won by a mother I often see out running. She has close-cropped hair, a body like a greyhound, and her face is set in an expression of grim determination. Her kids are nowhere to be seen. They obviously couldn't keep up with her and the concept of this being a Fun Run has been discarded somewhere along the route, along with so many Lululemon hoodies.

Adam and Bon jog up to the finish, in a very respectable time, and my stomach clenches involuntarily when I catch Adam's eye. He gives me a sheepish wave. I wish he would go back to Amsterdam. I feel like I've worked through what happened, but I'd still rather not see him every day. Ideally I'd just ignore him, but unless Tim and Bon have a huge falling out, I don't think that's going to be an option. I lose sight of them as they melt into the crowd.

For fifteen minutes Helen and I stand side by side, watching the runners finish. There's still no sign of Tim and Troy. Two dads accompanying a pair of stubborn four-year-olds straggle over the finish line to a huge round of applause, and finally Tim and Troy round the corner into the home straight. They are dead last. Tim is jogging virtually on the spot, and Troy is walking so slowly that Freya and Lola, at their most distracted, could leave him for dead.

By the time they reach the arch, most of the crowd has dispersed in search of sausages and ice cream.

'Hooray!' I yell. 'Come on, Tim! You can do it!'

He looks furious. 'I know I can do it. Dad's been so slow. We've come last. *Last*, Mum.'

Troy now appears to be limping. He's not looking very well.

'Darling, are you all right?' Helen rushes to his side.

'Yeah, yeah, I'm all good. Just rolled my ankle right after the race started, so I was a bit of a dead weight for poor old Tim.'

'Why didn't you stop?' Helen fusses. 'Tim could have run with someone else.'

'I couldn't let my boy down, could I?' Troy's leaning on Helen's shoulder now.

'Which ankle is it?' I ask.

He hesitates. Classic sign of a lie. 'Ah, the right.' He shifts his weight onto his left foot. Something's not right here.

'Look, I might just pop over to the first aid tent and get some ice for it,' he says, but before he gets a chance, Bon dashes over to us, followed by Adam and the woman I barged past before, who, now that I get a good look at her, can only be Bon's mother, such is their flaxen-haired similarity.

'Tim! My mum's here! Now she can be friends with your mum and she's brought all my Lego with her!'

Adam has the grace to look mortified. His wife looks at me without smiling and holds out her hand. 'Hello, again. I'm Ilse. I've heard so much about you and Tim.'

I'll bet what you've heard doesn't even scratch the surface of what there actually is to hear, I think, but I shake her hand. I'm about to apologize for bashing into her when Helen leaps in.

'Oh!' she says. 'You're Adam's *wife*?' Her voice is dripping with glee.

Shit shit shit. Don't say anything, Helen, I silently pray.

'I'm Helen, Tim's stepmother. This is his father, Troy. We must have you both over for dinner. We'd love to get to know Tim's little friends' parents more. Emma always seems to get to know them *so well* and we only have Tim every second weekend so we feel a little bit left out.'

This is going to get very ugly. I'm about to make my excuses, and leave them all to hear what Helen seems to be about one sentence away from telling them, when I hear a familiar voice calling my name.

'Emma! Emma!'

It's Philip. I don't know how it's Philip, but I turn to see him striding towards me. I'm so confused, but at the same time, strangely delighted.

'Hello,' he says, and wraps me in a huge hug. When he releases me, he kisses me firmly on both cheeks, and takes my hands.

'Philip!' I say, aware that all eyes are on us. 'What are you doing here?'

'Can I just borrow you for a moment, Emma?'

'Of course,' I say, and we move away from the others.

Philip takes a deep breath and begins. 'I arrived in Sydney yesterday, and I realized that I felt very sorry to have left you. It was such fun getting to know you, and I don't think I told you that. I wanted to ask you if I could see you again. And I didn't think you'd say "No, I won't see you again," but you never know with people, they might not want to see you again, so I thought I wouldn't risk not seeing you again by asking you that in an email or on the phone. And I remembered you were coming to this run thing—I remembered the name of your suburb, and I hope you don't find that creepy—so I thought I'd find you here. I came to ask you in person, that way if you said no then at least I would have seen you again anyway, if you know what I mean.'

I'm overwhelmed. Everyone is staring. Of course I want to see him again. He's wonderful. I can't begin to see how he would fit into my little life, but right now I don't care. He's still holding my hands.

I glance over at the others. Adam is looking at me like a kid who has just passed the parcel when the music stops.

Ilse is looking pleasantly baffled.

'Emma, is this *yet another* of your beaux?' says Helen, who seems to think she's in a Regency novel all of a sudden. She can't keep the delight from her voice. 'I'm impressed. I don't know how you find the time.' She comes over, holding her hand out to Philip. 'I'm Helen,' she says. 'You must be someone's husband.'

Before I can say anything, Tim pulls on my sleeve and I look down at him. There's an expression on his face I have never seen before. It's pure terror. I follow his gaze and what I see chills me.

Troy is a very strange colour. A sort of purplish grey, and over the next seconds, which take forever, I see every drop of that colour drain from his face. It's so dramatic that instinctively I glance down at his feet, expecting to see blood pooling around his shoes, for surely no one can go that colour unless they are bleeding out.

Slowly his knees buckle and he falls to the ground, eyes closed.

For a moment, no one moves. All faces are downturned, all eyes on Troy, who looks like a grey sack adorned with Nike swooshes.

Then all hell breaks loose.

Chapter Twenty-one

Helen and I are sitting on plastic chairs in a hospital waiting room. It doesn't smell like disinfectant, which I don't find confidence-inspiring. It smells like coffee. Troy is, to the best of our knowledge, at this moment, not dead.

He was though, earlier, at the Fun Run. For several minutes, actually, although heart attack minutes are like dog years—there are a lot more of them squished into a regular minute.

It felt like hours that he lay on the grass, a crowd of horrified onlookers gawking as first the St. John Ambulance officers, and then, remarkably quickly, real paramedics compressed his chest, squeezed air into his mouth, injected things into his veins, and finally, terrifyingly, shocked his body with a portable defibrillator.

All the time Helen stood ashen, her hands over her mouth.

Adam and Ilse turned Bon away from the scene, but they stayed where they were.

I knelt on the ground with Freya, Tim and Lola crushed to my body. I kept their faces away from seeing their dad, which meant I watched every moment of his resuscitation. Philip knelt beside me, gripping my shoulder.

The scene was eerily quiet. Suze, officious as ever, held the crowds back. Apart from the sounds of the children quietly weeping, all I could hear were the voices of the first responders. They were so calm. There was no bustle or drama, just methodical processes to be followed and outcomes to monitor.

I won't lie, I thought Troy was dead. I gave up hope around the time they started chest compressions. Just after a St. John's volunteer called Karen said, 'I can't find a pulse.' From that point on, my mind was working on the future.

While I watched what I assumed were vain attempts to revive my ex-husband, I was planning how I would now have to co-parent with Helen.

By the time they cracked out the defibrillator, which looked like an early 1980s educational computer game with its tough plastic casing and yellow handle, I was convinced there was no chance for Troy.

But after they shocked his heart, and obeyed the machine that told everyone to wait while it detected output, he had a pulse again. They loaded him onto a stretcher, put him in the back of the waiting ambulance with Helen by his side, and with sirens wailing, he was gone.

Everything started to move again then, and the babble of voices became so loud and chaotic that I didn't know where to look. My ears were ringing.

It was Philip who took charge. He did it unceremoniously, but quietly and capably he ascertained that I had no car there. He retrieved Helen's bag from where it had fallen from her shoulder onto the grass, which was now littered with detritus from the paramedics: swabs, plastic packaging, paper towels, and one of Troy's sneakers that somehow came off his foot while they were trying to bring him back to life.

Philip shepherded the three children and me off the sports field and pressed the unlock button on Helen's keys until her car revealed itself by flashing its lights. Together we buckled the kids into their seats.

On the way to the hospital, Lola and Freya cried, confused and frightened, while Tim sat, his tear-streaked face stony, and stared out of the window.

When we reached the doors of emergency, I leapt out, then came to a screaming halt when I realized I shouldn't take the kids inside. Whatever lay beyond those doors was not for their eyes. They'd seen too much already. My best option at this point was to send them off in the car with a man I barely knew.

I turned back. 'Philip, please will you take them to my dad's house? It's ten minutes from here. He's going away today but I hope he won't have left yet.'

'Of course,' he said. 'What's the address?'

I couldn't tell him. The address of the house I grew up in, the house where my own mother died, had vanished into the ether.

I stood on the sidewalk, gaping.

'It's the shock, Emma,' Philip told me. 'I'll bet Tim knows his grandpa's address, don't you, Tim?'

'We call him Grandad, not Grandpa,' Tim said, 'and his address is 15 Barker Place, um. . .'

'Philip,' said Philip, and I realized my children didn't have a clue who this stranger was.

'Hi, Philip, I'm Tim. This is my sister Freya, and my other sister, Lola.'

'It's a pleasure to meet you all. Shall we let your mum go check on your dad now, and go see your grandad?'

'Yep,' said Tim, and I'd never felt more proud.

* * *

On entering the hospital, I was immediately struck with déjà vu. It was only two weeks since Freya was here. Once again, the emergency waiting area was completely packed.

I approached the triage window and said my husband had been brought in by ambulance. They buzzed me through the big swinging doors and, in the absence of any other instructions, I followed the signs until I reached another desk with a nurse sitting at a computer.

I told her the same thing: my husband had come in by ambulance.

She looked at me with a furrowed brow. 'What's his name?'

'Troy Lawson,' I told her.

Her eyes widened and she looked stricken. 'Oh, um . . .' she started, then trailed off.

He's dead, I thought. That has to mean he's dead. This poor woman is unqualified and probably not even authorized to tell me Troy died in the ambulance, but that's what's happened.

My knees went wobbly and the world started to fade. Head between knees, Emma, I thought. Mum always said if you're going to faint, get your head down between your knees. I crouched down and hung my head. They must see a lot of that, because the nurse dashed around the desk and helped me to a chair.

'Is he . . . Did he . . .' I couldn't say the word.

'Oh!' she said in a tone of dawning realization. 'No, no, he's not dead, it's just well, this might be awkward or difficult, so I just want to prepare you.'

I wondered what on earth this woman was on about.

'It's just, when he was brought in he was in the company of a woman. And that woman told us—oh this is awful, I'm so sorry—but she said she's his wife.'

Relief coursed through me. 'Thank Christ,' I said.

The nurse looked confused. This wasn't the reaction she had been expecting.

I cleared things up for her. 'That woman is his wife. His new wife, I mean. I'm not married to him any more, but he's my kids' dad and I just wasn't sure they'd let me back here otherwise so I said he is my husband.'

Helen stuck her head out of a cubicle. 'Emma, you're here,' she said, sounding pleased to see me for the first time ever. 'He's in surgery. I don't even know what that means. They say he had a heart attack, well, he's still having a heart attack. I don't know. How long do heart attacks go for? Where are the kids?'

'It's all right, Philip's taking them to Dad's. When did he go into surgery? Did they say what they're doing? Who is the doctor?'

'I don't know. I don't know any of that. I don't know who to ask.' She looked confused and her eyes were filled with tears.

I put my arm around her shoulder. 'We'll figure it out, Helen.'

* * *

That was two hours ago, and since then Helen and I have been waiting for news.

Philip found my dad's house, and fortunately Dad was still in it. There has been no mention of Penny. I hope we haven't mucked anything up for Dad.

All three children are now, according to the text message updates I've received, eating everything they can find.

Lola and Tim are snuggled up on the sofa watching *The*

Railway Children—Dad's selection of DVDs is limited. This tells me they are really quite traumatized. Normally they wouldn't watch that kind of 1970s Victoriana for more than five minutes before begging Dad to sign up to a streaming service so they can have some decent content.

Freya and Dad, for reasons known only to them, are building a spice rack. Dad has excellent woodworking skills—as long as you want him to build a spice rack.

Some people, when they're upset, smoke cigarettes or drink Scotch. Dad saws wood and sands it and nails bits of it together so people have somewhere to put their cardamom. I've lost count of the number of spice racks he's made in my lifetime.

Helen's been on her phone nonstop, calling and texting, pretty much since they moved us from the cubicle in emergency up to this waiting room on the surgical floor. I was doing the same, until my battery died. Helen, now that I've returned her bag to her, has access to a charger, for she is the sort of person who carries one with her as a matter of habit.

I've been reduced to reading a pile of old issues of *New Idea* that have been either thoughtfully provided by the hospital or thoughtlessly left behind by other waiting families.

Every time we hear footsteps approaching, we both tense up and stare at the door, simultaneously wishing for that person to stop and tell us what's going on, and for them to walk on, keeping our future from us for as long as possible.

Helen sighs loudly, puts her phone back in her bag and folds her arms. She glances over at me. 'Do you want to charge your phone?'

'Only if you're done charging yours,' I say. 'There's not really anyone I need to contact. I reckon you've got Troy's family and friends covered.' As I say it, I realize how stupid I sound. Of course she has his family and friends covered. *She's his wife.*

What am I even doing here? Sure, he's my kids' dad, but really, I should be with them, not here, making his wife feel awkward and causing confusion among the staff.

'Helen,' I say, 'I'm sorry, I don't know why I'm still here. I should head off. Troy's mum and dad will be here soon, won't they? You guys won't want me hanging around like a bad smell.'

Helen pauses. 'You can stay. If you want, I mean. God, I spend my life wishing you weren't around so much.' She gives a bitter laugh. 'How ironic, that now I'd quite like your company. Troy's mum's had a panic attack and her doctor has given her something to make her sleep, so they're not coming down any time soon. And I don't really know who else to ask. It's not the normal way to spend a Saturday afternoon, is it, hanging out waiting to see if your husband is going to live.' Her voice cracks.

'He's going to live, Helen,' I tell her in my surest voice—the one I bring out to reassure my children that the miniature plastic squirrel they can't locate is definitely not lost forever.

'What if he doesn't? What am I going to do without him?'

'I don't know.'

We sit in silence for a while longer, and just as I'm about to suggest I go find us some coffee—or green tea for Helen—the door opens.

The woman who enters gives us one of those closed-mouth smiles that tells you absolutely nothing. I'm sure it's the look she gives before she delivers all news to families. It could be the smile she does before bringing in her eyebrows like a sad-face clown and telling Helen she's a widow. It could be the smile she gives before she tries to sound modest about unblocking a man's heart and giving him back his life. I just have to wait and see, and the seconds are endless.

'Hi,' she says. 'Who's Helen?'

Helen puts up her hand, like she's in class.

'Helen, I'm Dr. Zerafa. I'm a consultant cardiologist. I've been treating your husband this afternoon.'

'Hi,' Helen whispers.

'As you probably know, Troy has had what's called an acute myocardial infarction, commonly known as a heart attack. We have gone in and cleared the blockage that caused it, which was in the main artery that supplies the right side of his heart.'

'Gone in?' says Helen. 'Like, you cut open his chest?' She's very pale.

'No,' says Dr. Zerafa, 'we were able to avoid that. We did what's called angioplasty, which is where we go in through the groin and send a catheter up the artery. Then we used a balloon to widen the artery near the blockage, and once we removed the clot that was stopping the blood from getting through, we put in a stent to keep the blood vessel open.'

'So he's all right?' I say. 'He's going to be all right?'

'Look, the procedure went well, and we're hopeful that he'll make a good recovery, but I understand from the paramedics there was some delay in getting a normal heart rhythm. What that means is that there's a possibility his brain wasn't getting oxygen for longer than we'd like. So until he wakes up, we won't really be able to judge what effect that might have had.'

'He might have brain damage?' Helen says.

'We're going to keep him cool and sedated overnight in intensive care, and then tomorrow we'll start weaning him off the sedative and see how he does.'

'Can I see him?' Helen asks.

'Just give them about fifteen minutes to settle him in the ICU, and then you're fine to go up. Do you have any children, Helen?'

'One. I have one. But he has three. I don't want them to see him yet though. Is that all right? Is that the right thing to do? Or should they see him? They're little.'

'I'd probably hold off on bringing them in for now. The plan is to keep him very quiet. Let's see how he is tomorrow.'

'All right. Thank you.'

'No worries,' says the doctor. 'I'll leave you to it. Just head up to level seven in a bit, and ask the nurse on the desk which bed he's in. I'll see him again in the morning, unless there are any problems. Oh, and I understand Troy's been under the care of Dr. Lee recently, so although I'll be his consultant while he's here, once he's out, Dr. Lee will be the one to follow up with.'

'What?' says Helen. 'Sorry, who is Dr. Lee?'

'His cardiologist,' says Dr. Zerafa. 'The specialist he's been seeing for his cardiac issues.'

With that she gives us another all-purpose smile, this time with a distinct 'chin-up' hint to it, and leaves.

'I don't understand,' says Helen, who looks miserable. 'Is he all right? What cardiac issues? Why would he have brain damage? They got his heart started again so quickly, those ambulance guys, didn't they?' She leans her forearms on her thighs and hangs her head forward.

'I don't know,' I say. 'It was a few minutes after he collapsed. Maybe five? I'm not sure. And I don't know how long his heart wasn't going for. But that might have been long enough for the lack of oxygen to be a problem. There's nothing we can do, Helen.

We'll wait until we see him. And then wait until they wake him up tomorrow.'

Helen looks up. Her face is wet with tears. 'Emma, I can't lose him.'

'You won't,' I say, although of course I know nothing of the sort. I have no idea how this is going to turn out.

* * *

At ten o'clock that night Helen's parents arrive from Brisbane. I've never met them before. They seem very nice, worried about Troy, and Helen, and the kids, and even me.

I'm not sure why, but I thought they'd hate me. I assumed they'd have heard from Helen what an interfering cow I've been since she and Troy got together. But while Helen brings her mum up to speed on Troy's situation, her dad, John, offers to walk me down to the lobby and put me in a cab home.

We stand awkwardly in the dark corridor, waiting for the lift.

'It's terrible that it takes something like this for us to meet,' he says. 'Helen's told us a lot about you, and of course we've met your charming children, several times. It's a funny family set-up you have, but I think you all make it work just marvellously.'

'Helen must not have updated you recently,' I tell him. 'Things have gone a bit awry.'

He chuckles. 'Yes, she did say. And honestly, I thought to myself, good for Emma. It's about time she stopped letting Helen and Troy take advantage of her.'

The lift arrives and we get in. I press G.

John waits for the doors to close, and then continues musing. 'Of course I don't know the whole situation, only what I hear from

Hels, but it did seem to me that you've been really terrifically helpful to her for quite a long time, for not much reward. She must be some sort of saint, this Emma, I've thought at times. I mean, what's in it for her? What's she hoping to get out of this?'

It strikes me as a slightly odd, the way he talks about Emma, like she's a third person and not actually me, the person who is standing beside him right now in the lift. It also strikes me that this Emma person sounds like she needs her head read.

'Anyway,' he says, turning to me. 'You've been very good to Helen and Lola, so thank you. I hope Helen wasn't too rude. Sometimes she can be blunt when she's cross.'

'I think we've sorted things out now. And what matters at the moment is Troy.'

'Yes indeed. Quite right,' says John. 'We must hope for a full and speedy recovery. For all his faults, a lot of people need Troy to stick around.'

Chapter Twenty-two

When the taxi drops me off outside my house, it feels like I've come back to someone else's life.

I sort of remember this feeling from my travelling days in my twenties, the way everything that once was so familiar can feel foreign when you've been away from it for a while. It used to take a few months of backpacking, or at least a few weeks overseas for this to kick in. Not five nights. But then I suppose I'm out of practice at being anywhere but here. Five nights away from my life now might as well have been a gap year.

Inside, the house feels cold and empty. When there are no kids in a house that usually has kids, it feels like the life has been sucked out of it. I drop my bags in the hall and wander through to the living room. It's very tidy. It wasn't like this when I left on Monday. It was still in a severe state of post-camping. Dad must have sorted things out.

It's late. I should eat something. I think the last time I ate was on the plane this morning. But all I want to do is lie down.

I make a cup of tea, and while the kettle comes to a boil I stand in front of the open fridge, willing something to leap into my mouth. Eventually I eat a couple of string cheese sticks and a Sao cracker, and take my tea into the living room.

A week ago I was drunk in a tent, fighting with a bush rat. A week? That cannot be right. It feels like a year ago. Even seeing Adam today at the Fun Run feels like it happened in the distant past.

I don't even recognize my life any more. My life is repetitive. Predictable. Boring. For years, all I've done is the shopping, cook the meals, work, play with the kids, take Lola where I'm told. I'm not even exaggerating. That's all I do.

But this new life? This life is full of emotional upheaval. Drama. Unpredictability. Excitement. Between what's happened with Helen, Adam, Ilse, Wanda, Carmen, Philip, and now Troy, I can't see a time when it will be normal again.

It's like life was 'Hey Jude'—pleasant, monotonous to the point of being only just bearable—and now it's 'Live and Let Die', which feels like nineteen different songs squashed up against each other as if they're on a train at peak hour. It's thrilling and confusing and exhausting, with too many instruments and tempos and people playing trills on a piccolo when you least expect it.

I miss my kids so much. Lying on the sofa, all I want is for them to run in and hurl their warm heaviness onto me, giggling, 'Mummy, I'm a human blanket!' It's all I can do not to drive straight to Dad's and climb into bed with them.

And I miss Philip. That doesn't make any sense. I barely know him. But I really wish he were here with me.

The front gate screeches and my heart leaps. For a moment I'm sure it's Philip. By the time I've processed the unlikeliness of that, I know who is at the door, because as always, Laura doesn't bother waiting before she lets herself in.

'Are you awake?' she calls.

'In here,' I say.

She sits down beside me and hugs me tightly. She doesn't say anything. That's not like her.

Finally she pulls away and looks at me. 'You all right, you big idiot?'

'No,' I tell her, and burst into tears.

'Of course you're not all right. What a fucker of a thing to happen. Poor old awful, stupid Troy. Poor Helen.'

'I know. How can he be in intensive care? I just can't get my head around it. He can't die. My kids can't grow up without a father. That's not the deal.

'And it's not just Troy, Laura, it's everything. I can't get my head around anything. My life is a disaster. Adam's wife, she was at the Fun Run, and the way she looked at me, I think she knows I slept with him and I can't show my face at school ever again, I don't think. I'll have to sell the house and move to the other side of the city, and it will be exactly the same, except the kids won't all be called Olivia and Isabella, they'll be, like, Arlo and Enid and Esme, and I'll be really far from you and from Dad.

'Plus I think I've ruined my career. I went a bit weird and tried to tell Wanda how to write her book and I totally overstepped. She's going to complain to Carmen, the publisher, and that will be it—no more work from them.'

'Would that be such a bad thing?' asks Laura. 'You're a bit over editing, as a job, aren't you, really?'

'No. Well, maybe a bit, yes. But what else am I going to do? That's all I've ever done. I have no other skills, and now Troy's going to leave me a single mother—like properly properly single. A widow. No, an ex-widow. There isn't even a name for what I'll be.'

'Yes, by all means let's focus on that,' says Laura. 'On what the correct term would be if something happens that probably isn't going to. Anyway, bullshit, you do so have other skills, loads of them. We just need to find you something to channel those skills into. You're very skilled at telling people how to live their lives—that's a useful one. Also thinking you know best, again that's highly sought after in many industries.'

'Everything I know, I learned from you,' I tell her.

'Really though,' Laura says, 'I think you need a job where you aren't supposed to be invisible. I think you've done enough invisible work.'

'We shouldn't be talking about my career now. What kind of monster does that when her kids' father is lying in intensive care? He might be dead now. I might get a call any second.'

'He won't die,' Laura says confidently. 'You won't get rid of him that easily. Troy will live a long and annoying life. People like him always do. You have many years ahead of you to discover more and more annoying things about him, that will make you thank your lucky stars Helen came along when she did.'

I laugh so hard I snort.

'Oh, and by the way,' adds Laura. 'Who the fuck is this Philip guy everyone's suddenly obsessed with? The one who brought the kids over to Dad's place? Dad's very taken with him. Apparently he stayed and they hung out all afternoon.'

That doesn't surprise me.

'That's the other thing that's messy,' I explain to Laura. 'I just got to know Philip this week, up at Wanda's. He's . . .' How can I explain Philip? 'He's kind and handsome but he's much older than me and he doesn't even live in Australia—and I really think I might like him. And he seems to like me. But he has no idea the chaos he'd be letting himself in for.'

In an entirely unprecedented move, Laura doesn't raise an

eyebrow or tease me. She fixes me with a stare. 'Does he have a family? Where does he live?'

'No,' I tell her. 'He's from England, but he lives and travels all over the place for his job. He's been married, but no kids. He didn't get to say goodbye to me before he left Wanda's place and he happened to be in Sydney, so he popped by to say he liked meeting me, and I think he asked me out. I mean, I'd mentioned how I had to get back on Saturday for the Fun Run, and he must have remembered that and realized he could find me there. Is that really weird? Creepy? It's a bit stalkery, isn't it?'

'No, I don't think so,' says Laura. 'It's slightly odd, but it's thoughtful.'

'I don't know if it's even anything, Laura, so don't go getting all excited.'

'Who's getting excited? I'm just pleased you have a friend who showed up out of the blue and helped you when something terrible happened.'

'I like that too. That was unexpected. But I liked it a lot.'

'Look, Emma, I know you better than anyone. And you're right, going out with you would be no squirrel's picnic. You're all over the bloody place at the moment. But you're wonderful—there's nobody better, really—and if this Philip guy can see that, through all the ridiculous behaviour you've been exhibiting lately, then he sounds like someone worth keeping around.'

Laura ends up sleeping over. She climbs in beside me in my bed, and it feels like we are little again. We did this after Mum died, and again after Troy left me. After I turn the light off, she reaches for my hand in the darkness and holds it until I fall asleep.

* * *

When I wake the next morning, it's seven-thirty and Laura's sprawled beside me, mouth open, snoring lightly. Two of her sons do rowing and the other is a competitive swimmer, so between their transport requirements and the needs of Bledisloe the World's Worst Dog, Laura gets to sleep past five o'clock about one day a year.

I hear the quiet opening of a car door outside, followed by an equally hushed thunk as it closes.

'*Mum!*' yells a voice. 'Can you bring out my goggles?'

'*Georgina!*' comes Julia's voice in a furious whisper. 'The whole street does not need to be woken up because you cannot be bothered to go inside and get your own goggles. *For goodness sake.*'

I smile and stretch, and then suddenly yesterday comes back to me in a rush. Troy. Intensive care. Fuck.

I grab my phone. There's nothing from Helen. Just a message from Dad telling me to call when I'm ready for him to come round with the kids. I'm dying to see them, but I have to find out what's happening at the hospital first.

Slipping down the hall to the kitchen, so as not to wake Laura, I call Helen.

'Emma,' she says, picking up on the first ring. 'Everything's the same.'

I breathe out. 'Okay,' I say. 'Shall I come up?'

'Do you mind? I think it would be good. The consultant has been and she says they'll try bringing him out of sedation in another hour. I've sent my parents home.'

'I'll be right there,' I tell her. 'Can I bring anything for you?'

'No, I'm okay. Dad brought up clothes and a toothbrush last night. I'll see you when you get here.'

On my way to the hospital in a cab, I call my dad.

'Em, love!' he says. 'I have someone here who needs to talk to you.'

I hear a scuffling sound as he hands over the phone, then a small voice says, 'Mumma?'

'Hey, my Frey-Frey,' I say. 'It's so nice to talk to you. I've missed you so much.'

'Mumma, what scared Daddy?'

'What do you mean, sweetie? Daddy isn't scared. Didn't Grandad explain? Daddy's heart was a bit sick and it made him faint, and now he's in the hospital while they give him some medicine.'

'But he had a heart attack so what scared him?'

The penny drops. Whenever we play hide and seek, if I pretend I can't find Freya for long enough, eventually she leaps out and tries to scare me. And now that I think about it, when she does, I often say, 'Oh! You gave me a heart attack.'

'Darling, Daddy got sick because the blood couldn't get through to his heart for a little while, that's all. Not because he was scared. That's just an expression, and I won't say it any more.'

'Can we come home, Mumma? I miss you.'

'Yes, absolutely. I'm just going to visit Daddy to see how he's feeling today, and then you can come home. I love you. Can you please give Tim the phone now?'

Tim is guarded when I get him on the line. He's never great on the phone. I manage to ascertain that yes, he had a good sleep, yes, he's ready to come home, and no, there's nothing wrong. I can tell I'm not in his good books, which after almost a week away is fair enough. He perks up at the end of the conversation, to tell me Philip taught him to play solitaire at Grandad's house.

'It's like Uno, Mum, but better in a way because you don't

have to wait for someone to play with you. I won a lot of games. You should get Philip to teach you too. Or maybe I could.'

'I'd love that,' I tell him. 'I'll talk to you later, after I've seen your dad, okay?'

'Okay, bye!' He hangs up before I can ask to speak to my father again, but now I'm in the hospital car park anyway, so I away put my phone and go inside.

* * *

The intensive care unit does smell of disinfectant, as it rightly should. It's reassuring. It also has a hint of chocolate, but that's because I walk in just in time to catch the end of 'Happy Birthday', as a nurse pretends to blow out the unlit candles on his cake and his colleagues all cheer. It seems out of place in a ward where life hangs in the balance, but I suppose birthdays are birthdays, and if you have a job and a birthday you get a cake and a song. Besides, most of the patients here are unconscious. The nurses aren't going to wake anyone up with their singing.

Troy is in the second bed on the right. Helen is sitting beside him, her back to me. Her head is bowed and she's holding his hand in hers. For a moment I pause. I wish I could turn around and walk out. I don't want to know what's going to happen next.

But I steel myself and go over. Helen hears my approach and turns around. She looks horrendous. Well, horrendous for Helen. There are dark circles under her eyes, her face is pale, and her hair is limp, but on her it looks waifish and endearing. I, on the other hand, briefly caught sight of myself in a mirror in the lift and look like I've been dragged through a hedge backwards.

Still, I look better than Troy. I feel a jolt of horror when I stare down at him. He's no longer grey like a dead man, but he's as white as a sheet and has so many tubes and drains and drips and primary coloured monitor cords coming off him that he looks like a child has scribbled on a picture of Troy in anger.

Helen smiles. 'Hey,' she says. 'Good timing. They've just reduced the sedation a little while ago, so if he's going to wake up it might happen soon.'

'Shall I wait with you?' I ask.

'Yes, please,' she says.

We sit in silence for a while, listening to the sounds of the ward around us, and the steady beeps of Troy's heart monitor.

Then Helen speaks. 'I haven't called Lola,' she says. 'I'm too scared to talk to her on the phone in case I lose it. I know I have to keep it together for her, but I don't think I can right now.' Her voice is shaky.

'I think that's all right,' I tell her. 'They're all together. They're with Dad and they all love him. He's taking them to the hardware store this morning. And he's been in touch with your parents and they're all going to have coffee afterwards, at the café near the park with the fence around it. Dad's got everything sorted. Honestly, Helen, don't worry about Lola.'

'Thanks,' she says. 'I never thought I'd say this, but I'm lucky to have you, and your dad. It's pretty weird, to think our parents are hanging out together.'

'It's not the weirdest thing about our family.'

'No,' she agrees. 'You're right. I couldn't have imagined I'd end up in a . . . situation like this. It's not what you picture for your family, is it? Stepchildren and exes and ex-step-grandparents.'

'At least there are names for those things for you,' I tell her. 'What on earth are your parents to me? My children's sister's grandparents? We'll have to come up with something catchier.'

Helen laughs, and I join her, and so it's a moment or two before we realize Troy's eyes are open and he's looking utterly confused. Apart from the fact that he's waking from an induced coma after a heart attack, it's the first time he would ever have seen Helen and me enjoying each other's company. He probably thinks he's dead.

'Oh, you're back,' I say, surprised.

'Darling, thank God,' says Helen and she falls upon him with kisses.

'What am I doing here?' he asks.

'Kale poisoning,' I say with a straight face, before Helen shushes me.

'Darling,' she says seriously to Troy. 'You've had a little episode with your heart. But you're going to be all right.'

'My heart?'

'You had a heart attack.'

'A heart attack?'

He's already annoying me, repeating everything Helen says. My internal sigh of exasperation must be slightly external, because Helen shoots me a look of disapproval.

'Sweetie, the doctor says it's totally normal that you might have some memory loss about what happened.'

'What did happen?'

'You collapsed at the end of the Fun Run. Your heart stopped, but only very briefly. The ambulance guys got it started again. They brought you here and fixed the blockage in your heart, and then they kept you asleep for a bit, to rest you.'

'Fuck. I don't remember that. I sort of remember going to the run. Did I finish the race?'

'You came last,' I say.

'Emma.' Helen's warning me.

'I'm sorry,' says Troy, rather pathetically. 'I'm so sorry.'

'Apology accepted,' I say at the same time as Helen says, 'Don't you dare apologize, you didn't do it on purpose!'

Helen gives me a look that makes it very clear it is time for me to go. But I'm not quite ready.

'Troy,' I say, 'who is Dr. Lee?'

He sighs and closes his eyes. 'My cardiologist.'

'Why did you already have a cardiologist?'

'Because I haven't been feeling great for a few months. I didn't want to worry either of you, so I didn't say.'

Something comes back to me. 'Is that where you were when you missed parent–teacher night?'

He nods.

'So why did you let me think you were seeing a therapist?'

'I was embarrassed. I sell juice. I sell healthy lifestyles. How's having a weak heart going to look to people?'

'Oh my God, you're such an—'

Helen cuts me off. 'Emma, don't you have some calls to make?'

'Fine,' I tell them. 'I'll go let people know you're back from the brink. I'm glad you're not dead, Troy,' I say, and I realize, as I give him a little pat on the hand, that I probably mean it.

* * *

When I step out of the lift in the hospital lobby, Philip is standing there, waiting for me.

Because of course he is. My heart leaps to see this person I didn't really know a week ago and who now seems to pop up like a genie at the most opportune moments.

He's partially obscured by the gigantic arrangement of tropical flowers and foliage he's holding, but he spots me at once and smiles.

'Hello,' he says.

'Hello,' I say back.

We just stand there looking at each other, and smiling. Eventually it becomes awkward, but we don't stop smiling and staring, and finally it becomes hilarious.

When I stop laughing, we sit down on a mauve couch, with the flowers on the coffee table in front of us. It's like we're hiding in a little jungle. I tell him that Troy's still alive and probably no more brain deficient than he was before the heart attack. He's had a lucky escape.

'But they don't allow flowers in intensive care,' I add. 'Sorry.'

'These are not for your ex-husband,' he tells me. 'They're for you.'

'Thank you,' I say. 'They are beautiful, and they are by far the biggest bunch of flowers I've ever been given.'

'Well, what is it they say? "Go big or go home?" And I didn't really want to go home, so I went big.'

'Aren't you supposed to be in the Solomon Islands?' I ask him.

'I am, but the team can manage very well without me, and I thought I'd see if there was anything I could do to help before I leave.'

'You're very kind,' I say. I feel a bit overwhelmed. 'I don't know what you can do though.'

'May I take you out to dinner sometime?'

'Philip,' I say, 'my life is a mess. All those people back at the running race? They're my messy horror show of a life. It's all kids and ex-people and step-people and grandparents and people I was involved with and shouldn't have been, and school, and this tiny little suburb where you can't sneeze without everyone knowing about it. And then there's me. I'm a disaster. I've been sacked from half of my life, looking after my ex-husband's kid, because I was such an interfering know-it-all. I've probably buggered up my career by trying to tell Wanda what to write and how to write it. I act like I know what's best for everyone, but I really don't. I don't even know what's best for me. I don't think you want to get mixed up in this. And you don't live here, which is awesome for you, but how would that work if we . . . you know, started something?'

'Everyone's life is a mess, Emma,' Philip says. 'Lives aren't tidy. I'm older than you, which is something you kindly didn't include when telling me all the reasons we shouldn't, as you put it "start something". I've seen a lot of messes and they all work out in the end, in some way. Eventually it all dries and you can scrape it up and start again. All we can do is try to enjoy the parts we can and survive the rest so we can eventually look back and make some sort of sense of it.'

'I don't know how I'll ever make sense of my life,' I tell him. 'I don't know how to be a mother and an ex-wife and a stepmother and all the other people I have to be. I don't understand this story.'

'You will,' he says. 'You're an editor. You know how to see the shape in stories. But no one can really understand something while they're in it. You can't see all the parts. You can't get perspective and you don't have 360-degree vision, metaphorically speaking. There are bits of the story you can't see right now. I think you'll see the shape in this part of yours once you get a bit further along, when you get where you're going.'

'How will I know when I get where I'm going?' I ask him.

'That, I don't know,' he admits. 'Maybe there will be a big sign that tells you.'

'Philip,' I say, 'if I go out for dinner with you, can we talk about something other than my life in storytelling metaphors?'

He grins. 'At least for the entrée,' he says.

'Right then,' I tell him. 'It's a deal.'

'Where were you going,' he asks, 'when I ambushed you at the lift?'

'Oh, home. Well, wherever the kids are, actually. The hardware store, maybe, or the park. I need to see them.'

'If there's nothing I can do right now to help, I should head to the airport,' he says. 'But I'll be back in Sydney in a week. Can we have dinner then?'

'Yes, Philip, we can.'

Together we walk out to the street. There are three taxis waiting. Philip opens the back door to the first one for me.

He hands me the jungle flowers, and then he kisses me. Or he tries to. But there's about two hundred dollars' worth of greenery crushed between us, and a bird of paradise is stabbing my breast. In a movie I'd let them fall to the floor and wrap my arms around Philip, but these clearly cost more than the flowers for my whole wedding, and I'm not letting them go. So our kiss is awkward and his beard is scratchy but I'm so happy.

I get in the cab and roll down the window.

'I'll see you soon,' he says. 'And oh, wait, I have one more thing to give you.'

He passes a package to me. It's flat, square and wrapped in brown paper. 'It's a book. It's for Freya, and sort of also for you. Freya told me about her tiger book yesterday, and the situation with the ending. And I remembered this book, and I thought it might be a good one for her to have. Only she might be miffed because it's called—well, I'll let you read it. Anyway, I'm going to miss my flight unless I hop to it, so goodbye, Emma. For now.'

With that he kisses me again, very quickly, through the window, leaps into the cab behind and he's gone.

'Where're we heading, love?' asks the cabbie.

'Um, the hardware store at Shorewood, please,' I say.

'No worries. Those flowers are quite . . . big, aren't they?'

'They are. They are very big.'

I unwrap the package. It's a paperback children's book called *Timothy, An Extraordinary Tiger.* It looks old. I check the imprint page: 1979. It's older than me. It was also originally written in German. How in the name of God did Philip source an almost surely out-of-print English translation of an obscure children's book about a tiger, on a Sunday morning? He is a curious marvel.

At the risk of making myself car sick, I start to read.

It's the story of a toy tiger, Timothy, who a careless child leaves in the garden at the home of a hunter called Mr. Bang Bang. That night a tigress—who Mr. Bang Bang wants to kill—comes to the fence. Timothy cries like a cub, and although she thinks he is a strange little tiger, the tigress takes him away with her. Mr. Bang Bang gives chase, hunting them through the forest, and Timothy and the tigress learn from each other as they try to evade capture.

In the end, the tigress takes Timothy home to her cubs, as their new brother. The book ends when they set off to find themselves a new, safer, bigger lair.

It's a good ending—hopeful and warm. Freya will like it.

And so as I sit in a taxi that smells ever so slightly of sick, with half the Amazon's worth of flowers sticking into me and an old book in my hand, I drive away from Troy and Helen, and off to find the rest of my strange-shaped family, who are eating barbecued sausages and buying wood to build more spice racks.

Acknowledgements

My deepest thanks and most heartfelt gratitude are due to the following people:

My husband, Drew Truslove, who has stoically endured the writing of this book and who somehow understands that while I'm a lot of hard work when I'm writing, I'm even more when I'm not. Thank you for balancing so deftly the running of your business and our home, your own art, the raising of our children, the management of the bloody cats, and the care and feeding of an anxious would-be novelist.

My parents, Carol and Nicholas Dettmann—who made me watch *Fawlty Towers* and *The Young Ones* with them when all my friends were watching *It's a Knockout*—and my brothers, Sam and Pete. If there are any lines in this book that make anyone laugh, they probably had their origins in something one of these people said.

My children, April and Teddy. Before you I wasn't a writer and now I am. Let's face it, you're so wonderful that all I want to do now is show off and try to impress you.

My exceptional editorial team at HarperCollins: Catherine Milne, Anna Valdinger, Katherine Hassett, Belinda Yuille, Dianne Blacklock, and Shannon Kelly. Being the editor working on a book about an editor by an editor must be like being trapped in a mirrored change room wallpapered with overworked metaphors. I take my hat off to you all.

Sarah Barrett, for making sure the book got seen, and the HarperCollins sales team for convincing booksellers to take a chance on a new author.

James Kellow, for employing all the people I've just mentioned.

Janice Zawerbny, Kate Cassaday, and all at HarperCollins Canada for seeing the book on its first international adventure.

Frank Moorhouse and Ben Elton, for endless support, encouragement, and friendship over many years. People who say you should never meet your heroes obviously have the wrong heroes.

Natalie Yamey, who for more than a decade has made counselling sessions feel like storytelling practice.

Jo Butler, for her many years of friendship, which blurred into becoming my agent and selling this book when it wasn't even a book yet. Thanks also to Jeanne Ryckmans, and all at the Cameron Creswell Agency.

They say you should keep your friends close and your editors closer. It's easier if they're one and the same. Kate O'Donnell, Ellie Parker, Jessica Tory, and Ariela Bard gave their sound editorial advice and friendship, and Amy Kersey and Amy Maiden have been generous with their love, support, wisdom, and stern talkings-to when required.

Rachael Cordina, John Witzig, and Chris Effeney for helping me to understand cardiology, the geography of southeastern Queensland, and how fun runs work.

Finally, the small but dedicated band of readers of my blog, *Life With Gusto.* Their support, kindness, encouragement, and appreciation have been so important to me over the last seven years.